D0892508

THE LONDON BOROUGH
www.bromley.gov.uk

Please return/renew this item
by the last date shown.
Books may also be renewed by
phone and Internet.

The Men Who Make Christmas

Meet the Hammond brothers—will they find their own happiness under the mistletoe?

For James and Juan Hammond, Christmas should be the most joyful time of year. It's Hammond's Toy Stores' most profitable time of the year, and their Christmas window displays are legendary. Yet it reminds them of the most heartbreaking event in their family history.

But when they meet two delightful women for whom the festive season means everything, the Hammond brothers can't help but be captivated by their infectious Christmas spirit. This year, can they make Christmas the most magical time of all?

Don't miss this sparkling Christmas duet!

Christmas with Her Millionaire Boss
by Barbara Wallace
November 2017

Snowed in with the Reluctant Tycoon
by Nina Singh
December 2017

CHRISTMAS WITH HER MILLIONAIRE BOSS

BY
BARBARA WALLACE

This is a work of fiction. Names, characters, places, locations and incidents are purely fictional and bear no relationship to any real life individuals, living or dead, or to any actual places, business establishments, locations, events or incidents. Any resemblance is entirely coincidental.

First Published in Great Britain 2017
By Mills & Boon, an imprint of HarperCollins*Publishers*
1 London Bridge Street, London, SE1 9GF

© 2017 Barbara Wallace

ISBN: 978-0-263-92345-2

23-1117

Our policy is to use papers that are natural, renewable and recyclable products and made from wood grown in sustainable forests. The logging and manufacturing processes conform to the legal environmental regulations of the country of origin.

Printed and bound in Spain
by CPI, Barcelona

Barbara Wallace can't remember when she wasn't dreaming up love stories in her head, so writing romances for Mills & Boon Romance is a dream come true. Happily married to her own Prince Charming, she lives in New England with a house full of empty-nest animals. Occasionally her son comes home as well! To stay up to date on Barbara's news and releases, sign up for her newsletter at www.barbarawallace.com.

For Peter and Andrew,
who put up with a stressed-out writer trying to juggle
too many balls at one time. You two are awesome,
and I couldn't ask for a better husband and son.

CHAPTER ONE

OH, WHAT FRESH hell was this?

A pair of ten-foot nutcrackers smiled down at him with giant white grins that looked capable of snapping an entire chestnut tree in half—let alone a single nut. Welcome to Fryberg's Trains and Toys read the red-and-gold banner clutched in their wooden hands. Where It's Christmas All Year Round.

James Hammond shuddered at the thought.

He was the only one though, as scores of children dragged their parents by the hand past the nutcracker guards and toward the Bavarian castle ahead, their shouts of delight echoing in the crisp Michigan air. One little girl, winter coat flapping in the wind, narrowly missed running into him, so distracted was she by the sight ahead of her.

"I see Santa's Castle," he heard her squeal.

Only if Santa lived in northern Germany and liked bratwurst. The towering stucco building, with its holly-draped ramparts and snow-covered turrets looked like something out of a Grimm's fairy tale. No one would ever accuse Ned Fryberg of pedaling a false reality, that's for sure. It was obvious that his fantasy was completely unattainable in real life. Unlike the nostalgic, homespun malarkey Hammond's Toys sold to the public.

The popularity of both went to show that people loved

their Christmas fantasies, and they were willing to shovel boatloads of money in order to keep them alive.

James didn't understand it, but he was more than glad to help them part with their cash. He was good at it too. Some men gardened and grew vegetables. James grew his family's net worth. And Fryberg's Toys, and its awful Christmas village—a town so named for the Fryberg family—was going to help him grow it even larger.

"Excuse me, sir, but the line for Santa's trolley starts back there." A man wearing a red toy soldier's jacket and black busby pointed behind James's shoulder. In an attempt to control traffic flow, the store provided transportation around the grounds via a garishly colored "toy" train. "Trains leave every five minutes. You won't have too long a wait.

"Or y-you could w-w-walk," he added.

People always tended to stammer whenever James looked them in the eye. Didn't matter if he was trying to be intimidating or not. They simply did. Maybe because, as his mother once told him, he had the same cold, dead eyes as his father. He'd spent much of his youth vainly trying to erase the similarity. Now that he was an adult, he'd grown not to accept his intimidating glower, but embrace it. Same way he embraced all his other unapproachable qualities.

"That depends," he replied. "Which mode is more efficient?"

"Th-that would depend upon on how fast a walker you are. The car makes a couple of stops beforehand, so someone with...with long legs..." The soldier, or whatever he was supposed to be, let the sentence trail off.

"Then walking it is. Thank you."

Adjusting his charcoal-gray scarf tighter around his neck, James turned and continued on his way, along the path to Fryberg's Christmas Castle. The faster he got to his meeting with Belinda Fryberg, the sooner he could lock in his sale and fly back to Boston. At least there, he only had to deal with Christmas one day of the year.

"What did you say?"

"I said, your Christmas Castle has a few years of viability in it, at best."

Noelle hated the new boss.

She'd decided he rubbed her the wrong way when he glided into Belinda's office like a cashmere-wearing shark. She disliked him when he started picking apart their operations. And she loathed him now that he'd insulted the Christmas Castle.

"We all know the future of retail is online," he continued. He uncrossed his long legs and shifted his weight. Uncharitable a thought as it might be, Noelle was glad he'd been forced to squeeze his long, lanky frame into Belinda's office furniture. "The only reason your brick-and-mortar store has survived is because it's basically a tourist attraction."

"What's wrong with being a tourist attraction?" she asked. Fryberg's had done very well thanks to that tourist attraction. Over the years, what had been a small hobby shop had become a cottage industry unto itself with the entire town embracing the Bavarian atmosphere. "You saw our balance sheet. Those tourists are contributing a very healthy portion of our revenue."

"I also saw that the biggest growth came from your online store. In fact, while it's true retail sales have remained constant, your electronic sales have risen over fifteen percent annually."

And were poised to take another leap this year. Noelle had heard the projections. E-retail was the wave of the future. Brick-and-mortar stores like Fryberg's would soon be obsolete.

"Don't get me wrong. I think your late husband did a fantastic job of capitalizing on people's nostalgia," he said to Belinda.

Noelle's mother-in-law smiled. She always smiled when speaking about her late husband. "Ned used to say that Christmas was a universal experience."

"Hammond's has certainly done well by it."

Well? Hammond's had their entire business on the holiday, as had Fryberg's. *Nothing Says Christmas Like Hammond's Toys*. The company motto, repeated at the end of every ad, sung in Noelle's head.

"That's because everyone loves Christmas," she replied.

"Hmm." From the lack of enthusiasm in his response, she might as well have been talking about weather patterns. Then again, his emotional range didn't seem to go beyond brusque and chilly, so maybe that was enthusiastic for him.

"I don't care if they love the holiday or not. It's their shopping patterns I'm interested in, and from the data I've been seeing, more and more people are doing part, if not most of their shopping over the internet. The retailers who survive will be the ones who shift their business models accordingly. I intend to make sure Hammond's is one of those businesses."

"Hammond's," Noelle couldn't help noting. "Not Fryberg's."

"I'm hoping that by the end of the day, the two stores will be on the way to becoming one and the same," he said.

"Wiping out sixty-five years of tradition just like that, are you?"

"Like I said, to survive, sometimes you have to embrace change."

Except they weren't embracing anything. Fryberg's was

being swallowed up and dismantled so that Hammond's could change.

"I think what my daughter-in-law is trying to say is that the Fryberg name carries a great deal of value round these parts," said Belinda. "People are very loyal to my late husband and what he worked to create here."

"Loyalty's a rare commodity these days. Especially in the business world."

"It certainly is. Ned, my husband, had a way of inspiring it."

"Impressive," Hammond replied.

"It's because the Frybergs—Ned and Belinda—have always believed in treating their employees like family," Noelle told him. "And they were always on-site, visible to everyone." Although things had changed over the last few years as Belinda had been spending more and more time in Palm Beach. "I'm not sure working for a faceless CEO in Boston will engender the same feelings."

"What do you expect me to do? Move my office here?"

He looked at her. His gaze, sharp and direct, didn't so much look through a person as cut into them. The flecks of brown in his irises darkened, transforming what had been soft hazel. Self-consciousness curled through Noelle's midsection. She folded her arms tighter to keep the reaction from spreading.

"No. Just keep Fryberg's as a separate entity," she replied.

His brows lifted. "Really? You want me to keep one store separate when all the other properties under our umbrella carry the name Hammond?"

"Why not?" Noelle's palms started to sweat. She was definitely overstepping her authority right now. Belinda had already accepted Hammond's offer. Today's meeting was a friendly dialogue between an outgoing owner and the new CEO, to ensure a successful transition. She couldn't help it. With Belinda stepping down, someone had to protect what Ned had created. James Hammond certainly wasn't. To hear him, Fryberg's Christmas Castle was one step ahead of landlines in terms of obsolescence. She gave him two years tops before he decided "Hammond's" Christmas Castle didn't fit the corporate brand and started downsizing in the name of change. Bet he wouldn't blink an eye doing it either.

Oh, but she really, really, *really* disliked him. Thank goodness the corporate headquarters were in Boston. With luck, he'd go home after this visit and she'd never have to deal with him again.

"Our name recognition and reputation are important elements to our success," she continued. "All those people who line up to see Hammond's displays every Christmas? Would they still remember to make the pilgrimage if Hammond's suddenly became Jones's Toys?"

He chuckled. "Hammond's is hardly the same as Jones."

"Around here it might as well be."

"She makes an interesting point," Belinda said. Noelle felt her mother-in-law's sideways gaze. When it came to giving a pointed look, Belinda Fryberg held her own. In fact, she could probably do it better than most since she always tossed in a dose of maternal reproach. "While you may think our physical store has a limited future, there's no need to hasten its demise prematurely. Maybe it would make more sense for Fryberg's to continue operating under its own name, at least for now."

Leaning back in his chair, Hammond steepled his fingertips together and tapped them against his lips. "I'm not averse to discussing the idea," he said finally.

I'm not averse... How big of him. Noelle bit her tongue. Her mother-in-law, meanwhile, folded her hands and smiled. "Then why don't we do just that over lunch? I made reservations at the Nutcracker Inn downtown."

"I don't usually have lunch…"

No surprise there. Noelle had read once that sharks only ate every few days.

"Perhaps you don't," Belinda replied, "but for a woman my age, skipping meals isn't the best idea. Besides, I find business always goes smoother when accompanied by a bowl of gingerbread soup. You haven't lived until you've tried it."

Either Hammond's cheek muscles twitched at the word *gingerbread* or else they weren't used to smiling. "Very well," he said. "I have some calls to make first though. Why don't I meet you at the elevator in, say, fifteen minutes?"

"I'll see you there."

Returning Belinda's nod, he unfolded his lanky self from the chair and strode from the room. If only he'd keep walking, Noelle thought as she watched his back slip through the door. Keep walking all the way back to Boston.

"Well, that was a surprise." Belinda spoke the second the door shut behind him. "I hadn't realized you'd joined the mergers and acquisitions team."

"I'm sorry," Noelle replied. "But the way he was talking…it sounded like he planned to wipe Fryberg's off the map."

"You know I would never allow that."

She hung her head. "I know, and I'm sorry. On the plus side, he did say he would consider keeping the Fryberg's name."

"Even so, you can't keep getting angry every time he says something that rubs you the wrong way. This is Hammond's company now. You're going to have to learn to bite your tongue."

She'd better hope Noelle's tongue was thick enough to survive the visit then, because there was going to be a lot of biting.

"I just…" Starting now. Gritting her teeth, she turned and looked out the window. Below her, a school tour was lining up in front of the reindeer petting zoo, the same as they did every year, the Wednesday before Thanksgiving. Later on, they would make wish lists for their parents and trek over to the Candy Cane Forest to meet Santa Claus.

Her attention zeroed in on a little girl wearing a grimy pink snow jacket, the dirt visible from yards away, and she smiled nostalgically at the girl's obvious excitement. That excitement was what people like James Hammond didn't understand. Fryberg's was so much more than a toy store or tourist attraction. When you passed through that nutcracker-flanked gate, you entered a different world. A place where, for a few hours, little girls in charity bin hand-me-downs could trade their loneliness and stark reality for a little Christmas magic.

A warm hand settled on her shoulder. "I wish things could stay the same too," Belinda said, "but time marches on no matter how hard we try to stop it. Ned's gone, Kevin's gone, and I just don't have the energy to run this place by myself anymore.

"Besides, a chain like Hammond's can invest capital in this place that I don't have."

Capital, sure, but what about heart? Compassion was part of the Fryberg DNA. Noelle still remembered that day in sixth grade when Kevin invited her to his house and she felt the family's infectious warmth for the very first time.

"I don't fault you for wanting to retire," she said, leaning ever so slightly into the older woman's touch. "I just wish you hadn't sold to such a Grinch."

"He is serious, isn't he?" Belinda chuckled. "Must be all that dour Yankee heritage."

"Dour? Try frozen. The guy has about as much Christmas spirit as a block of ice."

Her mother-in-law squeezed her shoulder. "Fortunately for us, you have enough Christmas spirit for a dozen people. You'll keep the spirit alive. Unless you decide to move on, that is."

Noelle tried for tongue biting again and failed. They'd had this conversation before. It was another one of the reasons Belinda sold the business instead of simply retiring. She insisted Noelle not be tied down by the family business. A reason Noelle found utterly silly.

"You know I have zero intention of ever leaving Fryberg," she said.

"Oh, I know you think that now. But you're young. You're smart. There's an entire world out there beyond Fryberg's Toys."

Noelle shook her head. Not for her there wasn't. The store was too big a part of her.

It was all of her, really.

Her mother-in-law squeezed her shoulder again. "Kevin and Ned wouldn't want you to shortchange your future any more than I do."

At the mention of her late husband's wishes, Noelle bit back a familiar swell of guilt.

"Besides," Belinda continued, heading toward her desk. "Who knows? Maybe you'll impress Mr. Hammond so much, he'll promote you up the corporate ladder."

"Him firing me is more likely," Noelle replied. She recalled how sharp Hammond's gaze had become when she dared to challenge him. Oh, yeah, she could picture him promoting her, all right.

"You never know" was all Belinda said. "I better go get

ready for lunch. Don't want to keep our Mr. Hammond waiting. Are you joining us?"

And continue bonding with Mr. Hammond over a bowl of gingerbread soup? Thanks, but no thanks. "I think Mr. Hammond and I have had enough contact for the day. Better I save my tongue and let you and Todd fill me in on the visit later."

"That reminds me. On your way out, can you stop by Todd's office and let his secretary know that if he calls in after the funeral, I'd like to talk with him?"

"Sure thing."

Her answer was buried by the sound of the phone ringing.

"Oh, dear," Belinda said upon answering. "This is Dick Greenwood. I'd better take it. Hopefully, he won't chat my ear off. Will you do me another favor and give Mr. Hammond a tour of the floor while I'm tied up?"

So much for being done with the man. "Of course." She'd donate a kidney if Belinda asked.

"And be nice."

"Yes, ma'am."

The kidney would have been easier.

"You're not going to have an insubordination problem, are you?"

On the other end of the line, Jackson Hammond's voice sounded far away. James might have blamed the overseas connection except he knew better. Jackson Hammond always sounded distant.

Struggling to keep the phone tucked under his ear, he reached for the paper towels. "Problem?" he repeated. "Hardly."

With her short black hair and red sweater dress, Noelle

Fryberg was more of an attack elf. Too small and precious to do any real damage.

"Only reason she was in the meeting was because the new general manager had to attend a funeral, and she's the assistant GM." And because she was family. Apparently, the concept mattered to some people.

He shrugged and tossed his wadded towel into the basket. "Her objections were more entertaining than anything."

He'd already come to the same conclusion regarding the Fryberg name, but it was fun seeing her try to stare him into capitulation. She had very large, very soulful eyes. Her glaring at him was like being glared at by a kitten. He had to admire the effort though. It was more than a lot of—hell, most—people.

"All in all, the transition is going smooth as silk. I'm going to tour the warehouse this afternoon." And then hightail it back to the airstrip as soon as possible. With any luck, he'd be in Boston by eight that evening. Noelle Fryberg's verve might be entertaining, but not so much that he wanted to stick around Christmas Land a moment longer than necessary.

"Christmas is only four weeks away. You're going to need that distribution center linked into ours as soon as possible."

"It'll get done," James replied. The reassurance was automatic. James learned a long time ago that his father preferred his world run as smoothly as possible. Complications and problems were things you dealt with on your own.

"If you need anything from my end, talk with Carli. I've asked her to be my point person while I'm in Vienna."

"Thank you." But James wouldn't need anything from his father's end. He'd been running the corporation for several years now while his father concentrated on overseas and other pet projects—like his new protégé, Carli, for example.

Then again, he hadn't needed his father since his parents' divorce. About the time his father made it clear he didn't want James underfoot. Not wanting their eldest son around was the one thing Jackson Hammond and his ex-wife had in common.

"How is the trip going?" James asked, turning to other, less bitter topics.

"Well enough. I'm meeting with Herr Burns in the morning…" There was a muffled sound in the background. "Someone's knocking at the door. I have to go. We'll talk tomorrow, when you're back in the office."

The line disconnected before James had a chance to remind him tomorrow was Thanksgiving. Not that it mattered. He'd still be in the office.

He was always in the office. Wasn't like he had a family.

Belinda was nowhere in sight when James stepped into the hallway. Instead, he found the daughter-in-law waiting by the elevator, arms again hugging her chest. "Belinda had to take a call with Dick Greenwood," she told him.

"I'm sorry" was his automatic reply. Greenwood was a great vendor, but he was notorious for his chattiness. James made a point of avoiding direct conversations if he could.

Apparently, the daughter-in-law knew what he meant, because the corners of her mouth twitched. About as close to a smile as he'd seen out of her. "She said she'll join you as soon as she can. In the meantime, she thought you'd like a tour of the retail store."

"She did, did she?" More likely, she thought it would distract him while she was stuck on the phone.

Noelle shrugged. "She thought it would give you an idea of the foot traffic we handle on a day-to-day basis."

He'd seen the sales reports; he knew what kind of traffic they handled. Still, it couldn't hurt to check out the store. Hammond's was always on the lookout for new ways to engage their customers. "Are you going to be my guide?" he asked, reaching across to hit the elevator button.

"Yes, I am." If she thought he missed the soft sigh she let out before speaking, she was mistaken.

All the more reason to take the tour.

The doors opened, and James motioned for her to step in first. Partly to be a gentleman, but mostly because holding back gave him an opportunity to steal a surreptitious look at her figure. The woman might be tiny, but she was perfectly proportioned. Make that normally proportioned, he amended. Too many of the women he met had try-hard figures. Worked out and enhanced to artificial perfection. Noelle looked fit, but she still carried a little more below than she did on top, which he appreciated.

"We bill ourselves as the country's largest toy store," Noelle said once the elevator doors shut. "The claim is based on square footage. We are the largest retail space in the continental US. This weekend alone we'll attract thousands of customers."

"Black Friday weekend. The retailers' best friend," he replied. Then, because he couldn't resist poking the bee's nest a little, he added, "That is, until Cyber Monday came along. These days we move almost as much inventory online. Pretty soon people won't come out for Black Friday at all. They'll do their shopping Thanksgiving afternoon while watching TV."

"Hammond's customers might, but you can't visit a Christmas wonderland via a computer."

That again. He turned to look at her. "Do you really

think kids five or six years from now are going to care about visiting Santa Claus?"

"Of course they are. It's Santa."

"I hate to break it to you, but kids are a little more realistic these days. They grow fast. Our greeting card fantasy holiday is going to get harder and harder to sell."

"Especially if you insist on calling it a fantasy."

What should he call it? Fact? "Belinda wasn't kidding when she said you were loyal, was she?"

"The Frybergs are family. Of course I would be loyal."

Not necessarily, but James didn't feel like arguing the point.

"Even if I weren't—related that is—I'd respect what Ned and Belinda created." She crossed her arms. Again. "They understood that retail is about more than moving inventory."

Her implication was clear: she considered him a corporate autocrat who was concerned solely with the bottom line. While she might be correct, he didn't intend to let her get away with the comment unchallenged.

Mirroring her posture, he tilted his head and looked straight at her. "Is that so? What exactly is it about then?"

"People, of course."

"Of course." She was not only loyal, but naive. Retail was *all* about moving product. All the fancy window dressing she specialized in was to convince people to buy the latest and greatest, and then to buy the next latest and greatest the following year. And so on and so forth.

At that moment, the elevator opened and before them lay Fryberg's Toys in all its glory. Aisle upon aisle of toys, spread out like a multicolored promised land. There were giant stuffed animals arranged by environment, lions and tigers in the jungle, cows and horses by the farm. Construction toys were spread around a jobsite, around which cars zipped on a multilevel racetrack. There was even a wall of televisions blasting the latest video games. A special display for every interest, each one overflowing with products for sale.

"Oh, yeah," he murmured, "it's totally about the people."

A remote-control drone zipped past their heads as they walked toward the center aisle. A giant teddy bear made of plastic building bricks marked the entrance like the Colossus of Rhodes.

"It's like Christmas morning on steroids," he remarked as they passed under the bear's legs.

"This is the Christmas Castle, after all. Everything should look larger-than-life and magical. To stir the imagination."

Not to mention the desire for plastic bricks and stuffed animals, thought James.

"Santa's workshop and the Candy Cane Forest are located at the rear of the building," she said pointing to an archway bedecked with painted holly and poinsettia. "That's also where Ned's model train layout is located. It used to be a much larger section, but now it's limited to one room-size museum."

Yet something else lost to the march of time, James refrained from saying. The atmosphere was chilly enough. Looking around he noticed their aisle led straight toward the archway, and that the only way to avoid Santa was to go to the end, turn and head back up a different aisle.

He nodded at the arch. "What's on the other side?" he asked.

"Other side of what?"

"Santa's woods or whatever it is."

"Santa's workshop and Candy Cane Forest," she corrected. "There's a door that leads back into the store, or they can continue on to see the reindeer."

"Meaning they go home to purchase their child's wish item online from who-knows-what site."

"Or come back another day. Most people don't do their Christmas shopping with the kids in tow."

"How about in April, when they aren't Christmas shopping? They walk outside to see the reindeer and poof! There goes your potential sale."

That wouldn't do at all. "After the kids visit Santa, the traffic should be rerouted back into the store so the parents can buy whatever it is Little Susie or Johnny wished for."

"You want to close off access to the reindeer?"

She needn't look so horrified. It wasn't as though he'd suggested euthanizing the creatures. "I want customers to buy toys. And they aren't going to if they are busy looking at reindeer. What's that?"

He pointed to a giant Moose-like creature wearing a Santa's hat and wreath standing to the right of the archway. It took up most of the wall space, forcing the crowd to congregate toward the middle. As a result, customers looking to walk past the archway to another aisle had to battle a throng of children.

"Oh, that's Fryer Elk, the store mascot," Noelle replied. "Ned created him when he opened the store. Back in the day, he appeared in the ads. They retired him in the eighties and he's been here ever since."

"He's blocking the flow of traffic. He should be somewhere else."

For a third time, James got the folded arm treatment. "He's an institution," she replied, as if that was reason enough for his existence.

He could be Ned Fryberg standing there stuffed himself, and he would still be hindering traffic. Letting out a long breath, James reached into his breast pocket for his notebook. Once the sale was finalized, he would send his operations manager out here to evaluate the layout.

"You really don't have any respect for tradition, do you?" Noelle asked.

He peered over his pen at her. Just figuring this out, was she? That's what happened when you spent a fortune crafting a corporate image. People started believing the image was real.

"No," he replied. "I don't. In fact…" He put his notebook away. "We might as well get something straight right now. As far as I'm concerned, the only thing that matters is making sure Hammond's stays profitable for the next fifty years. Everything else can go to blazes."

"Everything," she repeated. Her eyes narrowed.

"Everything, and that includes elks, tradition and especially Chris—"

He never got a chance to finish.

CHAPTER TWO

FOUR STITCHES AND a concussion. That's what the emergency room doctor told Noelle. "He's fortunate. Those props can do far worse," she added. "Your associates really shouldn't be flying remote-control drones inside."

"So they've been told," Noelle replied. In no uncertain terms by James Hammond once he could speak.

The drone had slammed into the back of his head, knocking him face-first into a pile of model racecar kits. The sight of the man sprawled on the floor might have been funny if not for the blood running down the back of his skull. Until that minute, she'd been annoyed as hell at the man for his obvious lack of respect toward Fryberg tradition. Seeing the blood darkening his hair quickly checked her annoyance. As blood was wont to do.

That was until she turned him over and he started snarling about careless associates and customer safety. Then she went back to being annoyed. Only this time, it was because the man had a point. What if the drone had struck a customer—a child? Things could have been even worse. As it was, half of Miss Speroni's first grade class was probably going to have nightmares from witnessing the accident.

Then there was the damage to James Hammond himself. Much as she disliked the man, stitches and a concussion were nothing to sneeze at.

"How long before he's ready for discharge?" she asked.

"My nurse is bandaging the stitches right now," the doctor replied. "Soon as I get his paperwork written up, he'll be all yours."

Oh, goodie. Noelle didn't realize she'd gotten custody. She went back to the waiting room where Belinda was finishing up a phone call.

"Bob is working on a statement for the press," her mother-in-law told her. "And we're pulling the product off the shelves per advice from the lawyers. Thankfully, the incident didn't get caught on camera so we won't have to deal with that. I doubt Mr. Hammond would like being a social media sensation."

"I'm not sure Mr. Hammond likes much of anything," Noelle replied. She was thinking of the remark he made right before the drone struck him. "Did you know, he actually said he doesn't like Christmas? How can the man think that and run a store like Hammond's?" Or Fryberg's.

"Obviously, his disdain hasn't stopped him from doubling Hammond's profits over the past two years," Belinda replied. "What matters isn't that he like Christmas, but that he keeps the people in Fryberg employed, which he will."

"Hope they like working for Mr. Frosty. Did you know he wants to get rid of Fryer?"

"Well, some change is bound to happen," Belinda said.

"I know," Noelle grumbled. She bowed her head. She really did. Same way she understood that the retail industry was changing. She also knew she was acting irrational and childish about the entire situation. Ever since Belinda announced the sale, however, she'd been unable to catch her breath. It felt like there were fingers clawing inside her looking for purchase. A continual churning sensation. Like she was about to lose her grip.

James Hammond's arrival only made the feeling worse.

"Doesn't mean I have to like it though," she said referring to the prospect of change.

Belinda nudged her shoulder. "Sweetheart, you wouldn't be you if you did. Cheer up. Mr. Hammond will be out of your hair soon."

"Not soon enough," she replied.

"What wouldn't be soon enough?" Hammond's voice caused her to start in her chair. Turning, she saw a nurse pushing him toward her. He was slouched down in a wheelchair, a hand propping his head. Noelle caught a glimpse of a white bandage on the back of his scalp.

"The bandage can come off tomorrow," the nurse told them.

"How are you feeling, Mr. Hammond?" Belinda asked.

"Like someone split my head open. Who knew such a little device could pack such a wallop?"

"Lots of things pack a wallop when they're going thirty miles an hour. We pulled the toy from the shelves. Though I doubt it would have been popular anyway, once parents heard what happened."

"Don't blame them. Thing could slice an ear off." Groaning, he leaned forward and buried his face in both hands as though one was suddenly not enough to hold it up. "I'm going to have Hammond's pull them too as soon as I get back to Boston," he spoke through his fingers.

"That won't be anytime soon, I'm afraid. You heard what Dr. Nelson said," the nurse warned.

"What did she say?" Noelle asked. She didn't like the sound of the nurse's comment.

Hammond waved a hand before cradling his head again. "Nothing."

"Mr. Hammond has a slight concussion. He's been advised to rest for the next couple of days. That includes no air travel."

"You mean you're staying here?" No, no, no. Noelle's stomach started to twist. He was supposed to go away, not stick around for the weekend.

"The doctor merely recommended I rest," James replied. "No one said it was mandatory."

"Perhaps not, but it's generally a good idea to take doctors' advice," Belinda said.

"We're talking about a handful of stitches. Nothing I haven't had before. I'll be fine. Why don't we go have our lunch as planned and finish our conversation? I could use some food in my stomach. What kind of soup did you say they made?"

"Gingerbread," Noelle replied.

"The only place you should be going is to bed," the nurse said.

Much as Noelle hated to admit it, the nurse was right. He was looking paler by the minute. She remembered how unsteady he'd been right after the accident; he could barely sit up.

Funny, but he still looked formidable despite the pallor. A virile invalid. Noelle didn't think it possible. Must be the combination of square jaw and broad shoulders, she decided. And the dark suit. Black made everyone look intimidating.

Again, he waved off the nurse's advice. "Nonsense. I rested while waiting for the doctor. Why don't we go have our lunch as planned and finish our conversation? I could use some food in my stomach. What kind of soup did you say they made?"

"I just told you."

A crease deepened between his eyes. "You did?"

"Uh-huh. Two seconds ago."

"That only proves I'm hungry. I'm having trouble listening." He pushed himself to a standing position, squaring his shoulders proudly when he reached his feet. His upper body swayed back and forth unsteadily. "See?" he said. "Fine. Let's go."

Noelle looked over her shoulder at Belinda who shook her head in return. "I'm not going to negotiate anything while you're unsteady on your feet," her mother-in-law said. "I won't be accused of taking advantage when you're not thinking straight."

James laughed. "You're a smart businesswoman, Belinda, but I can assure you, no one ever takes advantage of me."

"That I can believe," Noelle murmured.

He looked at her and smiled. "I'll take that as a compliment, Mrs. Fryberg. Now how about we go get that lunch we missed…"

It took two steps for him to lose his balance. His eyes started to roll back in his head, and his knees started to buckle.

Noelle reached him first. "Okay, that's enough," she said, reaching around his waist. Thanks to the size difference, it took a minute to maneuver him, but eventually she managed to lower him into the wheelchair. Unfortunately, the downward momentum pulled her along as well. She landed with one hand pressed against his torso and knee wedged between his thighs. Man, but he was solid. A tall, lean block of granite.

She looked up to find herself nose to nose with him. Up close, his eyes were far more dappled than she realized, the green more of an accent color than true eye shade.

He had freckles too. A smattering across the bridge of his nose.

Cold-blooded businessmen weren't supposed to have freckles.

"Think you might listen to the nurse now?" she asked.

"I was lightheaded for a moment, that's all."

"Lightheaded, huh?" She pushed herself to her feet. To her embarrassment, the move required splaying her hand wider, so that the palm of her hand pressed over his heart. Fortunately, he was too dizzy or distracted to comment.

"Any more lightheaded and you would have hit the floor," she told him. "Are you trying to get more stitches?"

"I'm not..."

"Face it, Mr. Hammond, you're in no condition to do anything but rest," Belinda said. "We'll talk when you're feeling better. Monday."

"Monday?" He'd started to rest his head in his hands again, but when Belinda spoke, he jerked his head upward. The pain crossing his face made Noelle wince. "Why wait until then? I won't need that many days to recover."

"Maybe not, but that is the next time I'll be able to see you. Tomorrow is Thanksgiving. The only business I'll be discussing is whether the stuffing is too dry."

"What about Friday?"

Noelle answered for her. "Black Friday, remember? Around these parts, it's the kickoff for the annual Christmas festival, the biggest weekend of our year."

"I'll be much too busy to give you the proper time," Belinda added.

Noelle watched the muscle twitching in Hammond's jaw. Clearly, he preferred being the one who dictated the schedule, and not the other way around.

"Let me get this straight." Whether his voice was low by design or discomfort, Noelle couldn't guess. His tension came though nevertheless. "I'm not allowed to fly home for the next twenty-four hours..."

"At least," the nurse said.

The muscle twitched again. "*At least* twenty-four hours,"

he corrected. "Nor will you meet with me for the next five days?"

"That's correct," Belinda replied. "We can meet first thing Monday morning, and conclude our preliminary negotiations."

"I see." He nodded. Slowly. Anyone with two eyes could tell he didn't appreciate this change in plans at all. Noelle would be lying if she didn't say it gave her a tiny trill of satisfaction. Payback for his wanting to toss Fryer.

"Fine," he said, leaning back in his chair. "We'll talk Monday. Only because my head hurts too much to argue." Noelle had a feeling he wasn't kidding. "What was the name of that hotel?"

"The Nutcracker Inn," she replied.

"Right, that one. I'm going to need a room, and something to eat. What did you say that soup was?"

"Gingerbread." It was the third time he'd asked. She looked at the nurse who nodded.

"Temporary short-term memory loss can happen with concussions. It should recede soon enough. However, I think you might have a more pressing problem."

"I do?"

"He does?"

The two of them spoke at the same time. "I'm not sure the Nutcracker has any rooms," the nurse replied. "You know how booked it gets during the holidays."

"Wait a second." James tried to look up at the nurse, only to wince and close his eyes. "Please don't tell me there's no room at the inn."

"Wouldn't be the first time," the nurse replied. "Did you know that once we even had a baby born—"

"I doubt Mr. Hammond will have to do anything quite as dramatic," Noelle interjected. No need for the conversation to head down that particular road.

The nurse offered a tight-lipped smile. Apparently, she didn't appreciate being cut off. "Either way, you're going to need someone to look in on you. Doctor's orders."

"The concierge will love that request," Hammond muttered.

"We could arrange for a private duty nurse."

"Good grief," Belinda said. "That doesn't sound pleasant at all."

"Pleasant isn't exactly on the table right now." Hammond's eyes had grown heavy lidded and his words were slurred. It was obvious the entire conversation was exhausting him, and Noelle couldn't help but feel bad.

Although she doubted he'd appreciate the compassion. A man like Hammond, with his disregard for sentiment and tradition, would despise showing any hint of vulnerability.

"Of course pleasant is on the table," Belinda said. "This is Fryberg." The meaning behind her emphasis was obvious.

Hammond let out a low groan. Still feeling compassionate, Noelle decided the noise was coincidental.

Her mother-in-law continued as if the noise never happened. "We're not going to let you spend your weekend in some hotel room, eating room service and being attended to by a stranger. You'll spend the weekend with me. That way you can recuperate, and enjoy a proper Thanksgiving as well."

The strangest look crossed Hammond's face. Part surprise, part darkness as though her mother-in-law's suggestion unnerved him. Noelle didn't picture him as a man who got unnerved. Ever.

"I don't want to put you out," he said.

"You won't. I have plenty of room. I'll even make you

some…oh, shoot." A look crossed her features, not nearly as dark as Hammond's, but definitely distressed.

"What is it?" Noelle asked.

"The Orion House Dinner is this evening. I completely forgot."

In all the craziness, so had Noelle. Fryberg's was being honored for its fund-raising efforts on behalf of homeless veterans. "Would you mind?" her mother-in-law asked. "I don't want Orion House to think I don't appreciate the honor. The project meant so much to Ned."

"I know," replied Noelle. After Kevin's death, her father-in-law had channeled his grief into helping as many veteran programs as possible. Orion House had topped the list. "He was very passionate about wanting to help."

"That he was," Belinda said, getting the faraway look she always got when they discussed Ned. The family had been through a lot these past years, and yet they continued to channel their energy into the community. Their dedication in the face of grief made her proud to bear the Fryberg name.

"Would you mind stepping in instead?"

"Not at all," she told her. "I'd love to." It'd be an honor to accept an award for them.

"Thank goodness." The older woman let out a long sigh. "I was afraid that because of our words earlier… Never mind." Whatever her mother-in-law had been about to say she waved away. "Let me pull my car around. I'll help you get Mr. Hammond settled, and then go home to change."

Help her…? Wait… What exactly had she agreed to do?

Noelle opened her mouth, closed it, then opened it again. Nothing came out though. That's because she knew what she'd agreed to. As surely as the sickening feeling growing in her stomach.

Somehow, James Hammond had become *her* responsibility. She looked over to her mother-in-law, but Belinda was busy fishing through her purse. And here she thought she would be free of the man. Talk about your sick karmic jokes. If only she'd been the one hit in the head.

"Do you need an extra copy of the discharge instructions?" the nurse asked her.

"No," Noelle replied with a sigh. "I know what to expect."

There was only one consolation, if you could call it that. Hammond looked about as thrilled over this change of events as she was.

Goodie. They could be miserable together.

A few minutes later, James found himself being wheeled outside behind a tiny bundle of annoyance, who marched toward the waiting sedan with her arms yet again wrapped tightly across her chest. A voice behind his headache wondered if they were permanently attached to her body that way.

"Why don't you take the front seat?" Belinda opened the passenger door. "I've pulled it all the way back so you'll have plenty of leg room."

Front seat, back seat. Didn't make much difference. Neither were the cockpit of his private plane. His head felt split in two, the world was tipping on its axis and he wanted nothing more than to be in his bed back in Boston. Damn drone.

He pushed himself to his feet only to have the world rock back and forth like a seesaw. A second later, an arm wrapped around his biceps, steadying him, and he smelled the sweet scent of orange blossoms. The elf. He recognized the perfume from the confines of the elevator. Funny, but he expected her to smell Christmassy, not like Florida sunshine. Maybe they were out of sugar cookie perfume this week.

"Something wrong?"

Turning his head—barely—he saw her frowning at him and realized he'd snorted out loud at his joke. "Do you really need to ask?"

He was being an ass, he knew that, but with stitches in his scalp, surely he was entitled to a little churlishness?

The frown deepened. "Watch your head," she replied.

James did as he was told, and as his reward, the orange blossoms—as well as her grip—disappeared. In their absence, his headache intensified. He found himself slumped against a leather armrest with his fingers pressed against his temple to hold his head up.

"Fortunately, we don't have to drive too far," he heard Belinda say. "Noelle only lives a short distance from town."

"Great." What he really wanted to say was that two feet was too far what with the lights outside dipping and rocking as they passed by. Thankfully the sun had set. If those were buildings bobbing, he'd be lurching the contents of his stomach all over his Bostonians. He closed his eyes, and did his best to imagine orange blossoms.

"The nurse seemed to think the worst of the dizziness would pass by tomorrow," Noelle said from behind him.

"Thank God," he whispered. If true, then maybe he could snag a ride to the airport and fly home, doctor's orders be damned. He bet the elf would drive him. After all, she didn't want him at her house any more than he wanted to be there. He'd caught the look on the woman's face when Belinda foisted him on her.

Foisted. What a perfect word for the situation. Stuck

where he didn't want to be, dependent on people who didn't want him around.

Story of his life.

Great. He'd moved from churlish to pity party. Why not round out the trifecta and start whining too?

How he hated this. Hated having no choice. Hated being weak and needy. He hadn't needed anyone since he was twelve years old. Needing and foisting were incompatible concepts.

"It's too bad you can't look out the window," Belinda said. "The town looks beautiful all lit up."

James pried open one eye to see building after building decorated with Christmas lights. *Ugh.* One in particular had a giant evergreen dripping with red and green.

"That's the Nutcracker Inn. The Bavarian market is next door. It'll be packed on Friday for the festival."

"I doubt Mr. Hammond is very interested in a tour, Belinda."

"I'm merely pointing out a few of the landmarks since he's going to be here all weekend."

Not if he could help it, thought James.

"The man can't remember what kind of soup they serve—I doubt he'll remember what the place looks like."

"There's no need to be harsh, Noelle Fryberg."

"Yes, ma'am."

Actually, James rather liked the harshness. Beat being treated like a patient. "Pumpkin," he replied.

"Excuse me?" Belinda asked.

"The soup. It's pumpkin."

"You mean gingerbread," Noelle replied.

"Oh. Right." He knew it was some kind of seasonal flavor. His cheeks grew warm.

Belinda patted him on the knee. "Don't worry about

it, Mr. Hammond. I'm sure you'll be back to normal by tomorrow."

"Let's hope so," he heard the elf mutter.

James couldn't have agreed with her more.

CHAPTER THREE

THE NEXT MORNING James woke to what had to be the best-smelling candle in the universe—sweet with traces of allspice and cinnamon—which was odd since he didn't normally buy candles. Maybe the smell had something to do with the stinging sensation on the back of his head and the vague memories of dark hair and kitten eyes dancing on the edge of his brain.

And orange blossoms. For some reason, the first thought in his mind was that as delicious as the candle smelled, it wasn't orange blossoms.

Slowly, he pried open an eye. What the...?

This wasn't his Back Bay condo. He sprang up, only to have a sharp pain push him back down on the bed.

Sofa, he amended. He was lying facedown on a leather sofa, his cheek swallowed by a large memory foam pillow. Gingerly, he felt the back of his skull, his fingers meeting a patch of gauze and tape.

The drone. This must be Noelle Fryberg's living room. Last thing he remembered was leaning into her warm body as she led him through the front door. Explained why he had orange blossoms on the brain. The memory of the smell eased the tension between his shoulder blades.

Once the vertigo abated, he surveyed his surroundings. Given her slavish devotion to Fryberg's vision, he pictured his hostess living in a mirror image of the Christmas Castle, with baskets of sugarplums and boughs of holly. He'd been close. The house definitely had the same stucco and wood architecture as the rest of the town, although she'd thankfully forgone any year-round Christmas motif. Instead, the inside was pleasantly furnished with simple, sturdy furniture like the large pine cabinet lining the wall across the way. Brightly colored plates hung on the wall behind it. Homey. Rustic. With not a chandelier or trace of Italian marble to be found.

"You're awake."

A pair of shapely legs suddenly appeared in his line of vision, followed seconds later by a pair of big cornflower-colored eyes as the elf squatted down by his head. "I was coming in to check on you. I'm supposed to make sure you don't fall into a coma while sleeping," she said.

"I haven't."

"Obviously."

As obvious as her joy over having to play nursemaid.

She looked less elfish than yesterday. More girl next door. The red dress had been shucked in favor of a white-and-red University of Wisconsin sweatshirt and jeans, and her short hair was pulled away from her face with a bright red headband. James didn't think it was possible to pull back short hair, but she had. It made her eyes look like one of those paintings from the seventies. The ones where everyone had giant sad eyes. Only in this case, they weren't sad; they were antipathetic.

He tried sitting up again. Slowly this time, making sure to keep his head and neck as still as possible. He felt like an awkward idiot. How was it that people in movies bounced back from head wounds in minutes? Here he was sliding his legs to the floor like he was stepping onto ice.

"How did I end up here?" he asked.

Her mouth turned downward. "Do you mean the house or the sofa?"

"The sofa."

"Good. For a minute I was afraid you didn't remember anything." She stood up, taking her blue eyes from his vision unless he looked up, which didn't feel like the best idea. "You collapsed on it soon as we got through the door last night," she told him. "I tried to convince you to go upstairs to the bedroom, but you refused to budge."

That sounded vaguely familiar. "Stairs were too much work."

"That's what you said last night. Anyway, since you refused to move from the sofa, I gave you a pillow, threw an afghan over you and called it a night."

Out of the corner of his eye, James saw a flash of bright blue yarn piled on the floor near his feet. Tightness gripped his chest at the notion of someone tucking a blanket around his legs while he slept. Cradling his head while they placed a pillow underneath.

"Wait a second," he said as a realization struck him. "You checked on me every few hours?"

"I had to. Doctor's orders."

"What about sleep? Did you…"

"Don't worry—I didn't put myself out any more than necessary."

But more than she preferred. He was but an unwanted responsibility after all. The tightness eased, and the familiar numbness returned. "I'm glad. I'd hate to think you had to sacrifice too much."

"Bare minimum, I assure you. Belinda would have my head if you died on my watch. In case you hadn't guessed, she takes her responsibility to others very seriously. Especially those injured in her store."

His store now. James let the slip pass uncommented.

"Good policy. I'm sure your lawyers appreciate the extra effort."

"It's not policy," she quickly shot back. Her eyes simmered with contention. "It's compassion. The Frybergs have always believed in taking care of others. Belinda especially. I'll have you know that I've seen her literally give a stranger the coat off her back."

"I apologize," James replied. "I didn't mean to insinuate…"

She held up her hand. "Whatever. Just know that lawsuits are the last thing on Belinda's mind.

"You have no idea how special the Fryberg family is," she continued. Driving home the point. "Ned and Belinda were…are…the best people you'll ever meet. The whole town loves them."

"Duly noted," James replied. Must be nice, having a family member care so much they sprang to your defense at the slightest ill word. "I'll watch my language from now on."

"Thank you."

"You're welcome."

They both fell silent. James sat back on the sofa and rubbed his neck, an uncomfortable itch having suddenly danced across his collar. Normally silence didn't bother him; he didn't know why this lapse in conversation felt so awkward.

Probably because the entire situation was awkward. If they were in Boston, he would be the host. He would be offering to whip up a cappuccino and his signature scrambled eggs, the way he did for all his overnight guests. Instead, he was sitting on her sofa, feeling very much like the obligation that he was.

And here he'd thought he was done feeling that way ever again.

Noelle broke the silence first. Tugging on her sweatshirt

the way an officer might tug on his jacket, she cleared her throat. "I'm heading back into the kitchen. You might as well go back to sleep. It's still early. Not even seven-thirty."

"You're awake."

"I have cooking to do. You're supposed to rest."

"I'm rested out." Headache or not, his body was still on East Coast time, and according to it, he'd already slept several hours past his usual wake time. "I don't think I could sleep more if I wanted to."

"Suit yourself," she said with a shrug. "TV remote's on the end table if you want it. I'll be in the kitchen." The unspoken *Stay out of my way* came loud and clear.

She turned and padded out the door. Although James had never been one to ogle women, he found himself watching her jean-clad rear end. Some women were born to wear jeans, and the elf was one of them. With every step, her hips swayed from side to side like a well-toned bell. It was too bad the woman disliked his presence; her attractiveness was one of the few positive things about this debacle of a trip.

He needed to go back to Boston. It was where he belonged. Where he was...well, if not wanted, at least comfortable.

Slowly, he pushed himself to his feet. The room spun a little, but not nearly as badly as it had yesterday, or even fifteen minutes earlier, for that matter. If he managed to walk to the kitchen without problem, he was leaving. Grant him and Noelle a reprieve.

Plans settled, he made his way to the kitchen. Happily, the room only spun a little. He found his hostess in the center of the room pulling a bright yellow apron over her head. The delicious aroma from before hung heavy in the air. It wasn't a candle at all, but some kind of pie. Pumpkin, he realized, taking a deep breath.

His stomach rumbled. "I don't suppose I could get a cup of coffee," he said when she turned around.

She pointed to the rear cupboard where a full pot sat on the coffee maker burner. "Cups are in the cupboard above. There's cereal and toast if you want any breakfast. Do you need me to pour?" she added belatedly.

"No, thank you. I can manage." He made his way over to the cupboard. Like everything else in the house, the mugs were simple, yet sturdy. He was beginning to think she was the only delicate-looking thing in the house. "You have a nice place," he remarked as he poured.

"You sound surprised."

"Do I?" he replied. "I don't mean to."

"In that case, thank you. Kevin and his father came up with the design."

That explained the resemblance to the Christmas Castle.

"I'm curious," he said, leaning against the counter. She had bent over to look in the oven, giving him another look at her bottom. "Is there some kind of rule that the houses all have to look…"

"Look like what?" she asked, standing up.

"Alike." Like they'd all been plucked off a picture post-card.

"Well the idea *is* to resemble a European village. That's part of what makes us such a popular tourist attraction."

She was tossing around his words from yesterday. He'd insulted her again.

Which he knew before asking the question. Hell, it was why he'd asked it. Their exchange earlier reminded him how much he'd enjoyed her backbone yesterday. Next to her cute figure, pushing her buttons was the only other thing that made this trip enjoyable. "I'm sure it does," he replied.

"What is that supposed to mean?"

James shrugged. "Nothing. I was simply noting the town had a distinctive theme is all, and wondered if it was by design. Now I know."

"I'm sure you already knew from your research," she said, folding her arms. She had the closed-off pose down to a science. "You just felt like mocking the town."

"Actually…" What could he say? He doubted she'd enjoy knowing her anger entertained him. "Maybe I did."

She opened her mouth, and he waited for her to toss an insult in his direction. Instead she closed her lips again and spun around. Immediately, James regretted pushing too far. What did he expect? Surely, he knew she wouldn't find him as entertaining as he found her. Quite the opposite. She disliked him the same as everyone else. Pushing her buttons guaranteed the status quo.

There was one thing he could say that she might like.

"Your pie smells delicious, by the way. I'm sorry I won't get to taste it."

That got her attention. She turned back around. "Why not?"

Leaning against the counter, he took a long sip of his coffee. Damn, but she made a hearty cup. "Because as soon as I have my coffee and grab a shower, you're driving me to the airstrip so I can fly back to Boston."

Noelle almost dropped the pie she was taking out of the oven. Had she heard right? Not that she wouldn't be glad to see the back of him, but… "I thought the doctor said no flying."

"Doctors say a lot of things."

"Yeah, but in this case…" She flashed back to his falling into her at the hospital. "You could barely stand without getting dizzy."

"That was yesterday. Clearly, that's not the case today."

No, it wasn't. He appeared to be standing quite nicely against her counter, all wrinkled and fresh with sleep as he was.

The guy might be annoying, but he wore bedhead well.

Still, she couldn't believe he was serious about flying an airplane less than twenty-four hours after getting whacked in the head. What if he got dizzy again and crashed the plane? "It doesn't sound like the wisest of plans," she said.

From over his coffee mug, he looked at her with an arched brow. "You'd rather I stick around here with you all weekend?"

"No, but..."

"Then why do you care whether I fly home or not?"

Good question. Why did she care? She looked down at the golden-brown pie still in her hands. Setting it on the cooling rack, she took off her oven mitts, then nudged the oven door shut with her hip.

"I don't care," she said, turning back around. "I'm surprised is all. In my experience, doctors don't advise against things without reason.

"Why are you so eager to leave Fryberg anyway?" she asked. She could already guess the answer. It'd been clear from his arrival he didn't think much of their town.

Unless, that is, he had a different reason for returning to Boston. Something more personal. "If you have Thanksgiving plans with someone, wouldn't they prefer you play it safe?"

His coffee cup muffled the words, but she could swear he said "Hardly." It wasn't a word she'd expected him to use. *Hardly* was the same as saying *unlikely*, which couldn't be the case. A man as handsome as Hammond would have dozens of women interested in him. Just because he rubbed her the wrong way...

She must have misheard.

Still, it wasn't someone special calling him home. And she doubted it was because of Black Friday either. He could get sales reports via his phone; there was no need to physically be in Boston.

That left her original reason. "I'm sorry if our little town isn't comfortable enough for you to stick around."

"Did I say it wasn't comfortable?"

"You didn't have to," Noelle replied. "Your disdain has been obvious."

"As has yours," he shot back.

"I—"

"Let's face it, Mrs. Fryberg. You haven't exactly rolled out the welcome mat. Not that I mind," he said, taking a drink, "but let's not pretend the antipathy has been one-sided."

Maybe it wasn't, but he'd fired the first shot.

Noelle's coffee cup sat on the edge of the butcher-block island where she'd set it down earlier. Seeing the last quarter cup was ice-cold, she made her way to the coffee maker to top off the cup.

"What did you expect," she said, reaching past him, "coming in here and announcing you were phasing out the Christmas Castle?"

"No, I said the castle was near the end of its lifespan. You're the one who got all overprotective and jumped to conclusions."

"Because you called it a fading tourist attraction."

"I said no such thing."

"Okay, maybe not out loud, but you were definitely thinking it."

"Was I, now?" he replied with a snort. "I didn't realize you were a mind reader."

"Oh, please, I could hear it in your voice. I don't have

to be psychic to know you dislike the whole concept, even before you started making efficiency suggestions."

She set the pot back on the burner, so she could look him square in the eye. The two of them were wedged in the small spot, their shoulders abutting. "Or are you going to tell me that's not true?"

"No," he replied, in an even voice, "it's true. You shouldn't take it personally."

"Are you serious? Of course I'm going to take it personally. It's Fryberg's." The store represented everything good that had ever happened in her life since she was seven years old. "You didn't even want to keep the name!"

"I already conceded on that point, remember?"

"I remember." And considering how quickly he conceded, he'd probably already decided he didn't care. "That doesn't mitigate the other changes you want to make." The reindeer. Fryer. Those suggestions were the tip of the iceberg. Before anyone knew, her version of Fryberg's would be gone forever.

"Forgive me for wanting to improve the store's bottom line."

"Our bottom line is perfectly fine." As she glared into her coffee cup, she heard Hammond chuckle.

"So what you're saying is that you all would have been better off if I'd stayed in Boston."

"Exactly," she gritted.

"And you wonder why I don't want to stay in Fryberg."

Noelle's jaw muscles went slack. She looked back up in time to see Hammond tipping back the last of his drink. "I don't make a habit of staying where I'm not wanted," he said, setting the cup on the counter. "I'm certainly not about to start now. Would you mind if I grabbed that shower now? Then you can drop me off at the airstrip, and we'll both be free from an uncomfortable situation."

While he walked out of the kitchen, Noelle went back to contemplating the contents of her cup. She was waiting for a sense of relief to wash over her. After all, he was right; his leaving did free them both from an uncomfortable situation.

Why then wasn't she relieved?

Maybe because your behavior helped drive the man out of town? her conscience replied as she rubbed away a sudden chill from her right arm.

Perhaps she had been...prickly. Something about the man got under her skin. Everything he said felt like a direct assault on her life. Between the company being sold and Belinda moving to Florida, she felt cast adrift. Like a part of her had been cut away. The only things she had left were the castle, the town and its traditions. Without them, she'd go back to being...

Nothing. No, she'd be worse than nothing. She'd be the nameless little girl whose mother left her in the stable. She'd rather be nothing.

Still, regardless of how angry Hammond made her, she still had a responsibility as a host. Belinda would have never been as argumentative and...well, as bratty...as she'd been.

She found Hammond in the living room folding last night's cover. As he bowed his head to match one corner to another, he wobbled slightly, clearly off-balance. A stab of guilt passed through her. No way was he better.

"You're going to have to keep your head dry," she said, taking one end of the afghan for him. After making sure the folds were straight enough, she walked her end toward him. "That glue the doctor used to cover your stitches needs to stay dry until tomorrow. I could draw you a bath though." They met in the center, their fingers tangling slightly as he passed her his end.

"Anything that gets me clean works fine. Thank you."

Hammond's index finger ran along the inside of hers as he spoke. Coincidence, but Noelle got a tingle anyway. It had been a long time since a man's fingers touched her even accidentally. "It's the least I can do," she replied.

Tucking the afghan under her arm, she headed upstairs. The claw foot tub was going to be a tight fit for his long legs, she realized. Kevin had never been one for baths, and she'd never had any trouble, but Hammond was going to have to sit with his knees bent. Folded like a card table, as Belinda might say.

She felt another stab of guilt. Her mother-in-law would be mortified by Noelle's behavior this morning. In Belinda's world, everyone was welcome, no matter who they were. Hadn't she embraced Noelle that first afternoon? The Frybergs didn't pick fights like bratty children.

Or encourage men with concussions to fly home.

If he crashes, it's on your conscience.

He wasn't going to crash. He wouldn't take the risk if he didn't feel secure in his abilities. Right?

I don't make a habit of staying where I'm not wanted.

"That looks deep enough." Hammond's voice from behind her made her start. Looking at the water, Noelle saw the tub was three-quarters filled. Hammond's blurry reflection shimmered beside hers in the water. Tall and icy blue next to small bright red.

"The water?" he repeated.

Stupid her. "Spaced out for a moment, there," she said, reaching for the faucet handle. "I'll let some of the water out."

"No need. I think I can handle it. I didn't hit my head that hard."

"Right. Let me grab you a towel then and I…"

She sucked in her breath. Hammond had unbuttoned his shirt, revealing a white T-shirt beneath. Tucked tight in his waistband, the thin cotton emphasized the muscles in a way the dress shirt couldn't possibly. You could see the outline of his ribs. The bottom of the cage cut away to a narrow, trim waist. Above the ribs, a cluster of dark curls playing peekaboo at the V. It was to that spot that Noelle's gaze immediately zoned. Drawn by the contrast, of course, not by any memory of her hand splayed against the firmness.

Cheeks warming, she quickly yanked her gaze upward.

"There's blood on your collar," she said. It was the first thing that sprang to mind, and she needed something to explain her sudden loss of words. "Your shirt is ruined."

"Looks like the drone claims another victim." Hammond fingered the stiff corner. The red-brown stain covered most of the right side. "I'll toss it out when I get home. Who knew something so small could cause so much damage?"

"Consider yourself lucky it wasn't something bigger," Noelle replied. Her senses regained, she continued toward the linen closet. "Could have been a remote-control C-130."

"Or a crystal tumbler."

"What?"

"They can cause a lot of damage, is all."

"If you say so."

Was this knowledge from personal experience? Considering she'd thought about tossing a thing or two in his direction, she wouldn't be surprised. Taking a pair of towels from the cabinet, she piled them on a stool next to the tub along with a spare toothbrush.

"If you don't need anything else," she said, looking in his direction. Hammond had shed his dress shirt completely, and stood in his T-shirt studying the bloodied collar. Noelle struggled not to notice the way his biceps stretched his sleeves.

This sudden bout of awareness disturbed her. She'd never been one to check out other men. Of course, the fact that this was the first time a man had stood in her bathroom since Kevin probably heightened her sense of awareness. And while she didn't like Hammond, he was handsome. She had been struck by how much so when she'd checked on him during the night. He had been blessed with the most beautiful mouth she'd ever seen. Perfect Cupid's bow, full lower lip.

"What time do you have to be at Belinda's?"

His question jerked her back to the present. Dear God but she was having focus issues all of a sudden. "Not for a couple hours," she replied.

"Good. You'll have time to drive me to the airstrip."

Her stomach twisted a little. "So you're still planning to fly home today, then."

"What's the matter? Worried I changed my mind between the kitchen and here?" He grinned. Something else she'd noticed this morning. His mouth was capable of an annoyingly attractive smile.

Noelle scoffed. "Hardly. I doubt you ever change your mind."

"Only if I'm well and truly persuaded."

The intimate atmosphere made the comment sound dirtier than it was. Noelle fought to keep a flush from blossoming on her skin.

"That's what I thought," she said. He'd stick to his decision, even if the idea was a bad one. Nothing she could say would change his mind.

Oh, well. He was a grown man. If he wanted to risk his safety, it was his concern. She started to leave. "Do you need anything else?"

"No. I won't be long." From the corner of her eye, she saw him start to shake his head, then close his eyes.

He probably doesn't think I can see him.

Once again, Noelle's conscience twisted her stomach.

"You know…" she started. "Belinda isn't going to be happy with you. She was expecting you for Thanksgiving dinner."

"I'm sure she'll survive." There was an odd note to his words. Disbelief or doubt?

I don't make a habit of staying where I'm not wanted. His comment seemed intent on repeating itself in her brain.

"Survive? Sure," she replied. "That doesn't mean she won't be disappointed. Thanksgiving is a big deal to her. God knows she cooks enough for the entire state—and we're talking about a woman who gave up cooking when Ned made his first million. She'll hunt you down if you aren't around to try her sweet potato casserole."

"There's an image," he said with a soft laugh.

"But not far off. I'm willing to bet she was up early making something special for you."

"Something special?"

"That's the way the Frybergs do things. Seems to me the least you can do is stick around long enough to try whatever it is."

Noelle watched as his eyelashes swept downward and he glanced at the tile floor. He had pretty eyelashes too. When he raised his gaze, his eyes had an odd glint to them. The light looked right through her, and her argument.

"Is this your way of asking me not to fly?"

"I'm not asking you anything," she immediately replied. "I'm thinking of Belinda's feelings."

What was supposed to be nonchalance came out sounding way too affected, and they both knew it. Truth was, she didn't want to deal with a guilty conscience should something happen. "Belinda likes you."

The corners of Hammond's mouth twitched like they

wanted to smile. "Nice to know one member of the Fryberg family likes me."

"Don't get too flattered—Belinda likes everyone." Apparently, her conscience wasn't bothering her too much to stop being bratty.

To her surprise, he laughed. Not a chuckle, like previously, but a bark of a laugh that seemed to burst out of him unexpectedly. "Well played, Mrs. Fryberg. Tell me, are you always so upfront with your opinions?"

Honestly? Quite the opposite. She much preferred adaptation and assimilation to challenge. Hammond brought out an edge she hadn't known she had. "Not always," she replied.

"I'll take that as a compliment then." He crossed his arms, causing the T-shirt to stretch tighter. "There aren't a lot of people in this world who would say boo to me, let alone challenge me as much as you have these past twenty-four hours. It's been very entertaining."

Noelle wasn't sure if she should be flattered or feel condescended to. "I wasn't trying to entertain you," she said.

"I know, which makes me appreciate it even more. You've got backbone."

So, flattered it was. "You're complimenting me for being rude to you."

"Not rude. Honest. I like knowing where I stand with people. You may not like me, but at least you don't pretend, which is more than I can say for a lot of people."

He may have meant to be complimentary, but his words struck her uncomfortably. They pressed on her shoulders along with his comment from earlier. If he was trying to prick her conscience this morning, it worked. She took a long look at him. Tall, handsome, arrogant, and yet... Maybe it was the concussion misleading her, or maybe the injury shifted a mask, but she was seeing something in his expression she hadn't noticed before. It almost looked like…

Vulnerability.

The chip slipped a little off her shoulder. "I don't dislike you," she said, toeing the tile. "Not entirely. Like, I'd feel bad if you crashed your plane and died or something."

"Your kindness overwhelms."

"What can I say? I'm a giver." They smiled at one another, the air between them thawing a little more. The guy wasn't so bad when he wasn't talking about gutting tradition.

"Seriously," she said, "I wouldn't want to see anyone— you—do anything foolish."

"So now you're calling me foolish, are you?"

"I—"

"Relax, I'm joking. I know what you were trying to say. And I thank you."

"For what?" She hadn't done anything special.

His expression softened like she had, however, and she saw the man she'd watched sleep. "Caring about my safety," he replied. "Not many peop— That is, I appreciate it."

A tickle danced across the back of her neck at the gentleness in his voice. If he kept it up, they'd be friends before the bath water grew cold. "Does that mean you'll consider staying for dinner? I wasn't kidding about Belinda being disappointed."

"Well…" He ran his fingers across his mouth and along the back of his neck. "I'd hate to disappoint the woman who sold me her company. I suppose sticking around a few more hours wouldn't hurt."

"Good. Belinda will be glad."

"No one else?"

The cheeky question demanded a shrug in reply. "I

might be a little bit relieved. Lack of blood on my hands and all. Enjoy your bath, Mr. Hammond."

She closed the door before he could see in her eyes that she was way more than a little relieved.

Or that she was starting to like him.

CHAPTER FOUR

JAMES ADDED A LOG to the fireplace. The wood smoked and sputtered for a moment, before being hidden by the flames rising from the logs beneath. Warmth wrapped around his legs. Legs that were now clad in khakis, thanks to Noelle. She'd cajoled the Nutcracker's concierge into opening the hotel boutique so he could buy a fresh change of clothing. The casual pants and plaid sports shirt were more stylish than he'd expected, a fact Noelle took great pleasure in mocking once he'd completed his purchase. His rescue elf had a terrifically sharp sense of humor.

Then again, so did he. Tossing retorts back and forth in the car had him feeling as much like his old self as the bath and clean clothes.

Behind him, cheers erupted in the downstairs family room. Someone must have made a good play. A politer man would head down and join the other guests, lest he be labeled unsociable. Since James had stopped caring what people thought of him when he hit puberty, he stayed upstairs. He was content sitting in one of a pair of wingback chairs, studying the fire.

"People were wondering where you were." Noelle's heels click-clacked on the hard wooden floor until she drew up beside him. "Don't tell me you're not a football fan. Isn't that against the law in New England?"

"Only a misdemeanor," he replied. "I'll be down shortly. I was enjoying the fire. It's soothing."

"Hmm. Soothing, huh?" Perching on the arm of a wing-back chair, she looked up with a tilted glance. Before leaving the house, she'd swapped her sweatshirt for an angora sweater. The neon blue reflected in her eyes, giving them a gemlike glow. "Let me guess," she said, "you're not a fan of crowds either. Can't say I'm surprised."

"I don't dislike them," he replied. "But you're right, I prefer being by myself." It was easier that way. Less picking up on the negative vibes.

He shifted in his seat. The small space between the chairs caused their knees to knock. Laughing, they both pushed the seats back. "Let me guess," he said, "you love crowds."

"I don't love them, but they don't bother me either. I spent most of my childhood having to share my space, so I'm used to it."

An interesting choice of words. "You came from a big family then?"

"Not really."

Then with whom was she sharing space?

"Did you get enough to eat? There's more cornbread casserole if you'd like some."

"Dear God no," he replied. "Four servings is enough, thank you." Why such an abrupt change of subject? He was under the impression she was all about family. "I can't believe I ate as much as I did."

"That's what you get for sitting next to Belinda and her ever-moving serving spoon."

"Plus almost two days without eating." He literally had been the starving man at the buffet. The perfect match for Belinda's serving spoon.

Noelle wasn't joking when she said her mother-in-law cooked up a storm for the holiday. The woman must have served three times as much as the guests could eat. Granted, the turkey and side dishes were nothing like the five-star fare the family chef set out—on those rare occasions he and Jackson celebrated together—but James had enjoyed eating them ten times more. The food today came with wine and laughter and conversation. Real conversation. The kind where people debated, then joked the tension away. No stilted dialogues or pretend interest in each other's lives.

And not a single tumbler hurled across the room.

Funny how that memory had reappeared today, after twenty years of staying buried. Especially since it happened on Christmas Eve. Thanksgiving had been a Tiffany candlestick. Or had that been the dinner plate? The flying objects blended together after a while.

"You're frowning," Noelle said. "Is your head okay?"

"My head's fine." A faint headache at the base of his neck was all. The bulk of his dizziness had ebbed as well. Unless he whipped his head around quickly or hung upside down, he wouldn't have a problem.

"Guess that means you'll be able to fly home without a problem."

"Don't see why not," he replied. His original reason still stood. So long as he could control when and where he stayed, he would. "No sense overstaying my welcome, right?"

"Definitely not," Noelle replied. "Is it a long flight?"

"A few hours. One of the benefits of being the pilot, you save all that time waiting at the airport."

"No security pat down either. Is that why you fly? So you can avoid lines at the airport?" While she was talking, she slid backward off her perch and into the chair. The move left her sitting sideways with her calves balanced on the arm. "Wow, you really do hate people, don't you?"

Her smirk told him she was teasing. "Very funny," James replied. "I fly because it's more efficient. I don't like wasting time."

"Really? Who would have guessed?"

This time he smirked. Her sitting in such a cozy, casual position had made his muscles relax as well. He was at ease, he realized. An unusual experience outside the cockpit. The sky was the one place he felt truly at home. He would never tell that to anyone though. At thirty-nine-thousand feet, the sound of the engine roaring in your ears drowned out your thoughts. There was nothing to prove, nothing to forget.

"I was studying Belinda's mantel." He nodded toward the fireplace, and the collection of photographs and knick-knacks that lined the thick pine. Diverting the attention away from himself once more. "Couldn't help noticing you and she have a lot of the same pictures."

"No big surprise, considering I married into her family."

Family was definitely the theme. The largest photograph was a portrait of a man in a military uniform smiling from the passenger seat of a truck. Pushing himself to his feet, James walked over to take a closer look. A copy of the photo was on Noelle's mantel as well. "Kevin?" he asked. He already knew the answer. Who else could it be?

"He emailed the photo from Afghanistan a few months before the accident."

His jeep flipped over. James remembered from researching the sale. He'd been surprised to hear the Fryberg's heir had been in the military.

"He looks like he enjoyed being in the army."

"Guard," she corrected. "Signed up our senior year of high school." James heard a soft rustling noise, which he realized was Noelle shifting in her chair. A moment later, her heels tapped on the wood floor again. "He was so excited when his unit finally deployed. All he ever talked about was getting overseas. Ned and Belinda were crushed when they learned he'd been killed."

Was it his imagination or did all her answers go back to Ned and Belinda? "Must have been hard on you too."

"I was his wife. That goes without saying."

He supposed it did. It was odd is all, that she focused on her in-laws' grief instead of her own.

Then again, maybe it wasn't. Maybe that was how real families behaved.

The picture on the left of Kevin was from their wedding. The Fryberg quartet formally posed under a floral arbor. It too had a duplicate at Noelle's house. "How old were you when you got married anyway?" She looked about ten, the voluminous skirt of her wedding dress ready to swallow her.

"Twenty-one. Right after graduation. We were already living together, and since we knew Kevin was scheduled to leave after the first of the year…" She left the sentence hanging with a shrug.

No need to say more. "You didn't have a lot of time together."

"Actually, we had almost twelve years. We were middle school sweethearts," she added, in case that wasn't obvious. She smiled at the photograph. "I did a lot of growing up in this house."

"There you two are! Detroit's almost done letting everyone down." Belinda came strolling through the living room along with Todd Moreland, Fryberg's general manager. "I promised Todd here some pie for the road." When she saw he and Noelle were looking at her son's photo, she smiled. "I always liked how happy he looked in that photo."

"He was a real special kid," Todd added. "The whole company liked him. We always figured we'd be working for him one day. No offense, Mr. Hammond."

"None taken," James replied stiffly. "Everyone has their preferences." And it usually wasn't him.

"Noelle was filling me in on some of the family history," he said, turning to Belinda.

"You picked the right person for the job. She remembers more about the family history than I do at this point. In fact, she can tell you who those people in the portrait are. I forgot a long time ago."

"Ned's great-grandparents from Bamberg."

"See what I mean?" The older woman tugged at her companion's arm. "Come on, Todd. I'll get that pie."

"So, keeper of the family history, huh?"

"Someone has to. Family's important."

"That, Mrs. Fryberg," he said, shuffling back to the chairs, "depends upon the family."

He shouldn't have said the words out loud; they invited a conversation he didn't want to have. Taking a seat, he steered the conversation back to her. "What about your family? Do you maintain your own history as diligently as your in-laws'?"

A shadow crossed her face. "Like you said," she replied. "Depends upon the family."

It appeared they had both dropped curious comments. In her case, she'd dropped two. Was it possible they had more in common than he'd thought?

Catching her gaze from across the space, he held it in his. Trying to tell her he understood. "What's that old saying about families? You can't live with them...you can't take them out and bury them in the woods."

"I don't think those are the words."

Her expression clouded again as she added, "Besides,

you can't bury something you don't have." The words came out low and hesitant. Her gaze broke from his and returned to the photographs on the mantel as though she was speaking more to them than James.

Normally when a woman made coy remarks, he ignored them, seeing how coy was nothing more than an attempt at attention. Something about Noelle's remark, however, cut through him. There was weight to her words that spoke to a piece inside him.

Maybe that's why he decided to ask. "You don't have a family?"

Her sigh rattled signs in Chicago. "What the hell. Not like it's a secret.

"I was raised by the state," she said. "My mother left me in the town crèche on Christmas Eve and disappeared never to be heard of again."

That wasn't necessarily a bad thing, he thought. Better that she disappear altogether than sell you a fantasy and then unceremoniously pop the bubble.

He stared at the crease in his new pants. No wonder her comment affected him the way it had.

The two of them had more in common than she realized.

"Anyway, I grew up in the foster system. The Frybergs were the first real family I ever had. If it weren't for them, people would still be calling me the Manger Baby."

"The what? Never mind." He figured it out as soon as he asked. She said she'd been left in the crèche.

Something else dawned on him as well. "Is that how you got your name? Because you were found at Christmas?"

Her cheeks turned crimson as she nodded. "Nothing like advertising your past, huh? I shudder to think what they'd have called me if I were a boy."

"Trust me, I can imagine."

They both chuckled. When they were finished, he sat

back in his chair and took a fresh look at the woman he'd spent the last twenty-four hours with. "It suits you," he said. "The name."

He wasn't surprised when she rolled her eyes. "So I've been told by half the town."

"Half the town would be right." There was a brightness about her that reminded him of a Christmas ornament. He could only imagine what she'd looked like as a kid. All eyes and luminosity.

No wonder Kevin Fryberg fell for her.

Knowing her story, a lot of things made sense now. Her loyalty. Her attachment to every tradition Ned Fryberg ever started.

He sat back in his chair. "You know, hearing all this, I've got to say I'm surprised Belinda sold to me when she had you around to take her place."

The muscle on her jaw twitched. He'd clipped a nerve. "I said the same thing. I suggested she retire, and let Todd run the place while he groomed me to be his replacement, but she said this was the best move for the store. Hammond's would give us the capital we needed to stay modern. Plus, she thought selling would give me more freedom to do other things. She didn't want me to feel trapped in Fryberg because I was tied to the business."

Interesting. Made sense. While Noelle professed loyalty now, she was also young, with a host of options in front of her. Better to sell the business while Belinda could control the deal. That's what he would do. His father as well. Hell, if James weren't so good at making money, Jackson probably would have sold the store years ago—and not because he wanted his son to have freedom.

Still, he could hear the disappointment in Noelle's answer. A part of her felt rejected. Cast aside. He knew that sting. It made him want to pull her into his arms for a hug.

which was unsettling, since he didn't do comfort. And even if he did, she would deny the feelings.

Meaning they shared another trait in common as well: neither liked to show weakness.

"Look on the bright side," he said instead. "She could have fired you."

"You don't fire family."

"Speak for yourself, sweetheart. Not everyone is as family oriented as you are. There are as many people on the other side of the line who value profits over DNA."

She tilted her head. "I'm curious? Which side do you fall on?"

James didn't even have to pause and think. His answer was that reflexive. "The side that doesn't believe in family period."

Noelle stared at him. Unbelievable. No sooner did she catch a spark of warmth, then his inner Grinch came along to snuff out the flame.

"You do know how ironic that statement sounds, coming from the heir of Hammond's, right?"

Ask anyone in the industry and they'd tell you, Hammond's Toy Stores was the epitome of old-fashioned family values. Their history put Fryberg's hundred-year-old tradition to shame.

James's lashes cast shadows on his cheeks as he studied the palm of his hand. "Things aren't always what they seem," he said.

"They aren't? 'Cause I've studied Hammond's." And the last time she checked, Hammond's sure looked like a fifteen-decades-old success story. The Boston store dwelled in the same building where Benjamin Hammond originally opened it. Over the decades, the store had become a touchstone for people looking to recapture childhood innocence. Their window displays and decor was like walking into a magical piece of frozen history. And at Christmas time...

Noelle had seen the photos. It was the Christmas Castle, Santa's workshop and Rockefeller Center all rolled into one. "There's too much heart in your branding for it to have been pulled from a hat."

His reply was somewhere between a cough and a snort. "I'll let the marketing department know you appreciate their efforts. They put a great deal of effort into creating that 'heart.'"

She could feel the air quotations. There were exclamation points on the sarcasm.

"I hate to break it to you," he said, "but my family has made a small fortune selling a fantasy."

"For one hundred and fifty years? I don't think any company can fake their corporate culture for that long."

"Maybe once, a long time ago, someone believed in it," he said in a softer voice. "My grandfather or someone like that."

His fingers traced the plaid pattern on the chair arm. "Who knows? Maybe back then, life was different. But holidays are all manufactured now. There's no such thing as a 'family Christmas' except on TV. Divorce, dysfunction... most of the world's just trying to get through the day without killing each other."

Noelle didn't know what to say. She couldn't call him on his sarcasm, because he wasn't being sarcastic. He delivered his words in a flat, distant voice tinged with hopelessness. It took squeezing her fists by her sides to keep from hugging him. What was it he had said about glass tumblers?

"I'm sorry," she murmured.

"For what?"

Good question. She wasn't sure herself. "That you don't like Christmas."

Hammond shrugged before returning to his pattern tracing. "Don't have to like it to make money off it," he said.

"No," she said, "I don't suppose you do." And Hammond did make money. Lots of money. So, he was right. Who cared if he liked Christmas or not?

Except that the notion left her incredibly sad. Noelle didn't know if it was the cynicism of his words or something else, but this entire conversation left a pang in her stomach. She couldn't look at Hammond without wanting to perch on his chair and press him close.

To chase away his sadness. Talk about silly. Twenty-four hours ago she disliked the man and now here she was thinking about hugging him? As though a hug from her would solve the problem anyway. She didn't even know if he was sad, for crying out loud. Imagine what he would think if she suddenly nestled up against that hard torso.

That she was crazy, no doubt.

Still, possible personal demons aside, she wondered how long it would take before Hammond's cynicism bit him in the behind? She didn't care how good a marketing team he had, a store that didn't believe in its own brand couldn't last. Sooner or later the phoniness, as he put it, would seep through.

You can only bury the truth of your feelings for so long before the truth wins out.

The corner of her gaze caught the photo on the edge of the mantel. Noelle turned her head.

And thought of Fryberg's. Without sincerity at the helm, the castle would truly become a cheesy tourist destination. Wouldn't take long after that for Hammond to close the store down, in favor of his giant shipping warehouse.

The store was on borrowed time as it was. His cynicism shortened the timetable.

"Bet if you spent time here, you wouldn't be so negative."

"Excuse me?"

Oh, jeez. She'd spoken out loud, hadn't she? The point had merit though. "The magic of the place has a way of growing on you," she said.

"Is that so?"

Interesting that he hadn't said *no.* "Yeah, it's so. Do you think this cottage industry of a town sprang up because people wanted to live in Bavaria again?"

Her question made Hammond chuckle. "The thought crossed my mind."

It crossed a lot of people's. "The people here love the holidays. You want to see the Christmas spirit you need to see tomorrow's Christmas season kickoff. It'll convert the most frozen of hearts into holiday fans."

A light flickered in his eyes, along with an emotion Noelle couldn't quite recognize, but made her pulse quicken nonetheless. "Are you asking me to stick around, Mrs. Fryberg?"

"No. I mean, yes. Sort of." Articulating herself would be easier if he weren't chuckling. "So you could see how we do Christmas, is all."

"I've seen how you do Christmas. Part of the celebration struck me in the head yesterday, remember?"

"I meant how the town did Christmas. I thought, if you spent time with people who enjoy celebrating Christmas, it might make you less cynical."

"I see. Worried my cynicism will kill the Christmas Castle sooner rather than later?"

In a word? "Yes," she replied. Wasn't he already turning things upside down in the name of efficiency?

Damn if he didn't chuckle again. A throaty rumble that slid under a person's skin and brushed across her nerve endings. The sound left goose bumps on Noelle's skin. "No offense to your Christmas magic," he said, "but I highly doubt a few gingerbread cookies and a tree lighting will make me less cynical."

He had a point. She probably was giving the magic too much credit. "Once a Grinch, always a Grinch. Is that what you're saying?"

"Precisely. I always thought he was misunderstood."

"As misunderstood as a man with a tiny heart could be," Noelle replied.

This time, instead of chuckling, Hammond let out a full-on laugh. "I wasn't trying to be funny," she said when he finished.

"I know. I was laughing at how easily you're abrupt with me. It's so damn refreshing."

So he'd said this morning. "I'm not trying to be," she told him. "The words keep popping out before I have a chance to mentally edit."

"Making it all the more refreshing, knowing it's organic." He settled back in his chair and assessed her with, based on the tingling running up her arm, what had to be the longest look in the world.

"You know, I have half a mind to bring you along when I fly out of here so you could follow me around and make snarky comments."

"Excu—"

"Don't worry, I'm kidding." He wiped the words away with a wave of his hand. "I have no desire to move you from Fryberg. *Yet*."

Noelle let out her breath.

"What's this about flying to Boston?" Todd asked. He and Belinda came around the corner from the kitchen. The general manager had on his coat and carried a plastic bag filled with Tupperware.

"You're not planning to fly back tonight are you, Jim? They showed Foxborough on TV and the rain looks miserable there."

Partially hidden behind the chair wings, Hammond winced at the nickname, leaving Noelle to fight back a smirk. If there was anyone who looked more unlike a Jim...

"I've flown in rain before," he said. "I doubt it'll be a problem."

"If you say so. All I can say is better you than me. That wind was blowing so strong the rain was sideways. Won't be much of a passing game, that's for sure."

"How strong is this wind?" Hammond asked, swiveling around to face the man. Noelle noticed he already had his phone in his hand. Checking the forecast, probably.

"No clue. They didn't say."

"Maybe you should stay like you planned," Belinda replied. "I would hate for you to be bounced around during a storm and hit your head again."

"I'm sure I'll be fine. We fly above the weather."

"What about you?" he asked Noelle, once the others had departed. "You want to ask me to stay again too?"

The sparkle in his eye caused a rash of awareness to break out along her skin. "I didn't ask you to stay. I *suggested* staying for tomorrow's Christmas Kickoff might change your mind about the holiday. There's a difference." One of semantics maybe, but she clung to the argument anyway. "Besides, you made it quite clear this morning that you make your own decisions. If you want to risk flying in the wind, that's your business."

She fought back a frown. That last sentence sounded a

little passive-aggressive. It was his business and she didn't care—not that much anyway.

"You're right. It is my business," he replied.

Noelle watched as he tapped the keys on his phone and pulled up the Boston weather. An odd feeling had gripped her stomach. A cross between nervousness and disappointment. Something about Hammond had her emotions skittering all over the place. One minute she detested him, the next she felt a kinship. The man had turned her into a collection of extremes. It wasn't like her, being this mass of shifting energy.

Rather than continue staring, she turned to the pictures on the mantel. Kevin smiled at her from the Humvee and her insides settled a little. Good old Kevin who she'd loved for nearly fifteen years.

Loved like a brother.

No sooner did the thought rise than she stuffed it back down. How she felt about Kevin was her secret and hers alone. No one need ever know the truth.

Besides, she *had* loved him. He was her best friend. Her shoulder. Her rock. He'd given her so much. A home. A family. When she became his girl, her world went from being cold to one full of love and meaning. Kevin turned her into someone special. Wasn't his fault she couldn't feel the passion toward him that he deserved.

"Looks like you got your wish." Hammond's voice sounded above her ear. Startled, Noelle stepped back only to have her shoulders bump against his muscled chest, causing her to start again.

"What wish?" she managed to say as she turned around.

"Todd was right. There's a high-wind warning up and down the New England coast. Logan's backed up until the nor'easter moves on."

"What does that mean?" she asked. Focused on putting distance between their bodies, the significance of his words failed to register.

"It means…" He reached out and cupped a hand on the curve of her neck. His thumb brushed the underside of her jaw, forcing her to look him in the eye. The sparkle she saw in his left her with goose bumps.

"It means," he repeated, "that you're stuck with me another day."

It was the perfect time for a sarcastic remark. Unfortunately, Noelle was too distracted by the fluttering in her stomach to think of one. The idea of his continuing to stay around didn't upset her nearly as much as it had yesterday.

In fact, heaven help her, it didn't upset her at all.

James was disappointed when the barbed comment he'd been expecting didn't come. Instead, he found himself standing by the fire while Noelle went to tell Belinda he'd changed his plans. Again. Oh, well, what good was flying your own plane if you couldn't control your flight schedule, right?

He twirled his smartphone between his fingers. Christmas Kickoff, he thought with a snort. He'd go, but there was no way he'd change his thoughts on the holiday. The Hammond dysfunction was far too ingrained.

Turning his attention from the now empty doorway and back to his phone, James tried to settle the disquiet that was suddenly rolling in his stomach. He wished he could blame the sensation on being stuck in Christmas Land, but his phone screen told the truth. The conditions weren't that bad in Boston; he'd flown in worse dozens of times.

He'd used the wind as an excuse. To hang around.

He didn't rearrange his schedule on a whim for anyone, let alone a woman, and yet here he was making up reasons to spend additional time with Noelle Fryberg, a woman he was sure wasn't one hundred percent happy about the decision. He was breaking his own number one rule and staying where he might not be wanted. All because she made him feel energized and connected in a way no one ever had.

No wonder his stomach felt like it was on a bungee.

CHAPTER FIVE

SOMEONE HAD SHOT OFF a Christmas bomb. How else could he explain it? Overnight, fall had disappeared and been replaced by poinsettias and tiny white lights. There were wreaths and red bows on doorways and evergreen garlands draped the fascia of every downtown building. It was even snowing, for crying out loud! Big, fluffy flakes straight out of central casting. An inch of the white stuff already coated the ground.

"What the heck?" he said as he looked out the passenger window of Noelle's SUV. "Did you drag a snow machine over from one of the ski resorts?"

"Nope. A happy coincidence is all," Noelle replied. "Makes a nice touch for the start of the Christmas season, doesn't it? Snow always puts people in the Christmas spirit."

"Keeps people off the roads too. People hate driving in snowstorms."

"Maybe back in Boston, but in this town, we deal perfectly fine with snowstorms."

"Residents maybe, but what about all those out-of-town shoppers?"

"Oh, I wouldn't worry about them," she replied.

They turned onto the main drag, where the bulk of the

shops and restaurants were located. First thing James noticed was the steady flow of people looking into windows.

"See? The town will do very well economically over the next few weeks, weather or no weather."

"Yeah, but will they drive from downtown to the toy store?" That was the real issue. No one minded walking a few blocks; it was risking the roads that made people balk. Today, Black Friday, was the day retailers counted on to jumpstart their yearly profits. A healthy turnout was vital. "Conditions like this are one of the reasons why I want to push the online business," he said. "Bad weather encourages people to stay inside and shop online." Where there was a lot more competition for their attention.

Not surprisingly, she ignored his comment. "I wouldn't worry too much. We've got things under control."

She pointed ahead to where a bus stop had been decorated with a big gold sign that read Trolley to Christmas Castle Every Fifteen Minutes. "Like I said, we're used to snow. There's already a line too. Everyone loves to visit Santa's workshop."

The smugness in her voice begged to be challenged. "Crowds don't necessarily equal sales. Half the people coming to see the foolish window displays at the Boston store never buy a thing. Not a very good return considering how much we spend on them every year."

She gave him a long look. "If that's how you feel, then why continue having them? Why not scale back?"

"Because…"

James frowned. Why did he continue doing the windows on such a grand scale? Not even his own father wanted to continue the tradition. Yet, every year, he saw the numbers, and then turned around and approved something equally lavish for the following December. It was the one budget item where he deviated from his own rules of business and he didn't have a decent explanation.

"People have come to expect them," he replied. That was the reason. He was preserving Hammonds' reputation with the public. "Those window displays are part of the Hammond brand."

"I'm surprised you haven't figured out a way to support the brand in a less expensive way. Building brand new, custom animatronic exhibits every year is expensive."

Tell me about it, he thought. "Cutting back would send a negative message to the public. They might equate it with financial difficulties that don't exist." James could imagine how the business press might speculate.

"In other words, it's not always a good idea to mess with tradition."

"Unfortunately, no."

"You mean like Fryer and the Santa's reindeer corral at the castle."

Damn. She'd boxed him in. Quite neatly too.

Shifting in his chair, he tipped an imaginary hat. "Well played, Mrs. Fryberg. I see your point."

"I thought you might, Mr. Hammond," she said, nodding her head in return.

Neatly playing him, however, did not mean she was getting all her own way. "You still can't have people leaving Santa's workshop, and not reentering the store. The idea is to keep them around the toys as long and as much as possible."

He waited for a response, half expecting another argument. Instead, she daintily flicked the turn signal handle with her fingers. "Fair enough. What about Fryer?"

"Fryer?" Parts of the other day were still a bit fuzzy. James had to think a moment about whom she was talking about. Finally, he remembered. "You're talking about the giant stuffed moose eating up space at the rear of the store."

"Elk," she corrected.

"What?"

"Fryer. He's an elk, and people love taking selfies with him. In fact, customers have been known to bring friends specifically to see him. Much like your window displays."

So it was the moo—elk she wanted to save. Strange item to draw a line over. Then again, she did mention something about Ned Fryberg using the creature in his early ads and as he'd learned yesterday, his hostess had a very strong attachment to Fryberg history.

"Fine," he said. "The elk can stay. But only until I get a good look at the profit per square foot. If we need to re-design the floor plan, I make no promises."

"But he stays for now?"

"Yes," James replied, his sigh sounding more exasperated than he truly felt. "He can stay."

She turned and smiled. "Thank you."

That made twice in three days that she'd managed to convince him to bend on a decision. Granted, neither were major sticking points. Still, she had a better record than most of the experienced negotiators he'd faced.

Beginner's luck, he told himself. It definitely didn't have anything to do with how her eyes got bluer when she smiled.

He continued studying her after she'd turned her eyes back to the road. Today she was dressed for the holidays in a red sweater and a brightly colored scarf. Candy cane stripes, naturally. A matching knit cap sat on her head. The outfit made her look like a tiny character from *Where's Waldo*, only she'd stand out in any crowd, regardless of her size.

A blush worked its way into her cheeks as she sensed

him studying her. "How's your head this morning?" she asked. "You never said."

"Better," he replied. Better than better actually. The spot around his stitches was still tender, but the dull ache had disappeared and he could bend and turn his head without the room spinning. "Being able to shower this morning helped." Nothing like being able to stick your head under a stream of water to erase the cobwebs. "Having a bed helped too. No offense to your sofa."

"I'm glad you were awake enough to climb the stairs this time," she replied. "I was thinking that considering how tired you were last night, it was a good thing you couldn't fly home after all."

"Yeah, a good thing." James forced his expression to stay blank. When they'd returned from Belinda's, he'd gone straight to the bedroom, telling Noelle he was too tired for conversation. In reality, he wanted the solitude so he could process his decision to stay. He wanted to say it boiled down to attraction. Noelle wasn't stereotypically beautiful—more cute really—but the more he studied her eyes, the more he found her gaze hypnotically compelling. If that was even a thing. And her curves…he did love those curves, no doubt about it.

Problem was, attraction didn't seem like a complete enough answer. It wasn't the challenge either, even though she clearly challenged him. He was drawn to her in a way that went beyond attraction. What that meant, he didn't have a clue, other than knowing he liked her in a way that was different from other women he'd known. Whatever the reason, he didn't like feeling this way. He didn't want someone getting under his skin. Didn't want the awkwardness when things inevitably blew up.

Why break his cardinal rule then by sticking around

last night? To spend time with a widow devoted to her late husband and his family, no less?

Hell. Maybe he did want the awkwardness. Maybe he had some subconscious desire to punish himself.

Certainly would explain a lot of things.

A flash of color caught his eye. They were passing an open-air market of some kind, the perimeter of which was marked off by a banner of rainbow-colored flags.

"That's the *Christkindlmarkt*," Noelle said. "It's German for Christmas market."

"Yes, I know. I've seen them in Europe."

"Really? Only other one I've seen is in Chicago. Ned and Belinda told me about the one they visited in Berlin. Sounded wonderful."

James watched as they passed a woman moving her collection of knit scarves out of the snow. "If you like flea markets," he said.

"It's a lot more than a flea market," Noelle replied. Even with his head turned to the window, he could feel her giving him the side-eye. It made his stitches tingle. "We hold the market every year. There are crafts, baked goods. Did you even spend time at the market in Europe? Or were you too busy studying the traffic patterns?"

"Contrary to what you might think, I don't analyze every retail establishment I visit. And no, I didn't have time to visit the market in Germany. My car drove past on the way to a meeting."

"No wonder you are being so derisive!" she said. "We'll visit this one on our way back from the store. Besides the castle, it's the linchpin of our Christmas Kickoff festival. One of the vendors, Heineman's Chocolatiers, has the most amazing hot chocolate you've ever tasted. Kevin and I made a point of visiting his stall first thing every festival. Mr. Heineman would never forgive me if I skipped it."

"God forbid you break tradition," James replied. The strangest flash of emotion passed through him when she mentioned Kevin. Not jealousy—he hadn't known Noelle long enough to feel possessive—but the sensation had the same sharp kind of pang. Like a tear in the center of his chest.

He'd been feeling a lot of odd things these past two days. Maybe that drone had jarred something loose when it struck him.

All he knew was the idea of Noelle and her beloved late husband strolling through the Christmas fair made his sternum ache.

"I owe you an apology. That was the most organized chaos I've ever seen."

Noelle's chest puffed with pride. Store management had spent years perfecting their Black Friday routine, so she knew James would be impressed. What she hadn't counted on was how his positive reaction would make her feel. She took his compliments as a personal victory. Unable to contain her smirk, she let the smile spread as she looked to the passenger seat. "I take it you no longer think of the castle as a fading tourist attraction then."

"I still think our retailing future lies online," he replied, "but I'll concede that you all know what you're doing here. Those handheld wish list scanners are genius."

"Thank you. Ned installed them shortly before he passed away."

Borrowed from the supermarket industry, the scanners let kids record items they fell in love with. The lists were downloaded to share with Santa as well as their parents. Moms and dads could purchase the items then and there and have them stored for pickup at a later date.

"We've boosted our Black Friday numbers by thirty

percent since installing them," she told him. "Of course, our numbers drop a little at the back end, but we prefer to start the season high rather then sweat it out at the end of the quarter."

"Don't blame you there." He smiled again, and this time Noelle got a little flutter in her stomach.

Her assessment of his smile hadn't changed in the last twenty-four hours; if anything, she was finding it more magnetic. Especially when he let the sparkle reach his eyes. That didn't always happen. Noelle found those smiles— the ones with shadows—intriguing too.

Despite the voice warning her the shadowy smiles were the more dangerous of the two.

"When I was a kid, the store made paper lists. Kids wrote down ten items and put the letter in a mailbox for Santa. Parents could come by and pick up their child's list at the front desk."

James had taken out his phone and was typing a note. "This is much more efficient," he said. "I'm sending a message to our logistics department about the scanners right now."

"I had a feeling the system would appeal to you. Although, I've got to admit…" She paused to back out of her parking space. "There was something special about folding up the letter and dropping it into that big red-and-white mailbox." Christmas always brought out the nostalgic in her. "Scanning bar codes doesn't feel the same."

"Even Santa's got to keep up with technology," James replied.

"Yes, he does. By the way, did you see how popular Fryer was with the crowd? I had a half dozen people ask me if we were bringing back our stuffed animal version."

"So you told me in the store. Twice," he replied, as he

tucked the phone back into his coat. "I take it this is your way of saying 'I told you so.'"

"You've got to admit. I did tell you." A chuckle bubbled out of her, cutting off the last word. Didn't matter. He got the point.

In the grand scheme of things, Fryer's continued existence was a small victory, but one that made her happy. She'd saved part of Fryberg's, which was like saving part of her family.

"Don't hurt yourself gloating," James said.

His comment only made her chuckle a second time. Heaven help her, but she was starting to enjoy their verbal jousts. "I'm trying, but it's hard when I was so right. People really love that elk. We should have taken your picture."

"Why? For you to hang in your office?"

"Uh-huh. With a piece of paper underneath that reads The Time I Told James Hammond So." She waved her hand over the wheel as though painting the words in the air.

"Oh, well. Guess my memory will have to do."

From the corners of her eyes, she saw him shifting his position until he faced her. "Anyone ever tell you that you're cute when you're being smug?"

"No," Noelle replied.

The feel of his eyes on her turned her skin warm. It had been a long time since a man had studied her, let alone one with eyes as intense as his. She'd be lying if she didn't admit she found his scrutiny flattering. All morning long, she'd sensed him stealing glances here and there, checking her out as she reached for an item from a shelf or adjusted her rearview mirror. The sensation left goose bumps on her skin, not to mention a warm awareness deep inside her.

It felt good, being noticed by a man. That was, a man like him. Someone smart and savvy. Who took charge of a space simply by entering it. His scrutiny left her feeling decidedly female.

Plus, it kept her from feeling guilty about her own stolen glances. She'd been looking his way since their conversation in front of the fire.

She was stealing a look now.

"Getting ready to gloat more?" James's eyes had slid in her direction, catching her. Try as she might to stop them, her cheeks started to burn.

"No," she said. "I'm done gloating."

"Glad to hear it. Why the look then? You looked like you were about to say something."

Had she? "I was looking at your shirt," she replied. "You…" Her cheeks burned hotter. "You wear plaid well."

"Thank you." The compliment clearly took him by surprise, which was okay, because she was surprised she'd said it out loud. "I'm glad you like it since it's going to be a wardrobe staple while I'm here."

Interestingly, he didn't say anything about leaving. But then, the snow probably made flying impossible.

More interesting was how relieved she felt about his staying.

Again.

And heaven help her, it wasn't only the banter she was enjoying. She was enjoying James's company. A lot. "We can stop at the boutique and grab you a new shirt if you'd like."

"Are you saying you don't like this shirt?" he asked.

"Not at all. I mean, I like the shirt," she corrected when his brows lifted. "I told you, you look good in plaid."

"Thank you. You look good in…red-and-white stripes."

Sensing that another blush was working its way to the surface, she quickly turned her face to scan the left lane. "Color of the day," she murmured.

"Shouldn't it be black? Being Black Friday and all."

"Technically, maybe, but red is far more festive." They were stuck behind a returning trolley. Flicking her turn signal, she eased into the left lane to pass. A little boy with his face pressed to the window saw the car and waved. "I'm not sure a bunch of people running around in black would inspire Christmas spirit," she continued.

"Good point. All that really matters is that the red color stays on the people and not on my balance sheet."

"Said every retailer everywhere today."

"No one said we weren't predictable," he observed with a laugh.

"You can say that again," Noelle replied. Bad Black Friday jokes were as much a tradition as Santa in her office. Hardly surprising that a man raised in the retail industry knew his share of them. "Although not every retailer was born into a retail dynasty."

On his side of the car, James made what sounded like a snort. "Lucky me," he replied.

"I'm sure some people would think so. Ned used to tell me about the early days, when his parents weren't sure the store would survive. He considered it a point of pride that Kevin would inherit a thriving business. I know we're not talking the same thing as a multimillion-dollar national chain…"

"Yeah," James said, reaching back to rub his neck, "if there's one thing my father knows how to do, it's make money."

"As do you. According to Belinda anyway. It's one of the reasons she chose to sell to Hammond's in the first place. Because she liked the idea that you would be stepping into your father's shoes. As she put it, the apple didn't fall far from the tree."

"That isn't necessarily a compliment," James replied.

No, thought Noelle. She supposed it wasn't. Especially if his father was like the man who'd arrived at their store two days ago. She thought him brusque and unsentimental. Absolutely hated the way he'd been focused solely on product and profit.

Oddly enough, James's comments today didn't upset her. Oh, sure, he was just as focused on profit and efficiency, but rather than annoy her, James's suggestions this time around had sounded incredibly astute. Probably because this time around, she liked him better.

Which might also explain why she detected a bitter edge to James's voice when she compared him to his father. "Don't you and your father get along?" she asked.

"Let's say my father does his thing, and I do mine," he said when she cast him a look. "It's a system that's worked quite well for us for a number of years."

Work or not, it sounded lacking. "I can't help but wonder," she said, "if some of these cynicisms of yours are exaggerated."

"I beg your pardon?"

"Well, you can't hate your family too much if you work for the family business."

He stiffened. "I work for the family business because I'm good at it. Like you said, the apple doesn't fall far from the tree. Not to mention that if I didn't, Hammond's wouldn't be a family business anymore," he added in a softer voice.

"There aren't any other family members?"

"None that are around," he said in a chilly voice. Clearly, it was a touchy subject.

Figuring it best to move on, Noelle focused on the rhythm of her windshield wipers going back and forth in the snow. Too bad the wipers couldn't swipe away the awkwardness that had overtaken the car.

As they got closer to downtown Fryberg, the road narrowed to one lane. Thanks to the snow, the already slower than normal traffic was reduced to a crawl. Only the castle trolley, which traveled in the bus lane, made any progress. Looking to the passenger seat, James was attempting to lean against the headrest without pressing on his stitches and not having much luck. His brow was furrowed and his mouth drawn into a tense line. Was he agitated because he was uncomfortable or from her uncomfortable question? Either way, it made Noelle anxious to see.

The sign for Bloomberg's Pharmacy caught her eye, giving her an idea. "Think your head can handle the snow?" she asked.

"It won't melt, if that's what you're asking," he replied.

"Good." With a flick of her directional handle, she eased the car to the right.

"From here until the central parking lot, traffic's going to be slower than molasses. I'll park at the drug store and we can walk."

James's frown deepened. "Walk where."

"To the Christmas market, remember?"

"Hot chocolate and gingerbread cookies. How could I forget?"

"You left out Christmas spirit," she said. "I thought maybe we could find you some. That way you don't have to rely on your marketing department to give your business heart."

"I told you yesterday, it's going to take a lot more than some midwestern Christmas craft fair."

Maybe, but a day at the market might make him smile. And for some reason, that was suddenly important to her.

Noelle swore the Christmas Kickoff got larger every year. At least the crowds did. Seemed to her that in middle school, she and Kevin darted from booth to booth without having to fight the flow of traffic.

James cut through the crowd like it was human butter. Hands in his coat pockets, he walked past the various stalls and vendors with such authority, the people naturally parted upon his approach. Noelle walked beside him and marveled.

Part of the deference had to be caused by his looks. He was, by far, the most handsome man there. The wind had burned his cheekbones pink while his hair and coat were dappled with snowy droplets. Dark and bright at the same time.

He looked over at her with eyes that refracted the light. "Where is this chocolate maker of yours?" he asked.

"I'm not quite sure." Rising on tiptoes, she tried to scan the aisle, but there were too many people taller than her. "In the past, Mr. Heineman liked to take a stall toward the rear."

"Then to the rear we go," he replied. "Like salmon heading upstream. This cocoa better be everything you claim it to be."

"Better. I promise, you'll be addicted." Mr. Heineman had a secret recipe that made the cocoa smooth and spicy at the same time.

"Addicted, huh? You're setting a pretty high bar, Mrs. Fryberg."

"It's not high if it's true," she told him with a grin.

And there it was. The start of a smile. Like a lot of his smiles, it didn't reach his eyes, but they had all afternoon. After the way he'd closed off in the car, she was determined to pull a bona fide grin out of him before they were finished.

She'd contemplate why the mission mattered so much later.

"Coming through!" Four teenage boys wearing matching school jackets were pushing their way through the crowd with the obnoxious aggression of teenage boys. The tallest of the four crashed his shoulder into Noelle. As she pitched sideways, an arm grabbed her waist. Instead of taking a face full of snow, she found herself pressed against cashmere-covered warmth.

"Looks like it's your turn to get knocked over," James said, his chest vibrating against her cheek as he spoke. "You all right?"

"Right as rain." His coat smelled faintly of expensive aftershave while his shirt smelled of her orange body wash. A subtle combination that tempted a woman to rest her head. Okay, tempted *her*. Instead, she pressed a palm to his shoulder to steady herself. "We do have a habit of falling around each other," she said. "Thank you for catching me. In this crowd, I might have gotten trampled."

"That would definitely kill your Christmas spirit." Among other things. "Maybe you should hold on in case you get jostled again."

Noelle stared at the arm he was holding out for a moment, then wrapped a hand around his biceps. The curve of his muscles was evident even through the coat, reminding her that his vulnerability over the past few days was an exception. All of a sudden she felt decidedly dainty and very female. Her insides quivered. To steady herself, she gripped his arm tighter.

"Hey? Everything all right?"

He was looking down at her with concern, his eyes again bending the light like a pair of brown-and-green prisms.

"F-f-fine," she replied, blinking the vision away.

"You sure? You seemed a little unsteady for a moment."

"Must be your imagination. I'm steady as can be," she told him. Or would be, so long as she didn't meet his gaze.

She met his gaze.

"Are you sure? Because we could…"

It had to be a trick of the light because his pupils looked very large all of a sudden.

"Could what?" she managed to ask.

"Go…" His gaze dropped to her lips.

Noelle's mouth ran dry.

CHAPTER SIX

"Go," James repeated. "I mean… Back to the sidewalk. Where it's not as crowded." He shook the cotton from his brain. Was that what he meant? He'd lost his train of thought when she looked up at him, distracted by the sheen left by the snow on her dampened skin. Satiny smooth, it put tempting ideas in his head.

Like kissing her.

"Don't be silly," she replied. For a second, James thought she'd read his mind and meant the kiss, especially after she pulled her arm free from his. "It's a few inches of snow, not the frozen tundra. I think I can handle walking, crowd or no crowd. Now, I don't know about you, but I want my hot cocoa."

She marched toward the end of the aisle, the pom-pom on her hat bobbing in time with her steps. James stood and watched until the crowd threatened to swallow her up before following.

What the hell was wrong with him? Since when did he think about kissing the people he did business with? Worse, Noelle was an employee. Granted, a very attractive, enticing one, but there were a lot of beautiful women working in the Boston office and never once had he contemplated pulling one of them against him and kissing her senseless.

Then again, none of them ever challenged him either. Nor did they walk like the majorette in a fairy band.

It had to be the drone. He'd read that concussions could cause personality changes. Lord knows, he'd been acting out of character for days now, starting with agreeing to stay for Thanksgiving.

It certainly explained why he was standing in the middle of this oversize flea market when he could—should—be working. Honestly, did the people in this town ever do anything at a normal scale? Everywhere he looked, someone was pushing Christmas. Holiday sweaters. Gingerbread cookies. One vendor was literally making hand-blown Christmas ornaments on the spot. Further proof he wasn't himself, James almost paused because there was one particularly incandescent blue ornament that was a similar shade to Noelle's eyes.

The lady herself had stopped at a booth selling scented lotions and soaps wrapped in green-and-gold cellophane. "Smell this," she said, when he caught up with her. She held an open bottle of skin cream under his nose, and he caught the sweet smell of vanilla.

"It's supposed to smell like a Christmas cookie," she said. "What do you think?"

"I like the way your skin smells better." He spoke automatically. It wasn't until her eyes looked down and away that he realized how his answer sounded.

"I'm not a huge fan of vanilla," he quickly amended. "I prefer citrus smells."

"We have a holly berry scent which is fruity," the vendor said, reaching for a different sample. "Maybe you'll like this one better."

"I don't think..." Before Noelle could finish, the saleswoman grabbed her hand and squirted a circle of pale pink cream on her exposed wrist. "Scents smell different on than they do in the bottle," she said as she massaged the lotion into Noelle's skin. "That's why it's always best to try the sample out before you buy. What do you think? Fruity, eh?"

She started to lift Noelle's wrist, but James intercepted. Keeping his eyes on hers, he raised her wrist to his nose and inhaled. Traces of berry mingled with the orange blossom. "Better," he said.

Noelle was staring at him, her lower lip caught between her teeth, and he instantly thought about nibbling her lip himself. "But you don't need it," he finished. The scent and/or the nibbling.

He, on the other hand, was definitely going to see a neurologist when he got back to Boston.

For the second time, she slipped free of his touch. "I— I'll have to think about it," she told the saleswoman.

"Don't think too long," the woman replied. "I sell out every year."

"We'll keep that in mind," James replied. Noelle had already moved along.

"Sorry about that," he said when he caught up. He noticed she'd stuffed both her hands deep into her coat pockets. "I didn't realize she was going to make me smell your skin."

"The lady was definitely working for the sale."

"Vendors at these things always are."

They were conveniently ignoring that James was not a man who people made do anything, as well as the fact he could have sampled the scent without brushing the tip of his nose across her skin. "I hope my comment didn't stop you buying something."

"Of course not. I know what I like and don't like."

"I'm sure you do," he replied. In this case, as she'd twice

demonstrated, she didn't like sharing any more personal space with him than necessary.

Message received. Copying her, he stuffed his hands in his pockets.

"Heineman's Chocolatiers is straight ahead," she said, nodding toward the red-and-white-striped stall fifty yards away. "Doesn't look like there's too much of a line either."

Considering the crowds, that didn't bode too well for the chocolate. One would think the greatest cocoa in the world would have lines a mile long.

A burly man with gray bushy hair peeping out from beneath a Santa hat waved to them as they approached. "There's my Noelle! I wondered when I would see you!" Leaning over the table, he wrapped Noelle in a hug. His arms were so massive she nearly disappeared from view. "It's good to see you, child. Merry Christmas!"

Noelle replied something that sounded like "Murry Chrfmaf!" before breaking free. "It's good to see you too. I've been dreaming about your hot chocolate since last December."

"You say that every year."

"I mean it every year. You know it's not Christmas until I have my Heineman's Hot Chocolate fix."

James got a twinge in his stomach. Noelle wore a smile brighter than anything he'd seen on her face. Brighter than anyone had ever smiled around him actually.

"This is James Hammond," she said. "His company purchased the store."

"I read in the paper that Belinda had retired and sold the business. I'm surprised she lasted as long as she did after Ned's death. The store was always more his, and with Kevin gone…"

The man paused to wipe at a spot of dried chocolate with his hand. An impromptu moment of silence.

"I'm surprised she didn't have you take over," he said once the moment ended.

"I'm afraid I haven't worked long enough to have the experience," Noelle said. "I also didn't have the kind of money Mr. Hammond put up."

"I read that in the paper too. Nice to meet you, Mr. Hammond."

"Same here," James replied. "Noelle has been raving about your hot chocolate all day. She swears it has magical properties."

"I didn't say that," Noelle shot back. "I said it tasted magical."

"Auch! You and that man of yours were always saying that. Ever since you were in junior high.

"Did she tell you about her man?" he asked James.

"Some," he replied.

The old man nodded. "Kevin Fryberg. Belinda's son. Fine young man. A true hero."

"So I've been told."

"Left a hole in the town when he died," Mr. Heineman continued. "A huge hole. Can't imagine how Belinda coped. Or this one."

Noelle was looking down and fingering a tiny tear in the plastic tablecloth. Her cheeks had turned a darker shade of pink. "Mr. Heineman…"

But the vendor didn't get her hint. "Did she tell you how he died?" James shook his head, eager to learn details his research couldn't. "Truck rolled over and blew up while he was trying to pull one of his men free."

A true hero, like the man said. Bet he was a great guy through and through. The kind of guy who was easy to fall for. "Pretty amazing," James replied.

"The whole town loved him," Mr. Heineman repeated. "Isn't that so?"

Noelle, who still hadn't said anything beyond his name, nodded. "Everyone," she repeated softly.

"And this one... Joined at the hip, the two of them. Kevin Fryberg and the little Manger Baby. They made the perfect couple."

"Mr. Heineman..." This time, the words came out a little stronger, whether because of unwanted memories or the Manger Baby comment, James wasn't sure. Probably unwanted memories, considering how she started twitching the moment Kevin's name came up.

Personally, James wanted to hate the man—Kevin—but he couldn't. It was impossible to hate a saint. Instead he jammed his hands down deeper into his pockets.

"I don't mean to be rude, but I promised Mr. Hammond hot chocolate, not a trip down memory lane." Noelle did her best to smile brightly as she cut the older man off. "I need to prove to him that the drink's worth bragging about."

"Of course it's worth bragging about. Two cups of Heineman's Hot Chocolate coming right up."

"Prepare to be blown away," she said to James with an enthusiasm she no longer felt.

"My taste buds can hardly wait."

"Go ahead and joke. I will be vindicated."

Naturally, his responding smile didn't reach his eyes.

Dragging James to the market had been a bad idea. If she hadn't let his eyes get to her in the first place, they wouldn't have had to stand here listening to Mr. Heineman go on and on about Kevin. Normally, the man's effusiveness didn't bother her; people always talked about Kevin. Their marriage. His heroism. Being Kevin Fryberg's widow was part of who she was. This afternoon though, Mr. Heineman's reminiscing was too much like a spotlight. It left her feeling guilty and exposed.

Oh, who was she kidding? She was feeling guilty and exposed before they ever reached Mr. Heineman's booth.

It was all James's fault. Him and his stupid, sad, kaleidoscope eyes. Twice now, he'd looked at her in that intense way of his, and twice she'd had to move away before her knees buckled. Twice, she'd held her breath thinking he might kiss her. Which was stupid, because if a man like James wanted to kiss a woman, he would simply go ahead and kiss her.

And, since he hadn't kissed her, he obviously didn't want to. A point she should feel relieved over, but she didn't. She felt foolish. Mr. Heineman waxing on about her great love affair only made her feel worse.

James's voice pulled her from her thoughts. "Seems you and your late husband made quite an impression," he said.

"After a dozen years of buying hot chocolate, I should hope so." Her attempt at lightness failed, so she tried again. "That's the kind of person Kevin was. Everyone loved him. He didn't even have to try."

"Some people are naturally lovable," he replied.

"Only some?" Something about his comment struck her as odd. Looking over at him, she waited for his answer only to get a shrug.

"Not everyone is on that side of the bell curve," he said.

"Bell curve? What the heck's that supposed to mean?"

Mr. Heineman's arrival prevented him from answering. "Here you go. Two cups of Fryberg's finest hot chocolate. On the house," he added, when James reached for his wallet. "To celebrate you buying Belinda's company."

"That's very kind of you."

The old man waved off the compliment. "My pleasure. Besides, it's the least I can do for my longest and most vocal customer. You come back later in the season, okay?" he said to Noelle.

"Don't I always, Mr. Heineman?" There were customers waiting behind them. Leaning over the counter, she gave the chocolatier another hug and left him to his business.

"Moment of truth," she said to James. "What do you think?"

He took a long sip.

"Well...?" She was waiting to drink herself until she heard his verdict.

James smiled. "This is good. Like truly good."

"Told you." Her thrill at seeing his pleasure was ridiculously out of proportion. "And here you thought I was exaggerating."

"Yes, I did," he replied, taking another, longer sip, "and I take every thought back. This chocolate definitely qualifies as amazing. What's in it?"

"Beats me. Mr. Heineman won't share the recipe with anyone. Claims he'll take the secret to his grave." She took a sip and let the familiar delicious thrill wash over her. "That'll be a dark day for sure."

James was studying the contents. "I can't believe no one's suggested he bottle and sell it. A drink this good, sold in stores, would make him a fortune."

"He's been approached. So far as I know he's turned all the offers down. I think he feels it would lose what makes it special if you could have the drink all the time."

"Sort of like a store celebrating Christmas every day?" James replied.

"That's differ— Jerk."

He chuckled, forcing her to nudge him with her shoulder. It was like poking a boulder, and had as much effect, which made him chuckle again. Noelle hated to admit it, but the sound slid down her spine with a thrill similar to the cocoa. It was certainly as smooth and rich.

Quickly she raised her cup to her lips, before her reaction could show on her face. "You know exactly what I mean," she said.

"Yes," he replied, "I do. He's also a rare bird. Most people would willingly sell out for the sake of a fortune."

"Would you?" she asked.

His face had *Are you joking?* written all over it. "Weren't you listening yesterday? Hammond's already has."

Right. Their family fortune made by selling a fantasy.

Cocoa mission accomplished, the two of them began walking toward the market entrance. As their arms swung past one another, Noelle's muscles again tensed with a desire to make contact. She thought back to the lotion display and the way James's nose brushed her skin. Barely a wisp of contact, it nonetheless managed to send tingles up her arm. Now here she was having the same reaction from the memory.

Didn't it figure? All day, she'd been pulling away from his touch only to wish for it now, when the moments had passed.

But what if she touched him?

She snuck a glance through her lashes. Walking in the snow had left James's hair damp and shiny. At the back of his head, where the doctor had woven the stitches, there was a tuft sticking out at an odd angle. What would he do if she reached over and smoothed the unruliness with her fingers? Would his pupils darken the way they had before?

Would his eyes fall to her mouth?

She took a long swallow of cocoa. Thoughts like those were only asking for problems. Better to purge them from her brain.

"Before Mr. Heineman brought us our cocoa, you were talking about bell curves," she said. "You never explained what you meant."

He shrugged. "Ever take statistics?"

"In high school."

"Then you remember how results look when plotted for a spectrum, with the bulk of responses falling in the middle."

"The bell." Memories of mountain-shaped graphs popped into her head. "With the outliers on either end. I remember."

"Same thing works with personality traits, intelligence, etc. Most people are average and therefore fall in the middle. Every now and then, however, you meet someone who skews way over to one side. Like your late husband. He was clearly an outlier when it came to being well liked."

Noelle thought of how Kevin could charge a room with his presence. "He had a lot of personality. Like a big, enthusiastic teddy bear. It was easy to get caught up in his energy." So much so, a person could misread her own emotions. "All the Frybergs are like that."

"Having met Belinda, I know what you mean."

"I wonder where I would have fallen on the bell curve if I hadn't been with Kevin," she mused. "Probably in the middle." The poor little orphan girl dropped in the manger.

"Are you kidding?" They were passing a trash can, so he took their empty cups and tossed them away. "You are definitely an outlier."

"Don't be so sure. I'm talking about me without the Fryberg influence."

"So am I," he replied. "From where I'm standing, you'd be impressive, Frybergs or not."

Noelle was surprised the snow didn't melt from the blush spreading across her body. He'd looked her square in the eye as he spoke, with a seriousness to his gaze that matched his voice. The combination made her insides flutter. "Really? I mean, th-thank you." She cringed at the eagerness in her voice. Sounded like she was leaping at the approval.

Still, she'd been entwined with the Frybergs for so long. It was the first time anyone had ever suggested she was unique on her own. Well, Belinda had, but that was more maternal affection.

"You're welcome," he replied. "And..." He reached over and smoothed her scarf. Right before pulling away, his gloved fingers caught her chin. "Really."

Her insides fluttered again. Double the speed this time. "Wait a second."

They'd resumed their walk when the rest of his comment came back to her. "Didn't you say you were on the other side of the bell curve? That doesn't make sense."

"Why not?" Again, he shrugged. "We can't all be warm, huggable teddy bears. The world needs cool and efficient as well."

"True," Noelle replied. Why did his indifference sound forced, though? He was leaving something out of his comparison. Whatever that something was, its unspoken presence made her want to tell him he was wrong.

She settled for saying nothing. For his part, James seemed happy to see the subject dropped. "Traffic's eased up," he noted.

He was right. With the snow done and the bulk of the day over, there were fewer cars on the road. Most of the tourists were either on their way home or warming up before the evening festivities. "They'll start blocking streets for the Santa Light Parade soon." A few hardy souls were already setting up lawn chairs. "Santa will drive his sleigh down Main Street to light the town tree, and then Christmas season will be officially here."

"And you all do this every year?"

"Like clockwork," she told him. "I'm not the only one

who takes traditions seriously. You've got to admit it definitely kicks up the Christmas spirit."

"I'll admit the town has a certain marketable charm to it, but I still prefer Boston and its other three hundred and sixty-four days."

"Marketable charm? You spend a day surrounded by Christmas and that's the best you can come up with?" Worse, he still had those far away shadows in his eyes. "You really don't like Christmas, do you? I know..." She held up a hand. "We covered this last night."

They were coming up on the Nutcracker Inn. The hotel had been decorated to look like a real gingerbread house. "So much for my theory that Fryberg's enthusiasm could inspire anyone."

"Sorry." To her surprise, his apology sounded truly sincere. "You shouldn't take it personally. When it comes to Christmas..."

He paused to run a hand over his face. "Let's say my history with the holiday is complicated, and leave it at that."

In other words, sad. After all, people didn't hate the holidays because of happy memories.

"And here I thought I was the one with the juicy Christmas story," she said. "In fact, we're passing my birthplace now."

She pointed to the old nativity scene which had been relocated to the Nutcracker's front lawn. "Back when I was born, Mary and Joseph hung out in the park next to the Christmas tree. The Nutcracker took them in a few years ago."

"I'll refrain from pointing out the irony," James said.

"Thank you." Pointing to the baby in the center, she said, "That's where they found me. Bundled up next to the baby Jesus. I guess my mother thought he'd keep me warm."

They stopped in front of the display. "Anyway, a group of people walking by noticed there were two babies, alerted the authorities and a Fryberg legend was born."

"Manger Baby," James said.

"Exactly. And you say your Christmas history is complicated."

Noelle could make light of it now, but when she was a kid? Forget it. Being the odd man out, even at home. The foster families were decent enough and all, but she was never truly a part of them. Just the kid the state paid them to take care of. Whose mother abandoned her in a plaster nativity display.

Thing was, she could justify her mother giving her up, but why couldn't she have picked a fire station or somebody's doorstep? Why did she have to go with the cliché of all clichés on Christmas Eve, thus saddling her child with a nickname that wouldn't die?

"I hated that nickname," she said. "Every Christmas, without fail, someone would dredge up that story, and that's all I'd hear on the playground."

"I'm sorry."

"Don't be." Reaching across the gap separating them, she touched his arm. "I've gotten over it. People don't call me the name anymore, haven't since I was in high school." Or maybe they did, and she didn't notice because she'd had the Frybergs.

James looked down at her hand on his arm. Feeling her fingers begin to tingle with nerves, Noelle moved to break away only for him to cover her hand with his. "It's a wonder you don't hate Christmas as much as I do," he said. "Considering."

"Never even crossed my mind." She stared at the manger. "Christmas was never a bad holiday. I mean, yeah I got stuck with that nickname, but there was also all of this too."

With her free hand, she gestured at the decorations around them. "How can you dislike a holiday that makes an entire town decorated for your birthday?

"Besides," she added. "There was always Santa Claus. Every year, the school would take a field trip to Fryberg's and we'd tell him what we wanted. And every year, those very toys would show up under the tree.

"I found out when I was in high school that Ned Fryberg made a point of granting the low-income kids' wishes," she said. "But when I was six or seven, it felt like magic."

"At six or seven, everything seems like magic," James replied. Noelle could feel his thumb rubbing across the back of her hand. Unconsciously, probably, but the caress still comforted. "But then you grow up and stop believing."

"In Santa Claus maybe. Doesn't mean you have to stop believing in holiday magic. I believe that special things can happen at Christmas time. Like Ned making sure kids got their gifts. People come together during the holidays."

She waited for James to chuckle, and give her one of his cynical retorts. When none came, she looked up and saw him staring at the manger with sad, faraway eyes. "They also rip apart," he said in a low voice.

CHAPTER SEVEN

JAMES'S WORDS—or rather the way he said them—caught her in the midsection. Taking her free hand, she placed it on top of his, so that he was caught in her grasp. "Ripped apart how?" she asked.

"My parents broke up on Christmas," he replied. "Christmas Eve actually. I woke up on Christmas morning and my mother and my little brother were gone. Moved out."

"Just like that? Without a word?"

"Not to me."

Wow. Noelle couldn't imagine. At least she'd been a newborn when her mother dropped her off. Unable to notice the loss. "How old were you?"

"Twelve. Justin, my brother, was ten."

Definitely old enough to understand. She tried to picture James coming downstairs that Christmas morning and discovering his world had changed. "I'm sorry," she said, squeezing his hand. The words were inadequate, but she couldn't think of anything else.

"It wasn't a complete surprise. Whenever my parents got together it was a drunken screamfest. Mom liked her whiskey. Especially during the holidays," he said with a half smile. "And Justin had always been her favorite, so…" He shrugged. Noelle was beginning to realize it was his way of shaking it off whenever the moment got heavy. Or in this case, touched too close to a nerve.

"I'm sure she would have..." She stopped, realizing how foolish what she was going to say sounded. Mothers didn't always want their children; she of all people should know that. "Her loss," she said instead.

The right side of James's mouth curved upward. "From the woman who's only known me for seventy-two hours. And disliked me for at least twenty-four of them," he added, his smile stretching to both sides.

"Meaning I've warmed up to you for forty-eight. Besides," she added, giving a shrug of her own, "I don't have to know you for a long time to realize your mother missed out on knowing you. Same as my mother. Far as I'm concerned, they both didn't recognize what they had."

He squeezed her hand. Even trapped between her hands, his grip was sure and firm. Noelle felt it all the way up her arm and down to her toes. "Are you always this positive?" he asked.

"Me? Positive?" She laughed. "Only by necessity."

She let her gaze travel to the nativity set again. "For a long time, I dreamed about my mom coming back. She didn't have to take me away with her..."

"Just tell you why she left you behind."

Noelle nodded. He understood. "But she didn't. So, what else can I do but focus on being happy without her? Best revenge and all that, right?"

"You're right," James said. A chill struck her as he pulled his hand free from hers. Before the shiver could take true hold, however, gloved fingers were gripping her chin, and gently lifting her face skyward. James's eyes had a sheen to them as he smiled down at her. "Your mom lost out. Big time."

It might have been the nicest thing a man—anyone

really—had ever said to her. While the Frybergs—and Kevin, of course—complimented her, they always made a point of avoiding any mention of her mother. For as long as she'd known them, her past had been the great elephant in the room. Known but not spoken aloud.

She'd had no idea how good having her past acknowledged could feel. "Yours did too," she said, meaning it. "Your brother might be a modern-day saint for all I know, but your mom still missed out. On the plus side, though, at least your father didn't."

He dropped his hand away. "That, I'm afraid is debatable."

While he sounded self-deprecating, she'd clearly said the wrong thing. There was a cloud over his features that hadn't been there before. It made Noelle's stomach hurt. "I'm…"

"It's all right," James said, holding up a hand. "My father isn't the most lovable man himself.

"It's all right," he repeated. Noelle waited for the inevitable shrug to punctuate the sentence; she wasn't disappointed.

James was wrong though. It wasn't all right. The implication that he wasn't lovable wasn't right. Granted, she'd only known him a few days, but the man she was standing with right now seemed very lovable indeed.

She couldn't help herself. Rising on tiptoes, she wrapped her arms around his neck and pulled him into a hug. He stiffened, but only for a moment before sliding his arms around her waist.

"I think they're both idiots," Noelle whispered in his ear before laying her head on his shoulder. One of James's hands slid up her back to tangle in her hair.

They fit together well, thought Noelle.

Scarily so.

* * *

"What was I supposed to do? I mean, the guy's mother left him behind. On Christmas Eve, no less. I had to offer some kind of solace, didn't I?"

The photograph on the nightstand smiled knowingly. Kevin always did know when she was overjustifying. He would listen patiently, and when she finished talking, cock his head and say, "Who you trying to convince, Noelle? Me or you?"

"Me," she told the memory and flung herself face-first across the bed. Why else would she be in her bedroom talking to a picture?

Letting out a long breath, she splayed her fingers across her plaid duvet. The fresh air and snow had taken their toll. Fatigue spread through her body, causing her to sink deeper into the down filling. If she lay here long enough, she'd fall asleep.

James wouldn't care. He was locked in his own room, having retreated there as soon as they returned home. His head was bothering him, he claimed.

Could be true. Embarrassed was more like it though. Who wouldn't be when one of their new employees suddenly starts clinging to them in the middle of Main Street?

He'd hugged her back though. With warm, strong arms that made her feel safe all over. "Like the ones you used to give," she told Kevin.

Except for the way she'd flooded with awareness.

There had been a moment, when James slid his arm around her shoulder, that she swore the awareness was mutual. Apparently not. If James had wanted her, she thought, tracing the threading on her comforter, he would have kissed her. He wouldn't have retreated to his bedroom alone.

"Sorry," she said to Kevin. "S'not like I'm looking to

move on or anything. It's just I haven't been kissed in a long time—by a man, your mom doesn't count—and the idea is kind of nice."

Especially if the kiss came from a man with a mouth as beautiful as James's.

"You had a pretty mouth too, Kev," she said. Everyone in town used to say his smile was brighter than a Christmas tree. Once, when they were in high school, he'd taken her skiing, and face-planted in the snow getting off the ski lift. His laughter could be heard all over the mountain. God, but she missed that laugh.

She missed him. The private jokes. The Friday Old-Time Movie Nights.

"None of this would be a problem if you were here." She certainly wouldn't be drawn to her boss-slash-houseguest.

But, as her eyelids started to close, it was damp cashmere teasing her cheek, not brushed flannel, and the memory of warm arms cradling her close. Kevin's voice sounded in her ear. *Who you trying to convince, Noelle? Me or you?*

By all rights, James should have gone straight to bed, risen early and called a taxi to take him to the airport before Noelle was up for breakfast. Steps one and two went according to plan. Step three, on the other hand, had run into some difficulty. Instead of doing his preflight check, he was sitting on Noelle's leather sofa downing coffee number two and staring at her mantel.

She'd hugged him.

Flirting, kissing, sexual aggression, those he could handle. If Noelle had thrown herself at him, he would have gladly reciprocated, and the two of them would be waking up in tangled sheets.

But a hug? Hugs were tender. Caring. They reached into

vulnerable parts of you and offered compassion. How was he supposed to respond?

He'd hugged her back, that's how. Hugged her and took the comfort she was offering.

And when she put her head on his shoulder, it was like all the air had suddenly rushed to his throat. He'd nearly choked on the fullness. The last time anyone had bothered to comfort him was…

He couldn't remember. Certainly long before his mother left. God knows, she'd checked out on him long before that. His father even earlier. Was it any wonder he couldn't take the moment further?

Or were you afraid she'd say no?

The thought made his shoulders stiffen. Rejection had never been an issue before. Then again, a woman had never hugged him before either, or left him feeling so… so exposed. That made him want her even more, and he didn't mean sexually. He wanted to make her smile. Her eyes light up like a Christmas tree. To give her a dose of that magic she believed in so strongly.

Dear God. His mouth froze against his mug. He sounded like a sappy teenager. Could it be he was falling for Noelle?

"It can't be," he said.

"Can't be what?"

Noelle stood on the stairway in her Wisconsin sweatshirt and a pair of flannel sleep pants. Baggy plaid pants that obliterated her curves. He hated them.

"James? Everything okay?"

He blinked. "I was looking at your pajamas. They're very…" He sought for a decent adjective. "Plaid."

"Thank you," she replied, padding down the last couple steps. Barefoot, James noted. "I wasn't expecting you to be awake this early," she continued. "And you're dressed."

"You sound surprised. I didn't think you'd want me wandering around your kitchen in my briefs."

"Now that would have been a surprise. Is everything okay?"

"Huh?" James missed the question. He was too busy studying her bare feet. They were runner's feet—no painted toes for her—and to his horror he found them as attractive as the rest of her.

"I asked if you were feeling all right," she repeated.

"I'm fine. Why wouldn't I be?"

"Well, you didn't look good last night when you booked it to bed. I was worried you overdid it and made your headache return."

Dammit. Did she have to ask with concern increasing the vibrant blue of her eyes? It made his chest squeeze again, like yesterday.

"I'm fine," he said. "No headache. I got up to check the forecast."

"Oh." Was that disappointment darkening her eyes? "And what did you find out?"

"Actually…" He'd been too busy arguing with himself to look at his phone. It lay dormant on the coffee table.

"Is there coffee left?" Noelle asked.

He nodded, embarrassingly relieved that he didn't have to look quite yet. "I made a whole pot."

"Great. I'm going to grab a cup. Give me yours and I'll get you a refill." She held out her hand and waited while he finished the last swallow. "You can tell me about the weather when I get back."

Okay, the pajama bottoms weren't so bad after all, James decided as he watched her walk to the kitchen. Although, he would much prefer her bare legged.

The woman was definitely under his skin, big time.

Leaning forward, he picked up the phone and pressed

the weather app. As the radar loaded on his screen, he saw it was clear all the way to the coast. No excuse against flying home.

Fantastic, he thought, shoulders feeling heavy.

What a difference a few days made. Two days ago he couldn't wait to get out of the place. Now here he was dragging his feet.

Again.

"So, what's the verdict?" Noelle asked as she came around the corner.

Handing him one of the mugs, she took a seat in the opposite corner and waited.

"Smooth sailing," he replied. "Not a snowflake in sight. I'm back to thinking you had a hidden snow machine yesterday for ambience."

"Wouldn't surprise me if Ned considered it," she replied. "I know at one point he was looking for a way to make snow in July."

"Did he?"

"Apparently years ago he used soap flakes, but they got in the water and caused all sorts of problems. After that, Belinda put the kibosh on summer snow plans."

"Good thinking." He was beginning to think Ned Fryberg had been more than a little on the eccentric side. Envy twisted in his stomach. "Must have been fun, hanging out at their house as a kid."

"More like insane," she replied with a grin. "Ned was forever coming up with ideas. And they weren't all for the store. He went crazy at home too. You should have seen the to-do he made over Halloween. One year, he turned their living room into a haunted tableau. Kevin and his mom played haunted mannequins." James tried to picture the scene in his head. "What were you?" he asked.

"A flying monkey. Ned thought scary mannequins should be bigger than the fifth graders."

"I'm afraid he had a point there." Turning sideways, James rested his elbow on the back of the sofa, and propped his head with his hand. "I bet you made an adorable flying monkey."

"Scary! I was supposed to be scary!"

"Were you?" He waited while she sipped her coffee, noting her cheeks had grown the tiniest bit pink.

"No," she replied. Leaning in, she set the mug on the coffee table. The action brought along the orange blossom scent James had come to associate only with her. He breathed in deep through his nostrils. "I'm not surprised," he said once she'd left his senses. "I can't picture you as anything but adorable."

"Explains why we decided to decorate only outside the following year," she said, the blush James had been trying to deepen coming through. "Anyway, Ned was always coming up with something different. The neighborhood kids loved coming to the house to get candy."

"They sound like a fun family," he said. A true Rockwell painting. "My parents had the housekeeper pass out the candy." Bags of Hammond's brand goodies assembled by employees and doled out from a silver tray.

A hand suddenly covered his. Noelle's eyes were incandescent with unreadable emotion. "I'm sorry—I didn't mean to send us down that road again," she said.

"Road?"

"You know, our collective lousy childhoods."

James knew. But he wanted to hear how she framed the conversation.

"Bad enough we opened up all those wounds last night." She paused, reached for her coffee then changed her mind and pulled back. "I hope I didn't make you feel uncomfortable when I hugged you."

A loaded question. Depended upon her definition of uncomfortable.

"No," he lied. "Not at all."

"Good." He could hear her relief. "Because the moment seemed to call for one, you know? I didn't mean to overreach."

"You didn't," he told her. *You were the first person I'd ever shared my childhood with.*

Her eyes widened, and for a brief second, James wondered if he'd spoken his thoughts aloud. "So, you didn't go to bed early because you were avoiding me?"

Yes, I did. "Don't be silly. I had work to do, and I was tired."

"That's a relief. I... That is, we were..." A frown marred her features as she stared at their joined hands. "I wanted yesterday to jumpstart your Christmas spirit, not make things all awkward between us."

"They didn't make anything awkward," he told her. "As for the hug...it was nice. I liked it."

Soon as the words were out, his insides relaxed with a vengeance, as if they'd been gripped by tension for weeks, not a few days. He played with the fingers holding his. "I enjoyed spending time with you," he added.

"Me too," she said softly. "Even if we did get off on the wrong foot."

"More like wrong feet," James said, smiling. He took a good long look at her.

With one leg tucked under her body, she looked small and delicate against the dark leather. Only she wasn't delicate, was she? She was as resilient a person as he'd ever known. Strong, smart, loyal, gorgeous. A rare package.

Suddenly it struck him. Why he couldn't leave.

"What are you doing tonight?" he asked her.

As he suspected, her eyes got wide again. "Nothing. Why?"

"Because," he said, "I'd like to take you to dinner." And he knew the perfect place too.

"Dinner? You mean, like on a date?" From the look on her face, the question caught her by surprise. A good surprise, he hoped.

"Exactly like a date. Two minutes ago, we both said we enjoyed each other's company. I don't know about you…" Lifting his hand, he risked brushing the hair from her face. "But I'd like to continue enjoying it a little longer."

Wow. Noelle didn't know what to say. She'd gone to bed last night convinced she'd embarrassed both of them by hugging him, that this morning he would be flying back to Boston as soon as possible. Instead, he was asking her out. "But you're my boss," she blurted out. "Isn't that against some kind of rule?"

James chuckled. Noelle hated when he chuckled because the rumbling sound tripped through her every time. "I promise, where we're going, we won't run into a single coworker."

"Is that so?" Goodness, when did her voice grow husky? She sounded breathless.

"Absolutely. What do you say? Spend a few more hours with me? We can call it a thank-you for taking me in during my time of need."

His fingers were brushing her cheek again. Feathery light touches that made her mouth dry and turned her insides warm and liquid. Who exactly was supposed to be thanking whom in this proposal?

"All right," she said, fighting to keep from closing her

eyes and purring. His touch felt that good. "I'd love to have dinner with you."

"Fantastic. You have my word you won't regret a single second. This is going to make your Christmas Kickoff look like a roadside yard sale."

She laughed. Good to know his audacity was alive and well. "I'll have you know I happen to like yard sales."

"You'll like this better. Now…" To her dismay, he took both his touch and the hand beneath hers away. "Why don't you go get dressed while I make the arrangements? If we hurry, we'll have time to walk around before the show."

Show? There weren't any shows going on in Fryberg. The closest performances she knew of were at least a two hours' drive away.

"Are we going to Chicago?" she asked.

James was on his feet and taking her coffee cup. A man in command. "Not Chicago. I'm taking you to Radio City Music Hall."

"Radio what?" She'd heard wrong. "Isn't that in New York City?"

"Yes, it is," he replied. "Which is why you'd better hurry and get dressed."

CHAPTER EIGHT

SIX HOURS LATER found Noelle sitting in the back of an airport town car on her way to Manhattan, and wondering when—or if—her head would stop spinning. New York City for dinner? That was the sort of thing they did in movies. Yet there was the Empire State Building on the skyline ahead. And the Statue of Liberty alone on her island.

James's hand brushed her knee. "You haven't said much since we left the airfield. Everything okay?"

"I can't believe I'm actually in New York City for dinner" was all she could manage to say. "It's..."

"Amazing?"

"Yes. And overwhelming. When you said dinner, I never dreamed you meant—is that the Freedom Tower?" She pointed to a gigantic building with a large antenna, on top of which waved an American flag. She'd seen pictures of the structure built to replace the Twin Towers, but they were nothing compared to the real thing. "It's huge. Even from this far away."

"That was the idea," he replied before shifting a little closer. "To make a statement to the rest of the world about our resilience."

"They won't keep New York down."

"Precisely. New York Strong, as we'd say in Boston," he replied. He shifted again and unbuttoned the top of his

oat. Noelle caught a glimpse of pearl gray. Before leaving
Fryberg, they'd stopped at the boutique so he could pur-
hase another set of clothes, the plaid, he'd said, having
worn out its welcome. The soft color was a toned-down
ersion of the executive she'd met three days ago. That
nan, she thought with a smile, would never have flown
er to New York.

His hand slid along hers, breaking her train of thought.
"Would you like to see it up close?" he asked.

"Careful how often you ask the question. I want to see
everything up close."

Now that she'd accepted the ginormousness of where
hey were, excitement was quickly replacing disbelief.
"I've always dreamed of going to New York ever since I
was a little girl, but never got the chance."

"Never?"

"I almost went. Once. Right after Kevin and I got engaged. There was a merchandising conference I thought
of attending."

"What happened?"

"The conference conflicted with an awards banquet
Kevin had to attend. People expected me to be there too, so
cancelled. I could always go to Manhattan another time.
Wasn't like the city was going to go anywhere."

"At least not last time I looked," James replied. "And
ow you're here."

"Now I'm here." She sat back against the leather seat
nd watched the traffic. Despite being the middle of the
fternoon on a Saturday, the streets were lined bumper to
umper, with more cars than ten Fryberg Christmas Kick-
offs. Everywhere she looked, buildings reached toward the
ky. Big, square buildings jammed with people. She could
eel the city's energy pulsing through the limousine's win-
lows. It was fantastical.

Next to her, James was watching the window as well, his long fingers tapping on the armrest. He looked quite at home with the traffic passing by them. Same way he'd looked at home in the cockpit of his plane. Noelle had watched him the entire flight, his deftness at the controls far more interesting than the ground below. Surely he knew how gracefully he moved. If he didn't, the universe really should hold up a mirror for him to see.

"What?" He turned his face to hers. "Why are you staring at me?"

"Thank you," she replied, the words bubbling out of her. "For today."

"You haven't seen anything worth thanking me for yet."

Was he kidding? They were passing the biggest Christmas billboard she'd ever seen that very minute. "I don't have to see anything," she told him. "Being here is already amazing."

His eyes really did turn into sparkling hazel diamonds when he smiled. "You ain't seen nothing yet. You, Noelle Fryberg, are going to get the full New York Christmas experience."

"I can't wait."

It wasn't until she felt his squeeze that she realized they were still holding hands. Their fingers were entwined like puzzle pieces. Yet again they fit together with unnerving perfection.

James instructed the driver to pull over at the corner of Fifth and West Thirty-Third. Looking at the block of office buildings, Noelle frowned. "I might be a New York City virgin, but even I know this isn't Radio City Music Hall."

"There's no moss growing on you, is there?" James replied. Opening the door, he stepped outside and offered

ᴉer a hand. "Since we have time before the show, I figured
ᴠou'd enjoy a bird's-eye view of the city. Watch your step."

A blast of cold east coast air struck Noelle as she
ᵗepped onto the sidewalk. If not for James's warm hand
ᵒolding hers, she might have shivered. His grip, however,
ᵉft her impervious to the wind. "Bird's-eye view?" she
ᵃid. "I don't under... *Ohhhh!*" Spying the crowd ahead,
ᵗ clicked where they were. The Empire State Building.

"Precisely. Best view in the city, if you don't mind get-
ing cold."

What a silly comment. "I'm from the Midwest, remem-
ᵇer?" she replied. "We invented cold. Or have you already
ᵒrgotten what it was like walking around yesterday?"

Despite James's warnings of cold, the outside observa-
ion deck was lined with tourists. The two of them had to
ᵥait before finding a space near the rail. When they fi-
ᵃally made their way to a viewing spot, Noelle leaned as
ᶜlose to the barricade as possible. Below, the city spread
ᶠor miles. She squinted past the rooftops and spotted Lady
ᵼiberty. From up there, the majestic statue looked no big-
ᵍer than an action figure. "It's like standing at the top of
ᵗhe world," she said, only to cringe a little afterward. "Not
ᵗhat I'm being clichéd or anything."

"Hey, phrases become cliché for a reason." A pair of
ᵃrms came around to grip the rail on either side of her,
ᵇlocking the wind and securing her in a cashmere cocoon.

Noelle's fingers tightened their grip. She could feel the
ᵇuttons on his coat pressing through hers, letting her know
ᵒow close he was. So close that she need only relax her
ᵖine to find herself propped against his body. Did she
ᵈare? If she did, would he wrap his arms tighter? Her
ᵗomach quivered at the thought.

"I wonder if you can see the Christmas tree from the
ᵒther side," she said.

"The one at Rockefeller Center? I haven't a clue."

Turned out she didn't need to slouch, because James stepped in closer. "Want to know a secret?" he whispered in her ear. His breath was extra warm against her cold skin. "I've been to Manhattan dozens of times over the years and this is my first visit to the top of the Empire State Building."

"Really?" The sheepish nod she caught over her shoulder made her smile. "You're a virgin too?"

Several heads turned in their direction, earning her a playful shoulder nudge. "Say it a little louder," James replied. "There are a couple of people below that didn't hear you."

"Okay. James Hammond is a—"

The rest of her sentence died in a giggle as he grabbed her by the waist and pulled her to him. Her head leaned back against his collarbone. "I'm glad we could experience this together," she told him.

For a second there was silence, then his voice was back at her ear. "Me too," he murmured. Noelle swore he brushed the shell of her ear with his lips.

Like a kiss.

They took their time on the deck, making sure they saw all four views. Each was spectacular in its own right and Noelle decided that if her tour ended then and there it would still be an unforgettable day. "You really need to stop thanking me," James said as they left the observation deck. "I'm feeling self-conscious."

"Then you shouldn't have sprung for such a marvelous day," she told him. "Isn't the whole point of a day like today to make a woman feel grateful?"

She meant it as a tease, but he took her seriously, looking down at her with eyes filled with sincerity. "Not this time," he said. "Not you."

If they weren't trapped in a line of tourists, Noelle would have kissed him then and there.

The crowd herded itself downstairs and into the gift shop. "I see they've got the traffic flow issue managed," she remarked, hoping shop talk would distract the fluttering in her stomach. It didn't help that James's hair was windblown. The bonded strands around his stitches stuck out at an angle. "Considering all their years of practice, I'd be disappointed if they didn't," he replied.

Noelle only half listened. She was too distracted by those errant strands. Her fingers itched to run through them. Because those mussed-up strands looked all wrong, she argued. If she were him, she'd want someone to adjust his appearance, right?

"Hold on a second." Grabbing his arm, she stopped him from heading toward the doorway. "Let me…" As gently as possible, she combed his hair smooth, making sure her fingers barely grazed the bump on the back of his head. "Much better."

Did she just purr? Wouldn't surprise her. Stroking his hair was nearly as soothing as being petted herself.

"You realize the wind is going to mess up my hair again the second we step outside."

"Then I'll simply have to fix it again." She smoothed a patch around his ear, which was really an excuse to continue touching him.

Her reward was a smile, and a brush of his fingers against her temple. "Well, if that isn't incentive to spend the day stepping in and out of the wind, I don't know what is. Now, what do you say? Should we continue exploring?"

Noelle shivered. Explore could mean so many things. Whatever the meaning, she had the same answer. "Absolutely," she said. "Lead the way."

* * *

They were walking out of Radio City Music Hall when James's phone buzzed. "Maybe you should answer," Noelle said. "That's what? The fourth call today?"

While she was flattered he considered her to be the higher priority, she knew from experience that not all calls could be ignored. "Generally speaking, people only bother the boss on weekends if there's an emergency."

"And what makes you so sure these calls are from the office?" he asked. "How do you know I don't have an expansive social life?"

Like a girlfriend back in Boston? The thought passed as quickly as it popped into her head. James wasn't the type to play around. He was, however, the type to work all hours. "Okay, Mr. Social Life," she challenged, "what would you be doing right now if you hadn't been stuck with me all weekend?"

"A person can be dedicated to his job and have a social life, I'll have you know. And I'm not stuck with you."

Still, her point had been made and he pulled out his phone. "I was right. Nothing that can't wait," he said. He rejected the call. Not, however, before Noelle caught the name on the call screen—Jackson Hammond—and the frown that accompanied it.

Curiosity got the best of her. "You don't want to talk to your father?"

"Not particularly," he replied. "I'm sure all he's looking for is a trip update. I can fill him in when I get home."

Ignoring the unexpected pang that accompanied the words *get home*, Noelle instead focused on the rest of his comment. "I'm sure he wants to hear how you're feeling as much as he cares about the trip."

The sideways glance he sent her said otherwise. She thought about what he said yesterday, about his father and he doing their own thing. "He does know about your accident, doesn't he?" she asked.

James shrugged. "Word's gotten to him by now, I'm sure. I left a message with his 'protégé' that I was detained by a drone attack. She makes sure he's kept abreast of things."

"So you haven't spoken to him at all since your accident?"

"No." He stepped aside to let her exit the building first. "I told you," he continued, once he joined her, "my father and I aren't close. We don't do the family thing. In fact, I think I've made it pretty clear that the Hammonds are the anti-Frybergs."

Selling the world a clichéd myth. So he'd told her. Ad nauseum. "Still, your father is trying to reach you. You don't know it's all about business."

"I know my father, Noelle. When I was a kid and broke my leg, he didn't come home for two days because he was in Los Angeles meeting with a distributor."

Poor James. "How old were you?" Not that it mattered. A child would feel second-best at any age.

"Twelve and a half."

Right after his mother left. A time when he needed to feel wanted and special. Her heart clenched on preteen James's behalf. Being abandoned by her parents sucked. Still, James had something she didn't, and she needed to point that out. "He came eventually. I know it doesn't sound like much," she said when he snorted, "but I would have killed for even that much parental attention."

"Don't take this the wrong way, but you got the better end of the deal. At least you knew where you stood from the start."

"More like where I didn't stand. My parents were out

of my life from day one. So long as your father is around, you still have hope for a relationship."

Up until then, the two of them had been strolling the sidewalk. Now James stopped to look at her and for a moment, Noelle saw the twelve-year-old boy who'd been struggling to keep his hurt at bay. "Why hope for something that won't happen?"

And yet he did hope. She saw how his eyes flashed when she'd suggested his father might be worried.

"Never say never," she replied. "You can call me naive, but there's always hope. Look at me. For years, I burnt my Christmas wish on wanting a family, and then the Frybergs came into my life and poof! My wish came true."

"What do you wish for now?"

"I—" She resumed walking. "We're talking about you, remember?"

"We're also talking about hopes and dreams. You said you used to wish for a family. Since your wish was granted, you must hope for something else. What is it?"

"Peace on earth."

"I'm serious," he said.

"So am I." Every year, she, like every Fryberg's employee, filled out her Christmas wish list, and asked for large, conceptual things like peace or good health for all. There was no need for her to hope for anything personal. After all, hadn't she'd gotten everything she wanted when she'd become Noelle Fryberg? What more could she want?

James took her hand.

"This conversation is getting way too serious," he said. "Today is supposed to be about you getting the New York Christmas Experience. What did you think of the show?"

Noelle shook off her somberness with a laugh. "I loved it." She loved how he described the day with capital letters more. "If I were six inches taller, I'd start practicing my high kicks so I could audition."

"That's something I'd pay to see—you kicking your leg past your ears. I had no idea you were that limber," he added, leaning in to her ear.

Noelle's knees nearly buckled. It wasn't fair, the way he could lower his voice to the exact timbre to zap her insides. "Who said anything about ears? Waist-high is more like it.

"S'all a moot point anyway," she added. "With my size, I'd be more likely to get cast as one of the elves."

"And a right adorable one at that."

Noelle tried to shove him with her shoulder. Unfortunately, the impact had no effect. Instead, she found herself trapped against his side when he snaked his hand around her waist. The position left her arm no choice but to respond in kind and slip her arm around his waist as well.

"I mean it," he said, adding a side hug for good measure. "First thing I thought when I saw you was that you were Belinda's attack elf. So much feistiness in such a tiny package."

"I'm not sure if I should be flattered or actually try to attack you," she replied. With her luck, she'd end up wrapped in both his arms.

"Definitely flattered," he told her. "My second thought was I didn't know elves could be so beautiful. Are your knees all right?"

They wouldn't be if he kept purring compliments in her ear. "Careful," she purred back. "Keep up the sweet talk, and I'll get a big head."

"You deserve one. I've never met a woman like you, Noelle."

"You must not get out much."

Once more, he stopped, this time to wrap a second arm around her. Noelle found herself in his embrace. Heavy-lidded heat warmed her face as his eyes travelled to her mouth. "I'm not joking," he said. "You're an original."

If this were Fryberg, his features would have been hidden by the early darkness, but being the city that never slept, she could see his dilating pupils beneath his lashes. Their blackness sucked the breath from her lungs. She parted her lips, but couldn't take more than a shallow breath. Her racing heart blocked the air from going farther.

"I want to kiss you," she heard him say. "Right here, on this sidewalk. I don't care if people stare or make rude comments. I need to kiss you. I've wanted to since I—"

"Shut up, James." She didn't need to hear any more.

Standing on tiptoes, she met him halfway.

Kissing was something James thought he had a handle on. He'd kissed dozens of women in his lifetime, so why would kissing Noelle be any different?

Only it was different. With other women, his kisses had stemmed from attraction. He'd kissed them to stoke his sexual desire—and theirs. But he'd never *needed* to kiss a woman. Never had a bone-deep ache to feel their mouths on his.

The second his lips met Noelle's, a feeling he'd never felt before ballooned in his chest. Need times ten. It was the blasted hug all over again. Talking about his father and hope, she'd ripped open a hole inside him and now he couldn't get enough, couldn't get *close* enough.

Which was why he surprised himself by breaking the kiss first. Resting his head against her forehead, he cradled her face in his hands as they came down to earth.

"Wow," Noelle whispered.

Wow indeed. *Wow* didn't come close. "I think…" He inhaled deeply, to catch his breath. "I think we should get some dinner."

Noelle looked up her lashes. Her brilliant blue eyes were blown black with desire. "Is that what you want?" she asked. "Dinner?"

No.

And yes.

Some things were meant to simmer. "We've got all night," he said, fanning her cheek with his thumbs. The way her lips parted, he almost changed his mind, but inner strength prevailed. "Dinner first," he said with a smile. "Then dessert."

She nodded. Slowly. "All right. Dinner first."

"Wow. That might be one of the first times this weekend that you haven't disagreed with one of my suggestions." Maybe miracles could happen.

"What can I say?" she replied. "I'm hungry. Although..." The smile on her face turned cheeky as she backed out of his embrace. "Since you decided to postpone dessert, I'm going to make you work for it."

Her words went straight below his belt. Snagging a finger in the gap between her coat buttons, he tugged her back into his orbit. He leaned in, feeling incredibly wolfish as he growled in her ear. "Challenge accepted."

As seemed to be the theme of the past few days, James was completely wrong about the restaurant. He made their reservation based on an internet article about New York's top holiday-themed restaurants and wrote off the writer's ebullience over the decor as a marketing spin. For once, though, spin matched reality.

"Oh. My." Noelle gave a small gasp as they stepped inside. The place was completely done in white and gold to resemble an enchanted winter forest. Birch branches trimmed with tiny white lights formed a wall around the central dining room, making it look as though the tables were set up on the forest floor. There were Christmas ornaments and stockings strung about, as well as fluffy cottony-white snow on the window edges.

"Talk about a winter wonderland," Noelle said.

Indeed. Silly as it was, he actually felt the need to hold her hand tighter, in case some woodland creature tried to whisk her away. This was what she'd call magical. "I'm glad you like it," he said.

"Like it? It's unreal." She had her phone out and was snapping away at the various objects. Suddenly, she paused. "I'm not embarrassing you, am I?"

"Not at all." She was enchanting. "Take as many photos as you want. We'll be eating in a different room."

She frowned, and James almost felt bad for disappointing her. *Almost.* "You mean we're not eating in the forest?"

"Mr. Hammond requested a table in our crystal terrace," the maître d' informed her. He gestured to the elevator on the other side of the birch barricade. "Upstairs."

"We're eating on the roof," Noelle said a few moments later. He smiled at her disbelief as she stated the obvious.

Actually a glass atrium, the famed Crystal Terrace was decorated similarly to downstairs, only instead of recessed lighting, patrons ate under the night sky.

"I figured since this was our only meal in the Big Apple you should eat it with a view of the skyline," he told her. "By the way, this time you can see the Rockefeller Christmas tree. *And* the Empire State Building."

"Amazing."

Letting go of his hand, she moved toward the window while he and the maître d' exchanged amused glances.

"I had a feeling you'd like the view," James replied. He waited until the maître d' had disappeared behind the elevator doors before joining her at the glass. Noelle stood like a child pressed to a window display with her hands clutching the brass guardrail. Her lower lip was caught between her teeth in wonder. James stood behind her and captured her between his arms, the same way he had on the observation deck. "As good as the Fryberg town tree?" he asked.

"The Empire State Building really is red and green. I've read about how they projected the colors, but I had no idea they would be so vivid. The building looks like a giant cement Christmas tree."

"I'm not quite sure that's the analogy the city was going for, but..."

"I love it. Thank you for bringing me here."

Still trapped in his arms, she whirled around to face him. Up close, her smile knocked the wind out of him. He had to swallow before he could find his voice.

"I thought we agreed this afternoon that you could stop thanking me."

"We did, but a place like this deserves a special thank-you." She slipped her arms around his neck. "Makes sense now, why you wanted to have dinner. I'd have been disappointed if I'd learned... Are we the only people here?"

He was wondering when she'd notice. "No. There's a waiter and a bartender on the other side of the room."

"I don't mean the staff. I mean dinner guests. The other tables are empty."

"Are they, now?" He pretended to look over his shoulder. The Terrace only housed seven tables; the limited seating was part of how the place got its exclusive reputation. All seven tables were unoccupied.

"Well, what do you know. So they are empty," he said before turning back to her. "Must be because I booked them."

"You what?" Noelle's expression was worth every cent he'd paid too. Her eyes widened, and her lips formed an

O. She looked so charming; he had no choice but to press a kiss to her nose.

"You know how I like efficiency," he told her. "Service is so much better when you don't have to compete with other patrons for the server's attention. Besides, I wanted to give you something special since you took me in these last few days."

"I was under the impression flying me to New York was the something special," she replied. "This is…"

Shaking her head, she slipped from his arms. "Do you do this sort of thing often? Buy out restaurants?"

James wasn't sure of the right answer. Had he gone too far? The impulse had popped into his head when he'd read the internet article. Yes, it was over the top—this whole day was over the top—but he'd wanted to make it memorable.

Face it: he'd wanted to impress her. Because he liked her. And how else was he supposed to compete with a dead war hero who gave her the family she'd always dreamed of?

"I didn't mean to make you uncomfortable," he replied. "If you want, I can tell the maître d' to open the other tables…"

"No." She shook her head again. "You went to a lot of trouble, and I'm sounding ungrateful. It's just that you didn't have to do all this. Any of this. I would have been perfectly happy having dinner with you at the Nutcracker."

"I know. I told you, I wanted to do something special. To make you feel special. Because I kind of think you're worth it. Hell, after kissing you, I know you're worth it."

He scuffed the ground with his foot. Stumbling for words wasn't like him. But once again, she had him feeling and thinking uncharacteristically.

"Thank you," Noelle replied. Unlike the other times,

BARBARA WALLACE   129

she spoke in a gentle, tender voice that hung in the air.
"No one has ever put so much effort into trying to impress
me. Ever. You've made me feel very special. I think you're
crazy. But you make me feel special."

James smiled. So what if he was crazy? The satisfaction he was feeling right now far surpassed that of any deal
or successful investment. "So does this mean you'll stick
around for dinner?"

"What do you think?" she replied.

Turning to the first table within reach, James pulled out
a chair. "After you."

CHAPTER NINE

"HERE'S WHAT I THINK." It was an hour later, and the wine had loosened Noelle's tongue. "I think that you're not as anti-holiday as you claim."

"I'm not?"

"Nope." Giving an extra pop to the *p*, she leaned forward across the table. Shadows cast by the flame in the hurricane lamp danced on the planes of James's cheek, giving his handsome features a dark and mysterious vibe. She'd been thinking about this for a while, analyzing the clues he'd dropped. Tonight's rooftop surprise sealed her theory. "I think you're sentimental and I think you're a romantic," she told him.

He rolled his eyes. "Why? Because I bought out a restaurant? Hate to break it to you, honeybunch, but that doesn't mean I'm romantic—it means I'm rich and trying to seduce you."

And he was succeeding. Not even the wine and duck with truffles could wash the kiss they'd shared off her lips. James kissed like a man in charge. She might have met him halfway, but there was no doubt who dominated whom once the kiss began, and frankly, so caught up was she in the moment, that she didn't care. She liked being overwhelmed.

Right now, however, she didn't like him distracting her.

"Why are you so quick to paint yourself negatively?" she asked, getting back on track. "Last time I checked, a person could be rich and seductive and a sentimental romantic. This restaurant is only one example. The entire day…"

"Again rich and…"

"Trying to seduce me. I know," she replied.

James reached for the bottled water to pour himself a glass. "So far, I've got to say that your argument isn't too compelling."

"I have other examples."

"Such as?"

"You were tapping your toe during the show."

"It was a catchy tune!"

And the enthusiastic smile he wore at the end of the performance? He'd probably say he was rewarding a job well done. "What made you pick that particular show in the first place, huh? Why not that hot hip-hop musical everyone's gushing about, if you were simply out to impress me? Don't tell me you couldn't have scored tickets to that if you'd wanted them. Instead, you picked a Christmas show, and not just any show. The Christmas Spectacular. Heck, even your choice of restaurant," she said, gesturing at the winter wonderland around them, "is Christmassy."

"I didn't exactly pluck the theme out of thin air. Since I arrived in Fryberg, you've made your attachment to Christmas quite clear. For crying out loud, your in-laws celebrate Christmas year-round."

"All the more reason for a person who hates holidays to show me something different," she replied. "But you didn't. You went full-on Christmas. What's more, you enjoyed everything as much as I did. And not—" she wagged her finger "—not simply because I was having fun."

James raised his glass to his lips. "How could I not have a good time with such amazing company?"

Noelle blushed at the compliment. There was more though. She'd stolen enough looks during the day when he thought she wasn't looking. Saw the enjoyment on his face. Their adventure today had touched something inside him. The same sensitive part that was inspired to rent out the dining room.

She still couldn't believe he'd rented an entire rooftop for her. Talk about intimidating. She'd never been the focus of attention before, not by herself. Not without a Fryberg attached. The notion unsettled her.

Her thoughts were getting off track. "You're trying to distract me with compliments," she said, shaking her index finger. "No fair."

"*Au contraire*. I'm pretty sure all's fair," he replied.

"This isn't love or war."

"Yet."

He was joking. It was one date and, possibly, a few hours of intimacy. Neither of them expected anything more. Nevertheless, her stomach fluttered anyway. She reached for her wine, changed her mind, picked up her water and took a long drink to drown the sensation.

"Do you have any good memories of Christmas?" she asked, changing the subject.

He made a noise in his throat that sounded like an unformed groan. "We're back to talking about Christmas, are we?"

"We never left," she said. In spite of his efforts to dissuade her. "Surely, you must have some decent memories before your parents' marriage went sour." She was curious. There was a different James Hammond behind the cynicism, one that believed in moonlight dinners and making a woman feel like a princess, not for seduction purposes, but because he thought that's what a woman deserved. She wanted to get to know that James.

If she could coax him to talk.

He sat back and let out a long breath. "Easier asking for the Holy Grail. My parents never got along. Even before they separated, as soon as they spent extended time together, they would end up screaming and tossing dishes."

"Glass tumblers." She remembered.

"Exactly. Honestly, it's amazing they managed to have two kids." Frowning, he pushed his plate toward the center of the table. "There was this one Christmas. I was four. Maybe five. Hammond's was having some kind of event, for charity I think—I'm not sure. All I know is Santa was supposed to be there so my parents took Justin and me into Boston to see him. We had these matching wool coats and hats with flaps on them."

"Stylish," she said.

"Best-dressed kindergartener in the city."

His frown eased into a nostalgic-looking smile. "It was the first time I'd ever seen the Hammond's window displays. First time I remember seeing them anyway. We stood outside and watched them for hours. Although now that I say it out loud, it was probably more like ten minutes."

"Time has a way of slowing down when you're a kid."

"That it does," he said. "I read somewhere the passage of time changes based on how much of your lifetime you've lived. The author was very scientific. All I know is, on that afternoon, I could have watched those window displays forever."

He chuckled. "In one of the windows, a bunch of animals had broken into Santa's workshop. There was this squirrel inside a pot on one of the shelves that kept popping up. Every time he did, Justin would squeal and start laughing. Every time," he repeated. "Like it was the first time." And he rolled his eyes the way Noelle imagined his four-year-old self had. The image made her heart turn over.

"But you knew better," she teased.

"Totally. Who cared about some stupid squirrel when there was a polar bear looking in the window? At least the squirrel was inside the workshop. The bear was obviously in the store. What if he ate Santa Claus?"

"Obviously."

"Hey, don't laugh. Polar bears can be ruthless creatures."

"I'm not laughing." Not much anyway. His exaggerated earnestness made staying completely serious impossible. She could picture the moment in her head. Little James, his eyes wide and serious, worried about Santa's safety. "What did you do?"

"I thought we should call the police so they could tranquilize him, but my father assured me that all the polar bears at the North Pole were Santa's friends, and if there was one in the store, he was probably Santa's pet. Like a puppy."

"And that worked?"

His gaze dropped to the table. "Yeah, it did. If my father said the polar bear was a pet, then I believed him. Funny how at that age, you believe everything your parents tell you."

"The voice of definitive authority," Noelle said.

"I guess," he replied. "Anyway, we saw Santa, he told me the bear was taking a nap when I asked, and that Christmas I found a stuffed polar bear in my stocking. Damn thing sat on my bureau until junior high school."

When his world fell apart.

Afraid he'd come to the same conclusion, she reached

across the table and took his hand. He responded with a smile and a fan of his thumb across her skin.

"I bet you were an adorable little boy. Protecting Santa Claus from danger."

"More like worried I wouldn't get presents. I'd have gladly sacrificed Justin if it meant finding a race car set under the tree."

"Did you?"

"You know, I don't remember."

But he remembered the window displays, and the polar bear toy, and his childhood wonder.

"You know," she said, "they say Christmas brings out the child in people. That's why adults go so gung ho for the holiday."

"Oh, really?" He entwined their fingers. "In your case, I'd say that's definitely true."

"It is for you as well. Seriously," she said when he rolled his eyes. "You can talk about hating Christmas all you like, but today's little adventure proves that little boy who watched the window displays is in there, way down deep."

"That little boy also pulled off Santa's beard."

He was so determined to pretend he didn't have a soft side. "Fine, be that way," she told him. "I know better. Thou protest too much."

"I beg your pardon?"

"You heard me," she said, reaching for her glass. "You may act all cynical and talk about greeting card fantasies, but you don't one hundred percent believe it. If you did, you'd convince your father to redo the Boston store, tourist attraction or no. We both know you could do so successfully." Instead, he doubled down on the Christmas fantasy every year. The reason hadn't hit her until tonight, as she looked around the winter wonderland he'd rented.

He may never have had a greeting card family Christmas, but he wanted one. Over the years, whenever she'd looked at photos of the Boston store, she had sensed a secondary emotion hovering behind the nostalgia and charm, but she could never give the feeling a name. Until tonight. Like a completed jigsaw, now that the pieces had fallen in place, she could recognize the emotion clear as day. It was longing.

Hope.

That was why James authorized the window displays every year, and why he kept the Boston store unchanged despite his insistence they focus on the future. The Boston store wasn't selling a greeting card fantasy to tourists. It represented *his* Christmas fantasy.

How on earth had she missed it? If anyone knew what it was like to hope on Christmas... She'd bet he didn't even realize what he was doing.

"You're staring," James said.

"Am I?" Lost in thought, she hadn't realized. "I didn't mean to stare. I was thinking how stubborn you are."

"Me, stubborn? Says the woman who refused to move a moose?"

"Elk, and that's different. Fryer is part of our great tradition. And at least I fought to protect something the town has had for years. You're going out of your way to avoid looking sensitive."

As expected, he rolled his eyes again. At least, there was a blush accompanying it this time. She was making progress. "You know," she said, sitting back in her chair. "There's nothing wrong in admitting a vulnerable side. Some people might even be impressed."

He laughed. "Some people being you."

"Maybe." She shrugged. Truthfully, she was already impressed. Probably too impressed, if she stopped to think about it.

She waited while he studied their hands, a smile playing on his lips. "I never should have told you I enjoy it when you challenge me," he said.

"Yeah, well, hindsight is always twenty-twenty," she teased before sobering. "What I'm trying to say—very badly, apparently—is that it's okay for you to let your guard down around me. That is, you don't have to feel awkward about showing..."

Thinking of all the ways he'd already opened up, she realized how foolish she sounded. Psychoanalyzing and advising him on his feelings. "Never mind. You don't need my encouragement."

Slipping her hand from his, she pushed her chair away from the table and started folding her napkin. "I wonder what time it is? We probably won't get back to Fryberg until after midnight."

"Once," James said.

"Once what?" She set her napkin on the table and waited. James hadn't moved. His eyes remained on the spot where their hands had been.

"You wanted to know how often I bought out restaurants to impress women. The answer is once." He lifted his eyes. "Tonight."

Holy cow.

His answer rolling around her brain, Noelle stood up and walked to the window where, a few blocks away, the lights of Rockefeller Center created a glowing white canyon amid the buildings. "I was pretty sure you were joking about the whole rich-and-trying-to-seduce-you thing, but at the same time, I thought for sure you'd done stuff like this before."

She heard his chair scraping against the wood floor. A moment later, her back warmed with his presence. "Stuff?"

"You know... Sweeping a girl off her feet. Making her feel like Cinderella at the ball."

"Nope," he replied, mimicking the way she'd said the word earlier. "Only you."

She pressed a hand to her stomach to keep the quivers from spreading. "What makes me so special? If you don't mind my asking."

Silence greeted her question. The warmth disappeared from behind her, and then James was by her side, leaning against the chair rail. "I've been trying to answer that same question for two days," he said, "and damned if I know. All I know is you've had me acting out of character since Thanksgiving.

"Damn disconcerting too," he added under his breath.

"Most men would have answered a little more romantically," she said.

"I thought you knew by now that I'm not most men. Besides, you wanted me to drop my guard and be honest."

"Yes, I did," she replied, and James did not disappoint. What she hadn't expected was how enticing his honesty would be. Romantic words could be laughed off or discounted, but truth? Truth went right to your heart. Noelle liked that he didn't know why. Liked that his behavior frustrated him. That made her feel more special than any word ever could.

Suddenly, James wasn't close enough.

She moved left until they stood face-to-face, hip to hip. "I can't explain why you get to me either."

There was heat in his eyes as he wrapped her in his arms. "Then we'll just have to be confused together."

CHAPTER TEN

"I KNOW WHAT's topping my Christmas list this year."

Beneath Noelle's cheek, James's chest rumbled with his husky voice. She tucked herself tighter against his ribcage and let her fingertips ghost across his bare chest. "What's that?" she asked.

"A couple hundred more nights like this."

Sounded perfect. "You think Santa can fit them all in his sleigh?"

"He'll have to make them fit, because I won't settle for anything less. Wouldn't want to have to give him a bad online review. You know how he is about naughty and nice and all that."

"Sounds like someone gets silly when they're tired," she said, before planting a kiss on his skin. She liked silly. It was a side of him, she imagined, very few people got to see.

James rolled over and surrounded her in his embrace. They lay together like opposing spoons, with her head on his shoulder. "I'm not that tired," he said.

A yawn belied his words.

"All right, maybe a little. That was…"

"Amazing?" The word washed warm over her, causing her already boneless body to melt a little more.

"Mmm."

Noelle hadn't known. Sex with Kevin had been fine—she hadn't known anything else—but this… Her skin still hummed from being stroked. It was as if in touching her, James marked her inside and out, each caress and kiss seared into her skin like a brand.

The sensations went beyond physical though. She felt she'd woken from a long, unproductive sleep. When James sent her over the edge, he sent her to a place beyond her body. A place so high and bright, she swore she saw white. She'd wanted to float there forever.

And very nearly did.

James's fingers were tracing patterns along her arm. In her mind, she imagined them painting lines along her skin. To match the other marks he'd made.

"How about we fly to Boston in the morning, and lock ourselves in my apartment?" he suggested. "We can stay in bed until next year."

"We'd have to move though." Physical separation didn't seem possible at the moment. "Wouldn't it be easier to stay right here?"

"Nuh-uh. Boston's better." Sleep was turning his voice into a slur.

"Better than New York?"

"Better than anywhere. You'll see."

"I wouldn't say anywhere," she replied. "Fryberg's pretty special too, you know."

A soft snore stopped her from saying anything more.

So much for pillow talk. Shifting onto her elbow, Noelle used her new position to steal an uninterrupted look at the man beside her. Like she had on his first night in Fryberg, she marveled at James's beauty. The way all his features worked together to create the perfect face. Not perfect as in perfection, but perfect as in captivating. His cheekbones. His lashes. His parted lips. Leave it to him to make snoring seem attractive.

Awake, he looked older. There was a weight of the world behind his hazel eyes. When he slept, that weight faded, and hints of the boy he must have been leaked through. She would have liked to have known James as a boy. She would have told him he wasn't alone. She would have made him feel like he belonged, same way the Frybergs did her.

The Frybergs.

Her heart started to race. What had she done? She'd slept with another man. No, not slept with, *connected* with. What happened between her and James went beyond sex. Her entire love life with Kevin paled in comparison.

She felt awful just thinking the words. But they were the truth. She didn't feel guilty for sleeping with James; if anything, she felt guilty for enjoying the experience. She wanted to curl up in his arms and when James woke up, make love with him again. For crying out loud, she couldn't even use the word *sex*, because it was too inadequate a word.

"Damn you," she whispered. Why couldn't he remain the annoyingly dislikable boss she'd met on Wednesday morning? Why'd he have to get all romantic and vulnerable? Someone she could fall for?

If she hadn't fallen for him already.

She sat up, causing James's arm to slip away. He grumbled softly before rearranging himself, his head coming to rest on her hip while his arm wrapped around her thigh.

Reflexively, her fingers started combing his hair. The bump under his stitches was beginning to recede, she noticed. That was a good sign. She combed around the unruly patch where the hair and stitches met and tried to ignore the way her heart was expanding.

She *was* falling for him. Hard. And he was falling for

her—there was no way that tonight had been one-sided. No, they might be at the very beginning, but the emotions in this bed had the potential to become something very real and special. It was the last thing she'd expected, but there it was.

The air in the room was suddenly getting close. Her lungs wouldn't fill. She tried breathing in as hard as she could, but it was as if the air wouldn't flow past her lips.

Fresh air. That's what she needed. To clear her head so she could think.

Slipping out from beneath the covers, she padded toward the window only to find it couldn't open. Apparently New Yorkers didn't believe in throwing up the sash like they did in Fryberg. Very well, she'd risk a walk. A couple of moments of fumbling in the dark later, she was dressed and slipping out the door.

The brightness caught her off guard. She was used to seeing stars after midnight, not soft drink billboards and scrolling news feeds. After the soft lighting of their hotel room, the contrast hurt her eyes. Noelle leaned against the icy marble, and inhaled. The air was cold and sour smelling. A mixture of body odor and exhaust. A few blocks away, a trio of young women giggled their way toward her. They looked cold with their short jackets and exposed legs. Just looking at them made Noelle stuff her hands deeper into her pockets. If she were smart, she'd turn around and head back inside.

Back to James. No sooner did she think his name than her heart started racing again.

She was scared. She didn't want to be falling in love.

Was that what was happening? James certainly was someone she *could* love. Being with him these past two days, she'd felt like a different person. Not Kevin Fryberg's widow or the infamous Manger Baby, but like *herself*. For the first time that she could remember, she hadn't felt grateful for the attention. Maybe it was because they shared similar pasts, but when she was with James, she felt worthy. As though she was the gift.

She should be thrilled by the feeling. Why then was she standing panicked and shivering on a New York sidewalk?

"Like I would even be interested in the loser... Not that desperate... She's such a skank!" The female trio was crossing the street, talking simultaneously. They had their arms linked. Holding each other up, no doubt, since they swayed back and forth as they walked. A blonde on the far end looked to be swaying more than the others, and as they got closer, Noelle realized it was because she was bouncing to a song she was singing. Her movement caused the middle one to pitch forward and stumble.

"What are you looking at?" she slurred as they stumbled past.

Noelle blinked. "Nothing," she replied, but the trio had already passed on, the blonde turning the air blue as she heaved a string of crude obscenities in her direction. Half the words, Noelle had never heard a person actually say out loud. Feeling like she'd been punched, she tried to flatten herself farther against the building.

Something fuzzy brushed her ankle.

Oh, God, a rat! Noelle shrieked and jumped forward. City rats were rabid, weren't they? She whipped her head back and forth to see which direction the horrid creature went.

Except it wasn't a rat at all. It was a hand. A rattily gloved hand that had slipped free of a dark lump. In her distraction, she hadn't noticed the body rolled up tight against the building. The person moaned and rolled over to reveal a weathered dirty face partially covered by a winter hat. White eyes stared out at her in the darkness as he moaned again. Despite the late hour, there was enough light to see his lips moving. He was trying to tell her something.

Swallowing in nerves, she moved closer and crouched down so she could hear. As she did, she realized he was the source of the sour smell from earlier. Body odor and alcohol swamped her nostrils.

"Do you need something?" she asked, opening her pocketbook. She only had a few dollars on her, but if it would help...

The vulgar name he called her brought her up short.

Her head snapped back. "Wh-What?"

"You ain't takin' my vent. Get your own fraking spot. I ain't sharin' my heat with nobody."

The rant pushed her backward. Stumbling, she sat down hard. Tears sprang to her eyes from the impact, but she ignored them as she pushed herself to her feet. The homeless man was waving her off now as well, his voice growing loud and angry.

"I'm—I'm...sorry. I'm leaving right now." Dropping a handful of bills by his hand—which he snatched while continuing to swear at her—she scurried backward, afraid to turn around until she'd put a safe distance between them. She traveled no more than a yard or two when her foot slipped off the curb. A horn blared. A taxicab had stopped in the intersection.

"Hey, lady. Watch where you're going!"

Nodding, she hurried across the street, and didn't stop until she reached a sign indicating an all-night coffee shop. There was a waitress behind the counter playing with her phone. She looked up when Noelle entered, and pointed to an empty stool.

"Counter service only," she said, before going back to her phone.

Noelle took a seat between two bulky customers, both of whom glared at her desire for space. "Sorry," she heard herself murmur again.

"Coffee?" the waitress asked.

Not really, but Noelle was too shy to ask for anything else. "Yes, please," she replied.

The waitress slapped down a mug and a bowl of plastic creamers. Noelle shivered and wrapped her hands around the cup. Everything was so cold all of a sudden. Cold and angry. This was nothing like the New York James had shown her. But then, he'd gone out of his way to show her only the magical parts. What she was seeing now was the other New York, the part that dwelt beneath the twinkling lights and Christmas trees.

The realistic part, James would say. She'd been trying to keep this part of the world at bay since foster care.

What if falling in love with James was like that?

Sure, everything seemed wonderful now, but what if being with him was like New York and what looked beautiful at the beginning turned out to be filled with garish lights and cold, burnt coffee? It had happened before with Kevin. Hadn't she convinced herself he was the love of her life? What if she woke up one morning and discovered she'd made another mistake? Where would she be then? *Who* would she be then? She wouldn't be a Fryberg, not after betraying Kevin's memory, and they were the only family she'd ever had.

She'd be alone again. Back to the days when she was an outsider at the dinner table. Present but not truly belonging.

Manger Baby.

Suddenly, she felt very small and alone. Add in a few

schoolyard taunts and she'd be ten years old again. Lost and longing for a family to call her own.

"You want anything else?" a voice asked.

Noelle looked up to find the waitress looking in her direction. *Yeah*, she thought, *I could use a hug.* "No thanks. I'm good."

If she were home, Belinda would hug her. Like her son, she hugged fiercely. When a Fryberg encircled you in their arms, nothing in the world could harm you.

You come visit us anytime you want, Noelle. Any friend of Kevin's is a friend of ours.

Tears sprang to her eyes as Noelle remembered that wonderful first afternoon at Kevin's house. Had Mr. Lowestein known what he was giving her when he assigned Kevin as her lab partner? One step over the threshold and she had the family she'd always wanted.

And now, Kevin and Ned were dead. Belinda was moving. The store had changed hands. Everything she cared about and deemed important was slipping out of her fingers. If she lost Belinda's love along with everything else...

She couldn't lose it. She couldn't go back to being alone. She needed...

Needed...

"I need to go home."

Her announcement fell on deaf ears, but it didn't matter. Noelle knew what she had to do. With any luck, James would understand.

Slapping a five-dollar bill on the counter, she headed outside.

James woke up to the sound of his cell phone buzzing. At first he tried ignoring the noise by putting the pillow over his head, but no sooner did the call stop, than the phone started buzzing again.

"Whoever it is, they're fired," he groaned. Leaning over the side of the bed, he groped along the floor until he found his jacket and dug the phone from the breast pocket. The name on the call screen made his shoulders stiffen.

"It's the crack of dawn," he said. "Is something wrong?"

"It's early afternoon here," his father replied. "You're usually up this hour."

"I slept in." Sort of. Raising himself on his elbows, he looked to the other side of the bed, only to frown at the empty sheets. Noelle must have slipped into the bathroom. "Is everything all right?" he asked. "You don't usually call on Sunday mornings."

"Shouldn't I be asking you that question?" Jackson said in return. "Carli said there was an..." He cleared his throat. "An issue at the Fryberg store the other day."

How like Jackson to call his being struck in the head an "issue." "I had a minor accident is all," he said.

"So everything is all right there?"

"Everything is fine." He told his father he had the Fryberg deal under control. A bump on the head wouldn't change anything.

Jackson cleared his throat again. "I'm glad to hear it. Carli didn't have too many details so I wanted to make certain myself. When I had trouble connecting with you, I thought perhaps there had been a problem."

"No," James said. "No problems. I've just been very busy here, and with the time change and all..."

"Right. Right. I'm glad...things...are going smoothly." There was a pause on the other end of the line, like his father was reading something. Multitasking and distraction were par for the course with Jackson. "When do you think you'll be back in Boston?"

"I'm not sure." The irony of his answer made him smile.

Three days ago, he'd been champing at the bit to leave. "There are some…developments I want to look into."

"Developments?"

"Nothing problematic, I assure you."

On the contrary. If last night was any indication, he was on the cusp of something very significant. Noelle made him feel… He couldn't think of how to articulate his feelings. Special? Important? Neither word fit. How did he describe his heart suddenly feeling a hundred times larger?

"You'll keep me advised though, won't you? I want to know if there are any complications," his father said. "Doesn't matter if they are big or small. I'd prefer you not go silent again."

"Of course. I didn't mean to give you cause for concern."

"James, I'm always…" There was another pause. A longer one this time.

James couldn't help the way his breath caught. If he didn't know better, he'd say his father had been worried. "You're what?" he asked.

"I've decided to stop in Copenhagen before I head home."

"Oh." That wasn't what he was going to say. He looked down at the wrinkles on the sheets beneath him. Like tiny white rivers leading to Noelle's side.

Maybe it isn't all about business, she'd said. *You still have hope.*

What the hell. It was worth a try. "Hey, Dad?" The word felt odd on his tongue from lack of use. "Do you remember going into Boston to see the window displays?"

"I'm afraid you're going to have to be more specific. I examine the window displays every year."

"This was with me and Justin and…and Mom. Back when we were…" A family. "We went to see Santa Claus."

"I remember your mother hated those trips. She only went because Justin insisted. Why?"

So much for his wonderful family memory. "I was thinking about repeating one of the designs next year. Vintage is very trendy right now."

"But will it be in fashion next year, that's the question," his father replied. "Trends fall out of favor quickly these days."

As did memories. "It was just a thought."

"Well, you know my position on those displays. They outlived their expenditure long ago. I'll be back by the middle of the week. Why don't we connect then? Over dinner, perhaps."

"Okay," James said. With any luck he would have to cancel to take a certain sexy little elf sightseeing in Boston. "Have a safe trip."

"You too, James."

He let the phone drop to the floor. Stupid, his feeling kicked in the gut over one comment. Wasn't like his father was revealing some kind of family secret. At least Noelle wanted him. The way he felt with her trumped anything—everything—else. Simply thinking her name chased his dark thoughts away.

Damn, but he was falling hard for her.

He stretched his arm to pull her close, only to remember when he struck bare sheets that she was still in the bathroom. "You can come out of hiding! I'm off the phone," he called with a smile. It was sweet that she wanted to give him privacy.

When she didn't respond, he flipped over on his back. "Noelle? Babe? You okay?"

The bathroom door was wide open.

What the hell? Jumping from the bed, he rushed across the room and slapped on the bathroom light. The room was empty. He knew it would be empty. He'd just hoped…

That was the problem with hope. It always ended with a sucker punch.

Noelle was gone. While he'd been dreaming of waking up beside her, she'd gotten dressed and left.

Maybe she went to get coffee, a small, desperate voice in his head said. He angrily shoved the idea away before it could take hold. He didn't want to entertain possibilities, didn't want *hope*. His fingers squeezed the towel rod, his body trembling with the desire to rip it from the wall. He could still see the way she looked at him in the restaurant. Like she cared.

Dammit. He smashed a fist on the marble vanity, roaring through gritted teeth at the pain. Dammit, dammit, dammit! Why couldn't she have stayed a mildly attractive employee? No, she had to crawl under his skin and make him start to believe the damn greeting card was possible? He thought yesterday had been as mind-blowing for her as it had for him. He thought they were starting something here. He thought…

He thought she cared.

Joke was on him, wasn't it? Like he could compete with her dead war hero of a husband. For crying out loud, his own parents didn't want him; what made him think Noelle would?

If only she hadn't been so damn special.

Forget it. Taking a deep breath, James pushed the rage down as deep as possible. He tucked it away along with the crazy dream he'd had of sharing the holidays with Noelle.

Turned out, he'd been right all along. Things like family and holiday cheer, hope, love—they were pipe dreams.

Marketing concepts designed to manipulate emotions and sell products. They didn't really exist. At least not for him.

Lesson learned.

CHAPTER ELEVEN

IF NOELLE HEARD the guy on the sound system sing about
Santa coming to town one more time, she was going to
scream. The song, part of a continual loop in the store, had
been playing for the past three days. Usually, she embraced
Christmas carols, but she hadn't slept well since returning
from New York, and the lack of sleep had left her with a
throbbing knot at the back of her head. Like she'd been
smacked in the head by a drone.

If only she could be so lucky. A smack to the head and
temporary amnesia sounded pretty good about now. Anything would, if it meant whipping out Saturday's memories. She had her own continual loop of sounds and images
tormenting her. Every night when she tried to sleep, they
repeated in her head. James smiling. James propped on
his elbows above her. James raining kisses on her skin.
Over and over, the memories repeated until she ended up
clutching a pillow to her aching insides while she waited
for the clock to signal morning.

Not that daytime was all that much better. If she drove
past the Christmas market, she thought of James. If she visited Santa's workshop, she thought of James. If she walked
past her living room sofa…

For goodness' sake, they'd known each other four days!

Their relationship didn't warrant this kind of obsession. Yet, here she was obsessing.

Her guilty conscience didn't help. She should have gone back to the hotel and explained in person, but she'd been so freaked out by what she was feeling that she was halfway home before she'd thought things through. By then, embarrassment had kicked in, and the best she could do was a text reading *I'm sorry*. As far as regrets went, it was the stupidest, most immature thing she'd ever done.

Her gaze drifted to her telephone. It wasn't too late. She could still call and explain. What would she say? *Sorry I ran out on you, but I liked you so much I freaked?* While true, she doubted it would make a difference. When push came to shove, it was still only one night—one fantastical, mind-blowing, life-altering night—but one night all the same. And there was still the chance she'd read the situation wrong. After all, she was assuming he felt the same way. For all she knew, the way she felt after they'd made love was commonplace for James and his talk of showing her Boston was nothing more than pillow-talk promises. It had only been a few days, but he might have already moved on, and calling would simply make her look foolish.

A knock sounded on her door. Looking up, she saw Todd standing in the doorway. His arms were folded, and he wore a frown. "You okay?" he asked.

"Fine," she replied, pretending to shuffle some papers. "What can I do for you?"

"I was wondering if you've read the email from the Boston office yet."

Boston office meaning James. Her stomach did a little bounce. "No. What did it say?"

"Hammond sent a list of recommendations for how we can streamline operations and improve traffic flow in the store. Looks like he took a lot of mental notes during his tour last week. Pretty impressive for a guy with stitches in his head."

"Streamlining is his thing," she replied. Along with renting out restaurants and nipping at shoulders, she thought, fighting a blush.

Either she succeeded or Todd was too polite to say anything. "Some of his changes we won't be able to implement until after the holidays, but a few we can put in place now. Why don't you read the list and then you and I can talk?"

"Sure thing." Reaching for her mouse, she clicked on the email icon and brought up her inbox on the screen. "Has Belinda seen the list? What did she say?"

"Nothing. She officially stepped away from operations on Monday afternoon, remember?"

"Sorry. I forgot." This time, Noelle did blush.

"Totally understand," Todd replied. "It's going to take some getting used to, not thinking of her as being in charge."

Or being around, thought Noelle. The first thing her mother-in-law mentioned after Noelle's return on Sunday was that she planned to leave for Florida right after Christmas and not return until mid-April. So in the end, Noelle didn't have James or her family.

Todd cleared his throat. "You sure you're okay? You seem a little spacey."

"Sorry," she apologized again. "I was scanning the memo."

He nodded, even though the expression on his face said he didn't believe her for a second. "Soon as you've gone through it, come find me. I'm looking forward to hearing your thoughts. Especially about point number five."

Point number five, huh? She clicked open the email. Turned out, it wasn't from James after all, but rather a Carli Tynan. The suggestions were all James, however. She recognized the first two as ones he'd made during the tour. Quickly she scanned down to point five.

Remove the Elk statue from the rear of the store. In addition to taking up a large amount of space, the crowd that gathers around it impacts other shoppers' ability to maneuver in the aisles. Recommend statue be placed either outside on the grounds or in storage.

That rat! He'd promised Fryer would stay.

This was clearly revenge for her walking out. Completely unacceptable. It was one thing for him to be angry with her, but he had no business taking his anger out on a poor innocent elk. Fryer hadn't done a thing except uphold tradition.

Retrieving the Boston number from the bottom of the email, she picked up her phone and dialed.

"I want to talk to James Hammond," she snapped when the receptionist answered. There'd be plenty of time to regret her rudeness later. "Tell him Noelle Fryberg is on the phone, and that it's important."

Apparently, there was a part of her that didn't expect him to answer, because she nearly dropped the phone when James's voice drawled in her ear. "I'm in the middle of a meeting."

Nevertheless, he took her call. She might have taken that as a hopeful sign, if not for his chillingly businesslike voice.

She got straight to the point. "Fryer," she said.

"Carli sent out the memo."

"She sent it out, all right. What are you doing removing Fryer? We agreed he was a popular attraction, and deserved to stay."

"I changed my mind," James replied. "I had some time to think on my flight alone back to Boston and decided it wasn't a good idea. There's enough chaos in that store without teenagers blocking the aisles and taking selfies."

"On Friday you called that chaos organized."

"My perspective changed."

Noelle didn't think she'd ever heard his voice so emotionless, not even on his first day in Fryberg. He sounded like the warmth had been sucked out of him and it was her fault.

She grew sick to her stomach. "I'm sorry about the other night."

"I know. I received your text."

She winced. "I know I shouldn't have run out the way I did."

"Forget it, Noelle. I already have."

"You—you have?" Of course he had. Hadn't he said at the restaurant that he was a rich man trying to seduce her? She was the one who'd gone and attached deeper meaning to his behavior. Maybe all the importance had been in her head. "But Fryer..."

"Business, Noelle. The store is a Hammond's property now. It seemed silly to wax nostalgic about the previous ownership." She could hear him shifting in his chair and pictured him sitting straight and stiff behind his desk. "Besides, I'm taking the chain in a different direction after the first of the year. Your elk clashes with the new brand."

"But we agreed," Noelle said. The protest came out a whine. Worst of all, it wasn't Fryer she cared about. It was the chill in his voice. So cold and detached. She wanted the voice that scorched her skin.

"Disappointment's part of life."

Ouch. Then again, what did she expect his attitude would be? Relief? He was angry, and Noelle deserved every ounce of wrath thrown her way.

"James—" *I'm sorry.*

Too late. He'd hung up.

Noelle let the receiver slip from her fingers. What had she done? Handled the whole situation like a child, that's what. One-night stand or not, James deserved a proper goodbye.

Everything was messed up.

"Argh!" Squeezing her eyes shut, she ground the heels of her palms into her lids. "What a freaking idiot."

"Little harsh, don't you think?" she heard Belinda ask. "I'm sure whoever you're talking about isn't that stupid."

The blurry image of her mother-in-law carrying a newspaper walked into the office. She was dressed in her off-duty clothes—jeans and a soft hand-knit sweater—and looked so much like the day they first met, that Noelle immediately jumped up and ran into her arms. Immediately, Belinda's arms went around her in a bear grip more comforting than she deserved. Noelle's shoulders started to shake.

"Whoa, what's this all about?" Belinda asked. "Are you crying?"

"I c-can't help it." Noelle gulped between sobs. The safer she felt, the more she cried.

"Come now, I'm sure it's not that bad."

Did she want to bet? Sniffing back her tears, Noelle let herself catch her breath before speaking. "Fryer's gone," she said, sniffing again. "The Boston office wants him put in storage." And it was all her fault because she'd been a childish coward.

"Don't tell me all these tears are because of a battered old elk," Belinda said.

She stepped back and looked Noelle in the eye. "I know you're fond of tradition, sweetheart, but he's only an old statue. I tried to convince Ned to get rid of him for years. Thing takes up way too much space on the floor."

Great. In addition to dashing out on James, she'd been protecting a tradition no one else wanted.

How fitting.

"Then I guess you've finally gotten your wish." Backing out of her mother-in-law's embrace, Noelle turned back to her desk. "If I'd known you didn't care, I wouldn't have put up a fight."

"Don't be silly," Belinda said. "Of course you would have. You'll fight for every tradition. It's who you are. But something tells me all these tears aren't for our soon-to-be-departed mascot. Something's been bothering you all week."

"That obvious, is it?"

"Thirty seconds ago you were sobbing on my sweater. A billboard would be less obvious. What's wrong?"

Where to start? "It's complicated."

"Is it my retiring? I know my leaving for Florida is happening quickly."

"The business is only part of the problem," Noelle replied.

"I see." She wore Kevin's same skeptical expression as she folded her arms. "What's the other part?"

Shame burned in Noelle's stomach. Thinking her mistakes were bad enough, but speaking them aloud?

"I messed up," she said. "I did something really, really stupid."

"Oh, sweetheart." The older woman stepped up and rested a hand on Noelle's shoulder. "I'm sure you're exaggerating. Todd would have told me if it was super serious."

"Todd doesn't know, and worse, it's too late to fix things."

"You don't know that, sweetheart. Nothing is so horrible it can't be repaired."

"Not this time," Noelle replied, turning around. Taking a deep breath, she relayed what had happened in New York.

"Well," Belinda said when she finished, "that explains why James mysteriously cancelled our Monday meeting *and* why you were acting so strangely when you came by the house on Sunday afternoon. Why on earth would you run off and leave him like that?"

"Because I freaked out." She rubbed her forehead, the pain from the back of her head having decided to relocate there. "The way he made me feel. The emotions. They were too overwhelming. I've never felt like that before."

"Not even with Kevin?"

Noelle froze. Here she thought she couldn't mess up any further. "Kevin was… That is, I loved Kevin…"

"It's all right," Belinda said. "I know what you meant."

"Y-you do?"

"You and Kevin were practically babies when you started dating. Only natural the grown-up you would feel things a little differently.

"Maybe…" Her mother-in-law's smile was indulgent as she cupped Noelle's cheek. "Maybe even a little stronger."

How did she earn such a wonderful person in her life?

"You have to know, I loved Kevin," Noelle replied. "I wanted to spend the rest of my life with him." Who knows how things would have worked out between them if he'd returned? They'd already had a strong foundation. Passion might have blossomed eventually as well.

"No matter what, he'll always own a big piece of my heart."

Belinda smiled down at her. "I know, sweetheart. Now, the question is—does James Hammond own any of that heart? Are you in love with him?"

Was she? Noelle shook her head. "We've only known each other four days." Far too soon to fall head over heels.

"But…" She thought about how her heart felt fuller when he walked into a room.

"But you could see yourself falling in love with him someday," Belinda finished for her.

"Yes." Very much so, Noelle thought as she looked to the ground. She had the sinking feeling she was halfway in love now. Not that it mattered given her foolish behavior. "I'm sorry."

"Don't be ridiculous," Belinda replied. She forced Noelle to look up. "You never have to apologize for falling in love with someone else."

"But Kevin…"

"Kevin would want you to move on. So would Ned and I. You're much too young to spend your life alone."

Right, because Belinda was leaving. The reminder she would soon be alone in Fryberg only made the hollow feeling in Noelle's chest grow larger. "What if I'm wrong?" she asked. "What if James isn't as awesome as I think?"

"Then you try again," Belinda told her. "Relationships don't come with guarantees. Some work. Some don't."

"Yeah, but if I choose him, and we don't make it, then I'll be alone again." Her eyes had lost the battle and teared up again. One dripped down her cheek onto Belinda's fingers. "You're the only family I've ever had. I don't know what I'd do without you."

"My goodness, is that what you're scared of? Losing your family?"

She didn't see how she could move on and keep them. "I'm only family because I married Kevin. If I move on, I won't belong anymore."

"What are you talking about? Of course you'll belong. Don't you realize that with Kevin gone, I need you more than ever?"

Before she could say another word, Noelle found herself

back in Belinda's embrace. Her mother-in-law squeezed her tight. "You, Noelle Fryberg, have always been more than Kevin's wife," she said. "I love you like a daughter, and that's never going to change, whether you fall in love with James Hammond or a hundred different men. Family is forever, and you…"

She kissed Noelle's forehead. "You are my family. Got that?"

Noelle tried to keep her jaw from trembling as she nodded. What a fool she was. So busy being grateful for Belinda and Ned's affections, she couldn't see that when it came to Belinda, family wasn't an either-or proposition. Her heart was large enough to accommodate everyone. Take Thanksgiving and the mishmash of characters who joined every year. Todd, Jake from the mail room, Nadifa from sales. None of them blood related and yet all of them embraced like they were.

When she thought about it, Belinda had pulled Noelle into that welcoming web the day Kevin brought her home. She didn't inherit a family *because* she dated Kevin; dating Kevin was an added bonus. Chances are she would have been enfolded into the Thanksgiving Day group regardless. After all, the only qualification was being alone at the holidays.

"Your family was—is—the greatest gift I could ever ask for," she told Belinda. "Being a Fryberg was a dream come true. It was all I ever wanted."

By now Belinda's eyes were shining too. "Oh, sweetheart, you're my dream come true too. Don't get me wrong, I loved Kevin, but I always wanted a daughter to keep the family traditions alive."

Offering a smile, the older woman bent down and kissed Noelle on the forehead. "I never imagined I'd end up with a daughter who's more Fryberg than anyone with actual Fryberg blood."

They both laughed. "Does that mean I can still have Grandma Fryberg's recipe book?" Noelle asked, wiping her eyes.

"Absolutely. I'll even laminate the pages so you can pass the book along to your daughter.

"And you will have a daughter. Or daughter-in-law," Belinda added. Her smile faded and once again, her expression grew serious. "There's a whole world out there beyond this store and our family name. I fully expect you to build a happy life beyond Fryberg's. You deserve one."

"But I wouldn't have a life without Fryberg's," Noelle replied. Breaking out of her mother-in-law's grasp, she reached for the box of tissues on her desk. Her eyes and nose were runny with tears. "I can't imagine anything else."

"Really? Then why are you crying over James Hammond?"

All right, maybe Noelle could imagine a little more. The other night, in James's arms, she'd imagined all types of future. "Doesn't matter whether I'm crying over him or not," she said, blowing her nose. "He and I are finished."

"Are you certain?"

"Man said so himself."

Forget it, Noelle. I already have.

She blew her nose. "You should have heard his voice, Belinda." Remembering sent a chill down her spine. "I called him to discuss his email, and I might as well have been talking to a stranger."

A feeling of hopelessness washed over her. "I thought... That is, the whole reason I freaked out was because I thought we had some kind of special connection. Now I wonder if maybe I wasn't simply confusing good sex with affection and blew the weekend out of proportion."

Thankfully, Belinda chose to let the good sex comment slide. Hearing her thoughts out loud, however, made Noelle even more certain she was right, and had let the romanticism of Saturday night get the best of her. "Other than being angry with the way I took off, I wonder if James has even given me a second thought."

"I'm sure he has. He didn't strike me as someone who took...those kinds of encounters...lightly."

"Me either," Noelle replied. "He certainly sounded businesslike enough today though. Talking about the company's new direction and all."

"New direction?"

"Uh-huh. Based on the points in his email, I'd say he's back to focusing on streamlining and internet sales." She could see it now. Today Fryer. Tomorrow the Christmas Castle.

"Hmm."

Noelle frowned. "What?"

"I'm not sure," Belinda replied. "Did you see today's business headlines?"

"No."

"I think you should. There's something very interesting in it." Her mother-in-law retrieved the newspaper she'd dropped on the desk during their talk. It was folded in thirds, to highlight the headline on the weekly marketing column. Noelle's heart sank as she read.

Hammond's to discontinue iconic window displays.

The article below quoted James as saying he wanted to take the chain in a "new direction" and build a store for the next generation.

"'It's time Hammond's let go of the past,'" she read. "'We can't bring the past back, no matter how badly we may want to.'" It was a harsh-sounding quote, one she imagined marketing hadn't wanted to use.

"When I read the article this morning, something didn't hit me as right. Still doesn't, although I can't put my finger on what."

Noelle stared at the headline.

All week she'd been downplaying Saturday night to ease the giant ache in her chest, but her efforts hadn't worked. There were too many reminders in the Christmas music and lights. She wanted the holiday to go away so she could breathe again. She who held Christmas in her heart fifty-two weeks a year.

But ending the window displays? They represented the one decent family memory he had. It was why he kept them going year after year, regardless of the cost. Because there was a part of him, the ghost of that little boy, that wanted to believe family meant something. That he meant something to his family. Before his mother's midnight departure convinced him otherwise.

No. Noelle's heart seized. Dropping the newspaper, she stumbled toward a chair. The room had become a tunnel, a narrow dark tube with black all around.

"Are you all right?" she heard Belinda ask from far away. "Is something wrong? What is it?"

No. Yes. Everything. The answers flew through her head as her realization became clear.

She'd disappeared in the middle of the night without a word just like his mother. He'd spent the day revealing himself, at her urging, and she'd let her cowardice trample that vulnerability. In doing so, she solidified all of James's fears.

That was why he was closing the window displays. Not because he wanted to take the chain in a new direction—though he would and do so brilliantly—but because that little boy no longer believed in his own memory. James had retreated, quit, waved the white flag in defeat.

He had given up hope, and it was her fault.

It wasn't right. Someone needed to tell him he had too much sweetness and light inside him to hide behind profits and modern retail. Someone had to show him he was special.

Lovable.

Not someone. Her. Noelle needed to fix the horrible wrong she had done to him. And not by text or by phone either. In person.

"I need to go to Boston," she told Belinda. "As soon as possible."

She may have thrown away her chance to be with him, but Noelle would be damned if she cost him Christmas.

"Why are you still wearing your coat?" Jackson asked, as he slipped into his seat. As usual, he was dressed impeccably in a suit from his London tailor.

"I'm cold," James replied. "This table picks up a draft from the front door."

He and his father were meeting for a business lunch in the bistro across from Hammond's. Outside, Copley Square bustled with Christmas shoppers, many of who stopped to watch the Hammond's displays. In fact, there was a crowd of preschoolers clumped in front of them that very moment, watching the elves make mischief in Santa's kitchen. Why they were standing out in such blasted cold was beyond him. A shiver passed through him, and he looked away.

"If you're uncomfortable, we can move," Jackson said.

"That won't be necessary. I'll warm up soon enough." He hoped. He'd been chilled to the bone for days. At home, he'd cranked both his gas fireplace and the thermostat, and slept with an extra comforter. It was going to be a long winter, at this rate.

Maybe if he found someone to warm him up? He dismissed the idea as quickly as it appeared. Female company didn't appeal to him right now.

Meanwhile, for some reason, his father refused to let the subject drop. After the waiter took their orders, he laid his napkin on his lap and leaned forward. "Are you sure it's temperature-related and not something to do with the 'issue' you had in Fryberg?"

"I'm sure." Other than a minor case of temporary insanity, his "issue" had been side-effect-free. "A cup of hot coffee and I'll be fine."

Jackson stared at him for a beat or two. "If you say so," he said finally, before reaching for his water glass. "I saw the article in the *Business Journal* today about the window displays. I have to say I didn't think you would ever agree to eliminate them."

"What can I say? Even I couldn't ignore the numbers."

"I'm glad you finally came around. Although it would have been nice if you'd alerted me to your decision. I realize you handle these kinds of day-to-day operations, but..."

"You were in Copenhagen," James interrupted. "And I wanted to make the announcement early enough to take advantage of the entire Christmas season. I didn't mean to blindside you."

"*Surprise* is a better word."

James returned his father's flat smile and sipped his coffee. "Marketing tells me we're getting quite a bit of local press attention from the announcement. This could turn into a public relations bonus for us."

"That reminds me," Jackson said, "you need to talk to whoever wrote the press release. They should have drafted a less caustic quote."

James had written the quote himself. Molly, their communications assistant, had clearly wanted something else, but she hadn't argued.

Noelle would have. He suppressed a shiver. "Actually, I thought the quote went straight to the point."

"'We can't bring the past back, no matter how badly we may want to'?" Jackson quoted. "I would have preferred something a little less cynical."

"Why? It's true, isn't it?"

"Yes, but we're not in the business of selling truth, James—we sell toys."

"Don't worry. I've no intention of letting sales slide." Amazing how unaffected he was about the whole thing. Not too long ago, he would have argued the window displays brought in customers. But when he'd visited the store on Sunday afternoon and saw this year's intricate displays, he'd suddenly thought *Why bother?* All that money spent and what did it matter?

"The rest of the chain does quite well without window displays," James said, reaching for his coffee again. "Boston will too. A month from now, people won't remember what the display looked like."

"I could have told you that," Jackson replied.

The waiter arrived with their food. While he waited for the man to serve his soup, James let his eyes travel back to the crowd across the street. The preschoolers had been joined by several mothers with strollers. For a moment, he thought he saw a red-and-white knit hat mixed in the crowd and his pulse stuttered. His eyes were playing tricks on him. He hadn't thought about Noelle since he left New York—prolonged thought anyway—and he wasn't about to start.

Although yesterday's phone call nearly killed him. When the receptionist said her name, a tearing sensation had gripped his chest. The first intense feeling he'd had in days, it nearly knocked him to his knees. Then there was the way she'd lowered her voice to apologize. It took all his reserves, but thankfully he kept himself from breaking and asking why she left. No need to hear her excuse. He already knew.

The sound of his father clearing his throat drew back his attention.

"Are you certain you feel all right?" Jackson asked. "Perhaps you should see a specialist."

"I'm *fine*," he insisted.

"You say you're all right, but you're clearly not acting like yourself. You're difficult to reach. You're making sudden changes in company policy."

James let out a long sigh. "So this is about my not discussing the announcement with you beforehand." He knew this sudden interest in his health had to mean something.

"This has nothing to do with the announcement," Jackson said, killing that theory immediately. "I'm simply concerned about you."

"Why? You've never been before." The words came flying out before James realized what he was saying. They landed between them, causing his father to sit back, his features frozen in shock.

"You don't think I care?" Jackson said. He actually sounded stung.

What did he do now?

Aww, heck. Might as well put this bit of the past to rest too. "I'm not making an accusation," James said, holding up a hand. "I understand that you were stuck with me when Mom left and that put you in an awkward position."

His father stared at him. A long look similar to the ones he'd given James as a teenager. And like then, James had to fight the urge to tug at his collar.

Finally, Jackson put down his fork. "Are you suggesting that I was unhappy when your mother left you behind?"

Wasn't he? "I remember the look on your face when I came downstairs that morning and you definitely weren't expecting to see me. If anything," he added, looking down at his chowder, "you looked disappointed."

"That's because I was," Jackson replied. "For you." He let out a sigh. "Your mother was a very unpredictable woman. Doing one thing one day, and something else the next. She insisted that I encouraged your analytical side to spite her, and that I didn't understand what it took to raise a child. I had no idea she'd left you behind until you came downstairs that morning.

"She was right," he said, smoothing a wrinkle from the tablecloth. "I was completely unprepared."

Silence filled the table while his father paused to sip his water and James struggled for what to say next. It was true; his mother had been high-strung. Hence the flying crystal. He remembered preferring the quiet of his father's study to being around her whirling dervish personality.

"I'm not..." Jackson took another drink. "I'm not a naturally affectionate person. Your mother complained all the time that I was too detached. Too stiff. It's how I am. Looking back, I can see how an impressionable teenager might misconstrue my behavior.

"I can assure you, though," he added, "that at no time did I ever consider myself 'stuck' with you."

Slowly stirring his soup, James digested his father's confession. So he had been wanted after all. As far as family reconciliations went, the moment wouldn't win any prizes, but he got a tightness in his chest nonetheless. "Thank you," he said. "I appreciate you telling me."

For the first time in James's life, Jackson Hammond looked bashful. "You're welcome. Son."

By unspoken agreement, they spent the rest of the luncheon discussing business, a far more comfortable subject. When they were finished, Jackson suggested they meet for lunch again the next week. "Or you could come by for dinner," he offered.

"Sure," James replied. If his father could try, then so could he. "Dinner would be great."

Jackson responded with the most awkward shoulder pat in history. Still it was a start.

Not that he would ever say so, but his father had terrible timing. Short as it was, their heart-to-heart killed the numbness he'd so carefully cultivated when Noelle left. Granted, he'd been cold, but with one or two exceptions, he'd been able to function without thinking about what a fool he'd been.

But then, Jackson decided to pat his shoulder, and the first thought that popped into his head was *Noelle was right*. Suddenly, the entire weekend was replaying in his head.

Telling his father he had an errand, James hung back on the sidewalk as Jackson entered the building. He needed to clear his head of the frustration his father's apology had unleashed. It felt like a giant fist shoving upward in his chest. If he didn't push it back down, he was liable to scream out loud.

Why was he letting one tiny woman get to him so badly?

Dammit! He'd had one-night stands before. Some of them even told him to go to hell after they discovered they were nothing more than one-night stands. None of those experiences had ever turned into an existential crisis. His weekend with Noelle shouldn't have either, late-night escape or otherwise. Yet here he was, making long overdue peace with his father and wishing it was Noelle reaching out to him instead.

He never should have let her past his defenses. From the start, he knew nothing *real* could happen between them. Relationships didn't happen on his end of the bell curve. But then she'd hugged him, shifting around his insides and allowing things like hope and longing to rise to the surface. She'd made him believe their night together went deeper than sex. He hadn't just taken her in his arms; he'd shared his soul with her. Every touch, every kiss was his way of expressing the feelings she unlocked in him. Fool that he was, he'd actually started believing in Hammond's marketing pitch.

And now, thanks to his father's apology, those feelings threatened to return, this time to mock him. He didn't want to feel. He didn't want to hope anymore.

From here on in, it was about business. Profit and efficiency.

"Ooh, look, Andre! There's a monkey swinging in the lights. Do you see him?"

Lost in his thoughts, James didn't realize he'd joined the crowd in front of the window displays. Next to him, a young mother in a leather jacket stood holding a toddler. She had a second baby, bundled in pink bunting in a stroller beside her.

The woman pointed a manicured finger toward the window. "Look at him," she said. "He's trying to steal Santa's cookies."

The toddler, Andre presumably, had a frown on his pudgy puce-colored face. "Bad monkey," he said. "No cookies."

"You don't think he should take the cookies?" the mother asked, laughing as the toddler shook his head.

"Someone's taken the naughty list concept to heart," James caught himself saying.

"Let's hope he feels that way when he's ten," she replied. "You ready to see the next window, Dre?"

Watching the trio walk away, a pang struck James in the midsection as he realized Dre and his little sister wouldn't see the displays next year. Oh, well, at their age, they wouldn't even realize the loss. Most kids wouldn't. It was just James holding on to the memory.

Did his brother ever think about the window displays? Last time he saw Justin… When was the last time he'd seen him? The boat races maybe? Jackson had said something about his brother going to business school out west somewhere. James didn't even know what college his brother had attended. Or where he did his undergrad, for that matter. Like mother, like son, Justin had had little to do with them once he left. He'd apparently built quite a nice Hammond-free life and wasn't looking back.

James needed to do the same. It helped that at least Jackson had confessed he wasn't completely unwanted.

Just unwanted by his mother.

And by Noelle. Out of the corner of his eye, he saw another flash of red and white, causing the frustration to rise anew.

Four more weeks. Come January first, Christmas would be done, they would pack away the decorations, and he would be rid of any and all reminders of Fryberg. No more thoughts of blue eyes or snow-dotted lashes.

In the meantime, James had a business to run. The numbers at their Cape Cod store were especially troublesome and needed to be addressed.

Feeling his control return, he marched into the store.

His renewed focus lasted until he reached the top floor.

There, he barely managed to round the corner to his office when a red-and-white cap stopped him in his tracks.

So much for blaming his imagination.

Noelle rose from her seat. "I need to talk with you," she said.

CHAPTER TWELVE

SHE LOOKED...BEAUTIFUL. The image of her lying in his arms flashed before him, and his body moved to take her in his arms. Catching himself, James clasped his hands behind his back.

"If you're here about that blasted elk there's nothing more to talk about," he said.

"I'm not here about Fryer," she said.

"Good. Then we have even less to talk about. If you'll excuse me..."

He tried to brush past her and head into his office, but she stepped in front of him. A five-foot-two roadblock. "I read about you canceling the window displays."

"And let me guess, you're worried how the new direction will affect your Christmas Castle." Why else would she fly halfway across the country instead of emailing? All roads led to Fryberg, didn't they?

"You could have saved yourself the airfare. Our plans for the castle haven't changed. Your family business will live to bring another year of Christmas cheer."

Again, he moved to his office and again, she blocked his path. "I'm not here about the castle either."

"Then why are you here?" he asked. It was taking all his effort to keep his voice crisp and businesslike. What he wanted was to growl through clenched teeth.

"Because I owe you an apology."

Seriously? James ignored how her answer made his heart give a little jump. Not again, he reminded himself. No more being fooled into believing emotions existed when they didn't.

"You wasted your airfare. I told you on the phone, the matter has already been forgotten."

This time, he managed to pass her and reach his office door.

"I know what you're doing." Noelle's voice rang through the waiting area.

Don't take the bait. Don't turn around.

"Is that so?" he replied, turning. "And what is that, exactly?"

"You're trying to kill Christmas."

Someone dropped a stapler. Out of the corner of his eye he saw his administrative assistant picking up several sheets of paper from the floor.

"You're being ridiculous." He couldn't kill Christmas if he tried. Damn holiday insisted on existing whether he wanted it to or not.

"Am I? I know what those displays meant to you. How much you loved them…"

His assistant dropped her stapler again.

He closed his eyes. "Noelle, this is neither the time nor the place for us to have this conversation."

"Fine," she replied. "When and where would you like to have it?"

"How about nowhere and never?"

"Nice try, but I flew across five states to talk to you so I can say what I have to say now or I can say it later, but I'm not leaving until I speak my piece."

He expected her to fold her arms after her speech, but instead, she looked up at him through her lashes, and added, "Please?" Her plea totally threw him a curveball. No way he could resist those cornflower eyes.

"Fine. We'll talk." Opening his office door, he motioned for her to step in first. "But take off that hat." No way was he rehashing Saturday night with her looking adorable.

Unfortunately, she looked more adorable with tousled hat hair. He went back to clasping his hands to keep from combing his fingers through it.

Nodding to one of the chairs, he walked around to the other side of his desk and sat down figuring a three-foot cherrywood barrier would keep him from doing something stupid.

"Okay, you've got the floor," he said. "What was so important that you had to fly all the way to Boston to say?"

"Aren't you going to take off your coat?"

"No. I'm cold." Although that status was rapidly changing, thanks to his heart rate. It had started racing the second he saw her. "Now what is it you wanted?"

"Why are you closing down the window displays?"

"Because they're a financial drain on the company."

"Funny how you didn't think so before," she replied coming toward the desk.

"Well, I saw them with a new perspective. I realized we were spending a lot of money trying to sell a concept that no longer resonated." Was she coming around to his side of the desk? "My decision shouldn't be a surprise," he said. "My feelings about this kind of kitschy Christmas marketing were hardly a secret."

She stopped at the desk corner. "You didn't think them so kitschy on Saturday night when you told me about the polar bear."

"That's because I was trying to charm you into bed. And it worked. At least for a little while," he added. If she was going to stand so close, he was going to wield sarcasm.

God, but he wished she'd back away. It was easier to be furious with her when he couldn't smell orange blossoms.

"It was wrong of me to run out like that," she said. "It was stupid and childish."

The earnestness in her eyes left him aching. With his hands gripping the chair arm, he pushed himself closer to the desk. "Congratulations. We agree."

He didn't have to look to know his words hit their mark. "I don't suppose you'd let me explain," she said.

"Would it make any difference?"

"Maybe. No. I don't know."

"Thank you for summarizing everything so clearly." He didn't want to hear any more. Didn't want her orange blossom scent interfering with his anger. "I think you should go," he told her.

Noelle twisted her hat in her hands. This wasn't going at all the way she'd envisioned. Seeing him again reminded her how intimidating a presence he could have when he wanted. It also reminded her how much vulnerability there was beneath the surface. Icy as he sounded, she could see the flashes of pain in his eyes. She wanted to hug him and tell him how amazingly special he was. Only he wouldn't believe her. Not until she cleared the air.

Which was why she stood her ground. She came to explain and make amends for hurting him, and she would.

"I freaked out," she told him. "Saturday was…it felt like a fairy tale with me as Cinderella. You had me feeling all these emotions and suddenly they were too much. I felt scared and guilty and so many things. I needed to get some air."

"All the way back in Michigan? What, New York air not good enough?"

She deserved that. "At first, I only meant to stand outside for a little bit, maybe get a cup of coffee. But then there was this homeless man and these women and… It doesn't matter. Bottom line is, I got scared and ran home where I knew I'd be safe."

"I would have thought you'd find me safe, considering."

"You were. You made me feel incredibly safe. That was part of what freaked me out."

"How reassuring," James replied.

Yeah, listening to what she was saying, Noelle wouldn't buy it either. "I made a mistake," she said.

"No kidding." He shoved the chair away from his desk, causing her to jump. "I told you things I've never shared with anyone," he said, as he stood up. "I opened up to you—and you were the one who pushed me."

Shame at her behavior welled up inside her. "I know," she replied.

"You made me think…" The rest of his sentence died when he ran his hand over his face. "I should have known. When I saw that mantel full of photos, I should have known I couldn't compete with Kevin."

"What?" No, he had it all wrong. "That's not true."

"Noelle, listen to yourself. Thirty seconds ago, you said you felt guilty."

"Yes, but not because of my feelings for Kevin. I felt guilty because I realized Kevin couldn't measure up to you."

Confusion marked his features. "What?"

Noelle took a deep breath. After all his openness, he deserved to know her deepest secret. "Kevin was a special person," she said. "Every girl in school wanted to date him, so I couldn't believe how lucky I was that he wanted to be with me. Being Kevin Fryberg's girl was the best thing that ever happened to me. Being part of the Frybergs was the biggest dream come true."

"So you've told me," James replied.

"But what I didn't tell you was that Kevin was...he was like the big, wonderful brother I never had."

The confusion deepened. "I don't understand."

"That's the reason I felt so guilty," Noelle said, moving to look out the window herself. "I loved Kevin. I loved our life together, especially when his parents were around. But we never had that phase where we couldn't keep our hands off each other, and I just figured that was because we'd been together for so long. It wasn't until shortly after the wedding that I realized I didn't love him the way a wife should. But by that time, we were committed."

Her fingers ran along the blinds lining the window. "And I had the family I'd always wanted. If he and I ended... So I stuck it out, figuring I'd eventually fall more in love with him. Then Kevin deployed."

And then he died, leaving her the widow of the town hero and forced to keep pretending lest she hurt her surrogate family. She turned so she could study James with her damp gaze. "I didn't know," she whispered.

"Know what?"

"What it felt like to be truly attracted to someone. To have this continual ache in the pit of your stomach because you desperately want them to touch you. Until this past weekend. You made me feel out of control and off-balance and it scared the hell out of me."

"You could have told me," he said. "I would have understood."

"How was I supposed to tell you I could see myself falling for you, when it was those feelings that terrified me?" she replied. "Don't you get it? I was afraid my feelings would blow up in my face and cost me the only family I've ever known."

She waited, watched, while her confession settled over

him. After a moment, he ran his hand over his face again and sighed. "If it frightened you, why are you telling me now?"

"Because you deserved to know," she replied. "And because I've realized that family isn't an either-or proposition. Nor is it about being related. It's about love, pure and simple. So long as you have love, you have family."

Risking his rejection, she walked toward him. When she got close enough, she took his hand. "And maybe all that greeting card stuff you despise is a myth, but Christmas can still be wonderful if you're with someone special. Please don't close off the part of you that believes that too."

But James only looked down at their hands. Noelle could take a hint. Foolish of her to think an apology would change much. At least she'd tried. "Anyway, that's what I came to tell you. That you're on the lovable side of the bell curve, and that I wish I hadn't messed up, because there's nothing I would like more than to have been your someone special this Christmas."

"Are you still scared?"

A spark lit in her heart. There was hope in his voice. He trying to fight it, but it was there. "Terrified," she replied.

His grip tightened around her fingers. "Me too." Slowly, he lifted his gaze and she saw brightness sparkling in his eyes. "I've never had anyone think I'm special before," he told her.

"I've never been anyone's princess," she told him back.

"So maybe…"

She held her breath and waited.

"Be a shame for you not to see Boston since you flew all the way here," he said.

A hundred-pound weight lifted from her shoulders. She

felt like she had the day she met the Frybergs, times ten. "What about my flight home?"

Letting go of her hand, James wrapped an arm around her waist and leaned in until their foreheads touched. "Don't worry," he said. "I know a pilot."

EPILOGUE

Three weeks later

FOR THE LIFE of him, James was never going to get used to
those nutcrackers. They were the stuff kids' nightmares
were made of. Whistling to himself, he passed under them
and headed for the conductor's shack.

"Good afternoon, Ed," he greeted. "How's the train
business?"

The conductor blanched. "M-M-Mr. Hammond. We
weren't expecting you today. I'm afraid the castle closed
early."

"Are you telling me everyone has gone home?" James
asked in his sternest voice. "It's only two o'clock."

"Well, it…it is Christmas Eve…"

"James Hammond, stop scaring the employees." Noelle came bouncing out of the conductor's shack wearing a Santa Claus hat and carrying a gold-and-white gift
bag. Like it always did when he saw her, James's breath
caught in his throat.

"Don't mind him, Ed," she said. "He's not nearly as
Grinchy as he'd like people to believe." Rising on tiptoes, she flung her arms around his neck and kissed him
soundly. Completely confirming her charge, James kissed

her back with equal enthusiasm. Her gift bag crinkled as she wrapped her arms tighter.

"Merry Christmas," she said, smiling. "Nice sweater. You look very festive." He was wearing a red-and-white reindeer jumper purchased at the hotel on his last visit a few days before. One of the advantages of having his own plane was that it made long-distance relationships a lot easier.

"So do you," he replied. "Careful though. If Santa finds out you stole his hat, he'll put you on the naughty list."

"Then we'd better not tell him." Giving him one more kiss, she untangled herself and held out the gift bag. "This is for you. Merry Christmas Eve."

James fingered the red polka-dotted tissue paper peering out from the top of the bag. He might as well have been five again, for the thrill that passed through him.

No, he corrected, a five-year-old wouldn't get this choked up over a simple gift bag. "I thought we agreed to wait and exchange presents tomorrow night when we were alone."

Back in Boston, there was a stack of boxes with Noelle's name on them. More than necessary, probably, but he hadn't been able to help himself. Finally, he understood the joy that came from giving to the people for whom you cared.

"I know," she replied. "This is more of a pre-Christmas present."

Meaning she'd cared enough in return to shop for him. His throat constricted a little more. As far as he was concerned, he already had the best Christmas present in the world standing in front of him.

Her hand came down to rest on his forearm. Shaking off his thoughts, he focused on her shimmering blue gaze instead. "Consider it a small thank-you for asking me if

I'd help with next year's window displays," she said. "A very small thank-you. I'm poor from all my Christmas shopping."

"You didn't have to buy anything. Asking for your assistance was a no-brainer. No one is better suited to work on our chain-wide window display extravaganza than you, my little elf." It was true. Hammond's "new direction" involved rolling out Boston's iconic displays on a nationwide basis. The new displays would be more modern and inclusive to reflect the current consumer public, and focus on the message that Christmas was a time for spreading love and goodwill. James was excited for the new project, and for Noelle's involvement since she'd be making frequent trips to Boston. He didn't want to get too ahead of himself, but if things went well he hoped Noelle might someday consider spending even more time in Boston.

Seemed hope had become a habit for him these days.

"Aren't you going to open it?" Noelle asked.

"What?" The gift. He pretended to study the bag. "Considering the size, I'll go out on a limb and say you didn't buy me a drone."

Noelle stuck out her tongue. "Ha-ha-ha. You should be sending that drone a thank-you present. If you hadn't stood in the way, we might never have gotten past the dislike stage."

"True enough."

He shook the bag, only to hear the useless rustling of paper. "It's one of those stuffed Fryer collectibles, isn't it?" After he and Noelle made up, they'd compromised— sort of. Fryer was to be given one last season and then retired with an official ceremony after the first of the year.

"How about you stop guessing and open the package?" Noelle replied. "And don't forget to read the note. It's important."

James did as he was told and discovered a bag full of gingerbread cookies. Two dozen of them.

"I baked them last night," Noelle told him. "In case we get hungry on the way to Belinda's," she said. "Or on the flight tomorrow." They were spending Christmas Eve with Noelle's mother-in-law before flying to Boston for Christmas dinner.

"If you look," she said, "I gave them all little business suits."

Sure enough, she had. "So you can literally bite my head off?"

"Or lick your tummy."

"Sweetheart, you don't need a cookie to do that."

She slapped his arm, and he laughed. Like hope, laughter had also become a regular part of his life.

Funny how quickly things changed. A month ago he'd been utterly alone, and convinced he liked life that way. Now, for the first time in years, he was having a true family Christmas. He was making tentative strides with his father, and with the reappearance of his brother within the family business, it even looked like he and Justin might regain some of the bond they'd lost.

His brother had undergone his own collection of changes this past month. As a result, the two of them had discovered the Hammond family dysfunction had left a mark on both of them. Fortunately, they—and their father—were getting a second chance.

At the end of the day, though, the only person he really needed in his life was the woman in front of him. How right she'd been that day in his office when she said Christmas was wonderful when you had someone special.

And she was special. No longer were the two of them standing on the cusp of something extraordinary; they were over-their-heads deep in the middle. And with each passing day, he fell a little deeper. As soon as the timing was right, he planned to let Noelle know he'd fallen in love with her.

"The note," Noelle said prodding him.

Pretending to roll his eyes at her eagerness, he fished out the folded piece of paper. "For our first Christmas together. Made with all my love."

Damn, if he couldn't feel his heart bursting through his chest. "All your love?" he asked.

"Every ounce," she told him. "I love you, James Hammond."

Never had five words filled him with such hope and happiness. They were Christmas, Easter and every holiday in between. "I love you too," he said, pulling her close.

It was going to be a perfect Christmas.

* * * * *

Look out for the next great story in
THE MEN WHO MAKE CHRISTMAS *duet*

SNOWED IN WITH THE RELUCTANT TYCOON
by Nina Singh

Coming soon!
And if you enjoyed this story, check out these other
great reads from Barbara Wallace

WINTER WEDDING FOR THE PRINCE
CHRISTMAS BABY FOR THE PRINCESS
SAVED BY THE CEO
BEAUTY AND HER BILLIONAIRE BOSS

All available now!

"Here, try a bite."

He opened his mouth and relished the creamy, sweet taste bursting on his tongue.

"What do you think?" she asked.

"It's good." He withdrew a clean spoon from the drawer, dipped it into the small mixing bowl and offered it to her. "Your turn."

"Okay." Her mouth opened and closed around the spoon, tasting it herself. Then she ran the tip of her tongue over her lips.

His knees went weak, and an almost overwhelming urge rose up inside, pressing him to take her in his arms and kiss her. But he couldn't do that. He shouldn't anyway, and tamped down the compulsion as best he could.

Still, he continued to study her.

"Hmm, this is really good." Her voice came out soft. Sweet. Smooth.

He couldn't help himself; he reached out and brushed the flour from the tip of her nose.

Desire flared, his heart pumped hard and steady and his hand stilled. The temptation to kiss her senseless rose up again, stronger than ever. But he wouldn't do that.

He shouldn't.

Oh, why the hell not?

* * *

Rocking Chair Rodeo:
Cowboys—and true love—never go out of style!

A COWBOY FAMILY CHRISTMAS

BY
JUDY DUARTE

First Published in Great Britain 2017
By Mills & Boon, an imprint of HarperCollins*Publishers*
1 London Bridge Street, London, SE1 9GF

© 2017 Judy Duarte

ISBN: 978-0-263-92345-2

23-1117

Our policy is to use papers that are natural, renewable and recyclable products and made from wood grown in sustainable forests. The logging and manufacturing processes conform to the legal environmental regulations of the country of origin.

Printed and bound in Spain
by CPI, Barcelona

Since 2002, *USA TODAY* bestselling author **Judy Duarte** has written over forty books for Mills & Boon Cherish, earned two RITA® Award nominations, won two Maggie Awards and received a National Readers' Choice Award. When she's not cooped up in her writing cave, she enjoys traveling with her husband and spending quality time with her grandchildren. You can learn more about Judy and her books at her website, www.judyduarte.com, or at Facebook.com/judyduartenovelist.

To my aunties:
Dorothy Johnston Eggleston and Loraine Shaw.
Thank you for your incredible love and support
over the years. I love you both!

Chapter One

Dear Debbie,
I'm desperate and need your help.

Elena Montoya studied the first of several letters she'd been handed during her job interview at *The Brighton Valley Gazette*. She'd come here today, hoping to get her foot in the door at the small-town newspaper, but as a reporter. Not someone offering advice to the love-lorn in a weekly column.

Mr. Carlton, the balding, middle-aged editor, leaned forward, resting clasped hands on his desk. "So what do you think?"

Seriously? Elena would be hard-pressed to offer advice to anyone, especially someone with romantic trouble. But she didn't want to reveal her inexperience or doubt. "I'd hoped to land a different assignment—or another type of column."

"Let's see what you can do with this first." Mr. Carlton leaned back in his desk chair, the springs creaking under his weight, the buttons of his cotton shirt straining to contain his middle-age spread.

Elena knew better than to turn down work, even though this job wasn't a good fit. Worse yet, the pay he'd offered her wasn't enough to cover a pauper's monthly expenses. And since she was new in town, she needed a way to support herself.

But as an advice columnist? The irony was laughable.

"You look a bit...uneasy," the editor said.

She *was*. Either Mr. Carlton had neglected to read her resume or he'd confused her with another applicant.

"It's just that..." She cleared her throat and chose her words carefully. "Well, don't get me wrong. I'm happy to have this position, but I only took two psych courses in college. And since I majored in journalism, I'm more qualified to work as a reporter."

"Don't worry. It shouldn't be too difficult for a young woman like you, Elena."

She cringed at his use of her given name. The last thing she needed was for her new co-workers at the newspaper—or any rodeo fans in the small Texas community—to connect the dots and realize who she was. And why she looked familiar—in spite of her efforts to change her appearance.

"By the way," she said, "I go by Lainie." At least,

that's the childhood nickname her twin sister had given her.

"All right," Mr. Carlton said. "Then *Lainie* it is. But keep in mind you'll be known as 'Dear Debbie' around here. We like her true identity to be a secret."

A temporary secret identity was just what Lainie needed. After that embarrassing evening, when rodeo star Craig Baxter's wife had caught him and Elena together at a hotel restaurant in Houston and assumed the worst, Elena had done her best to lay low. The next day, she'd relocated to a ranch outside of Brighton Valley, where she could hide out until she could rise above those awful rumors—all of which were either untrue or blown way out of proportion.

Elena had tried to explain how she'd come to be there that night—how she had no idea that Craig was a rodeo star, let alone married—to no avail. Kara Baxter had been so angry at her husband, she'd thrown a margarita in Elena's face and read him the riot act. As if that hadn't been bad enough, someone at another table had caught it all on video, and the whole, ugly scene had gone viral. And now Kara's friends and Craig's fans blamed her for splitting up a marriage that wouldn't have lasted anyway.

"Do you have any other questions?" Mr. Carlton asked.

As a matter of fact, she had a ton of them, but she didn't want to show any sign of insecurity.

"I do have one question," she admitted. "Some of the people writing these letters could be dealing with serious issues. And if that's the case, I'm not qualified

to offer them any advice." Nor should she counsel anyone, for that matter.

Mr. Carlton shook his head and waved off her concern. "Our last Debbie used to have a stock answer
for the bigger problems. She told them to seek professional help."

Lainie nodded. "Okay. Then I'll use that response."
A *lot*.

"Just focus on the interesting letters or on those that
trigger a clever response," Mr. Carlton said. "It's really
just entertainment for most people. But keep in mind,
if the readership of the Dear Debbie column increases,
I'll give you a bigger assignment in the future."

At least, he'd given her a chance to prove herself,
something she'd had to do time and again since the
third grade, when she'd gone from a foster home to a
pediatric intensive care unit and lost track of her sister.
"I'll give it my best shot, Mr. Carlton."

"Okay, kid. What's the best number if I need to get
a hold of you?"

"I listed my cell on my resume, although that's not
the best way to reach me. I'm temporarily staying at
the Rocking Chair Ranch. Since the reception isn't
very good there, and the Wi-Fi is worse, you'd better
call me on the landline." She pointed to her resume,
which he'd set aside on his desk. "I included that number, too, and marked it with an asterisk."

"If you don't mind me asking, why are you staying
at a retirement home for old cowboys?"

"Because I'm filling in for the ranch cook, who'll
be gone for the next three weeks." When Lainie first

heard about the temporary position, she'd declined. But after that awful run-in with Kara Baxter, she'd changed her mind and accepted it out of desperation, realizing it would provide her with a place to stay until she could find something better and more permanent in town.

Oddly enough, she actually felt a lot more comfortable staying at the Rocking C than she'd thought she would. And she liked the old men who lived there. Most of them were sweet, and even the crotchety few were entertaining.

Mr. Carlton pushed back his chair and got to his feet, signaling the interview was over.

Lainie stood, too. Still hoping for something more respectable and better paying, she said, "I minored in photography, so if you need a photojournalist, that's another option."

"I'll keep that in mind. Consider this your trial run, kid."

Lainie nodded and reached for her purse.

Mr. Carlton headed for the door of his office and opened it for her. "I'll send you a copy of the letters electronically, and even if you're somewhere with terrible web access, your column is due by email before midnight on Wednesday. I can't wait to see it."

"You won't be disappointed. I'll channel my inner Debbie." Lainie tamped down her doubt, offered him a smile and lifted the letters in her hand. "You'll love what I do with these."

Mr. Carlton beamed, clearly convinced that she'd work a miracle of some kind, but Lainie knew better.

And she feared that by Friday morning, when her first column came out, her inadequacy would come to light.

Rodeo promoter Drew Madison drove his pickup down the county highway on his way to the Rocking C Ranch, listening to a Brad Paisley hit on the radio and sporting a confident grin. His plans for the Rocking Chair Rodeo were finally coming together, and a date had finally been set. The county-wide event would be held at the Brighton Valley Fairgrounds in April.

Drew's boss at Esteban Enterprises had granted him free rein on the project, although he'd insisted that Drew move in to the Rocking Chair Ranch for a few weeks, interview the old cowboys who lived there and write a few blog posts sharing their stories.

While Drew had graduated from college and certainly knew how to put a sentence together, he'd never considered himself a writer. But his promotion to VP of the company was on the line, so he'd brushed away his doubt and agreed to do it.

Besides, how hard could writing a few stories be?

His cell phone rang, the Bluetooth automatically shutting out the Brad Paisley tune. He assumed it was another business call, but when he looked at the dashboard and spotted his sister's name on the display, his heart clenched.

Kara Lee had been going through a lot lately, so he'd made it a point to check up on her each morning and evening. To have her contact him in the middle of the day was a little unsettling.

He answered quickly and tried to keep his tone up-beat. "Hey, sis. What's up?"

"Not much. I'm just bored, I guess. I called your of-fice, and they said you were traveling. Not that it really matters, but I thought you would've mentioned some-thing about it to me."

He hadn't meant to keep it a secret, but neither had he wanted her to worry about him being gone and un-able to get to the hospital in time if she went into labor. She'd nearly lost her baby last week and was on com-plete bed rest now.

"Actually," he said, "it's a new assignment. I meant to tell you about it, but I had to cut our morning call short."

"How long will you be gone this time?"

Longer than he wanted to admit, although he was looking forward to meeting the retired cowboys. "I'll be gone for a few weeks, but I'm not far from Hous-ton. If you need me, all you have to do is call. I can get there within a couple of hours."

"I'm sure that won't be necessary," she said, but the tone of her voice betrayed her words. "I'll be fine."

He certainly hoped so. Kara Lee had wanted to be a mother for as long as she could cuddle a dolly. And after three miscarriages, she'd made it to the fifth month this time around. For each day the little boy re-mained in the womb, the better chance he had.

"So where's this assignment?" she asked.

"The Rocking Chair Ranch. The rodeo will be spon-soring them in the spring, so I'm working on the pro-motion."

"Is that the retirement home for cowboys?"

"And ranchers." He'd been reluctant to mention anything about rodeos or cowboys since the night she found out her husband, rodeo star Craig Baxter, was having another affair. The stress from the confrontation with him and his lover had caused her to go into premature labor.

When Drew got word of the public blowup and learned that Kara Lee had been hospitalized, he'd wanted to beat the tar out of his brother-in-law. But Kara Lee had begged him not to, and he'd been reluctant to do anything to upset his kid sister, especially when the survival of her son was precarious. But that didn't mean he wouldn't be tempted to knock Craig's lights out the next time he saw him.

Kara Lee had told Craig to pack his crap and to get out of the house, which he did. But she hadn't yet filed for divorce, mostly because she wasn't able to deal with the legal proceedings when she was lying flat on her back. But once the baby came, Drew would do whatever he could to facilitate a fair and amicable split. One of his friends was a divorce attorney in Houston, and he'd already mentioned the case to him. He just hoped his sister didn't soften and take Craig back.

"You sure you're okay?" he asked her again.

"Yeah, especially since I've made it to the twenty-sixth week. At least the baby now has a chance to survive."

"That's good to know."

As silence filled the line, he decided to change the subject. "So what are you doing?" The moment the question rolled off his tongue, he wanted to reel it back in. Hell, what could a bedridden pregnant woman possibly do, other than read or watch TV?

She let out a sigh. "I wish I could work on the nursery, but I'll have to wait until after little Robby gets here."

"I'll tell you what," Drew said. "As soon as I finish this project at the Rocking C, I'll spend a few days at your place. Make a Pinterest board of stuff you like. When I get back, I'll be your hands and feet. We'll have it done before you know it."

"I love you, Drew."

"Aw, for Pete's sake. Don't get all sappy on me, Kara Lee." She'd been a tomboy when growing up—and a barrel racer in high school. So he wasn't used to seeing her softer side. It must be her hormones.

"You're the best, Drew."

"No. I'm not." He'd taken on a demanding job that required him to travel, so he hadn't been there for her recently, like he'd always been in the past.

He kicked himself for that now. If he'd been around more, he might have talked her out of marrying Craig. But that was all muddy water under the bridge now. From here on out, Drew was going to be the brother she deserved.

If Kara Lee suffered yet another miscarriage, losing the baby she'd already named and loved, there was no telling what it would do to her.

"By the way," he said. "I called an agency that provides home health services and asked them to send someone out to your house for a few hours each day.

She'll do some light cleaning and run errands for you while I'm gone."

"You didn't need to do that."

"I know, but I wanted to. It makes me feel better to know someone is with you or at least just a phone call away." He thought she might object, more out of pride than anything else. But she surprised him by accepting his effort to help.

"You know what, Drew? You're going to make some woman a wonderful husband."

He laughed. "My last two relationships didn't fare very well, thanks to all my travel." Well, that and the fact that he was beginning to enjoy being a tumbleweed, rolling through life on the whim of the wind.

Just like your old man? He winced, then discarded the thought as quickly as it came. He wasn't at all like his father.

"Besides," he added, "I'm not cut out for marriage, family or a home in the suburbs. If I was, I wouldn't enjoy being on the road so often."

"A woman who really loves you wouldn't complain about you being gone."

"I don't know about that. You'd be surprised."

"At least, you'd never cheat on her." She paused for a beat. "You wouldn't *cheat*, would you?"

"*Me?* No, I've always been honest with the women I date. From the very first time we go out, I make it clear that I'm not the domestic type."

"I'm not buying that," Kara Lee said.

Drew wasn't about to let his little sister psychoanalyze him. Who knew what assumptions she'd come to, right or wrong.

When he spotted the big yellow sign that indicated he'd reached the Rocking C, he said, "Listen, I have to hang up now. But I'll give you a call this evening."

"You don't have to. I know how busy you are."

"I'm never too busy for you."

And that was the truth. Kara Lee was the only family Drew had left, and after all they'd been through, especially *her*, she deserved to be happy—and to finally be a mom.

"I'm curious," she said. "Where will you be staying while on the ranch?"

"They're putting me up in one of the cabins so I can get a feel for the daily routine. It's not just a retirement home, it's a working ranch. So the whole enterprise is new and innovative. I'd like to check it out."

"Good luck."

"Thanks. I'm actually looking forward to having a change of pace—and to being in the same place for longer than a few days."

"So says the family rover. Maybe you're more cut out for home and hearth than you think, especially if you meet the right woman."

"Oh, yeah? We'll see about that." Drew turned onto the long, graveled drive that led to the Rocking Chair Ranch. "I'll talk to you later."

When the line disconnected, he slowly shook his head. If there was one thing he'd learned over his thirty-one years, it was easier to be a rover than to deal with the countless people who weren't what they seemed and were bound to disappoint you.

Thank goodness he wasn't likely to meet any of that type on the Rocking C.

It had been two days since Mr. Carlton had hired Lainie to write the Dear Debbie column, but she still hadn't made any headway in answering a single letter.

She'd been busy settling into her temporary job. But that wasn't the whole story. In fact, none of the problems of people seeking Debbie's advice had triggered a clever or witty response, and Lainie was stumped.

She sat at the kitchen table, reading through the letters, trying to choose an interesting one or two to include in her first Dear Debbie column. While she pondered, her fingers tapped softly on the keyboard without typing out a single word. She glanced at the clock on the microwave, noting how much time had passed since she'd done the breakfast dishes, and blew out a sigh. Her midnight deadline loomed.

"You can do this," she whispered aloud. Then she reread the letter on top of the stack.

Last year, I met John, the most handsome, amazing man in the world, and I knew I'd finally met Mr. Right.

Last month, Lainie had met Craig…

Darn it. She had to stop projecting that jerk into each of these stupid letters written by someone who'd either been jilted or disappointed by various people in their lives.

All I've ever wanted was to fall in love and get married, but now my heart is broken, and my life is a wreck.

"Tell me about it," Lainie muttered. Well, not the broken heart. She'd gone out with Craig only three times, but the rest of it sounded pretty darned familiar.

Then, a few weeks ago, a woman who works at John's office started hitting on him and lured him away from me.

Lainie leaned back in the chair and shook her head. From the comments left on the YouTube video of her that night at the Houston hotel, it seemed everyone in the rodeo world thought she'd targeted a married man and tried to lure him away.

During the blowup, his wife had told him off, implying that he was a serial cheater, a secret he apparently kept from his legion of fans.

"Aw, come on," Lainie scolded herself. "Focus on *this* woman, *this* letter, *this* problem."

Yet how could she? She was the last person in the world who should offer romantic advice to anyone, let alone a stranger who hoped for an easy fix.

Darn it. No matter how badly she'd wanted a job at the *Gazette*—and she *needed* one if she wanted to support herself—she'd been crazy to agree to taking over for Dear Debbie.

Footsteps sounded in the doorway, drawing her from her reading. She glanced up to see Otis "Sully" Sullivan enter the kitchen. The sweet, kindhearted old man had a jolly way about him. Each time she laid eyes on the retired cowboy, she couldn't help but smile. With a head of thick white hair and a full beard, he reminded her of Santa Claus, especially today when he wore a solid red flannel shirt.

"Hey, Sully."

"I'm sorry to bother you, but is there any more coffee?"

Lainie set aside the letter she'd been reading, pushed back her chair and got to her feet. "It's no bother at all. And you're in luck. There's still at least a cup left."

She poured the last of the carafe into a white mug. "I could make a fresh pot."

"No need for you to go to any extra trouble." Sully took the mug she gave him, gripping it with gnarled hands, and thanked her. "That was a nice breakfast you fixed us today. I haven't had good chilaquiles in a long time. My late wife used to make them for me every Sunday morning, but she usually overcooked them."

Lainie laughed. "Did she? How were mine?"

"Best I've ever had. Nice, crispy tortillas. Perfectly scrambled eggs. Mmm, mmm, mmm."

Lainie beamed at the compliment. She wasn't used to getting many. "Thanks, I'm glad you liked them. When I was a little girl, my grandmother used to make them for me and my sister."

"You got a sister?"

"Yes, a twin."

Sully brightened. "Where is she?"

Lainie had no idea. The two of them had been sepa-rated years ago, when Lainie had been taken from the group home and sent to the hospital to be treated for an undetected congenital heart defect. It had taken a while for the doctors to decide upon a treatment plan, and by the time Lainie recovered from her lifesaving surgery, a couple arrived at the children's home, adopted the healthy girl and left the sickly one behind. From what Lainie had gathered, her sister's new parents had been afraid to assume financial responsibility of a child with such serious medical issues.

As a result, she hadn't seen her twin since, but she offered Sully the happy outcome she'd imagined for Erica. "She's happily married to her high school sweet-heart and has a two-year-old daughter."

Before Sully could press further, Lainie turned the conversation back to the chilaquiles. "Anyway, my grandmother passed away before she could pass on her recipe. But when I got older, I did some research and a little experimenting until I came up with a batch that tasted nearly as good as hers. I hope they weren't too spicy."

"No," he said, "not at all. The salsa was perfect. In fact, that was one of the tastiest meals I've had since I moved in here. Not that Joy, our regular cook, isn't a good one, but she's more of a down-home, meat-and-potatoes gal. And I like good Mexican food once in a while."

"That's a relief. I knew I'd have some big shoes to fill, taking Joy's place in the kitchen while she's on her honeymoon."

"I haven't heard any complaints yet. And that's saying a lot, considering some of the old geezers who live here. They rarely keep their opinions to themselves." Sully glanced at the letters on the table. "I didn't mean to bother you. I'll just take my coffee into the living room and let you get back to whatever it was you were doing."

"Actually, I don't mind the interruption." Although she really should. With each tick and tock of the kitchen clock, her midnight deadline drew closer. And who knew if the ranch internet would work? She might have to drive into town and find Wi-Fi somewhere. *Darn it.*

"You look fretful, which doesn't do your pretty face any good. What's bothering you?" Sully nodded toward the stack of letters. "I hope it isn't bad news."

"It's just…a friend with a problem." Lainie chewed her fingernail and stared at the pile of unanswered letters. "I'm trying to come up with some wise advice, but I'm not feeling very wise."

Sully's smile softened the lines in his craggy face. "Wisdom comes with age and experience. Back when I was in my twenties, heck, thirties, too, I was under the false notion that I was as smart as I'd ever get."

Lainie had thought the same thing after her college graduation, which wasn't very long ago. Then Craig had taken her for a ride, leaving her with an unearned bad reputation and distrustful of sweet-talking men who couldn't tell the truth to save their souls. She'd learned a big lesson the hard way, but that hadn't made her an expert at facing romantic dilemmas.

"Want me to give it a shot?" Sully asked.

Was he offering his advice? Lainie wasn't sure what the dear old man might have to say, but at this point, she'd take all the help she could get. "Sure, if you don't mind."

Sully pulled out a chair, took a seat and rested his steaming hot mug on the table. "What's the problem?"

Lainie scanned the opening of the letter and caught him up to speed, revealing that her "friend" was twenty-four years old, relatively nice-looking with a decent job and a good sense of humor. Then she read the rest of it out loud.

"Three weeks ago, I found out the guy I was living with, the man of my dreams, was seeing another woman. We had a big fight, and he moved out. I've been crying every day, and I'm desperate to win him back."

Sully clucked his tongue. "A man who cheats on his partner, romantic or otherwise, isn't a prize worth winning back. That's what I'd tell her."

Lainie had once thought Craig was a prize, and boy, had she been wrong about that. It's a shame she hadn't had Sully nearby when she'd been taken in by that liar's soft Southern drawl. But Sully was here now. And providing the wisdom this letter writer needed.

"That's a good point," Lainie said. It was clever, too, and a good response for the column. "I'll mention that to…my friend."

Male voices sounded outside, growing louder until

the mudroom door squeaked open. A second later, Nate Gallagher, the acting foreman, entered the kitchen.

Sully acknowledged Nate with a nod, but Lainie focused on the man walking behind him. She guessed him to be a rancher or horseman, since his stylish Western wear suggested he could afford to hire someone to do the dirty work. He was in his early to midthirties, tall and nice looking, with broad shoulders and a rugged build.

He removed his black Stetson, revealing sandy-blond hair, which he wore longer than most of the rodeo cowboys she'd met. Not that she'd ever been a buckle bunny or even attracted to that kind of guy before she'd met Craig.

And after that awful night, she'd sworn off men indefinitely. Yet she found herself stirred by this one's presence. He also looked familiar. Had she met him before?

"Meet Drew Madison," Nate said. "He's handling the Rocking Chair Rodeo promotion."

Just the word *rodeo* sent Lainie's heart slamming into her chest. Had she seen him while on one of the few dates she'd had with Craig?

No, she'd never forget a man like him.

But if he and Craig ran in the same circles, he might recognize *her*. For that reason, she'd better get out of here. She didn't mind being around the older cowboys, some of whom had ridden in the rodeo back in the days before cable television and social media. But a recent connection spelled trouble—and further humiliation.

Nevertheless, she wouldn't be rude to a ranch visitor. So she placed the letter she'd been holding upside down on the rest of the stack on the table. Then she got to her feet and said, "It's nice to meet you. I'll put on a pot of coffee."

Then she did just that. If there was one thing she'd learned in her short time at the Rocking C, it was that the cowboys, young and old, loved a fresh brew.

As the coffee began to perk, Lainie studied the pot as if it might bounce off the countertop if she didn't stand guard.

She fingered the side of her head, checking to see if any strands had come loose. She used to wear it long, the curls tumbling along her shoulders and down her back. But after that video had gone viral, she'd pulled it up into a prim topknot—just one of several alterations she'd made to her appearance so she could fade into the background until that ugly incident was forgotten.

When the coffeemaker let out a last steamy gurgle, she poured two cups, then turned to face the younger men. They continued to stand in the middle of the kitchen, speaking to Sully, who was still seated at the table. She was about to excuse herself and leave them to chat among themselves, but her curiosity betrayed her and she took one last glace at Drew, who'd zeroed in on her.

"For some reason," he said, his gaze intense enough to see right through her, "it seems as if I've met you before."

"That's not likely," she said. "I'm not from around here."

"Where are you from?"

She wanted to ask, *What's up with the third degree?* Instead, she said, "I'm from up north—originally. But I'm sure we've never met. I just have that kind of face. I get comments like that all the time. Sugar? Cream?"

"I like it black."

His gaze continued to roam over her, as if removing her façade one piece at a time. But she pushed through the discomfort and handed him a mug.

He thanked her but didn't take a drink. Instead, those baby blues continued to study her as if trying to pinpoint where they'd met. But wouldn't she remember if they had? A woman wouldn't forget a man like him.

No, he was mistaken. She glanced down at the loose blouse and baggy jeans she wore today. She hadn't used any makeup. Her curls had been pulled into a bun.

But when she again looked at him, when their gazes locked, her heart soared and her hormones flared. For a moment she wished she'd been wearing that red dress Craig had given her for her birthday and insisted that she wear to the hotel that night, their first significant date, where they were to celebrate by having dinner. But she suspected someone who frequented thrift shops had already snatched it up, pleased with their find.

"If you'll excuse me," Lainie said, "I have work to do."

Then she left the kitchen and headed for her room.

After that awful night in Houston, she'd made up her mind to steer clear of handsome cowboys. And Drew Madison was as handsome as any cowboy she'd ever seen.

Chapter Two

Drew leaned back in his chair and watched the housekeeper stride toward the kitchen doorway. She wasn't the kind of woman he usually found attractive, but for some reason he did, and he hadn't been able to keep his eyes off her.

She had a wholesome, clean-cut way about her. Maybe it was the lack of makeup, which she really didn't need. She looked cute in those baggy overalls and plain white T-shirt, but there seemed to be real beauty underneath.

Her dark hair had been pulled up in a simple top-knot, but he imagined it'd be lush and glossy if she wore it loose. And those brown, soulful eyes? A man could get lost in them.

She'd said they'd never met, and she was probably

right. Her name didn't ring a bell. Laney? It wasn't one you heard every day.

Even though she'd already stepped out of the kitchen, he continued to watch the open doorway until Nate mentioned Drew's sister.

"How's Kara Lee doing?" he said. "It must have been devastating for her to lose another baby."

"She's still pregnant, thank goodness."

"Really?" Nate said. "That's good news. I'd heard otherwise, which would have been a real shame."

"There're a lot of rumors going around." Hell, Drew had heard most of them.

"Speaking of babies," Drew said. "How's little Jessica?"

Nate, who'd recently assumed custody of his new-born daughter, a preemie, broke into a proud papa grin. "She's doing great—and growing like a weed."

"And Anna?"

Nate's smile deepened. "She's the best thing that ever happened to me. I love being married."

"Better you than me," Drew said.

Nate chuckled. "Anyway, I'm glad Kara Lee's doing all right."

"Part of what you heard was true," Nate said. "She did go into labor the night she caught Craig cheating. Thankfully, her obstetrician managed to stop the contractions, but she's on bed rest for the time being."

"That's got to be tough," Nate said. "Especially for an active woman like her."

"You got that right, she's determined to have this baby. And she'll do whatever it takes."

"Well, give her my best," Nate said. "I know how badly she wants a kid."

"This one's a boy. And she plans to name him Robert. Bobby for short."

"I hate to even bring up his name, but how's Craig fit into the picture? I heard he's been begging her to forgive him."

Drew's back stiffened. "Where did you hear that?"

"Just around. There's been a lot of talk."

Drew wished that was one rumor he could debunk, but it was true. Craig had been calling her, promising her the moon. "I can't see her taking him back. Hell, I wouldn't be surprised if he was still seeing that sexy brunette who was with him in that hotel restaurant."

"Knowing Craig like I do, you're probably right." Nate crossed his arms. "I didn't see the video, but a couple of the other guys working here did. They say that woman looked like a pop-star wannabe. Did you see it?"

"Yeah." Way too many times. "I didn't get a clear look at her face, but she was certainly dressed the part in that curve-hugging red dress and high heels."

Other than that, Drew didn't know much about the woman, other than what he'd either heard through the rodeo grapevine or gathered from social media. Rumor had it her name was Elena, that she knew how to get what she wanted and that she'd set her sights on landing a champion bull rider, even if he was married to someone else.

Now there was another person he'd like to confront—if he ever crossed paths with her.

Kara Lee had told him that the brunette had claimed it was all a mistake, that Kara Lee had it all wrong. But there were plenty of nearby bars and restaurants where that woman and Craig could have met. So there was only one reason for them to be at a hotel.

Nate clucked his tongue and shook his head. "Craig never did deserve a woman like Kara Lee. And she sure as hell didn't deserve the way he treated her."

"You got that right."

As they both pondered the truth of that fact, the room grew silent for a couple of beats. Then Sully spoke up and snagged Drew's attention.

"Where did you two fellas meet?" Sully asked.

Drew glanced first at the retired cowboy, then at his buddy. "Nate and I competed in the junior rodeo as kids, and we went to the same high school. But when I left for college, I quit the circuit."

"I never could figure out why," Nate said. "Drew was always the guy to beat. He might not look it now, in those fancy duds and shiny new boots, but he's a damn good cowboy."

Drew shrugged off his friend's compliment, as well as the good-humored ribbing about his success in the business world. "Yep, don't mess with my hair."

They all laughed, but Drew suspected all the rodeo talk struck a tender spot in Nate, who'd suffered a career-ending injury and hadn't had an option when it came to hanging up his spurs.

"Do you guys miss the rodeo?" Sully asked. "I sure did when I had to give it up. But we all have to do that at some point. Our bones don't stay young forever."

Nate shrugged. "Sure, I miss it. I loved the thrill of competition. But now I've got a beautiful wife and baby, and they're more important to me than anything. I actually enjoy being at home these days." He winked at Drew. "Maybe you should consider finding a nice woman and settling down."

"You sound like Kara Lee, but I don't see that lifestyle in my future." He hadn't seen it in his past, either. He and his sister had grown up on their mother's run-down spread outside of Brighton Valley, and the only real memories they'd had consisted of hard work and sparse meals.

"Well, fellas," Sully said, "if you'll excuse me, I think I'll go check the football spreads. A couple of the guys have a Last Man Standing pool, and I'm still in contention."

"Not me," Nate said. "I had to drop out during the second week."

As Sully left the room, chuckling at his good fortune, Nate turned to Drew and pushed away from the table. "I've got to get back to work. I'll let you get started on that interview process. It'll be lunchtime before we know it."

Speaking of lunch, Drew wondered when the cook would be back to start the food prep. He'd like to see her again. Maybe he'd ask again where they might have crossed paths.

It really didn't matter, he supposed. Yet for some weird reason, it did.

Lainie had barely gotten to her room when she realized she'd left those darn Dear Debbie letters on the table. Sure, she'd turned them face-side down, but what if…?

Darn it. The last thing in the world she wanted was for someone on the ranch to see them. So, in spite of her plan to avoid Drew Madison while he was visiting, she hurried back to the kitchen.

She'd no more than entered the room when Drew pulled out a chair and took a seat at the table, right in front of those blasted letters. He placed his hand on them, pushing them aside, and her breath caught.

She'd better move quickly. All she needed was for him—or *anyone*—to learn that she was the new love-lorn columnist, especially since Mr. Carlton wanted Dear Debbie's identity to remain secret. Besides, Lainie wasn't looking forward to adding any failed journalism jobs to her resume.

So she scooped them up, clutching them to her chest. "Let me get rid of this mess for you."

She was about to dash out of the kitchen again when Nate said, "Lainie, you'll need to set out an extra plate for meals for the next few weeks."

"Sure, I can do that. But who…?" She paused, afraid to pose the question when she was already connecting the dots.

"Drew will be staying with us for a little while," Nate said. "He wants to interview the men who live here. Get to know them. Learn their daily routines. I think there's at least one empty cabin that's decent. I'm not sure what's available, but I know Joy gave you a tour of the ranch before she and Sam left on their honeymoon."

If you could call it a tour. Joy had taken Lainie on a quick walk and pointed out a few buildings, none of which she thought would be her concern for the short time she'd be here. But if Drew was going to stay on the Rocking C, she'd take him out to the cabin that was the farthest from the kitchen.

"Of course," she said. "I'll make sure it's aired out and ready for him."

"I hate to inconvenience you," Drew said, his gaze unwavering and kicking her pulse up another notch.

"It's not a problem." She feigned a lighthearted grin and tamped down whatever nervous energy he provoked, either through guilt or fear...or downright sexual attraction. "I'll take care of that cabin right away."

When Nate nodded, Lainie took her chance to escape.

"If you men will excuse me," she said, "I have chores to do." Then she headed toward the living area, clutching the letters to her chest.

As she reached the doorway, she overheard Nate say, "I've gotta get back to work. Next time you talk to Kara Lee, give her my best."

Kara?

Lainie nearly stumbled at the mention of a name that sounded similar to that of Craig's wife. Then she shook it off.

Boy, she was jumpy today. Nate had said Carolee. Or possibly Carrie Leigh. Either way, they surely weren't the same woman.

Thank goodness for that. If Kara Baxter was Drew Madison's friend, and if he realized who Lainie was and believed what people said about her, then having him on the ranch would be a lot more than an inconvenience.

It would be a humiliating disaster.

Lainie had no more than returned from Caroline's Diner, where she'd accessed the free Wi-Fi and emailed her first column to the editor, when she spotted Drew and Nate leaving the barn and heading for the house.

Her pride and enthusiasm waned, and her steps, once light and quick, slowed to a near stop. Her first impulse was to slip into the kitchen before they spotted her, but she couldn't very well do that, even if she did have the dinner meal to prepare.

The men waved to her, and she made her way toward them as if it was the most natural thing in the world to do and greeted them with a forced smile.

"There's the lady we've been looking for," Nate said. "Have you had a chance to get one of the cabins ready for Drew?"

Oops. Her first priority had been to make her deadline—well before the midnight cutoff. She lifted her hand to her throat and fingered the ribbed neckline on her T-shirt, as well as the bib of her overalls, both of which covered the long, thick scar that ran the length of her sternum. "I haven't made up the bed yet, but the cabin on the knoll behind the barn will work best. It's empty, and I'm pretty sure it's clean."

"Do you have time to check on it now?" Nate asked. "I'm sure Drew would like to get settled in before dinner, if possible."

Lainie was already behind schedule, but she couldn't shirk her responsibilities, especially when this job paid her a lot more than the newspaper did. "Of course. Just give me a minute to get fresh linens and a set of towels from the house."

"Thanks," Nate said. "I'd do it myself, but I'm going to be tied up for a while."

Lainie shot a quick glance at Drew, who was perusing her every bit as intently as he'd done before. Why did he keep doing that?

Her hand began to reach for her chest again, but she let it drop, her fingers trailing along the denim and brushing away imaginary dust. The scar wasn't visible, and she had to stop reverting back to the old habit she'd once kicked.

"I'll see you at dinner," Nate told Drew. "I need to have a chat with a couple of hands who are at odds with each other. It seems they're both dating the same cocktail waitress at the Stagecoach Inn. I couldn't care less what they do with their time off, but it's begun to affect their work."

"The woes of being a supervisor," Drew said.

Nate rolled his eyes. "That's *acting* supervisor. And you're right. It's not an easy job, especially with a young and inexperienced crew. Once Sam gets back from his honeymoon, I'm going to turn over my keys to the ranch and hightail it out of here."

"We're looking forward to having you join us at Esteban Enterprises," Drew said.

"I'm glad to hear that, because I can't wait." The

guys did some elaborate hand shake and fist pump ritual.

Lainie planned to move on once the honeymooners returned, too. Only problem was, she didn't have another job lined up, like Nate did.

Nate would undoubtedly be successful at Esteban Enterprises, but Lainie'd hate to work for a company that had anything to do with rodeos. Cowboys weren't her thing—except maybe for Sully and the other oldsters. But she'd prefer to never cross paths with the younger ones again.

She glanced at the handsome promoter. Drew might be dressed like a fancy Texas businessman, but his more casual demeanor shouted urban cowboy. So the sooner she could escort him to his temporary quarters and be done with it, the better off she'd be.

"I'll go inside for the linens," she told him. "Do you have your bags?"

"Just a suitcase and my briefcase. They're in the back of my pickup. It'll only take me a minute."

"Then I'll meet you back here."

Moments later, with her arms laden with freshly laundered sheets, pillowcases and towels, Lainie returned to the yard and found Drew waiting for her. He held a suitcase in one hand and a leather briefcase in the other.

"There it is." She pointed about fifty yards away from the barn, where a lone structure sat. The outside needed a coat or two of paint, but the inside was probably just fine. It looked sturdy enough and should keep him dry and cozy. "It doesn't look like much, but I think you'll be comfortable there."

"I don't require much."

No? She found that hard to believe. She glanced across the driveway at his spanking new Dodge Ram truck, then at his fancy denim jacket, his silver belt buckle and his shiny leather inlaid boots. No, this guy clearly liked the finer things in life.

"This way." She began walking along the graveled path toward the knoll, and he fell into step beside her.

"There's something you should know," she said. "The cell and internet access on the ranch isn't very good. There are some random spots here and there where you might get a bar or two, but it's sketchy at best."

"I won't need to get online right away."

"Okay, but when you do, it might be easier and faster to drive to town. Caroline's Diner offers free Wi-Fi now. And they also have the best desserts you've ever tasted."

"Thanks for the suggestion. I'll keep that in mind."

They turned to the right, following the incline to the cabin. A cool winter breeze kicked up a bit, sending the scent of his cologne her way. It was a clean woodsy fragrance—no doubt expensive—that suited him.

For a moment, her femininity rebelled, scolding her for not applying makeup earlier this morning, for choosing a plain white T-shirt and baggy overalls. But her days of enhancing her curves—whether they could be considered a blessing or a curse—were behind her now.

Yet despite her resolve to remain low-key and unaffected by Drew's presence, she stole a peek at him, hoping he wouldn't notice. But he caught her in the act. Her cheeks warmed, and she quickly looked away, placing her focus on the pathway.

"Have you ever been to Houston?" he asked.

The first image that flashed in her mind was the swanky hotel restaurant, where Craig had invited her for a birthday dinner. But she shook off the memory the best she could. "I went to college in Houston, but I'm originally from Amarillo."

He nodded, as if storing that tidbit of information away to use against her someday. *No, come on. That kind of thinking is crazy.* But she couldn't help being a wee bit suspicious. For some reason, he seemed to have locked onto the idea that they'd met before, and they hadn't. She was sure of it.

Still, there seemed to be something familiar about him. Probably his lanky, cowboy swagger.

She cut a sideways glance his way. "Why do you ask?"

"Just curious about everyone here."

She reminded herself that she'd have to stay on her toes around him.

They approached the small front porch, which appeared to have a rickety railing. Maybe the cabin wasn't so sturdy after all, but it would have to do.

"This is it," she said, hoping the inside was more appealing than the outside. "I probably should have checked things out before bringing you here."

"All I need is a place to sleep."

Lainie climbed the three steps ahead of him, when a crack and crunch sounded behind her.

"Dammit." Drew lurched forward and, apparently to steady himself, grabbed her hip, sending a spiral of heat to the bone and unbalancing her, too.

She didn't have to turn around to know what had just happened, but she couldn't help herself. Sure enough, he was removing his foot from a big crack in the wood, scratching his fancy boots in the process and banging his fancy leather suitcase against the steps.

He grumbled something she couldn't comprehend, then removed his hand from her denim-clad hip. Yet her skin sizzled from his touch, tingled from his grip.

"I'm sorry," she said. "I didn't realize that step was loose."

"The wood's completely rotten."

"I can see that. I know the owners plan to refurbish the cabins before the rodeo comes to town, but I don't think there's a lot of extra cash right now. Are you okay?"

Their gazes locked, and her pulse struck a wacky beat. His features softened, and his annoyance disappeared.

"Yeah, I'm fine. But this porch needs to be fixed pronto."

"I agree, but I think a repair like that'll have to wait."

"Seriously?" He straightened and slowly stepped onto the porch, testing the wood before placing his full weight on it. "Fixing that step can't wait. I might break my leg next time."

She clutched the linens to her chest. "Good point. But...like I said, Nate can't spare the extra cash right now."

He shrugged a single shoulder. "I'll fix it myself. I'm not too bad with a hammer and nails. Tomorrow morning, I'll go to the hardware store and get supplies I'll need to rebuild the broken step." He glanced around. "And the porch. It's just a matter of time before it falls apart, too."

"You're taking it upon yourself to do that?"

"I may as well pay for my keep."

"That'd be nice of you. And appreciated." For some reason, she hadn't expected him to actually do any physical labor. He didn't look like the kind of man who'd risk getting blisters or building up a sweat.

Lainie turned back to face the entrance and shuffled the linen to one arm. She reached for the knob and opened the door. As she crossed the threshold, into the tidy and modestly furnished interior, she caught a whiff of must and dust. "I guess we'd better open some windows and air it out."

"That's not a problem." Drew followed her inside. He set his suitcase on the hardwood floor near the small green-plaid sofa and his briefcase on the oak coffee table.

Lainie carried the linens to the bed and placed them on the bare mattress. Then she took the towels and washcloths to the bathroom. When she returned to the bedroom, she found Drew opening the window. He looked especially nice from the backside—broad shoulders, narrow hips...

Enough of that. Drew Madison was a cowboy—fancy duds or not. And what was worse, Lainie hadn't lucked out when it came to assessing the characters of men she found attractive.

"The pillows, blanket and spread must be in the closet," she said.

"I can take care of that. I'm sure you have other things to do."

She had a ton to do before her day ended. When she'd checked her email at Caroline's, Mr. Carlton had forwarded the next batch of Dear Debbie letters. But Nate had asked her to help their guest get settled. It wouldn't be right to take off and leave him on his own.

"No, I—" She'd just slid open the small closet door, when a brown furry streak jumped from the top shelf, landing on her head. She screamed and swiped at her hair to no avail. The damned creature dropped to her chest and scampered under the bib of her overalls. She shrieked again, and Drew was at her side in an instant.

"What's wrong?" he asked. "Are you okay?"

"No!" She continued to scream and shudder. She hopped up and down in an attempt to dislodge it, but it scurried around her waist and into her pant leg. She grabbed Drew's arm as if he could save her.

His brow furrowed, his expression one of concern. "What? What is it?"

"It's a mouse. And it ran down my…" *Oh, my God.* It was still in there, trying to find a hiding place.

A childhood memory replayed in her mind—the abandoned warehouse in their run-down neighborhood, the innocent game of hide-and-seek, the rat's nest that turned into a little girl's worst nightmare...

Lainie let go of Drew, who wasn't any help, unhooked the overall buckles and shimmied out of the baggy britches until they bagged at her ankles. She struggled to kick off her laced shoes.

"How can I help?" he asked.

If she wasn't in the midst of a mind-boggling crisis, she might have offered a suggestion. But all she could think to do was to scream yet again.

The nasty little creature was burrowing into the folds of the fabric, squirming to escape almost as frantically as she was. When she finally tugged off her second shoe and stepped out of the overalls, she turned to Drew and pointed at the pile of denim. "Get it. Take it *outside*."

Drew bent to do as she'd instructed, but not before the mangy little beast took the opportunity to zip under the bed.

Lainie shuddered and straightened, then she turned to him.

He stood there stoically, his gaze on her. Apparently, he didn't give a fig about the mouse that could easily burrow into his bed tonight.

He studied her for a couple of beats, then he looked away.

It took her those same beats and another to realize she was standing before him in her stocking feet, wearing only a baggy T-shirt and a pair of pink panties. And skimpy ones at that.

Her cheeks heated and her lips parted. Oh, no. Now what?

Drew snatched a folded sheet from the mattress and held it out to her.

She grabbed it and rushed to the bathroom, but it wasn't the blasted mouse she hoped to escape this time. It was the dashing cowboy who'd seen more of her than she'd wanted to reveal.

Chapter Three

Now that the crisis was over, some men might have found Lainie's reaction to a panicked field mouse a bit comical, but Drew had been too focused on her shapely, bare legs and those pink lacy panties. He hadn't realized what she'd been hiding behind all that denim, but certainly not curves that were that sexy.

Most women would flaunt them, but apparently Lainie didn't.

When the bathroom door creaked open, she came out with the sheet wrapped around her waist. Her cheeks were flushed a deep pink, and her brow was creased in worry. She scanned the room. "Is it gone?"

No, he suspected the critter was still under the bed and probably suffering from a massive coronary. He didn't want to lie, but neither did he want to risk having her freak out again. "You're safe."

Drew thought about making light of the situation and her reaction, but she was undoubtedly embarrassed by it. And he couldn't help sympathizing.

She pointed to the pile of denim on the floor. "Would you please shake those out, then give them to me?"

"Sure." He picked up the overalls, made an effort to examine them carefully, then gave them a vigorous shake before handing them to her. "Here you go."

It was a shame she was going to hide behind baggy clothes again.

She held the sheet in place with one hand and clutched the overalls with the other. Yet she stood her ground, her cheeks rosy, and gave a little shrug. "In case you hadn't figured it out, I hate mice."

"Apparently so." His grin broadened to a full-on smile. "But just for future reference, it wasn't going to eat you in a single bite."

She mumbled something directed at him, clicked her tongue then returned to the bathroom.

When the bathroom door swung open again, and she walked out wearing those damned overalls, he felt compelled to tease her. Instead, he bit his tongue. But he couldn't wipe the smile off his face.

"I realize you found this funny," she said, "and I admit that I overreacted."

"No," he lied. "Some people have an aversion to things like mice, bugs and snakes." He took a seat on the bed.

"And I'm one of them. But you see, one day, when

my twin sister and I were playing, we had a bad experience with rats. So that came into play just now."

"You have a twin?"

She paused a beat, and her eye twitched, just as it had a few minutes ago, when he'd asked her if she'd ever been to Houston. "Yes, I do."

"Identical?"

"No. People used to think we were, especially since there's a strong family resemblance and we were the same size and had the same coloring. But no, we're fraternal twins."

Had Drew run into her sister before? If so, that could be the reason Lainie seemed familiar.

"Where does your sister live?" he asked.

"I'm...not sure. I haven't seen her since... Well, it's been a while."

He was tempted to ask why, but he suspected they'd had a falling-out of some kind. And he'd had enough drama within his own family to last a lifetime.

"Anyway," Lainie said, "I need to go back to the house. I only have an hour to get dinner on the table."

"You sure you're okay?"

"I'll live. I'm just glad you reminded me that the darned critter wasn't able to eat me in a single bite." She smiled and winked. Then she bit down on her bottom lip. "Hey, do me a favor, please. Don't tell the guys about this."

"My lips are sealed. It'll be our little secret." This time, he winked. "Thanks for helping me get settled."

"And for providing you with a little entertainment?

You're welcome. I was just doing my job. Or trying to, anyway." Then she headed for the door.

He nearly added, *And thanks for the lovely vision I'll never get out of my head.*

Lainie had never been so embarrassed in her life. She couldn't believe she'd screamed like a wild woman and stripped down to her panties in front of a virtual stranger—and a handsome one at that.

So much for getting a fresh start in Brighton Valley. If word of this got out, she'd have to move again. Fortunately, Drew had been nice about the whole thing, but he must think she was a nut job, which she probably was. What normal woman would have reacted like that? And all because of a tiny little mouse.

She blew out an exasperated sigh. As much as she'd like to avoid Drew for the rest of her life—or at least, for the duration of his stay—she was going to have to face him again this evening, at the dinner table. And speaking of dinner, she didn't have a clue what she was going to fix. She'd been so focused on getting her column turned in on time that she'd neglected to do any prep work. And now she'd have to regroup and think of something that was quick and easy.

She had ground beef in the fridge. Hamburgers with all the fixings wouldn't be too difficult to pull off. By the time she'd gotten across the yard and near the house, she had a menu planned. Thank goodness for the canned beans in the pantry and the ice cream she'd stored in the freezer.

She'd no more than reached the back porch of the

main ranch house when she spotted Sully and Rex, another old-timer, sitting outside, swaying away the afternoon in rocking chairs. They were watching—or rather critiquing—a younger cowboy working with a horse in the corral.

"Damn fool kid," Rex said. "Someone had better fire his ass before he gets himself killed."

"You got that right." Sully slowly shook his head.

"Aw, hell." Rex got to his feet and reached for his cane. "I'm going to find Nate. This is crazy. That kid shouldn't be left to work on his own."

Rex had no more than taken a single step when he spotted Lainie and tipped his worn cowboy hat at her. "Little lady. If you'll excuse me?"

"Of course," she said.

Rex grumbled something under his breath as he took off in search of the acting foreman.

"So," Sully said. "I see you're finally home after your trip to town."

"Yes, I got back a little while ago. I've been helping Drew get settled in the cabin on the knoll."

Sully glanced at his wristwatch. "Looks like it's about time for dinner."

Yes, and if she didn't get inside quickly, she wouldn't have it on the table by five o'clock. Joy had warned her that the men were in the habit of eating at set times— and not one minute later.

"I know you're probably busy," Sully said, "but I thought about something after we discussed your friend's problem."

For a moment, the only problem Lainie could remember was her own. What normal woman dropped her pants in front of a stranger, and all because of a tiny mouse? But Sully hadn't been privy to that secret. At least, not yet.

"What problem is that?" she asked.

"You know," he said, as he got up from his rocker and followed her into the kitchen. "The friend who wrote you the letter about having her heart broken."

"Oh, yes."

"I thought about something else you can tell her," Sully said.

Too late. The column was already in Mr. Carlton's inbox. But Lainie wasn't about to turn down any sage advice she might be able to use later. "What's that?"

"You can't expect someone else to make you happy. You'll only end up miserable if you do because the time will come when the two of you will part ways, through death or divorce or whatever."

Wasn't that the truth? Time and again since childhood, Lainie had learned that lesson the hard way. She never knew her mother, and her father died before she and her twin entered kindergarten. Three years later, her grandmother followed suit and left them wards of the state. Then Erica was adopted and snatched away. Even while Lainie was in the hospital for her heart surgery, the nurses kept changing, thanks to their varied shifts.

So if there was anything to count on, it was that life was unpredictable. And the only one who could make her happy was herself.

She'd thought her luck might have changed when

she met Craig, but she'd never expected him to make her *happy*. She had, however, expected him to be honest with her.

"When my wife died," Sully said, "I missed her so much. For a while, I thought my life was over. I couldn't see a purpose for it after she was gone. But my buddies stepped in and gave me a kick in the backside. They told me to quit feeling sorry for myself and to focus on others."

Lainie opened the commercial-sized refrigerator and pulled out a huge package of ground beef. "What did you do?"

"I volunteered at a local soup kitchen. And it made all the difference in the world. Tell your friend to find something to do that's bigger than herself. Once she gets off the pity train, she'll be surprised at how good she'll feel."

"More wise advice," Lainie said. And more fodder for a future column.

"You might want to give her some options, like volunteering at the animal shelter or collecting blankets and toiletry items for the homeless."

Actually, that's exactly what Lainie would so. She'd go to the library and do some online research about the needs in the community. Then, when she found an opportunity to make a suggestion like that to someone, she'd have a good-size list of volunteer possibilities to provide as a wrap to the column.

"That's a great idea, Sully. I'll make that suggestion the next time I talk to my friend." She offered him a warm, appreciative smile, dropped the meat on the counter then opened the pantry and pulled out several packages of buns. "Thanks again for the advice."

"Sure. Anytime. Say, you need any help?"

Boy, did she. And on so many levels. But he was talking about dinner—and the need for her to get it on the table by five. "Sure, would you mind firing up the gas grill?"

"I'd be delighted." Sully went outside to the deck.

Before forming the meat into patties, Lainie washed her hands at the sink, then dried them with the dish towel that had been resting on the counter. She couldn't help glancing out the kitchen window at the cabin on the knoll. Her hand lifted, and she fingered the length of the scar that hid under the cotton and denim.

She'd just about reached her wit's end when it came to dealing with handsome men, especially those who left her feeling guilty or embarrassed or lacking in any way. Fortunately, she'd be moving on again soon. Only this time, when she chose a new job, it might be best to consider one at a convent.

Lainie had just finished wiping down the countertops and putting away the last of the breakfast dishes when the ranch telephone rang. She snatched the receiver from its wall-mounted cradle. The cord, stretched from years of use, dangled to her knees. "Rocking Chair Ranch. This is Lainie."

"Hey, kid."

She was more than a little surprised to hear Mr. Carlton's voice on the other end.

"I knew you could do it," he said, his tone almost

jubilant. "That column you sent to me yesterday was great. In fact, it was everything I'd hoped it would be."

Thank goodness. Or rather, in this case, thank *Sully*. Either way, she was relieved to know she'd hit the mark. "Thank you, Mr. Carlton."

"You mentioned the internet service wasn't very good at the ranch, so I hope you received the additional letters I sent. I hadn't gotten your column yet, but I had a good feeling."

"Yes, I did. I had to go into town to find Wi-Fi so I could send it to you. And while I was there, I checked my email and downloaded them onto my laptop." She hadn't looked at them yet. She was waiting until she found both the time and the enthusiasm to tackle the chore. But her boss didn't need to know that. "I'll read them over the weekend."

"Good, but you might want to get started on them right away. I'll need your next column turned in by Monday at noon."

"So *soon*?" Monday was only a few days away. She leaned against the wall and wrapped the curly phone cord around her index finger. "I thought my deadlines were on Wednesdays."

"Now that we're back on track, I'll need more time to review your column."

"I'm afraid I'm not following you."

"When the last Dear Debbie quit without notice, I had to find a replacement and make adjustments. The column comes out every Friday, so I pushed your deadline back to give you time to write it. But that meant I had to review it quickly. I'll admit that your column isn't a huge priority to me, especially since the reader-ship isn't that big. But the fans we do have are very loyal. And they're vocal."

Lainie didn't doubt that the lovelorn column was at the bottom of the editor's priority list. Not that she knew what was at the top. She had no idea what the Brighton Valley residents expected to see in terms of news and special interest stories. At least, not yet. She'd have a much better idea after she researched her new community and the various organizations needing vol-unteers the next time she went to town. She'd even take her camera with her. Who knew what photo op she might find? Or what interesting tidbit she might learn. There were sure to be plenty of people or ac-tivities going on that she could use for a future article.

Mr. Carlton cleared his throat. "A Monday deadline isn't going to be a problem for you, is it?"

She'd wrapped the phone cord so tightly around her finger that it had turned red, so she loosened it as she attempted to reassure her boss. "No, not at all. I'll get my next column to you with time to spare." Now all she had to do was to reassure herself that she'd come through for him again.

And to pull that off, she'd have to find Sully. Maybe she could bribe him with brownies.

"That's just the kind of response I like in my staff," Mr. Carlton said. "My *full-time* staff."

He didn't have to say any more. If Lainie wanted a bigger and more important position at *The Brighton Valley Gazette*, she'd need to keep her self-doubt at bay.

"You won't be disappointed, Mr. Carlton."

"We'll see about that." He muttered something under his breath—or possibly to someone else. "Listen, Debbie—or rather, Lainie. I have a meeting and need to get ready for it. I'll let you go so you can get started on the next column. I can't wait to see it." Then he hung up without saying goodbye.

Lainie completely freed her finger from the cord, released her death grip on the receiver and returned it to the wall mount. Then she straightened her stance and blew out a ragged sigh.

She had plenty on her to-do list today, like cleaning out the refrigerator and mopping the kitchen floor. She hadn't considered her usual household tasks to be a burden until she thought about those darned letters, just waiting for a clever response.

She'd better read them now, while she ate her own breakfast. That way, she could ponder her answers while she worked.

After retrieving her laptop from her room, where it rested on the pine dresser, next to her prized high-definition camera, she returned to the kitchen. She wanted to be available in case the on-duty nurse or one of the men needed her, so couldn't very well hole up elsewhere.

She toasted a slice of sourdough bread. After smearing it with peanut butter, she poured a cup of coffee and seasoned it with cream and sugar. Then she took a seat at the table and got to work.

Twenty minutes later, she'd chosen a couple of interesting letters. One of them gave her a perfect opportunity to share Sully's advice about getting off the pity train and thinking about someone else for a change. But she was still at a loss when it came to providing any suggestions for the other. Sure, she always had an opinion. But what if she steered someone in the wrong direction? Or what if her words came out dull and uninteresting?

In spite of her best intentions, she couldn't seem to wake up her muse or stir her thoughts. So she went about her chores, racking her brain to come up with something to write.

Darn it. Could she do this again? Heck, she hadn't even done it last time without help.

Once the kitchen was spick-and-span, she sat at the table again, a fresh cup of coffee beside her laptop. She tried to focus on Mr. Carlton's praise, but even that wasn't enough to instill a burst of confidence.

That column you sent to me yesterday was great. It was everything I'd hoped it would be.

Maybe so, but Lainie hadn't done it on her own. She'd been stymied until Sully…

Yep. Sully.

She needed to find the retired cowboy and ask for more of his simple but sage advice. So where was he?

He'd gone outside for a walk after breakfast, but he could be back now. She closed her laptop, scooted her chair away from the table then got to her feet. She made her way to the sink and looked out the window in search of the man who might be able to help her keep her job at the *Gazette*.

Sully wasn't in the yard, but when her gaze drifted to the cabin on the knoll, she spotted another man. A much younger one who'd shed his fancy duds for worn jeans and a long-sleeved black T-shirt that molded to his muscular form.

Well, what do you know? Drew Madison might *appear* to be a country gentleman with the financial resources to hire others to do physical labor. Yet there he was, tearing apart the old porch as if he wasn't afraid to roll up his sleeves and get the job done himself.

Apparently, he'd gone to the hardware store earlier this morning because a pile of new lumber was stacked off to the side. But it wasn't the tools or the supplies that commanded her interest. It was the man in action.

Rugged and strong.

Masculine and focused.

Heat rushed her face, and her tummy went topsy-turvy. But her visceral reaction only served to send up a host of red flags and set off alarms in her head.

She couldn't trust herself when it came to choosing a man. Neither of the two who'd struck her fancy in the past had turned out to be honest, kind or worthy of her time and affection. Not a single one. So what made her think this guy was any different?

Instead of gawking at Drew, she studied him carefully, trying to spot the flaws he hid behind his Western wear or under his hat.

He was handsome, that was a fact. But handsome men, especially the last one, had done a real number on her in the past. She turned on the tap water and washed her hands as if that simple act might rid her of a silly attraction to a guy who'd probably broken more hearts than wild horses.

* * *

Drew tore a rotted piece of wood from the porch railing, then slung it to the pile he'd made off to the side. It felt good to work with his hands for a change. And he took a sense of pride in the fact that he was, in some small way, helping out the Rocking C Ranch. Better than tackling that blog.

As he swung his hammer to break away the last stretch of porch railing, he got a weird feeling in his core, a second sense that suggested someone was watching him. Instinctively, he turned around.

At first, he didn't see anyone. But then he looked at the house, where a feminine shape stood at the kitchen window.

It had to be Lainie. Who else could it be?

Then she disappeared from sight.

Had he caught her watching him? Or had she merely glanced out the window in passing, a coincidence that he'd turned at just the right time to find her there?

"Whatever," he muttered, gripping the hammer tighter. It was hard to say for sure. Besides, it didn't really matter. He had work to do, and now that he'd built up a sweat, he wanted to finish. He kicked a rotting board out of the way, just as a familiar voice of one of the retirees called out to him.

"Hey, you. College boy. What's going on?"

Drew turned from his work and spotted Rex Mayberry, his late granddad's old friend, limping toward him, using a cane. He wore a tattered hat over his bald head, and a wooden matchstick wiggled in the corner of his mouth. Just the sight of him was enough to draw a smile.

"I'm just trying to pay for my keep." Drew lifted his left arm and wiped the sweat from his brow with a sleeve. "How 'bout you? Feeling okay today?"

"As long as you don't count bad knees, crappy vision and dentures, I'm doing just hunky-dory." With his wry, crotchety sense of humor, Rex was the kind of man who didn't usually say much. But when he did, people gave him their full attention.

At least, Drew always had. He'd been about six years old and living on his grandfather's ranch the first time they'd met. It hadn't taken him long to respect the wisdom behind the man's words. But it wasn't just his comments that had been notable. Rex had been a damn good cowboy, one of the best. So it was tough to see him now, stooped and gray.

Rex let out a chuckle. "I'll bet that rich, candy-ass uncle of yours would be pissed if he saw you now."

Drew smiled. "Yep, you've got that right. J.P. doesn't think much about cowboys, rodeos or ranching. But what he doesn't know won't hurt him."

"I'm sure as hell not gonna tell him. Not after him and me had words after your high school graduation."

Drew hooked his thumbs into his back pockets and frowned. "I wasn't aware of that."

"Yeah, well, I figured your granddad would have wanted me to speak up on his behalf. So I did."

"What'd you say?"

"I told him that you were one of the best horsemen I'd ever seen. And that you were a born rancher. You would've turned the Double M around—if you'd had the chance—and then you would have been able to keep it in the family."

"I might have. If Uncle J.P. would have loaned us the money to pay the back taxes." Drew had only been eleven when his grandfather died, so there hadn't been much he could do to keep the ranch going. His mother had inherited the Double M, but she hadn't been able to make a go of it, especially after her cancer diagnosis. But that had been her secret until her health deteriorated to a certain point.

"I thought it was lousy of J.P. to offer his help, but only if he could call all the shots."

Drew had hoped his great-uncle would loan them the money to pay the back taxes, but J.P. had refused, saying he hadn't reached financial success by squandering his holdings.

Andrew, J.P. had said at the time, *you have a hell of a lot more going for you than being a cowboy. And you're too smart to risk your neck at a foolhardy way of life. So I'll tell you what I'm going to do. I'll pay for your college tuition, which is an investment in you— and in your future.*

"It was probably just as well," Drew said. "My mom had been in remission, but about that time, she got word that the cancer had come back. So J.P. told her to sell the ranch and move to the city with Kara Lee. Mom had access to better medical care there. And selling the ranch provided her with the money to pay for it."

Rex chuffed. "I know it was probably the right thing

to do for her, but I'm not so sure about your sister. She had a hard time changing high schools."

Neither of them mentioned the fact that Drew's mom had died anyway, leaving Kara Lee in Drew's care until she graduated.

"And what about you?" Rex asked. "You gave up your boyhood dreams at the request of your uncle."

"Yes, but not completely. I'm still a cowboy at heart."

And so was the old man leaning on his cane.

"Hold on," Drew said. "I'll bring out a chair for you. That way, you can watch what I'm doing. I'd hate for you to think I'm too book smart for my own good."

"Sure, I'll sit here for a spell. And just for the record, I never had much use for a man who thought he was too good to get his hands dirty or work up a good lather."

"Yes, I know."

"Your grandfather and me, we were cut from the same bolt of cloth. We thought a hard day's work and good deeds never hurt anyone. No, sir."

"I might work indoors most of the time," Drew said, "but I haven't forgotten any of the lessons you guys taught me."

"I'm glad to hear that. I was afraid those college professors would ruin you." Rex lifted his worn felt cowboy hat and raked his gnarled fingers through what was left of his graying hair. "Now get me that chair."

Drew winked at his old friend and mentor before climbing onto the porch. He entered the cabin and returned with one of two chairs from the small dinette table. He placed it in a shady spot.

The old man took a seat and leaned the cane against his knee. "I still think you could have been a champion bronc rider if you'd continued on the circuit."

"Maybe so. But under the circumstances, I don't have any major regrets. I have a good career with Esteban Enterprises. And someday soon, I'm going to create my own company, Silver Buckle Promotions."

"That's one heck of a name. I like it."

"Yep. I'm putting my education to good use. Besides, I still work in the rodeo world, only now I'm a promoter."

Drew had just turned back to his work when Rex asked, "So what's this I hear about you interviewing us? Are you writing an article for the newspaper?"

"No, I'm going to write a blog."

Rex let out a humph. "I'm not sure what that is, but I hope it'll help keep this ranch afloat."

Drew tore up a piece of the floorboard and tossed it on top of the pile of old wood. "That's just one part of the plan. And you'd better believe I'll give it my all." He wasn't so sure about the blog, but he knew he'd do a good job with the rest of the promotion. The Rocking C provided the old cowboys with an affordable and familiar place to live out their last years. So it was too important not to help them get the financial support they needed.

"That's good to know because I like it here—especially the food. That Joy is one fine cook. I was afraid that her temporary replacement wouldn't be worth a darn, but she's actually doing okay. What's her name? Lonnie? Lindy?"

"Lainie."

Rex nodded. "Yeah, well, she's been holding her own so far."

Drew glanced toward the house. When he didn't spot Lainie standing at the window, a pang of disappointment struck. But he shook it off. He wasn't here for fun and games. He had work to do.

Only problem was, he hadn't planned on meeting Lainie. Nor had he expected to get a glimpse of her wearing a pair of sexy panties. As the memory replayed in his mind, a smile spread across his face.

"She's a pretty one," Rex said.

Drew peeled his gaze away from the empty kitchen window and turned to his old friend. "I'm not sure I'm following you."

"The hell, you say." Rex laughed and pointed his thumb at the house. "Kid, I've always been able to read your face like a book."

That might have been true when Drew was a kid, but he'd learned to mask his expressions over the years. That is, unless he was caught off guard.

To throw Rex off course, he reached for the first excuse he could concoct. "I'm getting hungry and wondered if lunch was ready."

"Don't lie to me. The food won't be on the table 'til noon. And I watched you pack it away at breakfast. You might be working hard, kid, but not enough to want lunch at ten o'clock."

Okay, so he'd been caught. "If you haven't noticed, I've been working my tail off here."

"Yeah, right." Rex chuckled.

Rather than let the conversation continue, Drew turned back to demolish the rest of the porch. He wasn't going to give Rex further reason to connect romantic dots that weren't there.

Only trouble was, Drew couldn't help but wonder if there actually might be a few dots that could use a little connecting.

Chapter Four

Lainie had no sooner whipped up a batch of corn bread to go with the chili simmering on the stove, when Sully entered the house through the mudroom, whistling a spunky tune.

"Hey," she said, as she continued to pour the batter into the large, rectangular pan. "You're just the guy I was looking for. Where've you been?"

"Me?" He furrowed his bushy white brow. "I was out taking a morning walk. Then Nate asked me if I wanted to ride into town with him. What's up?"

"Not much. I talked to my friend and shared your advice with her. She realized you were right about the jerk she'd been dating. But then she told me about another friend of ours with a problem, and we're at odds on what to tell her."

Sully pulled out a chair and took a seat at the table. "So what's troubling that gal?"

"She's been saving her money for nearly a year and has enough to purchase a used car, which she desperately needs. Her old one keeps breaking down, and the repairs have been costly. On the upside, she now has a new, better-paying job. She needs dependable transportation, but her kid brother wants to borrow a thousand dollars to cover his rent and the late fee."

Sully rested his clasped hands on the table and steepled his fingers. "Can she spare the money?"

"Yes, if she doesn't buy the car." Lainie placed the pan into the prewarmed oven and set the timer. "Her brother promised to repay her next month, but to complicate matters, he hasn't always repaid the loans she's given him in the past."

"Sounds like she has every reason to turn him down this time."

"I think so, too, but she's been taking care of him ever since their parents died." Lainie could certainly relate to the woman's love and compassion. If she and her twin hadn't been separated, she'd feel the same sense of responsibility.

"How old is the boy?"

"He's twenty-four now and living on his own. But she's worried about him getting evicted, especially since he can't seem to keep a job."

"Apparently, he hasn't had to. His sister keeps jumping in to save the day."

"She means well," Lainie said.

"Yes, but by bailing him out every time he gets into

a jam, she's robbing him of the ability to learn from his mistakes."

Wow. That was an interesting way to look at it. And wise, too.

"Listen," Sully said. "If her no-account brother can't come up with the money to cover his rent this month, how is he going to pay it next month and also be able to repay her as promised?"

"Good point."

"Your friend is allowing her heart to get in the way of her brains. Her brother might have one sob story after another, but it's time for him to grow up. And it's time for his sister to let him."

"You're absolutely right. Thanks." Lainie could work with that sound advice. She'd just have to put her own spin on it.

The back door squeaked open. When she glanced up, she spotted Drew entering the kitchen. His hair was damp and freshly combed, suggesting that he'd recently showered. He'd changed clothes, too.

White button-down shirt. Clean jeans. Shiny cowboy boots.

Their eyes met, and Lainie found it impossible to look away.

He closed the gap between them, and she caught an alluring whiff of masculine soap. Her breath caught, and her voice squeaked out a greeting. "Hey, Drew."

He responded with a "Hey" of his own, his deep voice rumbling through her. She wasn't sure she'd be able to conjure a response until Sully cleared his throat, drawing Lainie's attention away from the handsome man who stood a mere arm's length away.

"If you two will excuse me," Sully said. "I'm going to rest up before the noon meal." Then he shuffled out of the room.

"Something sure smells good," Drew said.

He clearly meant the food, but by the way his gaze caressed her, she wasn't sure. Nevertheless, she couldn't very well stand here like a ditz. So she gathered her wits and said, "I saw you earlier when I glanced out the window and into the yard. I thought you were only going to fix a couple of steps. I had no idea you were going to replace the porch."

"The whole thing was shot. I wasn't going to nail new lumber to bad."

"That makes sense." But what didn't make sense was the way her pulse was racing. Or the way he was looking at her right now. It seemed as if he could see right into her heart.

She touched her throat to check the top button on her flannel shirt before trailing her fingers along the soft blue fabric that covered her chest. When she reached the waistline of her jeans, she realized what she'd been doing and placed her hands on her hips.

He grinned.

And why wouldn't he? He probably thought she was flirting with him, that she had something romantic on her mind, but she didn't. Well, maybe just a little, but she wouldn't allow her curiosity and sexual awareness to get the better of her.

"No overalls today?" he asked, arching a single brow.

"They're in the laundry. I have two pairs, actually. But I don't always wear them. I like them, though. I got them on sale at the local feed store. Very utilitarian. You know?"

She nearly winced at her response. Could she sound any more ditzy or moonstruck?

He nodded, his gaze again scanning her from the topknot on her head to her shoes, then back again. Her toes curled inside her sneakers, causing her to sway. Oh, for Pete's sake. She had to put a stop to the girlishness. She was practically swooning.

Back to business. She turned to the counter, picked up a spoon and started stirring the chili in the pot.

"So when will you finish those repairs?" she asked, her back to him.

"I tore apart the old porch and hauled off all the bad wood. I'll start on the new carpentry tomorrow."

"That'll make entering the front door a little awkward. It's a big step."

"Not for me."

No, she supposed it wouldn't be. The man had to be six feet tall or more. Looking at his handsome face was hard enough. But when he spoke with a faint Southern drawl, his voice had a lulling effect on her.

She placed the spoon on a plate, stepped away from the stove, then brushed her hands on her denim-clad hips, as if her jeans had somehow gotten dusty.

Oh, my gosh. Stop fidgeting and get it together, Lainie.

She offered him her best attempt at an unaffected smile and changed the subject yet again. "I hope you like chili beans and corn bread because that's on the menu for lunch."

"It sounds good."

Her face heated. She hadn't meant to tell him something he could figure out for himself by looking at the stove, but the man was too distracting.

"I was going to interview one of the retired cowboys before we eat," he said. "But now that I've caught a mouthwatering aroma of what's to come, I'd rather hang out in here. Is there anything I can do to help you?" He nodded toward the cupboard. "I'd be happy to set the tables."

"Sure, thanks."

Nate and the young ranch hands usually ate in the kitchen. The retirees were served in the dining room. But he'd know that from being there for several meals, so there was no need to offer further instruction.

Off he went with the plates into the dining room. Moments later he returned for the silverware.

As he moved about the kitchen, close enough to bump into her, close enough for her to catch his musky scent, it was difficult to think, let alone respond to any friendly chatter.

She ought to be thankful for his help, but the only thing that would truly help her right now would be for him to go in search of one of the cowboys, like he'd planned to do.

"I can finish up," she told him. "Why don't you round up someone to interview before lunch?"

And take your sexy smile, hunky self and mesmerizing scent with you.

Drew didn't know why he'd insisted on helping Lainie in the kitchen. As a kid, he'd resented doing what he'd considered women's work. But later, after his mother started chemo and was sick more often than not, he'd taken on meal preparation for their family of three. That included the planning, shopping and cooking. So he'd gained a new respect for cooks—male or female.

But that still didn't explain why he'd stepped up and was now counting out mismatched flatware from the drawer. Lainie was certainly capable of handling things on her own.

The fact that he found her attractive was undoubtedly a contributing factor. And if anything, the more time he spent with her, the more appealing he found her to be.

She didn't wear makeup, which gave her a wholesome, girl-next-door look, which he found alluring. Hot, even. And her faint floral scent? It was enough to make a man perk up and take notice of her every move.

She rocked those baggy jeans and that oversize T-shirt like an urban model, the kind that didn't give a damn about what other people thought. And she pulled it off right down to her sneakers.

Once again his mind drifted to the mouse encounter, when he'd gotten a peek at her shapely legs and those sexy panties, and he'd begun to see her in a whole new light. An arousing one.

He found the contradiction, the soft femininity of silk and lace hidden behind durable denim, to be incredibly sensual. It not only spiked his testosterone, it piqued his curiosity. And that, he decided, was what prompted him to offer his help today.

After he finished setting both tables, he returned to the kitchen, pausing just inside the doorway to watch Lainie work. Her back was to him, so she was unaware that he'd stolen the opportunity to study her.

She snatched a potholder from the counter, then opened the oven door, withdrew the corn bread and placed it on one side of the stovetop to cool. Next she checked the chili beans simmering in a pot.

Rather than continue to admire her, Drew said, "I finished setting the table. Is there anything else I can do?"

She turned to face him, her cheeks flushed a deeper shade of pink. She touched her collar, fiddling with the top button. When she caught his eye, her hand dropped to her side.

"You can fill the glasses with ice." She nodded to the countertop, where two large gallon jars held tea. "Most of the men like to have sweet tea with all their meals."

"Consider it done."

As Drew made his way toward the cupboard and near Lainie, she bit down on her bottom lip. "Don't get me wrong. I appreciate this, but I'm not used to having help."

"It's no problem."

She offered him a waifish smile. Something in those expressive brown eyes suggested that she'd been on her own for a while. And that it hadn't been by her own choosing.

He pulled glasses from the cupboard. "You mentioned having a twin—and that you hadn't seen her in a while."

When Lainie didn't immediately respond, he realized that he'd overstepped. He didn't have the right to pry or to ask about the dynamics of her family, but for some reason, his curiosity grew too strong to ignore.

"I take it you and your sister aren't very close," he said, prodding her.

"We used to be." Her voice came out soft, fragile, stirring his sympathy along with his interest.

"Did you have a falling-out?" he asked.

She paused for the longest time, and he just stood there, a glass in hand, waiting while the moment turned awkward.

He was about to apologize for getting too personal when she said, "Her name is Erica, but I called her Rickie. We haven't seen each other since we were nine and she was adopted."

Wow. Drew hadn't seen that coming.

"Were you adopted, too?" he asked.

"No, I…remained in foster care."

The waning sense of awkwardness rose up again, stronger than ever. Under any other circumstances, he might have turned away, changed the subject. Yet he felt compelled to dig for more information, even though each time she answered one of his questions, it only served to trigger another.

"Have you considered looking for her?" he asked. "I mean, now that you're adults."

"I think about that all the time, but it was a closed adoption, so there's not much I can do."

"Feel free to tell me to mind my own business, but why didn't her parents adopt you, too?"

"It's complicated." She reached for her collar again. A nervous habit, he supposed. "We were both living in foster care at the time. I... Well, I had a few health problems back then and was moved to a home with better access to medical care. While I was gone, a family came along and chose her, but not me."

"I'm sorry." That must have hurt like hell.

"Don't be. I was sad, but I understood why. I've dealt with it."

"Have you?"

"I just said I had."

"I mean, most kids would have felt hurt, left out, rejected. Some might even carry those feelings for years."

"Not me. Don't worry about it."

"I'm sorry if I stirred up any sad memories."

She shrugged. "Like I said, I've dealt with it." Then she turned her back to him and returned to her work, ending a conversation that had gotten way too personal and revealing for his own good.

Yet for some crazy reason, he was tempted to embrace her, to press her head to his shoulder and tell her he sympathized with her over the rejection and the loss of her sister. But he didn't.

He might be a sucker for innocent, vulnerable women, but he wasn't about to take on another one now. Not when he had his plate full with a pregnant sister on bed rest.

"How about you?" Lainie asked. "Do you have any siblings?"

"Yes, a kid sister." And she was the only family he had left. Well, so far. "She's expecting a baby boy at the end of March."

"That's nice. Uncle Drew, huh?"

He grinned. "That's right."

"I take it you're close."

"Yeah, we're pretty tight." At Kara Lee's wedding, Drew had been the one to give her away. Then he'd stood back, his head held high, a smile on his face.

He'd been glad to know that she'd finally grown up, that she'd have a home and family of her own. That she'd have the happiness she'd always deserved. He'd assumed that Craig was an honorable man. That he'd step up and take care of Kara Lee from that day on, for richer or poorer, in sickness and in health.

But that wasn't to be. And it hadn't been death that parted them, but a parade of lovers. The last straw was the sexy brunette whose video had gone viral.

A woman who hadn't had any more respect for sacred wedding vows than Craig Baxter had.

While Lainie tidied up the kitchen after the evening meal, Drew and one of the retired cowboys remained at the table, having a cup of decaf.

Drew had set up a small video recorder, a real nice one. The kind that, if Lainie hit the lottery, she'd buy.

"Damn it. I can't get this thing to record."

Lainie had planned to stay in the background, but she couldn't help going to the rescue. "Here. You have it on the wrong mode. That's all." She triggered the right one. "There you go."

The elderly cowboy, Gilbert Henry, laughed. "Guess you're an old soul like me, Drew. Can't figure out that newfangled equipment."

"Something like that."

Lainie scrubbed a counter that didn't need cleaning and listened to Gilbert talk about his time in the Marine Corps during the Korean War, his return to the States and his marriage to Pearl, his high school sweetheart.

"We bought a house in Wexler," Gil said. "We had dreams, me and Pearl. She wanted a big family, and I was prepared to give that little gal anything she wanted. But I guess God or Fate had other plans. We tried to have a baby for nearly ten years. Finally, we adopted two little boys—brothers who'd been orphaned at a young age."

Lainie couldn't help but wish that a couple like Gil and his wife had been around when she and Rickie needed a home.

"Ray was the oldest," Gil said. "And was he a real pistol. Sharp as a tack, but never did like school. Jimmy was the youngest. And quiet. For a while, we never thought he'd ever say a word. But once he did, he jabbered from morning until night."

"Where are they now?" Drew asked.

"When Ray was sixteen, he got caught up with the wrong crowd and ended up on drugs." Gil clucked his tongue. "And he got sent to the state pen for a while, too. Damn near broke Pearl's heart and caused a divorce when I refused to bail him out. But hell, he was going to have to serve time anyway and I didn't trust him to show up in court."

"That must have been very hard on you and your wife."

"Yep. But in the long run, Ray's incarceration turned out to be a blessing. Thanks to a prison ministry, he turned his life around. Believe it or not, he's a preacher in Louisiana. He doesn't have a big fancy church. He spends a lot of his time on the street corner, passing out Bibles and giving sandwiches to the homeless. But he seems to be happy doing that."

"How about the younger boy?" Drew asked.

"We lost him in Desert Storm."

Lainie stopped scrubbing and looked over her shoulder at the man.

Gil's voice cracked. "I keep his Silver Star on my nightstand to remember him by."

"I'm sorry to hear that," Drew said.

"Me, too. But you should have seen the letters some of his buddies sent to us and the articles written in the paper. I'm damn proud to know I raised a boy who didn't balk when it came to dying to save the men in his platoon."

Lainie had already tidied up the kitchen, but rather than leave the men alone, she began reorganizing the pantry, which really didn't need it. Joy kept an organized kitchen. She also kept two bottles of wine in there and had told Lainie she was welcome to open either or both. But Lainie wouldn't do that.

She shuffled some of the canned goods, wasting time so she could continue to eavesdrop and hear what Gilbert had to say. But after mentioning Pearl's death two years ago, just days after their sixtieth wedding anniversary, the interview stalled.

"Well," Gil said, as he got up from his seat. "I guess that's pretty much all I have to say."

"Thanks for your candor and your time," Drew told him.

Lainie watched Gil shuffle from the room, her heart heavy with the bittersweet memories he'd shared. She knew each of the retirees at the Rocking C had unique backgrounds, filled with both sad and happy times, but hearing Gil's story reminded her that they weren't forgotten stories.

Drew shut off the video recorder and blew out a ragged breath. "Writing this blog is going to be even more difficult than I thought it'd be."

"Because of Gil's interview?"

"Yes. You were in here and heard his story. My heart goes out to that guy. His life seems pretty tragic, and I'm not sure how to go about writing it."

Lainie closed the pantry door, turned to face Drew and leaned against the kitchen cupboard. "All you have to do is put the right spin on it. You can choose to portray Gil as a tired, grieving old man. Or you can show him as a loving husband and proud father who raised sons who have made this world a better place."

"Good point. The older boy spent time in prison, but he learned from his mistakes."

"And the younger brother made the ultimate sacrifice for his country."

"Yeah. Gil and his wife were good parents, whose sons have sacrificed for others. I'm not sure if I can do them all justice."

"Sure you can. Follow your heart, and you'll do right by them."

He stared at his notes and frowned. "But I don't even know where to begin."

"I could help out. I have a degree in journalism." Shoot. Why had she made an offer like that?

"No kidding?"

She crossed her arms and shifted her weight to one hip. "Don't look so surprised. This job at the ranch is only temporary. And while it's come in handy for the time being, I'm going to work at a newspaper someday."

Actually, she was working for one now, but that was her secret. Besides, writing the Dear Debbie column certainly didn't make her an investigative reporter or a photojournalist.

A grin stretched across Drew's face, lighting his eyes. "I'm impressed. I don't suppose I could hire you to give me some editorial direction for that blog? Would you be up for that?"

Did he mean to pay her for her time? She was going to offer her services for free, but she could sure use the additional income. "You want to hire me?"

"Absolutely. I'm not sure what the going rate is, but I'll gladly pay it."

Lainie tempered her enthusiasm and said, "Sure. I'd be glad to help. Besides, it's for a good cause."

"It certainly is. I'd hate to see this place close."

"Me, too. The men seem happy here, even when they complain about the competency of some of the young ranch hands."

He laughed. "Sully calls them 'whippersnappers.'"

Lainie had heard plenty of comments from all the men. And she'd watched out the kitchen window one day when a couple of them, using a cane and a walker, approached the corral and gave one of the young hands a scolding for doing things wrong. It was a real sight. She'd wished she'd had her camera handy.

"You know," Lainie said, "I also have a minor in photography."

"No wonder you knew how to work my video recorder. Do you have a camera?"

"Yes. And I can take pictures of the ranch and the men to go along with your blog."

"That'd be great. We can show the young cowboys at work, as well as the old guys."

Lainie had a feeling she was going to like collaborating with Drew on the blog project. She might not have the perfect job at the *Gazette* yet, but at least she could get some more experience on her resume.

"I feel like celebrating," he said. "Too bad we don't have any champagne handy."

Toasting with crystal flutes and drinking sparkling wine with a handsome rodeo promoter sounded tempting. And while she knew where Joy's wine was, she wasn't about to lower her guard around a man like him. She'd been attracted to two other men in her life, and both had proven to be lacking in character.

And now here was another. Would the third time be the charm? Or another disaster?

Either way, she'd need to keep her wits about her.

"I have cookies and milk," she said in her best kindergarten teacher's voice.

"Then that'll have to do." Drew tossed her a dazzling smile, his eyes sparkling like fine champagne.

Yes, it would have to. Lainie removed several snickerdoodles from an airtight plastic container in the pantry and placed them on a plate. Then she poured them each a glass of milk.

All the while, Drew watched her. His gaze intensified, as if he knew that she wore white lace lingerie under her clothes, the one feminine luxury she'd refused to give up during the last reinvention of herself.

He reached for a cookie. "I'm looking forward to putting our heads together on the blog."

The thought of their heads touching, their breaths mingling...

Oh, for Pete's sake, Lainie. What were you thinking?

She took a sip of milk in an attempt to shake the inappropriate thought, but when she stole a peek at him and spotted his boyish grin, it didn't work. Images of romantic scenes continued to hound her.

She should have known better than to offer to help him with that stupid blog. With her luck, the assignment would end up being more trouble than it was worth.

So she did her best to shake off his mesmerizing gaze and her heart-stirring reaction to it by stuffing a cookie into her mouth.

Like it or not, she was stuck working closely with the gorgeous cowboy, and she'd just have to keep her growing attraction to him in check. Or she'd have to stuff herself with more milk and cookies.

Chapter Five

Over the next few days, while Lainie washed the dinner dishes, Drew conducted his first interviews in the kitchen.

"Since you offered to help me write that blog, or however many stories we have to tell," he'd told her, "you should hear what the men have to say."

Lainie agreed. And it certainly wasn't a hardship. The retired cowboys' memories and reflections were both touching and entertaining.

But their stories weren't the only thing that held her interest each evening. Drew's voice had a mesmerizing effect on her, and in spite of her efforts to ignore his soft Southern drawl, she found herself increasingly drawn to the rodeo promoter.

She was also touched by the kindness and respect

he'd shown the old guys, which made her think he might be different from the men who'd let her down in the past. Clearly, her first impressions of him hadn't been on target.

After placing a meat loaf in the top oven and the russet potatoes in the bottom, she washed her hands at the sink and peered out the window at his cabin, which now had a new front porch.

Drew wasn't anywhere in sight, so she leaned to the right and arched her neck to get a better view of the barn and yard. She still didn't see him, but she spotted Nate working with a fidgety colt in the corral. She'd heard about the acting foreman's skill with horses, but to see him in action was an amazing sight.

She'd already taken a number of shots of the cowboys, old and young alike, and this was a perfect opportunity to get another. She shut off the faucet, dried her hands on a dish towel and hurried to get her camera.

Moments later, she opened the mudroom door and stepped into the yard, her camera lens raised.

"Good job," a familiar, mesmerizing voice called out. "I'm glad to see you're taking advantage of a photo op."

Lainie didn't have to glance over her shoulder to see Drew's approach, but she turned to him anyway.

He looked good today in that black hat cocked just right and that chambray shirt, pressed with a dash of starch—thanks to a laundry service, no doubt. And those jeans? He wore them as if they were a part of him.

As he closed in on her, his scent—something alluring, manly and no doubt expensive—stirred her senses.

Her heart rate soared, and her arm wobbled, nearly causing her to drop her camera.

Oh, for Pete's sake. Get it together, girl.

Determined to shake off the effect Drew had on her, she nodded toward the corral. "The men told me that Nate was the resident horse whisperer, so I thought I'd get a couple pictures of him for the blog."

"Good idea." Drew offered her a heart-strumming smile and followed it up with a playful wink that would tempt the most diligent female employee to play hooky from work. "I'd better not interrupt you."

He had that right. She had a job to do, a photo to take. So she adjusted the lens and checked the light. After catching several shots of Nate, she lowered the camera to her side and focused on Drew. "I missed seeing you this morning. Where'd you run off to?"

"I met a friend for breakfast at Caroline's Diner."

She wondered if his friend was male or female, but decided it would be rude to come right out and ask. However, that didn't mean she couldn't prod him for a little more information.

"From what I saw, it seems that Caroline's is the place where all the locals eat. The food is good, and the desserts are amazing," she said. "Don't you think?"

"That's for sure." He splayed a hand on his flat belly and grinned. "But I'd better not make a habit of filling up on her hotcakes and maple syrup."

Maybe not, but he still hadn't given Lainie a clue about who he'd met, so she pumped a little more. "You and your friend must've had a lot of catching up to do. It's nearly lunchtime."

"Before heading back to the ranch, I stopped by the hardware store to buy more lumber. My cabin isn't the only one with a rickety, worn-out porch."

"You mean you're going to fix each one?"

"I might." He lifted his hat long enough to rake a hand through his hair.

"That's a nice thing for you to do." It was also generous, which was yet another reason to believe he might be a man worth her time and affection.

Lainie lifted her camera to take a picture of him, but he waved her off, blocking his face with his hand.

"Cut that out," he said, his tone playful and light. "That blog isn't about me."

"Okay, cowboy." She lowered her lens, but her gaze lingered on him. She really ought to return to the house, but she couldn't seem to make a move in that direction.

The thump of her heartbeats counted out several seconds until footsteps sounded and she spotted Bradley Jamison approaching.

The young ranch hand cleared his throat. "Excuse me. I hate to interrupt."

It was probably best that he did. Lainie offered him a smile. "What's up?"

"Nate said I could use one of the cabins for a few days. I don't want to cause you any trouble, ma'am, so I'd be happy to clean it up, if it needs it."

Drew answered Brad before Lainie could. "I thought you slept in the bunkhouse. Is someone giving you a hard time in there?"

"Oh, no. The cabin's not for me. It's for my mom.

She just got hired to work at the new children's home down the road. Once she's on their payroll, she'll get room and board there, but she doesn't start until Monday, and her lease is up tomorrow. So it would only be a couple of days."

"The new *children's* home?" Lainie asked.

Brad nodded sagely. "It's a place for abused and neglected kids. A man and his wife bought the old Clancy place and opened it up last month."

"I know where that ranch is," Drew said. "It's got a big house, but it's pretty old. I doubt it's up to code."

"It wasn't at first. But last summer, the community church got involved with the project, and so did the Wexler Women's Club. The couple in charge are trying to get a grant of some kind, but in the meantime, they'll have to slowly add kids as they go."

Still stunned by the idea of a children's home down the road, Lainie asked, "How many kids live there?"

"I think about twelve. Most of them are from the city. My mom told me the idea was to move them to a country environment so they could see a new way of life."

"That's an interesting concept," Drew said.

"Yeah." Brad replaced his hat on his head. "My mom was pretty impressed when she went out and saw it for herself. From what I understand, each kid is given certain chores, and they're also assigned a few animals to take care of—like pigs, sheep, goats and rabbits."

Lainie hoped they didn't plan to work the children too hard. She'd had one set of foster parents who'd been awfully strict and expected more out of her than seemed fair.

"What's your mom's job going to be?" Drew asked.

"They hired her as a counselor. After she divorced my stepdad, she went back to school. It took a while because she had to work during the day and take classes at night, but she finally got a degree."

"Good for her." Lainie liked the woman already.

"Yeah, I'm proud of her." Brad kicked the toe of his boot at the ground, stirring the dirt. "She's glad she'll be there before Christmas. A lot of those kids never had a tree or presents before. Their funds are limited, though, so she can't go all out with decorations and stuff, but she doesn't think it'll take much to make them happy."

"Actually," Lainie said, "regular meals and a warm, safe place to sleep helps a lot." Of course, that wouldn't change the reality those kids lived with each day, the memories they carried. "Don't worry, Brad. I'll make sure the cabin is ready for your mom."

Drew placed his hand on Lainie's shoulder, giving it a gentle squeeze. "No, you don't have to do that. I'll do it for you. You never know, a mouse might be lying in wait."

Lainie's cheeks warmed. She was tempted to plant an elbow in his side and shoot him a frown. But in truth, he'd just offered to do her a huge favor.

"Thanks," Brad said. "I really appreciate this. And just so you know, my mom said she'd be happy to help out around here. She'll cook, clean, run errands…whatever. She'll even keep some of those pesky old cowboys out of your hair. She's good with people, even difficult ones."

"I'm looking forward to meeting her," Lainie said. "And I'm sure we'll keep her busy while she's here."

"Well, I'd best get back to work or Nate'll have my hide." Brad tilted the brim of his hat to Lainie, turned and strode toward the barn.

Rather than let the subject of their conversation drift back to that embarrassing mouse encounter, Lainie steered it in another direction. "I hadn't given Christmas much thought, but I really ought to put up some holiday decorations, including a tree."

"I'm going to my sister's house on Christmas Day, but the rest of the time I'll be on the ranch, so I can help you." Drew nodded toward a couple of older men rocking on the porch. "Imagine the memories Christmas must dig up for these guys."

True. More fodder for Drew's blog...and for another human interest column for her to propose to Mr. Carlton. She could see it now: *A Cowboy Christmas.*

As Lainie began making a mental list of the chores to be done, she had a lightbulb moment. "Oh, wow."

"What's wrong?"

"Nothing. I just had an idea. What if we have a joint Christmas party for the children here at the Rocking C?"

"That'd be nice, but it would be a huge undertaking."

"Maybe, but I'm sure Rex, Sully and the others would help. And it would give the men a special purpose, not to mention something to look forward to."

Drew looked out in the distance, his brow creased in

concentration. After a couple of beats, he brightened. "You know, a party like that would lend itself to one heck of a blog post."

"You read my mind." A grin slid across Lainie's face, and a tingle of excitement spread through her.

She couldn't remember the last time she'd looked forward to Christmas, but she'd do whatever she could to create a special holiday for those kids. Decorations, a tree, holiday baking...

"We can do this." Lainie clutched Drew's arm in camaraderie, but she nearly jerked away when the body heat radiating through his shirt sent an electrical zing through her.

She tried to blame the spark on the energy emanating from their new joint venture, although she feared it was more than that.

"I'll find out who's in charge of the children's home," Drew said. "And I'll see how they feel about joining us for a Christmas party at the Rocking Chair Ranch."

"And I'll talk to our nursing staff," Lainie said, "although I can't see why they'd object. A party would be good for young and old alike."

"There's only two weeks before Christmas, so we have our work cut out for us. We'd better get busy." Drew gave Lainie's shoulder a nudge with his arm, reminding her of his presence, of his heat. They'd become a team, and by the way he was looking at her, he liked that idea.

She liked it, too.

As Drew turned and walked away, she studied his

back, admiring his sexy swagger, his broad shoulders
and the perfect fit of his jeans.

A romantic wish tingled through her, warming her
cheeks once again. Maybe Santa would be good to her
for a change.

And if she was lucky, she just might wake up on
Christmas morning and find a cowboy under her tree.

Drew was always up for a challenge, which is why
he'd searched every nook and cranny of his cabin to
find a cell signal. He was determined to set up a temporary but functional home office, although he wasn't
having much luck. About the time he considered giving up and driving to town for Wi-Fi, he picked up a
signal near the kitchen area.

As long as he moved the dinette table about three
feet from the east wall, he could connect to the internet, which would make it a lot easier to work while he
stayed at the ranch for the next two weeks.

Once he set up his laptop and got online, he did
some research on the children's home Brad had mentioned earlier this afternoon. It was called Kidville,
and from the pictures posted on the main website page,
the outside looked like a small town in the Old West.

"Interesting," he said, as he continued to read up
on the place that had been founded by Jim and Donna
Hoffman, an older couple who had a heart for kids.

The more Drew learned about the Hoffmans and
Kidville, the more determined he was to meet with
them and see it for himself. With the Wi-Fi service
he now had, it didn't take him long to find the num-

ber for the administrative office and ask for whoever was in charge.

A couple minutes later, Mr. Hoffman answered. "This is Jim. How can I help you?"

Drew introduced himself and revealed his affiliation with Esteban Enterprises, the rodeo and the Rocking Chair Ranch, and his admiration for what the Hoffmans were doing.

"Thanks," Jim said. "For nearly ten years, my wife and I dreamed of creating a place in the country where we could provide a safe, loving environment for abused and neglected city kids. So when we retired from our county jobs, we set our plan in motion. We've had a few hurdles along the way, so Kidville has been nearly two years in the making."

"I'd imagine funding would be one of those problems."

"Yes, that's true. But thanks to the help of the community church, the Wexler Women's Club and the Brighton Valley Rotary, we were able to remodel the house and get it up to code, paint the barn and set up a playground. But until we get more financial backing, we're nearing our capacity."

"I think it would be fairly easy to drum up support for such a worthy cause." Drew went on to explain his promotional plan for the retired cowboys' home.

"As a nonprofit, I'm afraid we don't have the funds to pay for any advertisements or PR companies," Jim said.

Apparently, Drew hadn't made himself clear. "I didn't expect you to hire me or Esteban Enterprises.

To be completely candid, I'm not exactly sure what I can do to help you and Kidville, but just for the record, nothing tugs at my boss's heartstrings more than rodeos, aging cowboys and children."

Drew didn't mention anything about a Christmas party on the Rocking C, but he did suggest a meeting with the Hoffmans. He could propose the idea at that time.

"Why don't you come by Friday afternoon?" Jim suggested. "We'll talk more then, and I can give you a tour of Kidville."

"Sounds like a plan. And if it's okay with you, I'll probably bring my…um, associate. It was her idea to do some joint promotion, and there's no telling what we might come up with if we all put our heads together."

"I'll make sure my wife is available. Would two o'clock work for the two of you?"

"That's perfect. We'll see you then." After the call ended, Drew continued to sit at the dinette table, his cell phone in hand. He had a good feeling about Kidville. And he couldn't wait to share the news with Lainie.

He glanced at the clock on the microwave. It was closing in on five o'clock and would soon be time for dinner. If he'd learned one thing in his week spent on the Rocking C, it was that the meals ran on a strict schedule.

He wouldn't say anything about it at the table. Instead, he'd wait until after everyone ate, when it was quiet in the kitchen.

And when he had Lainie to himself.

* * *

Other than several murmurs of appreciation for a tasty meal, the men had eaten quietly, their focus on the meat loaf, buttered green beans and baked potatoes. Even Drew, who sat at the kitchen table with the young ranch hands, hadn't said much, but by the glimmer in his eyes and the grin on his face, he seemed to be pleased about something.

Lainie tamped down her curiosity for now. She'd wait until after dinner to question him.

In the meantime, while the men had ice cream and chocolate chip cookies for dessert, she carried the plates and flatware to the sink, rinsed them off and placed them in the dishwasher. By the time she returned to the table for the empty bowls and spoons, the ranch hands were already filing out the back door, with Drew in the midst of them.

Lainie continued her work, putting away leftovers and wiping down countertops, but she couldn't help wondering what Drew was up to. For the past few evenings, he'd interviewed the retired cowboys in the kitchen, a routine she'd come to look forward to.

She glanced out the kitchen window. The lights were off in his cabin, so he hadn't turned in for the night. She'd just placed the detergent in the dishwasher when the back door swung open and clicked shut. She turned to see Drew striding through the mudroom on his way back inside.

His smile, as dazzling as it'd ever been, lit his eyes, and her pulse rate kicked up a notch.

"Got a minute?" he asked.

"Sure. What's up?"

He pulled out a chair from the table for her. "I thought you might like an update."

She sat down, and he took a seat next to her. "I did a little research, and Kidville, that children's home, appears to be everything Brad said it was and more. So I made an appointment for us to take a tour on Friday at two. Can you slip off for an hour or so?"

"I'd really like to, but I'm not sure. I'm usually busy with the meal prep for dinner at that time."

"I've got you covered. Brad's mother will be here by then, and a few minutes ago, when I mentioned what I had in mind, he called her. She said she'd be happy to cook dinner—or do anything else to help out. She's coming to stay that day anyway, so she's going to arrive a few hours early. You'll have plenty of time to show her around the kitchen."

"You've thought of everything."

"I try to cover all my bases." His wink turned her heart inside out.

They'd not only become teammates, but it seemed as if they were well on the road to being friends.

She liked the thought of that.

"Did you know that Kidville has a small orchard and a good-size vegetable garden?" Drew asked. "They're going to grow most of their produce, and they're raising chickens."

A niggle of concern crept over her, stealing her smile. "I know the kids will have chores, but I hope they won't be expected to do all the work."

"Jim Hoffman and his wife believe children should

be given age-appropriate responsibilities, and I see the reasoning behind that."

"Me, too. I just hope this doesn't turn out to be a farm run by child labor." Lainie's thoughts drifted to the time she'd lived with the Bakers, the memory taking her back to a place and foster family she'd hoped to forget.

"You have a faraway look in your eyes," Drew said, drawing her back to the here and now.

"I'm sorry. My mind wandered for a moment."

"To a bad personal experience?"

Lainie didn't usually talk about her early years—at least, not in detail. But she'd grown close to Drew in the past few days, and if they'd truly become friends, she should be up front with him. "I told you that I grew up in foster care. For the most part it wasn't too bad. If I'd been able to stay with the first family…" Tears filled her eyes, and she blinked them away. So much for the candor of friendship.

"I'm sorry that you had such a crappy childhood," he said.

"It wasn't all bad." She swiped at her lower lashes, stopping the overflow. "Most of the families I lived with were decent. In fact, I actually liked Mama Kate, the first foster mother my sister and I had. She was an older, dark-skinned woman who had an easy laugh and a loving heart as big as her lap. She never turned down a kid needing a placement, so there were a lot of us. Yet she managed to find special time for each of us. My sister and I counted ourselves lucky to live with her."

"Why'd you have to leave?" Drew asked.

"One night, about six months after we moved in, Mama Kate had a stroke and had to give us all up."

"That's too bad. Where did you go next?"

Lainie bit back a quick response. She wasn't sure she wanted to be that up front. She and Rickie had moved to a receiving home, where her heart condition was finally diagnosed. She endured several back-to-back hospitalizations, which was when she and her sister were separated. After her surgery and a long inpatient recuperation period, she learned that Rickie had been adopted. Sadly, they'd never had a chance to say good-bye to each other.

But Lainie wasn't going to share that.

She reached for her collar, fingered the top button then skimmed the next three before dropping her hand to her lap. "Next stop was to the Bakers' house. Talk about all work and no play."

"So that's why you're worried about the children and their chores at Kidville," Drew said.

"The Bakers seemed to think that I was there to cook, clean the house and do the laundry."

"An unpaid servant, huh?"

"Pretty much. At least, as far as my foster mother was concerned." Lainie tilted her hand and flicked her fingers at a crumb she'd neglected to wipe off the table. "Her name was Glenda, which always reminded me of the good witch, only spelled differently. But she wasn't very good—or nice. She once called my fifth grade teacher to complain about the amount of homework I was assigned. She told Mrs. Fleming that I wouldn't be allowed to do any of it, especially the reading, until after my household chores were done. But by then, I was exhausted."

Drew reached across the table and covered her hand with his, warming it. He brushed his thumb across the top of her wrist. She suspected he meant to have a comforting effect, a calming one. But his touch spiked her pulse, arousing her senses instead.

"I'm sorry, Lainie. That must have been very difficult for you."

"It was." Her voice came out a notch above a whisper, and when she met his gaze, she spotted sympathy in his eyes.

She was glad for the connection they'd made, for his understanding, but she didn't want his pity. She had the urge to jerk her hand away from his and to reach for the collar of her blouse. But she couldn't seem to move.

As her heart pounded a strong, steady cadence, an unfamiliar emotion rose up inside, one that stirred her senses and reminded her just how inexperienced she was. Especially when it came to things like openhearted discussions, honest emotion and a friendship drifting toward romance.

She was at a complete loss. Should she pull her hand away from him now?

Or should she leave it in his grip forever?

Drew made the decision for her when he turned her hand over, palm side up, and clasped her fingers in his. He squeezed gently, relaying compassion and reassurance. Yet at the same time, it triggered a blood-swirling feeling she'd rather not ponder or put a name to.

"I don't think you need to worry about the Hoffmans," he said. "I have a good feeling about them. And if we all work together, I think we can boost financial support for both the Rocking Chair Ranch and Kidville."

Lainie withdrew her hand from his, albeit reluctantly. "Are you talking about the Christmas party?"

"Yes, but why stop there? What about an Easter egg decorating party, pumpkin carving… I could go on and on."

"Wow. That's creative," she said.

"Just doing my job," he said, shrugging off her compliment. Then he brightened. "You know, something tells me this is going to be a successful venture. We should celebrate."

"That's a little premature, don't you think? We haven't even toured the children's home or met the people in charge."

"Okay, then we can toast our new venture." His playful, boyish expression made it difficult to tell him no.

So Lainie returned his smile. "With a glass of milk and cookies?"

"Do you have anything better suited for adults?"

"Coffee?"

He lifted an eyebrow. "How about something stronger than caffeine?"

The wine stash. Lainie hesitated.

Oh, why not. Joy had told her to help herself.

"As a matter of fact," she said, "I do. You have your choice of merlot or chardonnay."

"Either works for me. You pick. I'll find a cork-screw."

Lainie watched Drew head for the kitchen drawer and realized this wasn't going to be a celebration. It was more of a christening, like breaking a bottle of bubbly on the bow of a ship ready to set sail for the very first time.

As she went to the cabinet and selected the merlot, she hoped that if she and Drew were about to launch a romance, it wouldn't end up a disaster of *Titanic* proportions.

Chapter Six

Lainie handed Drew the bottle of merlot, and he pulled the cork, releasing the scent of oak and blackberries.

She'd been right. It was too early to actually celebrate anything, but he'd had another motive to consider tonight a special occasion. He wanted to get to know her better, to spend some time with her, and he hadn't been able to come up with a better reason to stick around in the kitchen this evening.

She removed two wineglasses from the small hutch and set them on the table, allowing him to fill them halfway.

Then he lifted his glass in a toast. "Here's to helping the young and old alike."

"To cowboys and children." She clinked her glass against his, then took a sip.

He did the same, yet it wasn't their team effort to encourage charitable contributions for both ranches that he was thinking about. He actually liked the idea of working closely with Lainie. He liked it a lot.

"Are you looking forward to visiting Kidville?" he asked her. "Or…" He paused, realizing that her time spent in foster care might make a visit to a children's home, even one as unique as that one appeared to be, stir up bad memories. And he didn't want to open a Pandora's Box of emotion.

"I'd like to take that tour," she said softly. "Thanks for including me. Besides, it'll be good for the blog, right?"

"Yes, that's true. At this rate, we'll have enough blog content for months." He studied her face, those big brown eyes, the soft, plump lips. Her high cheekbones, like those of a top model, bore a slight blush.

Once again, it struck him that he'd seen her somewhere before. In his dreams, most likely. But in those nocturnal musings, she hadn't been dressed in baggy denim or blouses buttoned to the throat. She'd worn sexy silk panties, which she kept hidden from sight and only revealed to her lover.

"Have you started the blog yet?" she asked.

Not really. When it came to sitting down in front of his laptop and actually opening up a Word document, he'd been dragging his feet.

"I'm still conducting the interviews," he said. "I plan to talk to the younger men, too. Nate has an interesting story."

"Does he?" Lainie ran the tip of her tongue across her top lip, licking a drop of wine.

Drew sucked in a breath. For a moment, he lost his train of thought. So he focused on his wineglass. Anything but that mouth, those lips and that tongue.

"I'd heard that Nate got married recently," she said, "but not to the mother of his baby."

Oh, yeah. They'd been talking about Nate.

"You heard right," Drew said. "A few months back, a woman he'd once dated showed up here at the ranch, pregnant and battered by her new husband. She was looking for Nate and claimed the baby was his."

"How tragic." She did that thing with her tongue on her lip again, and he nearly forgot what they were talking about.

Nate and the baby. Right.

"Because of that beating, she went into premature labor," Drew said, "she gave birth to little Jessie, then died from a brain bleed."

Lainie cupped her hands around the stem of her goblet and scrunched her brow. "That poor woman. How sad."

"It sure was. Her husband is now in prison for murder." Drew reached for the bottle and replenished his wine. "More?"

She shook her head and placed her hand over the top of her glass. "What happened next?"

"Nate took custody of the baby and hooked up with Anna, the hospital social worker who'd been assigned to his case." Drew took a sip of wine. He wondered if Lainie liked the merlot. She wasn't drinking much.

She fingered the stem of the glass, her brow slightly furrowed. "Nate fell in love with his social worker?"

"Do you find that odd?"

Lainie smiled. "I can't imagine a handsome young cowboy falling for any of the ones I had as a child."

"Then Nate was lucky. Anna's both pretty and loving. But for a while, he was afraid she'd find him lacking as a father, and that he'd lose custody of the baby as a result. But he was wrong, and now they're married."

"You were right. That's an interesting story. But I have a question. You said the baby's mother 'claimed' Nate was the father. Was he?"

"At first, Nate wasn't sure. He told me that DNA didn't make a man a daddy. And that you don't have to be born into a family to belong to one."

"That's true," Lainie said, brightening. "It's an interesting take—and a good piece of advice. I'll have to keep it in mind."

"Advice? I'm not following you."

She blinked a couple times, then let out a little giggle and shrugged her shoulders. "I'm sorry. I was just thinking out loud."

And probably ruing the fact that she didn't have a family of her own. Drew was about to comment, then realized he'd be wading into a slew of emotion he didn't want to deal with. He had enough of that with Kara Lee, which had been made worse by maternal hormones. So he let it go.

He looked at Lainie's left hand, the one he'd once touched, once held. She wasn't wearing a ring, so he concluded she wasn't involved with someone.

For a man who never mixed business with pleasure, he was tempted to make an exception this time.

"Is there a special man in your life?" he asked.

"No, not anymore. Actually, there really never was. Not one who was special."

Drew sat up straighter, pumped by what sounded like good news. "That's a little surprising."

"What is?" She lifted her glass, studied the burgundy color in the kitchen light, then took a drink. "That I'm not engaged or seeing someone right now? Actually, the few men I thought were decent ended up disappointing me. I can ferret out the heart of a story, but apparently, I'm not very good at judging a man's heart and character."

"Sounds like you're recovering from a painful breakup."

Her shoulder twitched. Not quite a shrug, but a tell just the same. One that told him she'd been hurt in the past and possibly betrayed.

"I was too trusting," she said. "But I'll be a lot more careful in the future."

Drew couldn't say he blamed her. He'd built a few walls of his own, although that didn't mean he hadn't found the time for a casual but intimate relationship every now and then. And when he did, he was pretty selective.

The truth was, he found Lainie to be both attractive and completely acceptable in that regard. Would she feel the same way about him? To be blunt, would she be interested in having a short-term affair while they were both on the Rocking C?

Oh, hell. That was a crazy thought.

Lainie was the type of woman who was probably looking for a husband and kids—just like Kara Lee, who'd been on the prowl for Mr. Right and thought she'd found him in Craig Baxter.

And look how that had turned out. No, Drew didn't have any misperceptions about love and living happily ever after.

So who was he to mess with Lainie's heart?

He threw down the last of his merlot and said, "I'd better turn in for the night. Thanks for talking to me. I'll see you tomorrow."

"I'll be ready."

He returned the cork to the nearly empty bottle and placed it in the fridge. But before turning to go, a thought overtook him. "Do you have anything other than jeans or overalls to wear?"

Her brow furrowed. "Yes, why?"

"I realize we're just going to a ranch, but I told the Hoffmans you were my associate. So I thought you might want to... You know, dress the part?"

She looked down at her jeans and baggy blouse, then rolled her eyes. "Don't worry. I know how to dress professionally."

"I'm sorry. I didn't mean to offend you. In fact, you have understated class and look great no matter what you wear. Forget I said anything."

"You're forgiven." Her smile was pretty convincing. "Would business casual be acceptable?"

"That'd be perfect." He lobbed her an appreciative grin, then headed outside.

By the time he'd shut the back door, his lips had quirked into a full-on smile. Now he had something to look forward to.

And so did his nocturnal musings.

At nine o'clock on Friday morning, Brad's mother, Molly Jamison, arrived at the Rocking C Ranch driving a white Ford Taurus that had seen better days—or make that years. Lainie had been looking forward to meeting her, so she went outside to greet her in the yard.

But when a petite redhead in her midthirties climbed out of the car and pulled out a suitcase that was nearly as big as she was, Lainie's steps slowed.

Brad had to be close to twenty, so Lainie had imagined his mother to be in her forties or fifties. But she must have been a teenager when she'd given birth.

Not that it mattered. Tamping down her surprise, Lainie crossed the yard, introduced herself and reached out her hand in greeting. "It's nice to meet you. Do you need help with your luggage?"

"I don't have much," Molly said. "Just a single suitcase and an overnight bag."

Before Lainie could offer to show her where she'd be staying, Brad came out of the barn wearing a great big grin on his face. "Hey, Mom. I'm glad you're here. I'll take your stuff and put it in the cabin. I know you're eager to get a tour of the house and meet the men who live here."

"Thanks, honey." Molly blessed her son, who stood

a good six inches taller than her, with a warm smile. "I'm also ready to roll up my sleeves and help out."

"Let's start with a tour of the kitchen," Lainie said.

Molly resembled a young, red-haired Dolly Parton, but without the big hair, double Ds and the sparkle. Still, she had a sweet smile and a happy voice. Lainie liked her instantly.

She and Molly also had a lot in common, including the fact that they'd had to pull themselves up by their proverbial bootstraps, a fondness for the elderly and underprivileged children and a willingness to work.

So when it was time to go with Drew to Kidville, Lainie didn't have any qualms about leaving. The men would be in good hands with Molly.

Now, as Drew slid behind the wheel of his black pickup, which boasted all the bells and whistles, Lainie sat in the passenger seat, checking out the GPS and what appeared to be an upgraded sound system. The impressive, late-model truck had that new-car smell. At least, it did until Drew shut the driver's door, filling the cab with his faint, woodsy scent. "Ready?" He glanced across the console at Lainie, stirring her senses to the point of distraction. "Buckle up."

"You bet." But it wasn't just her body that needed to be secured with a seat belt. When it came to Drew, she feared her heart might be in for a bumpy ride.

She tried to keep her mind on the road ahead—and not on the bigger-than-life cowboy driving. But that was hard to do when he cut another glance her way, his eyes sparking. "You look great, Lainie."

Her cheeks warmed at the compliment.

"It wasn't easy to lay aside my overalls."

"Seriously?" He shot another look across the console, his brow furrowed.

She laughed, made a fist and gently punched his arm. "I'm kidding."

"Seriously," he said, "that's exactly the professional style I had in mind."

"I told you that I knew how to dress." She'd chosen a pair of low heels, black slacks and a tailored white blouse. She'd topped off her outfit with a red plaid scarf, then pulled her hair up into a topknot.

"I'm sorry for doubting you. You look great." He grinned, then winked before returning his gaze to the road ahead. A couple of miles later, he pointed to the right. "There it is. It sure looks a lot different than it did when the Clancys owned it. The perimeter used to be surrounded by rusted-out barbed wire and leaning posts. But not now. The Hoffmans have made a lot of changes to the place. If I hadn't seen pictures on the internet, I wouldn't have recognized it from before."

Lainie noted the solid, six-foot fence made of cinderblock posts and wooden slats. "It looks like they meant to protect the property and keep the children safe."

Drew turned into the driveway, where they stopped in front of a black, wrought iron gate. Using an intercom/phone system, he called the office. Once he identified himself, the doors swung open, granting them access to the property.

He continued on to a graveled lot and parked between a white minivan and a red sedan. They got out of his truck and headed for an arched entryway made of adobe brick. A wooden sign overhead read: Welcome to Kidville, Texas. Population 134.

"Do you think they have that many children living here?" Lainie asked.

"Brad said there was about a dozen, and Jim gave me the impression they'd just begun taking in kids. I think that's just their way of making Kidville sound like a real town."

She nodded, then continued along the dirt road, passing under the sign. Her steps slowed as she took in the grassy areas, a red schoolhouse, a newspaper office and even a hotel. The only areas without the quaint, Old West look were a volleyball court, a baseball field and a playground that provided a swing set, several different slides and a colorful climbing structure.

"Kidville's layout is amazing," she said. "No, it's actually mind-boggling."

"Yeah, it's pretty cool." Drew gestured for her to take the wooden sidewalk that led to the hotel.

"I've never seen anything like it." Sure, she'd watched television shows with similar settings, carefully constructed building facades and wooden sidewalks that portrayed Western life in the late 1800s. She'd also experienced living in a children's home for a while, but she'd never imagined seeing the two combined into one.

Drew had to be equally impressed because he took out his cell and began to take a picture.

"No, don't." She reached for his arm to stop him. "I would have brought my camera with me, but I'm sure they have privacy rules in place to protect the children. We should get permission from the Hoffmans first."

"Good point." Drew returned his cell to his pocket. "I hadn't thought about that. I'm glad you did."

"Where are we supposed to go?" she asked.

"Jim told me that the main office is located in the hotel, although he and his wife live in that white, two-story house next to the ball field."

Lainie spotted it right away. "Do you think all the children sleep in the house?"

"It looks big enough for some of them, but I didn't ask him about the number of kids they had or the living arrangements. Brad mentioned that his mom would be staying here, so there could be other staff members supervising children at night in some of the outbuildings."

In spite of the quaint setting, apprehension crawled through Lainie's stomach. Her thoughts drifted back to the day her caseworker had taken her from the hospital to the receiving home, where she was to complete her recovery.

She'd been walking slowly that day, more from fear and loneliness than pain. The woman had sensed her distress and had taken her hand to provide comfort and reassurance.

That lasted only about five minutes. Then Lainie was handed over to an employee who cared more about her need for a cigarette break than Lainie's need to feel safe and secure.

How odd, she thought, that those feelings would

creep back again today, as if she were being taken to a new home and to yet another, unfamiliar placement.

She wiped her palms on her slacks. When Drew's arm bumped her shoulder, she was tempted to take his hand in hers for reassurance. And it annoyed her that, at times, the past still seemed to have power over her.

"It sure is quiet," Drew said. "I wonder where all the kids are."

"Probably in school. A lot of children who come from broken, neglectful homes have never lived in an environment that encouraged education. So many of them lag behind in the classroom and struggle with their studies."

"Did you?" he asked.

"Yes, before my dad died. After that, I tended to bury my nose in a book and focus on my homework."

"Instead of boys?"

"Absolutely. Boys were a dead end." And in her experience, so were the grown-up versions for the most part. "My studies helped me forget what was going on around me." She scanned the quiet grounds. "I wonder if the kids are tutored here or if they go to a public school in town."

"Let's find out."

As she and Drew approached the hotel, a balding, heavyset man in his late fifties opened the door and came outside to welcome them. "I'm Jim Hoffman."

Drew introduced himself and Lainie, and they all shook hands.

"Come inside. My wife wants to go on the tour with

us, but she's got some business to take care of first." Jim led the way into the hotel.

Lainie didn't know what she'd been expecting. Something to match the exterior façade, she supposed, but the reception area looked more like a modern living room, with overstuffed sofas and chairs upholstered in faux leather, a southwestern style area rug and potted plants throughout.

A tall, slender redhead in her late fifties sat on one of the sofas, next to a boy with messy, dark hair who appeared to be seven or eight. She was telling him to be patient, that he'd see his little brothers soon.

"But you don't understand." The boy's brown eyes filled with tears. "They don't have nobody but me to take care of them. What if someone doesn't turn the light on for them at night? Abel is scared of the dark. And what if they don't know how to rub Mario's tummy when it hurts?"

"I promise to call their foster parents," the redhead told the worried child. "I'll make sure they know what to do."

The boy swiped at his tear-streaked face. His frown eased a bit, but he didn't appear to be completely convinced that all would be well.

"Donna?" Jim said, "I'd like to introduce you to Drew and Lainie, the people I told you about from the Rocking Chair Ranch."

"It's nice to meet you." She offered them a warm smile, then turned to the boy and placed her hand on his small, thin shoulder. "This is Andre. Mrs. Tran, his social worker, just brought him this afternoon to stay with us. He's going to join us for the first part of our tour, which will be the schoolhouse, and then we'll introduce him to his new friends and teacher."

The child sniffed, then bit down on his bottom lip.

"Hey, Andre," Drew said. "It's nice to meet you."

The boy studied Drew, scanning him from his hat to his boots. Sizing him up, it seemed. "Are you a cowboy?"

Drew smiled. "Yes, I guess you could say that."

The boy's eyes widened, and his lips parted. "A *real* one?"

"Well, I grew up on a ranch. And I work with the rodeo now."

"Do you have your own horse?" the boy asked.

"I used to."

Andre's shoulders slumped, clearly disappointed. He glanced down at his sneakers, one of which was untied, then looked at Drew. "But you do know about horses, right?"

"I sure do."

The boy looked at the Hoffmans and frowned. "Mrs. Tran told me there were horses here. But that's not true. They don't have any."

"We don't have any *yet*," Donna said. "We're working on it, though."

"We do have plans to buy a couple of good riding horses in the future," Jim interjected. "But in the meantime, we have plenty of other animals, like rabbits and sheep and goats. We even have barn kittens and a couple old dogs who'll lick your face and play ball with you."

"I know," the boy said. "But..." He scrunched his face and blew out a sigh, clearly perplexed about something. Then he looked at Drew. "Can I ask you a question?"

"Sure. Go ahead."

"When people have a bad leg and can't walk too good, can they still ride a horse?"

"I'm sure they can." Drew looked at Donna, who placed her hand on Andre's small shoulder.

"When Andre was four," she explained, "he broke his foot. The bone wasn't set properly, and there wasn't any follow-up treatment. So it left him with a pronounced limp. But fortunately, we have an appointment for him to see an orthopedic surgeon next week, and we're hopeful that they'll be able to correct that for him."

"But in case they don't," Andre said, his big brown eyes seeking out Drew, "do you think I can still learn to ride someday? I want to be a cowboy when I grow up, and you can't be a very good one if you don't have a horse."

"I'll tell you what," Drew said, "if it's okay with the Hoffmans, I'd be happy to give you a riding lesson, even if I have to borrow the horse."

The boy turned to Jim. "Is it okay? Will you let me?"

"I don't see why not. I'll talk to Mr. Madison and see what we can work out. But for now, you'd better go to the schoolhouse and meet your new teacher and the other children."

Donna stood and reached for Andre's hand, helping him up. Then she walked with him to the door.

Lainie followed behind, observing the boy's uneven gait. One of his legs was clearly shorter than the other. Her heart ached for him, and she lifted her hand to finger her chest. She knew how it felt to have her medical care neglected, to face a painful surgery without anyone to offer comfort and reassurance.

Would one of the Hoffmans stay at Andre's bedside, like the loving parents of other hospitalized kids had done? She certainly hoped they would.

When they reached the red schoolhouse, they went inside. The classroom smelled of crayons and white paste, reminding Lainie of days gone by. The teacher was collecting a math worksheet from her six students—seven, now that Andre had arrived.

"This is a combination class," Jim explained while his wife led Andre to the teacher. "They're in first, second or third grade."

The teacher, a blonde in her midthirties, offered the boy a kind smile. "I'm Mrs. Wright, Andre. I heard you were coming, and I'm so glad you're here. You're just in time for recess and an afternoon snack."

After leaving Andre with his new classmates, Donna led the tour outside, letting the door close behind them.

"That poor child has had a real time of it," Donna said. "He's the oldest of three boys, and up until child protective services stepped in to rescue them from an abusive home, he did his best to look out for his younger brothers."

"Where are the other boys?" Lainie asked Donna.

"In a separate foster home. We'd like to bring them

here, but we don't have the staff or the resources to take in preschoolers yet."

"That's something else we're working on," Jim said.

Lainie hoped adding younger kids would be a priority over the horses. And that the Hoffmans would be able to take in Andre's brothers soon. It was so unfair, and the injustice of the situation sparked her into action.

"Siblings shouldn't be separated," Lainie said. "I can tell you right now, we'll do whatever we can to help you get more funding—and to provide Andre's brothers a home at Kidville."

Donna pressed her hand to her throat. "I'm overwhelmed—and so glad to hear that."

Lainie glanced at Drew, aware that he might not approve of her making a commitment like that without talking it over with him first. It would be nice to have his blessing, but she'd meant what she said. Kidville was going to be her newest project—and she hadn't even gotten the full tour.

Chapter Seven

Drew had been impressed with Jim Hoffman, even before seeing him in person, so he was ready to climb onboard. But he wouldn't have blurted out a half-baked commitment without first discussing it with his "associate."

He might have been annoyed with Lainie for making a unilateral decision for them both, but when she looked at him with those soulful brown eyes, he'd been toast.

Hell, how did a man say no to a woman like her?

Besides, Kidville was a good cause.

"Here's what I have in mind," he said, as he fell into step beside Lainie. "Rocking chairs are associated with young kids, as well as the elderly. So Esteban Enterprises can easily cross-promote Kidville and the ranch at the same time."

"Don't get me wrong," Jim said. "We'd appreciate your efforts to bring in more financial support, but I worry about splitting the pot. I'd hate to see the Rocking C only get half of what they expected."

"Actually," Drew said, "I think we'll double the pot."

Jim glanced first at his wife, who gave him a cautious nod of agreement, then back to Drew. "Then we're game if you are."

An animated smile erupted on Lainie's face. "We'd like to start by inviting your children to attend a Christmas party at the Rocking C. We'll provide the refreshments, of course. And I'll even coax one of the retired cowboys to play Santa."

That'd be a nice touch, Drew thought. He could even publish a blog post about it afterward.

Lainie continued to lay out her plan. "If it's all right to take pictures of the children, it might make the promotion more personal and touching, which would encourage potential benefactors to be more generous. Christmas and kids should be a heartwarming draw."

"You're probably right." Jim scrubbed his hand over his receding hairline. "But we have a couple of children who should stay out of the limelight, if you know what I mean. So I'd like to look over any pictures you take before they're published or posted."

"Absolutely," Lainie said. "And just so you know, I plan to propose an article for *The Brighton Valley Gazette*. That is, if you don't mind. I'd let you look it and the pictures over before we go to press."

"Well now," Jim said, "this meeting is proving to be very productive."

"I think so, too," Lainie said. "Should we schedule the party on Christmas Eve? That would give us time to decorate the ranch, buy some gifts for the children and locate a Santa Claus suit."

"That would be awesome," Donna said. "Some of our children have never had a real Christmas."

"I know." Lainie's voice was soft and almost fragile. "I spent a few years in foster homes when I was a girl. And some of the kids I grew up with had sad backgrounds."

"I'm sorry to hear that," Donna said.

Lainie shrugged. "It's all in the past. But that's why I want to help your kids now."

Drew was a little surprised she'd been so forthcoming, but then again, the Hoffmans were an easy couple to like and to trust.

"I hope we can get some donations rolling in quickly," Lainie added. "I'd like to see you be able to bring Andre's brothers here as soon as possible."

Donna placed her hand on Lainie's arm. "Believe me, Jim and I want to see that happen, too, but since you're no stranger to foster care, you probably have an idea how long these things can take. It's not just the funding we need, it's licensing and paperwork, too. I'm afraid you'll have to be patient until Jim and I work through the system."

Lainie's cheeks turned a deep shade of pink. "Yes, of course. Sometimes I let my heart and enthusiasm run away with me."

Drew realized she was eager to see Andre's family reunited because, after losing touch with her twin sister, she knew how the poor kid felt. He could certainly understand that. He felt sorry for Andre, too, but for a different reason. He admired the wannabe cowboy's loyalty to his younger brothers and his determination to look out for them.

Family came first. Drew understood that. His mom might have passed away, but he was committed to looking out for his sister—whether she was a preschooler or a grown woman—for the rest of their lives.

"Let's continue the tour." Jim led them toward the barn. "Like I said, we don't have any horses yet, but I'll show you what we do have. We've done a lot of research on animal therapy and have put it to work here. It's a big part of our program."

Donna chimed in. "Each child will have their own animal to look after, which will give them something to love. And it will also teach them responsibility."

Twenty minutes later, after seeing two frisky Australian shepherds, four fluffy kittens, a chicken coop called the Peep-Peep Palace, a mama duck and her ducklings, as well as goats and sheep, the tour ended.

Lainie and Drew thanked the Hoffmans and promised to be in touch soon. Then they climbed into the pickup and headed back to the Rocking C.

They'd barely gone a mile down the road when Drew glanced across the seat and spotted Lainie sporting a grin.

"You sure look happy," he said.

"You're right. Helping the Hoffmans and those children has given me a real purpose."

"You've got good instincts. I'll give you that much."

Her smile deepened. "Thank you."

"However, don't ever pull a stunt like that again."

Her brow furrowed, and she cocked a sideways glance at him. "What are you talking about?"

"In the professional world, we don't offer services until we've discussed them with the entire team. Lucky for you, I agreed wholeheartedly with your idea and plan to run it past my boss for his approval. But if I'd had any qualms, I would have had to do some fancy backpedaling, and then we'd both look like idiots."

Her once happy expression sobered. "I'm sorry. You're right."

"Don't get me wrong," he said, "I appreciate your enthusiasm, and I'm glad supporting the Hoffmans and Kidville gives you a sense of purpose, but it's not the same for me. Promoting them is my *job*."

"I'm sorry if I overstepped. I shouldn't have used the word *we*."

A pang of guilt, as well as sympathy, lanced his chest. He hadn't meant to scold her, especially since this was more than a job to her. But he couldn't get carried away with soft, tender feelings—especially for Lainie. He had enough to worry about without taking another waif under his wing.

Yet just looking at her now, seated next to him in the truck, her eyes bright and focused on whatever she had on her mind, he wouldn't consider her vulnerable. She looked strong, proud…and lovable.

Whoa. Don't even go there. Drew returned his focus to the road. He'd better watch his step when he was around Lainie. Not to mention his heart.

* * *

In spite of being reprimanded by her "business associate" for being unprofessional, Lainie entered the house with her heart nearly bursting and her head abuzz with holiday plans. She'd thought she might be too excited to eat. That is, until she took her first step into the mudroom and the warm aroma of tomatoes, garlic and basil accosted her.

Molly stood at the stove, holding a wooden spoon in one hand and a potholder in the other.

"Something sure smells good," Lainie said. "Thanks for covering for me."

"You're welcome. I love to cook." Molly lowered the flame, then turned away from the pot simmering on the stove. "How'd the tour go?"

"Oh, my gosh." Lainie wasn't sure she could put her thoughts and feelings into words. "Kidville is amazing."

Molly burst into a smile. "That's exactly how I felt after my first visit. I'm so glad I get to work there."

"I can see why." Lainie scanned the kitchen. "Need any help?"

"No, I've got it all under control. But do you mind keeping an eye on the spaghetti sauce for a couple of minutes? I forgot to give Brad a letter that came in yesterday's mail, and he's waiting for it."

"No problem. Take your time."

Molly had no more than shut the back door, when the telephone rang. Lainie answered and was surprised to hear Mr. Carlton's voice on the other end.

"I've gotta tell you," the editor said. "If you continue to turn in quality columns like the one we just published, I might have to hire an answering service to handle all the calls we're receiving from Dear Debbie fans. I told you they're pretty vocal, and this time they weren't complaining. They like the direction the column is going. Of course, we did change the font and the layout."

Seriously? He was taking credit for the positive reader response?

Okay, so the advice she'd given had come from the mouth of a wise old man. But Lainie had written the column herself, using her own words, and she was going to stake a claim on some of that success, if not all of it.

"We also made it easier to find the column—right next to the obituaries." He chuckled. "Kind of apropos, don't you think? Life's a bitch, and then you die."

Lainie went silent. Did she really want to work for this guy?

"Just a little editorial humor, kid. But I'm glad Dear Debbie is finally back on track."

"Thanks. It's nice to know that you and the readers like what I've done. I also want to give you a heads-up about something else. I'm sending you a proposal for an article about a local children's home called Kidville. I took a tour, and it was impressive."

"I've heard about that place. What do you have in mind?"

She told him more—about the unique setting, the administrators and their animal therapy plan. But just enough to whet his appetite.

"Send me that proposal," he said, giving her the green light she'd been hoping for.

When the call ended, she was tempted to hole up in her room and outline her proposal, but she couldn't neglect the Dear Debbie column when she was on a roll. And that meant she'd have to come up with a clever answer to at least one of the latest letters.

Lainie had just checked the spaghetti sauce when Molly returned to the kitchen.

"What else can I do to help?" Lainie asked.

"Actually, not much. The tables are set, and I have everything else under control."

It certainly looked like it. The salad was made and in a bowl on the counter. The garlic bread was wrapped in foil and ready to pop into the oven.

"Are you sure?" Lainie asked.

"Absolutely."

"Then if you don't mind, I'll take off for a while, but I'll be back to help you serve dinner."

"Take your time."

Lainie thanked her, then with her confidence bolstered by Mr. Carlton's phone call, she slipped off to her room to look over the latest Dear Debbie letters.

Only trouble was, five minutes turned to ten, and as the tick-tocks of the windup clock on the bureau grew louder and louder, she feared she was going to be a one-column wonder.

There was, however, one letter that struck an interesting chord. It had been written by a woman who'd dreamed of getting married, creating a home of her own and having babies.

I met a great guy at work and was immediately attracted to him. He's sweet, funny and cute. I couldn't believe someone hadn't snatched him up already, and before long, I fell head over heels for him.

And that's my problem. I just found out that he's a widower with four small children.

If I marry him, I'd have to give up my dream of having a family of my own.

Lainie understood the woman's dream as well as her dilemma, but she sympathized with those poor, motherless kids. Her first impulse was to tell the woman that the two adults involved would have to be fully committed to the children or everyone would be miserable.

I fell head over heels for him…

Did she love the man enough to be his life partner? To join his team and mother those children as her own? It was impossible to know.

Lainie blew out a sigh. Doling out the wrong advice would be devastating.

What would Sully tell the woman? She glanced at the clock on the bureau. There was no time to ask him now. It was almost five o'clock, so she shut down her laptop and left it in her room. Then she went to help Molly serve the meals.

When she entered the kitchen, the young ranch hands had already gathered, and Brad was introducing them to his mom.

But it wasn't Molly or the cowboys who caught Lainie's eye. It was Drew, who stood off to the side, leaning against the doorjamb, his arms crossed in an alluring, masculine pose. When his gaze zeroed in on her, any plans she might have had scattered to the wayside.

"Got a minute?" he asked.

For him? She was tempted to say, "I've got all night." Instead, she nodded and let him lead her out to the front porch.

Once Drew and Lainie stepped outside and out of earshot, she asked, "What's up?"

"I'm not sure if you had a chance to speak to any of the nurses yet, but Chloe Martinez called a few minutes ago. She and her husband Joe own the Rocking C and plan to be home for Christmas. So I mentioned our plan to host a party for the kids."

"What'd she say?"

"Chloe loved the idea. In fact, she'd like to help pull it all together, but she and Joe are just finishing up their graduate programs at the university in Houston, and they can't leave school until the twenty-third."

"So the party's still on." Lainie beamed, her enthusiasm impossible to ignore. "That's awesome. There isn't any reason we can't get started with the planning and prep work."

"I guess not, but there could be a few bumps in the road."

Lainie's smile paled, and her lips parted. "What do you mean?"

"There's no telling what the old guys will think about it. Some of them, like Rex and Gilbert, can get a little crotchety. They might not appreciate having a bunch of children running around."

"Seriously? You think they'd be upset?"

Drew hadn't meant to steal her happiness, but he'd wanted to warn her of the possibility so she wouldn't be disillusioned if things didn't work out the way she wanted them to. He'd had his share of disappointing holidays.

"There's no way to know how they'll react until we tell them," he said. "And the sooner the better."

Lainie nodded, worry etched on her face.

He placed a hand on her shoulder to offer support and comfort. "Come on, let's go."

Then as he guided her into the house, his hand slipped around her in a show of solidarity. At least, that's what he told himself he was doing as they continued to the dining room, where the retired cowboys sat around the table.

"While you're all together," Drew said, "we wanted to share something we have in the works." He glanced at Lainie, who was biting down on her lower lip, which he found arousing. And distracting, so his words stalled for a beat.

Fortunately, Lainie shook off whatever apprehension she'd been having and spoke up for both of them. "Earlier this afternoon, Drew and I visited a home for abused and neglected children that's located a few miles down the road."

"You mean the one at the old Clancy place?" Sully asked.

"Yes, that's it." Lainie went on to sing the praises of

the Hoffmans and their innovative home. "So we had this brilliant idea about hosting a Christmas party for those kids here on the Rocking C."

Drew's hand slipped from her shoulder, his fingers trailing along her back until he drew away and moved closer to the table. "What do you say, guys?"

"Christmas is a lot more fun when little tykes are around," Gilbert said. "We'd better get a bigger tree than that scrawny stick we had last year."

Rex agreed. "My Jennilyn used to make a big deal out of decorating the house, baking all kinds of sweets and wrapping gifts. And that reminds me, we ought to have something under that tree for those kids."

"How many are living there?" Gilbert asked. "It might be nice if we took up a collection, then sent someone shopping for us."

At that, Sully chimed in. "I'm pretty good at wrapping. A few years back, I helped the local Four H Club at their gift wrapping booth they had at the Wexler mall."

"I'm glad to hear you're onboard," Lainie told Sully.

"Hey," he said. "I like kids."

"Good," Lainie said, "because you'd make a perfect Santa."

"Ain't that the truth?" Rex howled with laughter. "And Sully won't need any stuffing around his middle, either."

Sully puffed out his chest. "I'd be delighted to be Santa Claus." Then he turned to Rex. "I'd rather have a little meat and muscle on me than look like a bony ol' scarecrow."

Gilbert slapped his hand on the table and let out a hoot. "Now there's an idea. If we host a Halloween party for those kids, we can prop Rex up in the cornfield and let him play the part."

Lainie's excitement lit her pretty face. "You guys are the best, you know that?"

"Ah, shucks," Sully said. "No, we aren't."

"Speak for yourself, Sully," Gilbert said. "I'm thinking I'm pretty dang good."

Drew couldn't help but laugh at the men's humor. When Lainie looked at him, he gave her a wink.

And not just because their Christmas party was a go. If he had his way, promoting Kidville and the Rocking Chair Ranch wasn't the only joint venture they'd start up.

Four days later, Drew shook his head in disbelief. Somehow, he'd let Lainie rope him into making Christmas cookies.

"You do realize it's still more than a week before the party." He draped the red-and-white checkered apron she'd suggested he wear over the back of a chair. He didn't mind assuming kitchen duties. Heck, he'd done most of the cooking and cleaning after his mom got sick. But he'd never dressed the part. "I don't know why we have to bake cookies tonight."

"Because there's so much to do at the last minute." She sprinkled flour on the open breadboard, then handed him a rolling pin. "And this is something we can do ahead of time."

"But the cookies won't taste very good if they aren't fresh."

She didn't seem the least bit concerned. "I plan to freeze them and thaw them the night before the party. Don't worry. I know what I'm doing." Then she reached out, touched his forearm and smiled. "You agreed to help me, remember? You said you'd do anything that needed to be done."

"Yes, but when I made that offer, I was thinking more along the lines of getting the tree and decorating it."

"You can do that, too."

He'd had every intention of doing his part and more. He just hadn't expected to work in the kitchen. Or to be swayed into doing so by the singe of Lainie's touch or the warmth of her smile.

She placed a lump of dough on the floured board. "I appreciate your help. Do you know how to do this?"

"I'll manage." He'd seen his mom make biscuits before. And once, while she'd been on chemo and sicker than a dog, he'd stepped in and taken over for her. They'd purchased the heat-and-serve variety at the grocery store after that.

Lainie unscrewed the lid of a mason jar to use for cutting out circles. "I wish I had some real cookie cutters. Then we could make trees and stars and other Christmas shapes. But this time, plain round ones will have to do." She pointed to the lumpy side of the dough. "Roll it out evenly or the cookies will be lopsided."

Okay, boss." Drew rolled out the dough flat and

even, but the edges were cracked. "Am I doing this right?"

Lainie took a moment to look over his work. "That's perfect." She handed him the jar lid. "Make the circles as close together as you can."

He followed her instructions, then placed them on the pan.

"Let's get the first batch in the oven," she said, setting the timer.

He glanced at the large mixing bowl on the counter. They'd hardly made a dent in the dough. "How many of these are we going to make?"

"Dozens and dozens. I love frosted sugar cookies, don't you?" She didn't wait for his answer and went back to work, her holiday excitement impossible to ignore.

It was also easy to appreciate. She had a girlish look to her, not to mention a little flour on her nose. Yet at the same time—maybe it was the yellow gingham apron she wore—he saw a domestic goddess.

Lainie was going to make a good wife and mother. A pretty one. He imagined coming home each night after work and finding her in the kitchen, preparing his meals, and a zing shot through him.

He quickly shook off the thought. Was he nuts? Bumping elbows with her tonight was one thing. But words like *permanent*, *long-term* and *forever* weren't in his vocabulary.

Before long, a sweet cookie aroma filled the room. After Lainie pulled the first pan from the oven and replaced it with the next, she removed powdered sugar and a bottle of vanilla from the pantry. Then she took milk from the fridge and placed it on the counter, next to a cube of butter that was already softening.

From the amount of dough still in the mixing bowl, Drew figured they were going to have a boatload of cookies, yet Lainie measured out only a small amount of powdered sugar.

He studied her as she worked. She still had a dusting of flour on her nose, although she wasn't aware of it. And her sweet smile made him smile, too.

"Aren't you going to frost all of them?" he asked.

"Not the ones we're going to serve at the party. I'll do that the night before."

"I don't understand."

"I'm going to frost a couple of them now. Don't you want to see how the finished product is going to look and taste?"

Actually, Drew loved sweets. "Sure. Why not?" He watched as she whipped up the frosting in a bowl with a handheld mixer, then she added a couple drops of green food coloring and blended it together with a spoon.

"Mama Kate used to make the best cookies," Lainie said.

"Your first foster mom, right?"

Lainie nodded. "She always let me help her since I didn't play outside with the other kids."

Drew could understand why a girl might prefer time in the kitchen, cooking and baking. But by the way Lainie had said it, he got the idea that she rarely went outdoors. "Did you prefer being indoors?"

The spoon she'd been using to mix the frosting

stilled, then she started stirring again. "Back then, I wasn't really able to."

A bad memory? Or maybe it was just a simple, heartfelt reflection of the days she'd lived with Mama Kate and it made her sad.

He told himself it really didn't matter which, but for some reason, it did. "Why not?"

At first, she didn't answer and continued to mix the frosting. A couple of beats later, she said, "I was a little sickly back then."

She'd mentioned something about having health issues, but he hadn't considered them serious. "You mean, from an illness?"

She clicked her tongue and continued stirring. "It was no big deal. It's all in the past."

He was about to quiz her further, but she switched the subject on him as swiftly as a champion stock car driver shifted gears and changed lanes.

"Donna gave me a list with the children's names, ages and sizes," she said. "The men chipped in to buy gifts for them, and I volunteered to do the shopping. Do you want to go with me?"

"Not on a bet."

She laughed at his quick and telling response. But he didn't mind. He liked the sound of her laughter, the lilt of her voice.

"I hate to shop," he said.

"But you dress so well."

"That's different. I go to my favorite men's store sometimes, but not all that often. There's a clerk who works there and knows what I like. So I usually just give her a call and bam. Done. But in general, I'm not into shopping."

"Why?"

He shrugged. "When my mom was sick, that job fell on me. So I've always considered it a chore."

"But one that needs to be done." Lainie dripped more food coloring into the bowl. "You were responsible—and a good son. I'll bet your mom was proud of you."

"She was, but she hated having to rely on me to do everything." Drew could still remember her stretched out on the living room sofa, weak and pale and only a wisp of the woman she'd once been. Tears streaming down her cheek as she apologized for not being strong enough to take care of him and his sister anymore.

"I'm sure she enjoyed being your mom and felt badly when she had to give it up. That's how I'd feel, if I were a mother."

Drew glanced at Lainie, who had a maternal air about her this evening, especially when she wore an apron and baked cookies.

"Do you plan to have kids?" he asked.

"Yes, someday. But for now, I have the children at Kidville."

He was glad she'd taken those kids under her wing. She was clearly eager to make them happy. He suspected she'd do the same with her own someday.

She turned to him with a spoonful of green frosting in her hand. "Here, try a bite."

He opened his mouth and relished the creamy, sweet taste bursting on his tongue.

"What do you think?" she asked.

"It's good." He withdrew a clean spoon from the drawer, dipped it into the small mixing bowl and offered it to her. "Your turn."

"Okay." Her mouth opened and closed around the spoon, tasting it herself. Then she ran the tip of her tongue over her lips.

His knees went weak, and an almost overwhelming urge rose up inside, pressing him to take her in his arms and kiss her. But he couldn't do that. He shouldn't, anyway, so he tamped down the compulsion the best he could.

Still, he continued to study her.

"Hmm, this is really good." Her voice came out soft. Sweet. Smooth.

He couldn't help himself; he reached out and brushed the flour from the tip of her nose. Their gazes locked. Her pretty brown eyes darkened, and her lips parted.

His heart pumped hard and steady, and his hand stilled. The temptation to kiss her senseless rose up again, stronger than ever. But he wouldn't do that.

He shouldn't, anyway.

Yet as he struggled to do the right thing, the smart thing, desire trumped common sense.

Chapter Eight

Drew cupped Lainie's jaw, and his thumb caressed her cheek. Now was the time to release her and apologize for making such an intimate move, such a presumptive one, but the moment dissipated in a heartbeat.

Her lips parted a little wider. Whether it was in anticipation or surprise, he wasn't quite sure. But at this point, he didn't care which it was—as long as she didn't stop him. He set the spoon on the counter.

At least, he tried to. It clattered to the floor, but neither of them looked anywhere but at each other.

He took her in his arms, bent his head and lowered his mouth to hers.

The kiss was hot, yet sweet. And the taste? Sugar and vanilla and everything a man ever craved.

His tongue swept into her mouth. Her breath caught,

but she didn't pull away. Instead, she clung to him as if she might collapse if she didn't.

The kiss intensified, and so did his hunger. He couldn't seem to get enough of her taste, enough of *her*. He might have suggested that she go with him to the privacy of the cabin if he hadn't heard approaching footsteps and someone clearing their throat.

Lainie damn near jumped through the roof as she broke away from Drew's embrace, landing on the tip of the spoon and sending it sliding toward the doorway and ending at Sully's feet.

The jovial old man grinned from ear to ear. With his white hair and beard and wearing a red-and-green plaid shirt, he looked a lot like old St. Nick himself. Just the sight of him put a new spin on the old tune of "I saw Mommy Kissing Santa Claus."

In this case, it was Santa Sully who'd gotten the romantic eyeful.

"Hey, kids." Sully looked around the kitchen. "What's cooking?"

Besides Drew's blood pressure?

"I'm...sorry," Lainie said, lightly touching her lips. Her fingers trailed down to her collar. The top button of her blouse, barely visible under her apron, had come undone, and she fumbled to close it up tight. It was almost as if she was trying to hide behind that blouse, just as she'd hidden the pink, sexy panties under the denim overalls the day of the mouse encounter.

Drew would give just about anything to know why she seemed compelled to cover up. Was she wearing skimpy undies now?

"What are you sorry for?" Sully asked her, as he stooped to pick up the spoon. He set it on the counter, then turned to them with a big ol' grin that sparked a Santa-like glimmer in his eyes. Even his chuckle had a ho-ho-ho quality about it.

"Because I'm supposed to be working." Lainie quickly turned her back to them, reached for a cookie on the cooling rack that sat on the counter and showed it to Sully. "Would you like one? I'd be happy to frost it for you."

"Don't mind if I do," the oldster said. "I came down here looking for a bedtime snack. And a sweet one sounds pretty darn good."

Lainie got right on it, frosting not one but two cookies and handing them both to Sully. She waited while he wolfed one of them down.

"What do you think?" she asked.

"They're great. Best I've had in ages."

"Too bad I didn't have a Christmas tree cookie cutter."

Sully chomped into the second cookie. "You could call these ornaments."

"You're right."

As Lainie and Sully launched into a conversation about baking, the tree decorating and the gifts she planned to purchase and wrap for the kids, Drew retreated to the sink and started washing the bowls.

To him, it was just a bunch of nervous jabber, an attempt to put the kiss behind them and to pretend it hadn't happened. But it *had*.

And if it had the same effect on her that it had on him, it wasn't one either of them was likely to forget.

More than twelve hours had passed since the cookie baking session turned into a romantic moment and ended with an earth-shaking kiss. Yet Drew's memory of Lainie's sweet taste and the feel of her body in his arms hadn't faded a bit.

He'd tried to broach the subject with her after Sully left the kitchen last night, but she hadn't wanted to talk about it. She claimed she wasn't feeling well, that she needed to get some sleep and that she'd finish the baking in the morning.

She had looked a little tired. It was hard to say for sure, but he suspected, in reality, she was both shaken and troubled by the kiss.

He could understand why. He'd been stunned by it, too. But since he hadn't been ready to face any of those *now what* questions, especially when he didn't have an answer, he'd counted himself lucky and had gone back to his cabin.

All during breakfast, Lainie had bustled about the kitchen, but she'd hardly glanced his way. And the only thing she'd said to him was, "Good morning."

Even when Sully came in from the dining room for a second cup of coffee and thanked her for a tasty meal, she'd followed it up with a simple, "You're welcome."

Her cheeks bore a constant flush, though. So he decided the only thing bothering her was that kiss.

It might have been an ornery move on Drew's part,

but he'd set up an after-breakfast interview with Sully in the kitchen.

He doubted Lainie'd like having both men return to the scene of the passionate crime, but after Sully went on his way, Drew would broach the subject. And who knew? He might even instigate another kiss.

But things hadn't worked out the way he'd planned. Moments after Sully took a seat at the table and Drew poured them each a cup of coffee, Lainie slipped out of the kitchen and didn't return.

"Something's bothering Lainie," Sully said. "Is she upset because you kissed her last night? Or just about being caught?"

"I'm not sure." Drew took a sip of coffee. "Some women aren't easy to figure out. And Lainie's one of them. But just for the record, I don't have any regrets. It was a great kiss."

"She certainly seemed to be enjoying it," Sully said. "My guess is that she's not sure what to do about it."

Drew wasn't, either. But that didn't mean he wouldn't like to kiss her again. Lainie was proving to be... Well, intriguing, to say the least.

"I really like that little gal," Sully said.

"I do, too." Drew stared at his coffee for a second. "What do you know about her?"

Sully lifted his mug, blew at the steam rising from the top and took a sip. "Not much. She's a sweetheart. Pretty, too. But her friends are a little iffy."

"Seriously? That surprises me."

"Yeah, me, too. But it's probably because she has a big heart. Too big, I suspect."

"What do you mean?"

Sully sat back in his chair. "It's nothing, I guess. It's just that, over the last couple weeks, she's come to me with one question or another. It seems that either one of her girlfriends or someone she knows has a problem, usually due to their own making." Sully slowly shook his head. "I gotta tell you, Lainie really needs to choose some new friends. Some of them don't have the sense the Good Lord gave a goose."

Was that a red flag? Had Sully spotted a flaw in Lainie that Drew had failed to notice? Or were her questionable friendships merely the sign of a warm, loving heart? Either way, Drew intended to find out.

Sully clucked his tongue. "I guess everyone has a weakness."

"You're right." And Drew figured some of them also harbored a few secrets.

For a while the men didn't say anything.

"Cookies aside," Sully said, "how're the party plans coming along?"

"Everything seems to be on track."

"Say," Sully said, "I was thinking. Why don't we wrap up that Christmas party with a good, old-fashioned hayride and a sing-along? The church my wife and I used to attend would have one each summer to celebrate the children's promotion to their Sunday school classes. And we all had a lot of fun."

"Good idea. The kids would probably like that."

"There's an old wagon in the barn," Sully said. "You should check it out. It's probably an antique by now and hasn't been used in years. So you'd need to clean it up and fill it with straw. They don't have any draft horses on the Rocking C, but you could hitch it up to the John Deere. Might be a good idea to mention it to Nate and see if he agrees."

"Yeah. I'll share the idea with Lainie, too."

That's not all Drew would like to share with her, but for the time being, his romantic plans had hit the skids.

That might not be a bad thing. Maybe he should back off for a while—or at least, take things slow and steady.

Yet that didn't mean he wouldn't dream about her tonight and relive that sweet, arousing kiss all over again.

Lainie stood in the kitchen, chopping celery, pickles and hard-boiled eggs to mix into the potato salad she was preparing for lunch. But her mind wasn't on her work. It was on that luscious, romantic moment she'd shared with Drew in this very room last night. A tingle raced up her leg to the back of her neck.

As he'd held her in his arms and kissed her senseless, she'd completely lost her head until Sully interrupted them. At that point, she'd finally returned to earth. Yet even now, she wasn't back on solid ground, and she didn't know what to do about it.

One kiss would surely lead to a second, but then what?

Dread picked at her. She wasn't ready for an intimate relationship—and not just because of that horrible debacle at that hotel lounge in Houston, when Craig Baxter's wife caught him and Lainie together and assumed the worst.

Lainie didn't blame Kara Baxter for thinking that her husband had a lover. To be honest, that's the direction the relationship had been heading, but Lainie had been reluctant to become intimate. And for good reason.

She fingered her chest, felt along the cotton fabric that hid the raised ridge. In college, her first real boyfriend and almost-lover had balked at the sight of the long pink scar.

"Why didn't you warn me?" he'd asked.

She'd cried, and he'd apologized, but the whole evening had turned out to be disappointing and they'd broken up. After that, she'd vowed to be more careful with her affections.

Then Craig came along, and she'd decided to give him a chance. Looking back at the way things had ended between them, she thanked her lucky stars—and her ugly scar—that she hadn't let him convince her to make love.

But tell that to the world. While the cell phone cameras focused on Craig and his pregnant wife, Lainie had rushed to her car in the parking lot, but she hadn't been able to outrun the internet. By nine o'clock the next morning, the scene had gone viral, the comments devastating. You'd think people would consider Craig the villain, but they seemed more focused on how he hovered over his wife, how he cooed to her, caressed her...

And that left Lainie to take all the heat. Even the blogosphere and all the network gossip shows got on the bandwagon, leaving her both hurt and angry.

She took out her frustration on a stalk of celery, chopping it hard and nicking her finger in the process.

"Ouch!" She tossed the paring knife in the sink.

See? That's what happens when you let your emotions get in the way of good sense. You screw up.

She sucked her finger, the metallic taste of blood lingering like a bad memory and an unearned reputation as a temptress and a home wrecker, when all she'd ever wanted was to love and be loved.

Now, here she was, considering another attempt at a relationship.

Was Drew different from Craig? Could she trust him to see past her scar and into her heart? Quite frankly, she wasn't sure, but she was tempted to give him the benefit of the doubt and risk being hurt again.

She glanced down at the flannel and denim she'd pulled out of the closet after her morning shower. She'd kept her curls contained in a topknot, but on a whim, she'd applied a coat of pink lip gloss and a little mascara.

It felt good to tap into her femininity again. Maybe it was time to start dressing the part. She might not have the money to buy expensive clothes, but she'd always been style conscious. And she wasn't going to wear loose tops and baggy pants the rest of her life.

For now, though, she'd focus on preparing lunch.

"Hey, Lainie?"

She turned toward the doorway, where Drew stood, his hair stylishly mussed, and wearing a dazzling smile. Why did he have to be so appealing?

Drew made his way into the kitchen. "Sully had

a suggestion for the party. What do you think about wrapping up the festivities with a hayride and a sing-along?"

"I think that's a great idea."

"There's an old wagon behind the barn. We'd have to clean it up, but it should work out perfectly for what we have in mind. Do you want to see it?"

"Absolutely." She turned to the sink, and washed her hands then grabbed a dish towel to dry them. "Let me put the potato salad in the refrigerator."

Minutes later, they'd left the house and walked around the barn, where a large, buckboard style wagon was parked on a thick patch of grass in the back.

"This is it," Drew said.

At first glance, it looked to be about a hundred years old and weather-beaten. It didn't just need a good cleaning, it could use a coat of paint, too.

"It has potential," she said.

"I've already checked out the structure, and it looks all right. One of the wood slats on the side needs to be replaced, but with a little work, it'll do just fine."

"The kids are going to love a hayride, especially Andre. I'll bet he'll be in seventh heaven."

"I was thinking about him," Drew said. "The next time I'm in town, I'm going to buy him a child-size cowboy hat."

Lainie leaned her hip against the wagon's open tailgate and gazed at him. "That'd be really sweet. I'm sure he'd love it."

He shrugged a single shoulder. "I figured he would."

"You know," she said, pressing her palm on the open

tailgate and finding it sturdy, "you promised to let him ride a horse. He'll be disappointed if it doesn't work out for some reason."

"I know. That's why I've already talked to Nate about it. He suggested we use a gentle mare named Felicity."

Lainie hopped up on the tailgate and took a seat. "I'd planned to call the Hoffmans later today to talk about the party plans. If it's okay with you, I'll ask them if Andre can come here before the party to ride Felicity."

"Sure, go ahead. I'd be happy to work around their schedule."

"Then if they don't have any objections, I'll set up a day and time that works for everyone."

Drew continued to study her, his gaze sweeping her face. "You're something else, Lainie."

She wasn't entirely sure what he meant, but her chest warmed and her heart fluttered at what was surely a compliment. She crossed her ankles and swayed her legs, a nervous reaction that might seem a little girlish, but there was something very grown up about what she was feeling—and about the way Drew was looking at her.

"There's something else I wanted to bring up while we're out here alone," he added.

Uh-oh. Here it comes. The kiss chat she'd been dreading. Yet for some reason, she wasn't the least bit worried about having it now.

"It was fun last night. I'd like to finish what we started."

Was he talking about the kiss? Or the baking session? Either way, she didn't dare ask.

"After that," he said, "maybe we can roll out the remaining dough and make more cookies."

Heat singed her cheeks, and her heartbeat kicked up to a lively pace. So he'd been referring to the kiss. She was tempted to slip off the tailgate and make a mad dash to the house, but before she could move, Drew closed in on her, blocking her escape route.

"I hadn't meant for that to happen," she said, "but it...just did."

"It was a nice kiss, don't you think?"

That's not how she'd describe it. She'd use words like *sweet, arousing* and *sensual*.

"Just *nice*?" she asked.

"Actually..." His lips quirked into a crooked grin. "On a scale of one to ten? I'd rate it an eleven or twelve."

Now it was her turn to smile. "Something tells me you've had plenty of kisses to compare it to, so I'll take your word for it."

"You haven't?" he asked.

She wasn't about to admit that she lacked any real experience worth counting. "I thought it was pretty good."

"Good enough to try it again someday?"

She ought to tell him no, to set up some boundaries between them, to protect herself from entering another bad relationship, but she couldn't deny the truth.

"Sure," she said. "Maybe someday."

He closed the two-foot gap between them, which seemed to be his way of saying, *Then why not now?*

For the life of her, she couldn't come up with a single objection.

He placed his right hand along her jaw. His fingers slipped under her ear and reached the back of her neck. The pad of his thumb caressed her cheek, scrambling her brain and setting her senses on high alert. All the while, he studied her face as if he could read every single detail about her life, every memory in her heart.

Lainie could've sworn he was going to kiss her again, and she wasn't sure what to do about it—if anything.

Fight? Flight?

Or should she just roll with it?

Preparing to make a move of some kind, she placed her palms on the tailgate and shifted her weight. As she sat back down, one side of the tailgate cracked and her seat gave way. She let out a scream, grabbed Drew and brought him crashing to the ground with her.

Chapter Nine

Drew had been blessed with quick reflexes, but when the wood cracked and the bracket broke, he didn't have much time to react.

He tried to catch Lainie, as her fingernails dug into his arm, but she still slid down the slanting tailgate, pulling him to the ground with her.

He rolled to the side, thankful for the thick patch of long grass that softened their landing, and propped himself up on his elbow. He hovered over her, brushed a silky strand of hair from her face and searched her eyes. "Are you okay?"

"I think so." She blinked a couple of times. "Nothing hurts."

"Good." He probably ought to help her up, but he liked being stretched out beside her, gazing at her pretty face, taunted by her soft floral scent. It was an arousing position.

Admittedly, there were better, more romantic places for a proverbial roll in the hay than a patch of grass, next to an old buckboard wagon, but he wasn't about to suggest a change in position, let alone location. Not while he had Lainie in his arms again. He felt compelled to kiss her long and hard.

He really shouldn't. But she was studying him intently, practically inviting him to do it.

When her lips parted, he was toast.

As their lips met and his eyes closed, they returned to that blissful, intimate state they'd reached last night. Their bodies naturally took off from where they'd left off.

Drew rolled her with him to the side, finding a comfortable spot away from the wagon, and continued to kiss her thoroughly. Tongues mated, breaths mingled and hearts pounded out in need.

He stroked her back, his hands bunching up the flannel fabric that separated his fingers from her skin. But a simple article of clothing, no matter how blousy, couldn't hide the soft, feminine body underneath.

He slid his hands along the curve of her spine and down the slope of her hips. As his mouth continued its gentle yet demanding assault, Lainie let out a soft whimper, sending a rush of desire coursing through his veins.

Unable to help himself, he slipped his hand under the hem of her shirt, seeking the woman inside. As he felt along her warm skin and explored the curve of her waist, his testosterone flared. He inched his way up to the edge of her satin bra, soft and sleek, and sought her breast. But the moment he cupped the full mound, she jerked away as if he'd crossed an invisible line.

And hadn't he? Considering the circumstances, where they were and how they came to be there, she probably thought he was way off base.

She'd seemed more than willing, though. That is, until now.

"I'm sorry," he said. "I guess I got a little carried away."

She sat up, lifted her hand to her collar, fingering the flannel fabric, and slowly shook her head. "No, I'm the one who should be sorry. I didn't mean to overreact. I hope you don't think I was being a tease."

A flush covered her throat, indicating her own arousal. She bit down on her lip, which was still plump from the gentle assault of their kiss. "It's just that…" She scanned the area around them. "This isn't the time or the place."

She had a point, but he made light of it by tossing her a playful grin, hoping to ease her discomfort or embarrassment. "Well, the timing was okay with me. And I admit this probably isn't the place. But no one saw us, so we're the only ones who know what happened."

She got to her feet and, after righting her shirt, she pointed at the wagon. "I think, once that tailgate is fixed, this will work out perfectly for what we have in mind."

He wasn't about to mention what *he'd* had in mind,

what he was still thinking, but he followed her lead and rose from the grassy ground.

"Or better yet," she said, "maybe we should ask around the neighboring ranches and see if we can borrow something similar."

Avoiding a person or a subject seemed to be her primary line of defense.

His first thought was to mention it, to take her back to the subject at hand, but it was probably in his best interests to let it go for now. Did he really want to talk about what they'd just done and what it might mean?

He was definitely attracted to her. And the clock was ticking since he'd be leaving the Rocking C after the party.

"I planned to call the Hoffmans later today," Lainie added. "So I'll ask if they have any concerns about the kids having a hayride, although I don't think they will."

She clearly didn't want to address their undeniable attraction, the heated kiss they'd just shared or where it might lead. He should leave it at that, right?

"While I'm on the phone, I should probably lock in a time for the party. How do you feel about two o'clock? Or should we include the children for lunch?" She bit down on her bottom lip again, but this time, when she looked up, her eyes glistened like warm honey. "There's so much I want to do."

"You're really excited about this party, aren't you?"

"More than you know." She ran a hand through her hair, which had gotten mussed with the tumble and the kiss. Her fingers caught on a tangle, and she tugged through it. "But it's not just about this particular party.

After Christmas, I'm going to stay in close contact with the Hoffmans and do everything I can to support Kidville. My heart's gone out to those kids, especially Andre."

Drew felt the same way. "I'd like to continue helping them, too. I mean personally and not only through Esteban Enterprises."

"Jim and Donna will be happy to hear that. They're going to need all the support and manpower they can get." Again, she pointed to the buckboard. "And speaking of manpower, who's going to refurbish this wagon and make sure it's safe to carry the kids? And where do we get the straw?"

"I'll take care of it. And I'll rope Sully and Rex into helping me. It'll be good for them to have a job to do and something to look forward to."

Lainie smiled. "That reminds me, I need to get back to the kitchen, or lunch won't be on the table by noon." Then she turned and walked away as if nothing had happened, as if they'd never kissed.

Drew studied her from behind, watching the sway of her denim-clad hips and the way that flannel shirt ruffled in the light afternoon breeze. He felt badly about feeling her up, especially if that's what had unsettled her. But he'd felt compelled to learn what she was hiding underneath her unflattering fabric façade.

And if things worked out the way he hoped they would, one day soon he'd find out.

Lainie hurried toward the house, determined to escape Drew and the powerful yet unsettling feelings he stirred up inside her. But now that she'd kissed him and experienced his heated touch, she doubted her efforts would work.

He'd set her soul on fire, and as he'd caressed her, she'd nearly melted into a puddle on the grass. His touch created an ache deep in her core, and she'd nearly forgotten she had a physical flaw.

But when his hand moved dangerously close to her chest, she'd suddenly realized that he was just one tantalizing stroke away from stumbling upon her scar. And she'd freaked out like a feral cat. How embarrassing was that?

If things progressed between them, if they became lovers—and if truth be told, she wasn't opposed to that any longer—she'd tell him about the surgery and prepare him for what he was about to see. The last thing she wanted was for him to be repulsed, just as Ryan had been when he'd frozen up and turned a romantic moment ugly.

But then again, Drew seemed to be different from Ryan—and certainly from Craig. Could she risk being completely honest with him?

She was healthy and whole now. Besides, it might not matter to Drew that she bore a hardened ridge and a pale white line that would never go away.

At the possibility that he might accept her completely, an idea sparked and a new game plan arose.

She'd start looking like herself again. First step: wearing lipstick instead of the gloss she'd applied earlier. And she'd choose clothes that were more feminine, more stylish. More flattering. Then, when the subject came up again, and the timing was right, she'd level with him about her surgery.

By the time she opened the back door and entered the house, she felt much better and a lot more confident. And when she spotted Sully seated at the table, she burst into a smile.

"There you are," her old friend said. "I've been looking for you."

Thank goodness he hadn't gone in search of her behind the barn!

"I went with Drew to see the wagon he'd like to use for the hayride," she said. "Is everything okay?"

"Everything's hunky-dory. I just wanted to share some good news."

"What's up?"

Sully leaned back in his seat, clasped his hands and rested them on his rounded belly. "A few years back, I used to be a member of the Brighton Valley Moose Lodge. Every December they'd have a holiday party, and Santa Claus always made a showing. So I called an old friend who's still active with the group and asked if I could borrow their suit after they finish with it."

"What'd he say?"

"They'll loan it to us. And after I told him why we needed it, he offered to have it dry cleaned and promised to deliver it himself." Sully grinned from ear to ear, clearly pleased with his contribution to the party.

"That's great," Lainie said. "Things are coming together nicely. Getting a Santa suit is one thing I can mark off my list, but there's still a lot to do."

"Let me know if there's anything else I can do to help."

"Thanks, I'll keep that in mind." She'd also have to remember to place that phone call to Kidville. She didn't want to make any more plans before talking things over with the Hoffmans first.

After Sully left the kitchen, Lainie glanced at the clock over the stove. She'd better get the chicken in the oven or it wouldn't be ready by noon.

Ten minutes later, using the old-style phone that hung on the kitchen wall, she placed the call to Kidville.

When Donna answered, Lainie launched into their party plans, including the hayride that would wrap up the day. Just as expected, Donna gave her full approval, and they settled on a one o'clock start time.

"There's something else I had on my mind," Lainie said. "We offered Andre a horseback ride, and Drew found the perfect horse for him, a gentle mare named Felicity. Would it be all right if Andre came to the Rocking C for a lesson within the next few days?"

"That would be awesome. He seems to be adjusting pretty well to being here with us, but he's still very concerned about his little brothers. Maybe visiting the ranch and riding a horse will help him take his mind off his worries, at least for an hour or two."

"Are the younger boys together in the same foster home?" Lainie asked.

"I wish they were. Sadly, there are more children in the county who need a place to live than families willing to take them in. But Mrs. Tran, their social worker, believes siblings should be together whenever possible. So I hope and pray they won't have to be separated too long."

Lainie's heart clenched, and her grip on the telephone receiver tightened. "Are the children adoptable?"

"I expect the youngest boys to be cleared soon. Their father is serving a life sentence without possibility of parole. And from what I understand, he's going to surrender parental rights, which would make Abel and Mario eligible for adoption."

"But what about Andre?" Lainie's grip on the receiver tightened until her knuckles ached.

"I'm not sure. His father ran off years ago, and no one knows where he is. On top of that, the poor kid is facing several surgeries and some extensive rehab, so he's in limbo. At least, legally. Jim and I are doing all we can to make him feel loved and safe."

Lainie had no doubt about that, but still...

"I'd take all three boys in a heartbeat," she said, "if that meant they could stay together. But I'm not prepared to provide them with a permanent home just yet."

"That's sweet of you to even consider it," Donna said.

Lainie wasn't just blowing smoke and offering something she didn't expect to follow through on. It had been a heartfelt offer, and she wanted to make sure Donna realized it.

"I'm serious," Lainie said. "I'd have to do some footwork first. I have a small apartment in town, so I'd need to find a bigger place." Not to mention a better-paying job.

Then again, if Lainie went to work full-time to support a family, she'd need day care for the kids. And that wouldn't allow her to give them all the time and affection they needed—and deserved.

Or would it? A lot of single parents had to work, yet they still found a way to spend quality time with their kids.

"Would the state allow me to adopt as a single woman? Or at least, become a foster mother?"

"I can place a call to Mrs. Tran and ask," Donna said. "Or better yet, I can give you her number."

Lainie sucked in a deep breath, then let out a wobbly sigh. "My position at the Rocking C is only temporary, so I'd need to find a different job first. Maybe it would be best if I called Mrs. Tran after I get settled."

The more she thought about it, the more the idea sounded like a pipe dream that couldn't possibly come true. By the time she was capable of providing those children with a home, Mrs. Tran might have found a better living situation for all of them. Or by then, Kidville would be able to expand and accept younger children.

Hopefully, Andre's little brothers were in loving environments and would have a nice Christmas this year, even if they…

"Say," Lainie said, "could we invite Andre's brothers to the party? We'd include their foster families, too, of course."

"That's a great idea, and I know Andre would be thrilled if they came. I'll call Mrs. Tran and see what she has to say. It might be difficult to coordinate something like that on Christmas Eve since everyone could have different holiday plans. But it might work. In the meantime, when did you want to schedule that riding lesson for Andre?"

"As soon as possible."

"I'm happy to hear that," Donna said. "That little boy has had to face a lot of broken promises in the past."

Lainie could certainly relate to that. The two men she'd once cared about had been big disappointments, too.

But then she'd met Drew. Hopefully, if she were to consider having a relationship with him, it would prove to be a lot more promising than the other two.

Drew stood on the front porch, drinking a cup of coffee and waiting for Jim Hoffman to bring Andre for his riding lesson. The morning air was crisp—not exactly cold, but chilly enough to know winter had crept in on them.

When the screen door creaked open, Lainie stepped outside with a plastic container in her hand. He'd already seen her at breakfast this morning and noted the change in her. She'd ditched the baggy denim for a pair of snug black jeans and a stylish, curve-hugging sweater. She'd even applied lipstick.

But seeing her now, without the full-length apron to cover her up, he realized he was going to have a hell of a time keeping his eyes off her and focused on Andre and his riding lesson.

"What have you got there?" he asked.

"Just a couple of carrots and an apple. I thought Andre could give them to Felicity before or after his ride. But I thought I'd better ask you first." She glanced out to the corral, where Felicity was saddled and tied to a hitching post. "Is that her?"

"She isn't used to getting much special attention, so she'll like having a treat."

"Sounds like she and Andre have something in common," Lainie said.

Drew was getting some special treatment today, too. Not only was Lainie a lovely eyeful, she was wearing a new fragrance, something soft and tropical, which seemed out of place at a ranch. Actually, now that she'd ditched the baggy denim and blousy cotton, she seemed out of place here, too.

He'd found her attractive before, but today, she was beautiful and downright sexy.

From what he'd seen so far, it appeared that she had a good heart, and an unusual thought struck him, one that was a little too domestic for a man who'd made up his mind to remain single the rest of his life.

That decision had been fairly easy to make, when the people who should have loved and supported him as a kid had all failed him one way or another—whether through sickness or desertion.

Okay. So Kara had never let him down, but that was different. She wasn't supposed to look after him. It was the other way around.

"Come on." Drew gave Lainie a gentle nudge with his elbow. "I'll introduce you to Felicity."

They'd just stepped off the porch when a white mini-van pulled into the yard.

"Oh, good," Lainie said. "Andre's here."

The moment Jim and the boy climbed out of the vehicle, Andre broke into a happy grin.

"I've never been on a ranch before." His small brown eyes glowed with excitement. "I didn't think today would ever get here."

"That's true," Jim said. "He hardly got a wink of sleep last night, and he's been jabbering nonstop about cowboys and horses ever since we told him about the riding lesson."

"I'm glad we can provide a little fun for him," Drew said.

"So am I." Jim placed his hand on the boy's small shoulder. "I'd love to stay in the yard and watch you guys, but I'm taking a new medication for the next week or so, and I'm supposed to stay out of the direct sunlight."

"Why don't you sit on the porch," Drew said. "I have a feeling several of the retired cowboys will soon join you. They like sitting in those rockers in the shade."

"Great. I'd like to meet them." Jim placed his hand on the pint-size, wannabe cowboy's head. "Have fun, Andre." Then he turned and headed toward the porch.

"This is so cool." Andre scanned the pastures, the corral and the barn. "I wish Abel and Mario could be here to see this."

Drew glanced at Lainie, whose glassy eyes revealed her sympathy. Rather than stir up any sadness—hers or Andre's—he decided to let the boy's comment ride.

But Lainie faced it head-on. "I'll try to set up a visit for your brothers to come to the Rocking C, too."

Why had she offered something she might not be able to pull off? If it didn't work out for any reason, it would only make the poor kid feel worse.

"That'd be awesome." Andre looked up at Lainie as if she held all power, all knowledge... All hope. "Can I come again when they get their lesson?"

"Of course you can. They won't have as much fun without you."

There she went again, committing Drew to something without running it by him first.

Of course, she hadn't actually included him in her plan, but she wasn't going to be living on the ranch much longer. How did she think she'd find time to set up another visit with two separate families?

"Andre," she said, as she stooped to tie the boy's shoes, "tell me about your brothers. I can't wait to meet them."

Aw, man. Why'd she have to go and do that? The poor kid didn't need those sad, painful feelings stirred up. He needed to learn to tamp them down. If Drew had allowed himself to get sucked into the emotions his mom and sister had once faced, he wouldn't have been able to stay strong for them.

"Mario is four," Andre said, "and Abel is six. They have a different dad than me, and I'm glad about that because he's in prison." Andre glanced down at his sneakers, which were now double knotted, then back at Lainie. "I never met my dad, but my mom told me he was a cowboy. And the best one ever. So when I grow up, I wanna be just like him."

Drew's gut twisted at the thought that Andre's dead-beat dad had become a superhero, a mythical cowboy who'd bailed out on his own flesh and blood, just like Drew's old man had done.

"Do you have any idea where your father might be?" Lainie asked.

"No, but he's probably working on a ranch like this one. He's a nice man, and not like Pete. My dad would never hurt a kid or a mom."

At that, Drew's hand fisted, and his heart clenched so hard it almost choked off his air supply.

He wasn't about to stand here and let Lainie resurrect the past, ruining the boy's day—and possibly his future. So he had to put a stop to it here and now.

"Come on," he told Andre. "I've got a hat for you in the barn. Once you're dressed like a real cowboy, I'll introduce you to Felicity, the mare you're going to ride."

"Cool," the boy said, as he limped along with Drew. "I can't wait to ride her."

When he and Andre returned from the barn, Lainie was waiting for them inside the corral and next to the mare.

"You look like a real cowboy." She tapped the top of his new hat. "Now let's see how you look mounted on Felicity."

Apparently she intended to stick around and witness the boy's first ride, which was okay with Drew.

He liked having her around—at least, as long as she didn't pry or poke at tender feelings.

As Drew walked toward the gate, Andre limping along beside him, Lainie lifted the plastic container. "I brought this so you could give Felicity a treat before you ride her. I have an apple and two carrots. Which do you want to give her?"

Andre looked at Drew. "Which one would she like best?"

"Let's give it all to her." Drew reached into his pocket, pulled out a Swiss Army knife his sister had given him last Christmas and cut the apple into chunks.

"Is it bad for her to eat big pieces?" Andre asked.

"No, but she'll gobble it up so fast she won't get a chance to taste it. Let's make her work for it." He handed a chunk of apple to Andre, then showed him how to keep his hand open flat while he offered it to her.

Just like the cowboy he wanted to be, Andre took to feeding a horse quickly. All the while, he beamed and giggled.

Felicity seemed to take a real liking to him, too.

"Let's get you in that saddle," Drew said, "so we can start your riding lesson."

Minutes later, as Drew adjusted the stirrups, he glanced up and caught the happy smile on Andre's face. His chest filled with warmth, just knowing he'd had a part in putting it there.

The lesson began, and Andre was a natural. Before long, Drew was able to step back and let the horse and boy move about the corral.

As he leaned against one of the posts, Lainie stood next to him, only the white wooden railing separating them.

"Look at him," Drew said. "He's having the time of his life."

"You're good at this," Lainie said.

At what? Surely she didn't mean he was good with kids. His expertise was horses, although he had to admit to having a soft spot for a disabled kid who wanted to grow up to be a cowboy. But he thanked her just the same.

Then he looked over his shoulder, caught her profile, the thick dark lashes, lengthened by mascara. The turned-up nose. The fresh application of dark pink lipstick.

"You look pretty today," he said.

"Thank you."

"What's the big occasion?"

She shrugged a single shoulder. "I just wanted to look nice for Andre's big ride."

"Then it worked."

Her smile reached her eyes, sparking a glow that made the color look amber.

"Those black jeans are a lot more flattering than overalls," he said, wondering what style panties she wore today. Were they pink and lacy like before? Or maybe satin like the soft bra he'd touched the other day?

He didn't ask, and she didn't comment further. Instead, he checked on Andre, who had a steady grip on the reins. The kid was a quick study, which was good since Drew couldn't keep his mind or his eyes off Lainie.

Maybe it was her scent, which reminded him of a big, frozen piña colada, complete with a slice of fresh pineapple.

She was pretty damned tempting—sweet and intoxicating. What he wouldn't give to get her alone. To see if she tasted as good as she smelled.

He really didn't know that much about her, though. But since he didn't make long-term commitments, did that even matter?

The next time he had a moment alone with her, he just might suggest they have an affair while they were both here.

That reminded him, time was slipping away.

"Are you still planning to edit my blog posts?" he asked.

"Sure. Have you started it yet?"

"I wrote about one of the cowboys, but it's still in draft form and needs work. I thought that you might want to look it over and tell me what you think. It'd be nice to know if I'm heading in the right direction."

"I'd be happy to." She offered him another smile, and he was again struck by her beauty. And by the appeal of a romantic distraction until Christmas.

"I've got some things to do in the kitchen," she said. "So this isn't a good time to see what you've pulled together. What about after dinner tonight?"

Bedtime? He liked the sound of that.

"Perfect," he said. "I'll have my laptop all set up.

Once you think the first blog post is ready to go, I'll schedule it and start work on the second one."

"I'm looking forward to it," she said.

So was he. Hopefully, she'd be agreeable to love-making. Only trouble was, they'd both be moving on and going their own ways soon. So he'd better suggest it tonight.

Chapter Ten

Lainie could hardly wait to finish her evening chores, slip away from the house and head to the cabin where Drew was staying. And she suspected that he felt that same eagerness.

Several times during dinner she'd caught him gazing at her so intensely that it seemed as if he was looking beyond her outward appearance and into her very heart and soul. It had been a little unraveling, but in a good way.

He didn't know about the scar yet, but she planned to tell him about it tonight.

She ought to be nervous about that, but she wasn't. She'd come to realize Drew was special. A flood of warmth had filled her chest when she saw him with Andre today, when she'd observed the kindness he'd shown, the sensitivity. She'd nearly melted when she'd watched him slow his steps so the limping boy could keep up with him.

And that's when she'd lowered her guard and finally faced what she was really feeling for him.

They would work on his blog tonight, but they'd also have a heart-to-heart talk. No more secrets. No surprises.

Besides, Lainie's congenital heart defect had been corrected years ago. And that scar was her badge of courage, as one of the nurses in the pediatric intensive care unit had told her.

She'd have to tap into that bravery while she waited for his reaction to her revelation like a timid little girl being wheeled into the operating room to face the unknown. Would he accept or reject her?

Shame on him if he didn't, yet her heart swelled with hope. She'd come to care deeply for Drew. She might even love him. At least, that's what she'd imagined love might feel like. And if he gave her any reason to believe he felt the same way, she'd come out and tell him to his face.

Once Lainie had washed the dishes and put them away, she blew out a ragged sigh, then glanced at the clock on the wall, ticking out the minutes until she could see him again. It was nearing showtime. So she returned to her bedroom to freshen up—and pull out all the stops.

As she stood in front of the bathroom mirror, she ran a brush through her hair and let the curls tumble down her shoulders the way they used to. She'd gotten tired of hiding her looks, her identity.

Heck, she might even tell him about that fiasco with Craig. That way, in case he ever heard about it, he'd know the truth.

After reapplying her lipstick and mascara, she used a little blush, although she probably wouldn't need it. Excitement and nervous anticipation were sure to paint her cheeks a warm, rosy hue.

Before leaving for Drew's cabin, she took one last look in the mirror. She wanted to put her best foot forward before knocking on his door tonight.

Pleased by the familiar image looking back at her, she said, "This is it."

Now was the time to let Drew know who she really was. And to find out if he would accept the real Lainie.

After eating dinner in the kitchen with the ranch hands, Drew returned to his cabin to get ready for Lainie. He was excited about her visit—and not just because he wanted her help on writing up his interviews.

Something told him that tonight was going to be special, and that he should be prepared for anything. So he'd taken a shower, slipped into a clean pair of worn jeans and put on a Texas A & M polo shirt. Once an Aggie, always an Aggie. Right?

His hair was still damp when he sat down at the dinette table, his makeshift home office, and booted up his laptop. He may as well set the scene so Lainie would think that work was the only thing he had on his mind, but his hormones had already caused his thoughts to stray in a sexual direction.

He wished he could offer her a glass of wine or a cold bottle of beer. All he had to drink was coffee or soda pop, which would have to do. But an adult beverage would be a lot more conducive to romance.

Then again, so was a sugar cookie.

And a broken tailgate.

He'd just logged on to the internet when an online call from his sister came through. The last time they'd talked, Kara had insisted that she was doing well. Hopefully, that was still the case.

"Hey," he said, once they connected. "What's up?"

"Not much. Just the same old, same old. But I'm hanging in there."

He could see her stretched out on her bed, where several big, fluffy pillows propped up her head. She appeared to be a little pale, but maybe it was just the lighting.

"When's your next doctor visit?" he asked.

"I see her on Monday. Since I've made it another week, she might let me start moving around again."

"I don't blame you for wanting to get out of bed. You've been housebound for so long."

"Yeah, I know. Who'd think going to an obstetrical visit would be something to celebrate?"

He laughed. "Not me. How's that woman I hired to help you working out?"

"She's great. She sits with me during the day and keeps me company. We're watching entire seasons of *Downton Abbey.*"

Drew'd pass on that. "And how's her cooking?"

"The best mac and cheese this side of the Mississippi."

"Don't get fat."

She patted her tummy. "Ha, ha." Then her expression turned a little more serious. "How's life on the Rocking Chair Ranch?"

"Not bad. A couple of the retired cowboys are a real hoot. And all of them are pretty cool, with interesting pasts."

"Have you started writing the blog?"

"Yeah, but it's still just a draft. I've asked a woman who lives here to edit them for me."

Kara readjusted herself in bed. "Who is she?"

"Her name is Lainie. She's filling in temporarily for the ranch cook. She's a nice woman, and she's talked me into helping her plan a Christmas party."

"Hmm." A slow smile stretched across Kara's lips, providing a little color to her face. "Do I sense a little romance in the air?"

A zing hit his stomach. "No, but I have to admit, the thought has crossed my mind." Drew glanced at the clock on the microwave. Maybe he ought to end his call before Lainie arrived. His sister was more than a little nosy and could be pushy at times.

Then again, he could always introduce them. What would it hurt?

He was still pondering a decision when a knock sounded at the door. He didn't have to open it to know who'd arrived.

Aw, what the heck. Why not?

"Hang on, Kara. She's here now."

"Ooh. You mean I get to meet her? That's cool. You usually keep the women you date at a distance."

"Just from you." He scooted his chair back and got to his feet. "And just so you know, we're not dating. Not yet, anyway."

He heard Kara laugh in the background as he answered the door and let Lainie inside.

Damn, she looked good tonight. She was dressed to kill in a pair of sleek black slacks and a white blouse. And that hair? A man could get lost in soft, flowing curls like that. She'd freshened her lipstick, too. Red this time.

Clearly, Drew wasn't the only one who had romance on the mind, and it took every ounce of self-control not to welcome her with a heartfelt, hormone-driven kiss.

"Are you going to invite me in?" she asked.

"Sorry. Of course." His tongue tripped over the words, and he stepped aside.

Again, he regretted that he didn't have anything to offer her stronger than root beer or an after-the-lovin' midnight snack.

As they crossed the small living area to the laptop, he said, "You're just in time to meet my sister."

Lainie scanned the interior of the tiny cabin, which was obviously empty, and her brow creased.

"She's not actually *here*. She's online—I'm talking to her now." He led her to the laptop, where his sister waited on the screen. A smile tugged at his lips. Kara had been right. He'd always kept his relationships private and hadn't introduced her to any of his lovers in the past. But Lainie was different. Maybe he did have a domestic side he'd kept hidden.

"Kara," he said, waiting to witness their first interaction. "This is Lainie."

Drew wasn't sure what he'd expected, but certainly not his sister's strangled gasp.

He shot a glance at Lainie, who'd slapped her hand to her throat and recoiled as if she'd just spotted another mouse in the cabin. No, worse than that.

"What in the hell is *she* doing with you?" Kara asked.

Drew didn't understand. He glanced first at his startled sister on the screen, then at Lainie, her eyes wide, the color fading from her face.

"I'm sorry," Lainie said. "I had no idea…"

"About what?" Drew was at a loss. What was happening?

He looked back at the screen to see Kara sitting up in bed, no longer resting her head on a pile of pillows, her finger raised and shaking. "Oh, my God, Drew. I don't believe it. You're dating the woman who broke up my marriage."

"Lainie? No way." He'd seen the brunette in question—or rather, her image when that bar scene video had gone viral. Her hair was the same color, and her curls bounced along her shoulders when she strode away from the restaurant confrontation in a huff.

But now that he thought about it, their faces *were* similar. Especially with Lainie's red lipstick.

"I have no idea what's going on," Drew told his sister. "But I'll get to the bottom of this. And when I do, I'll call you back."

Drew disconnected the call, turned to Lainie and folded his arms across his chest. "I don't understand. Who are you? And what's my sister talking about?"

"I can explain," Lainie said. "I did date Craig, but not very long. And just so you know, I haven't seen him since that awful day at the hotel."

Dammit. "You're Elena?"

"Yes, but I can explain."

No wonder she'd seemed familiar to him. And now he was looking at the woman who'd slept with Craig, destroyed his and Kara Lee's marriage and nearly caused his sister to lose her baby. Apparently, he'd been wrong about Lainie or Elena or whatever her name really was.

"Go ahead." His eyes narrowed. "I'm listening."

"I had no idea Craig was married," she said. "I didn't even know who he was—I don't follow the rodeo circuit. He lied to me and led me on."

Drew's stomach twisted into a knot. Craig was an ass, that's for sure. But the whole idea sickened him. Damn. He'd almost gotten involved with a woman his ex-brother-in-law had slept with.

And worse, just seeing Lainie at the cabin with Drew was going to kill his sister. Hell, it was bothering the crap out of him just to think about it.

"Don't look at me like that," Lainie said. "There's no way I would have gone out with Craig if I'd known he was married."

"I can't buy that. How could a journalist be so naïve? That is, if you actually *are* a journalist."

"Now that—" she stabbed her finger at him "—is insulting."

"You can't be a very good one if you didn't figure out Craig was married. He's not a hermit. And practically everyone on the circuit knows Kara."

She sucked in a breath. "I screwed up. Okay? I'm human."

And one who was sexier than he'd ever seen her before. Just look at her all dolled up. Had she planned to come on to him tonight? And if so, for what purpose?

He raked his hand through his damp hair, stymied. Perplexed. Pissed.

"Apparently, you believe the worst about me," Lainie said.

He didn't want to. But maybe it was easier that way, to get angry and cut his losses before she inflicted even more pain on his family. Besides, he couldn't very well choose between Lainie and Kara. And he damn sure couldn't sleep with his ex-brother-in-law's lover.

"Believe it or not," Lainie said, "your sister wasn't the only victim in all of this."

Maybe so, but the only victim who really mattered right now was Kara.

"You should leave," Drew said.

"No. Talk to me."

How could he? "You've put me in an awkward position." And an impossible one, it seemed. "Tell me something. Did you know Craig was my brother-in-law?"

"No, of course not. Do you think I'm scheming you or something?"

"Either that, or again, you're a lousy journalist. If you had even an ounce of investigative chops, you would have found out about my family."

Her expression went from angry to hurt, and she threw up her hands. "I give up. It isn't worth it." Then she turned on her heel and headed for the cabin door. Before reaching for the knob, she paused and turned back to him. "I hope your anger at me won't stop you from helping Andre and the other children at Kidville."

"I wouldn't do that," he said. "I intend to follow through on my commitment to get financial support for those kids."

"That's a relief. And for the record, I plan to make that Christmas party special—with or without your help. Those kids have had too many disappointments in life."

She gave him only a beat to answer, but a flurry of emotion balled up in his throat, making it hard to speak, even if he could have found the words to say.

Then she let herself out, the door clicking shut behind her, severing what little connection they'd once had.

Drew flopped onto his bed and scrubbed his hands over his face. He should be relieved that she was gone, but an ache settled deep in his chest. Now what? He'd always been a fixer, but he didn't have a clue how to clean up this mess.

A hodgepodge of emotion swirled around his heart like a Texas twister. Regret that his sister had been hurt. Disappointment that Lainie wasn't the woman he'd thought she was. And worse yet, fear that she actually was that woman and that he couldn't pursue her now. Not after she'd slept with Craig and had been involved in his sister's divorce.

But he wouldn't try to sort through his tangled up feelings when he had a phone call to make and a sister to calm. The last thing he needed right now was for Kara to go into premature labor again.

Tears streamed down Lainie's cheeks as she marched across the yard and away from the cabin, but she was too crushed and disappointed to swipe them away. She'd been let down yet again by a man she'd once cared about. Only this time, it was different—worse. She'd allowed herself to become way too invested in Drew, when she should have known better than to take that risk.

On top of that, she was angry as hell. He'd not only considered her a floozy and a liar, which was bad enough, but he'd accused her of being a lousy journalist, the one thing she had pride in.

Sure, she should have done a background check on Craig. And on Kara. Heck, she should have done one on Drew, too. But was she supposed to dig into the lives of everyone she met?

"Ooh!" She had to walk off some of the built-up steam before entering the house. She circled the outside of the empty corral, trying to shake off her grief and come to grips with her emotions.

Drew had assumed the worst about her and wouldn't

let her explain. Gosh, you'd think he'd at least listen to her side of the story. After all they'd done together—the long talks, the visit to Kidville, the Christmas plans they'd made…

And what about the amazing kisses they'd shared?

Darn it. She'd actually begun to care about him, to believe he was different, that he was worth her affection. Given time, she might have fallen in love with him.

But who was she kidding? Her feelings for him bordered on love already, if she hadn't actually taken a hard tumble into a romantic abyss.

Her heart ached, but as she circled the corral a second time, hurt gave way to anger. She wanted to lash out at someone. Anyone.

It was almost funny, though. In the past, she might have gone undercover or run away, like she'd done after that horrible confrontation with Craig's wife—or rather, Drew's sister—at the Houston hotel restaurant.

But Lainie wasn't about to slip into old habits. She might have had a lousy childhood and faced some difficult hurdles, but she'd come a long way since then. That, in itself, demanded that she hold her head high from now on.

She was Elena "Lainie" Montoya, up-and-coming journalist. She was also "Dear Debbie" to Mr. Carlton. And from this day forward, she didn't give a rip who knew her true identity or what she stood for.

And she'd no longer struggle with her outward appearance, either. She liked what she saw in the mirror and would embrace it, whether she chose to wear denim or silk, overalls or stilettos.

Lainie had a *lot* going for her. She was a recent college graduate with a bright, shiny future ahead of her. Someday she'd be an investigative reporter who would change the world, one story at a time.

Tired of circling the corral, she headed toward the barn. She paused near the buckboard, which was barely visible in the darkened yard. Her heart clenched as she looked at the grassy ground, where she'd been so swayed by Drew's kiss that she'd nearly convinced herself that he was the guy she'd been waiting for all of her life. And that they could have something special together, but she'd better forget that crazy idea.

One day soon, she'd have it all—a successful career, a family of her own *and* a loving husband. She just hadn't met him yet.

Feeling much better and back in control of her thoughts and emotions, she turned toward the house, but she wouldn't go inside just yet. She wanted more time to suck in the cold ranch air, to remain in the shadows and form a game plan from this night forward.

She'd hardly taken a single breath when the mudroom door swung open, and Sully walked out.

"There you are," Sully said. "I wondered where you ran off to."

Lainie continued to stand outside the ring of the porch light, where Sully couldn't detect any lingering moisture on her face.

"I just wanted a little fresh air and exercise," she said. "Did you need to talk to me?"

"Only to tell you I'm going to Tennessee, but I plan to be back for the Christmas party."

"Seriously?" Panic at the unexpected announcement laced her voice. "Why?"

"My brother's in the hospital."

"I'm so sorry to hear that. What's wrong?"

"His ticker is giving him grief, but the doctors say he's going to be okay. He wants to move to the Rocking Chair Ranch as soon as he's discharged, but his family isn't onboard. I plan to talk to them on his behalf, and then I'll bring him back with me."

"How long will you be gone?"

"A few days. You gonna miss me, sweetie?"

"Of course I will." And on many levels. Lainie certainly understood why Sully had to go, but her next column was due before he could possibly return. "When are you leaving?"

"First thing in the morning. And way before breakfast, so I thought I'd better tell you goodbye now."

How in the world was she going to be able to offer advice to the lovelorn without the wise old man's help?

Worse yet, who was she going to confide in about her own heartache and disappointment?

"You look worried," Sully said.

"Just about the party," she lied. "The kids will be disappointed if Santa isn't here."

"Don't worry, Lainie. I'll be back at least three days before the party. You can count on me."

Apparently, Sully was the only man she could count on, so she eased into the light emanating from the porch, swiping her eyes with the back of her hand and forcing a carefree grin.

As she continued forward to offer Sully a goodbye hug, he squinted and crunched his craggy brow. "Don't you look pretty tonight. But are you crying?"

"No, I had something in my eye."

"That better be all it is, because if one of those cowboys around here has hurt your feelings or toyed with your heart, he'll hear from me."

"Just a piece of straw or an eyelash. But it's out now." She embraced her sweet old friend, breathing in the faint scent of laundry soap on his green flannel shirt and catching a whiff of chocolate. "Did you get into the leftover brownies for another bedtime snack?"

"Don't tell the nurses," he said. "They think I'm getting fat."

If Lainie's heart hadn't been so heavy, she might have laughed. Instead she smiled. "I won't say a word about you raiding the kitchen to appease your sweet tooth. At least, not until after the party. I wouldn't want the kids to see a skinny Santa."

"No worries about that." Sully chuckled. "And just so you know, I've been practicing. How's this? *Ho, ho, ho! Merry Christmas.*"

At that, Lainie did laugh. "It's perfect." Then she followed him into the house.

"I'd better turn in," he said. "It'll be time for me to head for the airport before you know it."

And it would be time for Lainie to turn in that blasted column before she knew it, too.

Once inside her bedroom, she was tempted to crawl

into bed and forget about her deadline until tomorrow. But the sooner she took a look at the latest batch of letters, the better off she'd be.

Interestingly enough, and right off the bat, she spotted a problem she could respond to.

Dear Debbie,

I'm so upset with my sister (I'll call her Connie) that I can hardly see straight. We had a crappy childhood and grew up in a dysfunctional home. Since we only had each other, we've always been very close. But recently, Connie started dating this guy (I'll call him Mike). I told Connie I didn't like him, but she didn't care. Now she spends every waking hour with him and doesn't have time to go to lunch or a movie with me. We don't even talk on the phone anymore.

Last night, Connie came home with an engagement ring. She announced that she was going to marry him in a couple of months and asked me to be her bridesmaid. I told her that was way too soon. She needs to get to know Mike better. I mean, he's still in college and works as a barista at a local coffee place. So it's not like she's marrying a guy who can support her the minute they say "I do."

We argued, and things got ugly. I refused to attend her wedding, so she told me she'd ask Mike's sister to stand up with her. How's that for loyalty?

I'm tempted to disown her—or whatever it is

*siblings do when they don't want to be related
anymore. But I'm not quite ready to do that. At
least, not yet.*

*So here's my question, Dear Debbie: How do
I talk her out of marrying a guy she's only known
for three months? That's not enough time for her
to find out if he's going to turn out to be a mean
drunk like our father was. I'm only trying to protect her, but Connie doesn't see it that way. How
do I convince her she's wrong?*
Brokenhearted Sister

An answer came to Lainie right away, so she
cranked up her laptop and got to work. The words
flowed easily, and her advice was heartfelt and sound.

Apparently, she'd learned a lot from talking to
Sully in the past, from listening to the way he rea-
soned things out.

For the first time, she'd responded to the writer as
Elena Montoya, sharing things she'd never told anyone.
She knew a thing or two about being hurt, about having
people betray her. And, sadly, about betraying people
herself, even if it had been completely unintentional.

But it felt good be authentic. To give advice from
her heart. She just wished she'd been authentic with
Drew, too.

Or course, it was too late for that. And maybe that
was just as well. It was one thing sharing her heart and
soul to a stranger and under the guise of Dear Debbie,
and it was another to reopen old wounds and lay herself
open and vulnerable to a man who'd broken her heart.

After shutting down her laptop, she walked over to the bedroom window and peered out into the night. She didn't expect to see Drew's cabin in the dark, but with the inside lights blazing, she spotted it right away.

Was he still awake? Was he working on the blog?

Or was he, like Lainie, mulling over what they might have had and lost?

Chapter Eleven

It was nearing midnight, but Drew wasn't ready for bed or even close to falling asleep. Just a couple of hours ago, he'd called Kara and told her to think about the baby. He'd reminded her that her tiny son needed a peaceful environment in which he could grow, and that's all it had taken to convince her to calm her down.

On the other hand, Drew was still wound up tighter than a guitar string ready to snap. He couldn't get over the revelation that Lainie had been Craig's lover.

Now, as he paced the floor of the small cabin like a caged mountain lion, he wished he could relax. He probably ought to use his time wisely by working on his blog, but the only thing he could focus on was Lainie.

Who was the woman who'd nearly stolen his heart? Angel or vixen?

He wished he knew. His gut told him she wasn't the type to intentionally date a married man. He'd always been a good judge of character. Shouldn't he trust his instinct when it came to Lainie?

Then again, she had a deceptive side, a major flaw he'd failed to see. Even Sully had pointed it out.

I guess everyone has a weakness, the old man had said.

It seems that one of her girlfriends or someone she knows has a problem, usually due to their own making. Then he'd added, *Lainie really needs to choose some new friends. Some of them don't have the sense the Good Lord gave a goose.*

Drew hadn't met any of her friends, and after what Sully had told him about them, he hadn't wanted to.

Still, if she had some loser friends, was that a bad sign? Or was it the result of having a naïve and loving heart?

She was good with the old cowboys—and with kids like Andre. Didn't that prove she was kind and thoughtful? But then again, was that just an act?

There'd been other incidents and comments made that might've offered him a clue. Like the day she'd touched his forearm and dazzled him with a pretty smile. *You'll help me, won't you? You said you'd do anything that needed to be done.* She'd practically batted her eyelashes, working her wiles on him.

He'd failed to pick up on the possibility that she might've been playing him. Instead, when she'd zapped his nerve endings with her touch and gazed at him sweetly, he'd been captivated and completely swayed.

Sure, helping her plan a Christmas party for the children wasn't a bad thing. But that wasn't the point. Hadn't she just blurted out the idea, committing him to help before asking him first?

Then there was that sexually charged embrace near the barn earlier today. She'd been kissing him back like there was no tomorrow, when all of a sudden she'd torn her mouth from his and pushed him away as if he'd been a real horn dog. Yet just a heartbeat before, she'd made it pretty clear that she wouldn't mind if he'd taken her right there, in the soft grass and under cover of an old buckboard.

I didn't mean to overreact, she'd said. *Or to be a tease.*

He'd accepted her response at face value, but now he couldn't help wondering if she'd known exactly what she'd been doing.

Had she played on Craig's attraction to her in that same way?

Drew didn't want to believe so, but he supposed it was possible. Hadn't Lainie taken to wearing makeup recently? Was that an attempt to draw Drew deeper under her spell?

There lay the crux of his problem. He couldn't figure her out.

Even if she was as goodhearted as he'd once thought she was and Craig had duped her, like he had so many other people, Drew would still have to give her up for good. How could he date her knowing how his sister felt about her? Besides, no matter what the circumstances had been, she'd also slept with Craig.

Wasn't it easier—and safer—to believe the worst?

Drew blew out a ragged breath. More than two hours had passed since their online showdown, and he still wasn't anywhere near a decision or a judgment. He stopped pacing and glanced at the bed. He really ought to turn in for the night, but his thoughts kept tumbling and rumbling through his brain, making it impossible to rest.

Damn. He'd probably be up until dawn, stewing about Elena.

And ruing the fact that he'd never kiss "Lainie" again.

Much to Lainie's surprise, Drew hadn't avoided her. He showed up in the kitchen for breakfast the next day. But then again, he had to be hungry, and there weren't many other mealtime options in this neck of the woods.

She couldn't help noticing that he didn't look nearly as handsome as he had before. His hair was mussed as if he'd raked his hand through it a hundred times, and dark circles under his eyes suggested he hadn't slept a wink.

Was he worried about his sister? Had she gone into premature labor?

Lainie certainly hoped not. She didn't want Kara to lose her baby or to suffer any more than she already had.

Still, Drew looked worn. Tired. Uneasy.

She'd like to think his haggard appearance had to

do with guilt for being so mean to her last night, but his tight-lipped scowl told another story. Clearly, he hadn't softened toward her at all.

Only yesterday, he'd smiled as she bustled about, checking on the older men in the dining room, as well as the young hands who ate in the kitchen. He'd seemed to take pleasure in her movements. But today, as she served the men, replenishing their cups with fresh coffee and putting warm biscuits, butter and honey on the table, he didn't seem to notice her at all.

No, things had clearly changed between them—and permanently, it seemed. His frosty silence was pretty convincing.

As she continued to work, she did her best to ignore both him and his grumpy expression. But it wasn't easy.

She'd considered looking for a replacement to cover for her until Joy returned from her honeymoon and took over the kitchen duties. But Lainie couldn't leave before the party. The invitation had already gone out to Kidville, and there was no way she'd do anything to disappoint Andre or the other children. So she was determined to soldier on and see it through, at least until Christmas.

Besides, pouring herself into the party plans, baking cookies and creating inexpensive, homemade decorations would keep her busy and, hopefully, ease her heartache.

"These buttermilk biscuits sure are good, ma'am," Brad said.

Lainie thanked him. "Would you like another? I have more warming in the oven."

"No, ma'am. I've already had three and filled my belly to the brim. If I don't quit now, I won't be able to move, let alone work."

As the men began to push away from the table, she placed her hand on Drew's shoulder to stop him. "Can we talk a minute?"

His corded muscle tensed, and his eyes narrowed, creasing his brow. In some ways, his suspicion and distrust hurt her more than if he'd said, "There's nothing to talk about," and stomped off with the others.

"It won't take but a minute," she said.

He neither agreed nor objected, but he remained in his seat while the ranch hands filed out of the kitchen, into the mudroom and then out the door.

Once they were alone, she pulled out the chair next to him and asked, "How's your sister?"

Apparently he hadn't seen that question coming because the furrow in his brow deepened. "She's all right, I guess. It didn't help her to flip out after seeing you with me in the cabin."

Ouch. Yet in spite of the painful barb, she wasn't going to cower or apologize for something that had been all Craig's fault and none of her own doing.

"I'm glad to hear she's okay," she said.

His only response was a slight nod.

"I meant what I told you last night. I had no idea Craig was married. If I had, I would've run for the hills. Granted, I should have done a background check of some kind, an internet search of his name, but I didn't.

It won't happen again, though. I'll be more careful and skeptical from now on. And just for the record, I regret not checking up on you, too. I really should have, but I guess there's no need to anymore."

His eye twitched, but he didn't comment. If she were one to resort to violence, she might have shaken him until his teeth rattled. Instead, she pushed away from the table, standing tall, head high, her tears in check. "Someday, you're going to want someone's under-standing and forgiveness, and I hope you get it."

"Maybe I won't deserve it."

She took a deep breath, wondering why she was wasting her time on him. Misplaced hope and a ro-mantic delusion, she supposed, but her feelings and disappointment weren't the only things to consider. She had the Hoffmans and the children to think about.

"Do you still plan to support Kidville?" she asked.

"I told you I would."

"Yes, but I thought you might have changed your mind during the night. Of course, it's clear you haven't changed your opinion about me."

When he didn't respond, not even with a telltale blink of the eye, she bit down on her bottom lip, strug-gling with what to say next. They obviously didn't have a romantic future together, but they still had to cross paths.

"I realize there isn't a snow cone's chance in hell of us becoming friends," she said, opting not to use the word *couple*.

"And just so you know, I didn't ask you to stick around after breakfast so I could convince you otherwise. But we have a party to get through. Can we strike some kind of a cordial truce until I leave the ranch?"

"Sure, we can do that."

She let out the breath she'd been holding, relieved that they might be able to put things behind them. Yet, for some reason, it was important for him to know that she had a loving heart and good intentions.

"I'm going to adopt Andre and his brothers," she said. "Or if that doesn't come together for some reason, I'm going to take them in as foster children."

His response was sharp and immediate. "Are you kidding? How are you going to do that? You can barely support yourself and don't have a home. Why would you subject kids to an uncertain life?"

Lainie wasn't sure what hurt worse—his sharp tone or his lack of compassion. She never should have shared her innermost hope with a man who clearly didn't trust her or care about her feelings.

Sure, Drew had a point. She couldn't very well bring three young children into her life until she found a full-time job and a bigger place to live than a studio apartment. But she wasn't going to be bullied, hurt or taken advantage of any longer, especially by the likes of Craig or Drew.

Instead of fingering her scar and retreating, as she'd been prone to do in the past, she rose up to him and lifted her finger, jabbing his chest. "You're a self-centered jerk. You might not think so, but you're not any better than Craig Baxter. First you hurt my feelings, then you insult me."

As Drew gaped at her, his surly expression morphed into one of surprise.

"Cat got your tongue?" she asked, her own ire rising at a deafening speed.

"There's really not much to say."

"You're right."

She'd never wanted to clobber anyone so badly in her life, other than her drunken father. But he'd died in a barroom brawl when she and Rickie were seven, so she hadn't had to rise to the occasion. Besides, she'd never resort to violence, even if Drew made it oh so tempting.

"To make it easier for both of us," she said, "I'm going to try and find a temporary cook to cover for me until Joy returns. Either way, I'll stay out of your way until after the party. Then, by hook or crook, I'm going to create a home for Andre and his brothers. And you mark my words, I'll pull that off, or I'll die trying."

Then she turned on her heel and marched off, her head held high, but her heart and soul aching.

Drew stood alone in the kitchen, stunned by Lainie's anger and spunk.

Okay, so maybe he'd been an ass and deserved a good tongue-lashing after his gut reaction to her announcement that she intended to adopt not one, but three kids.

Her family plan was probably heartfelt, but so was Drew's response. He hadn't meant to come across so harsh, but she wasn't the only one thinking about the kids.

To this day he remembered going to bed hungry

as an adolescent, his belly empty and growling. After his mom got sick and could no longer work, money was tight and food was scarce, especially at the end of the month when her disability check ran out. So Drew often took less than his share at mealtimes to make sure his mother was able to keep up her strength and his sister had enough to eat.

Andre and his siblings might be separated, but at least they had warm beds and full stomachs at night.

Lainie couldn't blame him for connecting the dots to her living situation. She'd made it clear that she needed to find another job and another place to live. It didn't take a rocket scientist to realize she lacked the resources to provide for herself, let alone a family. What had she been thinking?

He supposed she'd been thinking with her heart. And that being the case, he had to admit that he and Kara might be wrong about her. Needless to say, he'd have to apologize to her, but he had some things to sort through before he chased after her.

The old-style ranch telephone, which hung on the kitchen wall, rang a couple of times. The nurses had their own phone back in the office, so it wasn't a call for them. Still, Drew doubted it was for him and waited for the answering machine to kick on.

When it did, a man's voice filled the room. "Lainie! It's Stan Carlton at *The Brighton Valley Gazette.* I've got good news, girl. I love that story proposal and want you to get started on it right away. And what's more, the Dear Debbie readership has grown impressively since you took it over. You're doing a great job. I can't wait to hear what the readers have to say when your next column comes out on Friday. Give me a call back at your convenience and we can talk about a raise in pay."

What the hell? Just about the time he thought he'd have to apologize for being a jerk, he hears this?

Lainie had lied to him. She'd told him that she hoped to land a job with *The Gazette*, but she already had one.

To top it off, she'd proposed an article, and it had been accepted. Did she have something underhanded in the works? Something that might exploit the old cowboys on the Rocking Chair Ranch or the children living at Kidville?

Dammit. Rather than offering up an apology, he was going to confront her with her lie.

Lainie tossed her freshly washed bedsheets into the dryer, albeit with a little more force than necessary. There was no point in taking out her anger, frustration and pain on the damp cotton percale, but it did help her work off some steam.

"There you are," Drew said from the doorway, his voice terse and not the least bit remorseful.

She glanced over her shoulder. "What do you want? Did you have more cruel barbs to sling at me, more false accusations to make?"

He leaned his shoulder against the doorjamb and crossed his arms. "Just one. You lied to me."

At that, she slammed the dryer door shut, turned to face him and slapped her hands on her hips. "How do you figure?"

"Stan Carlton from *The Gazette* called and left a message for you."

"What'd he say?"

"That your proposal was accepted, the Dear Debbie column is going great and that he's giving you a raise."

Finally. Some good news for a change. For a moment, she was so stunned—and pleased—that she forgot Drew had called her a liar. Well, more or less.

"You told me that you wanted to get a job at *The Gazette*," he said, "but apparently you already have one."

"Actually, it was a part-time position as the lovelorn columnist, and it didn't pay squat."

"You?" he said. "What do you know about love, let alone offering advice to people?"

"Not much, but thanks to Sully, I'm learning to problem solve."

Drew pushed away from the doorjamb and straightened. "What's that mean?"

"It's really none of your business. And you probably won't believe me anyway. But I needed to get my foot in the door at the paper, so I took the Dear Debbie position. Since I was at a loss on how to respond, I ran a few problems by Sully, who has more kindness, common sense and understanding of people in his little toe than you have in your big ol' cowboy body."

"You mean you don't have a bunch of troubled friends?" he asked.

She scrunched her face. "I have plenty of friends—smart ones. Nice ones from good families. But we all went different directions after college, and I'm new in Brighton Valley. I haven't made any local ones yet. Except for the men who live here."

"What about the article you proposed? What's that all about?"

What was this, the third degree? She wanted to tell him to take a very long walk off a short pier, one that stretched over shark-infested waters. But lashing out wasn't going to help much. She needed vindication.

"I proposed a big Sunday spread about the rodeo, the ranch and the children's home in hopes of gaining financial support."

His expression softened. Apparently, he'd begun to realize his assumptions and accusations might have been wrong. "I owe you an apology."

"Yes, you do. But right now, I'm not so sure I want to accept it." She turned around, set the dryer on high and pushed the start button.

When she turned around, he was still standing in the doorway, blocking her exit.

"Excuse me," she said. "I have work to do."

He stepped aside to let her out, and she marched off to find something to do. There was no point in arguing with a man who would never accept her for who she was.

Drew might not have faith in her, but she had faith in herself. Whether he believed it or not, she was going to help Andre reunite with his brothers. And somehow, in the process, she'd finally have a family of her own.

Chapter Twelve

Over the next couple days, Drew kept to himself, but by Friday, his niggle of guilt grew to a steady throb in the chest. He'd been wrong about Lainie, but he had no idea what to do about it.

He could tell her he was sorry, and she might accept his apology. But what about Kara? She wasn't apt to be as understanding or forgiving. And if not, that would really complicate his life.

Before breakfast, Drew climbed into his pickup and drove several miles down the road to the mom-and-pop market, where some of the locals hung out to while away the time and shoot the breeze. Once he'd parked in front, he entered the store.

A tall, wiry clerk sitting behind the register looked

up from the crossword puzzle he'd been working and smiled. "Howdy. Just let me know if I can help."

Drew sniffed the warm air. "Is your coffee fresh?"

"Sure is." The clerk got to his feet. "I just made a new pot. Can I get you a cup?"

"Yes, large. Black and to-go."

"You got it. Want a donut to go with that?"

Why not? He hadn't eaten breakfast. "Chocolate, if you have it."

As the clerk took a disposable, heat-resistant cup from the stack and filled it, Drew asked, "Do you carry *The Brighton Valley Gazette*?"

"You bet." The clerk pointed a long arm to the left of the register. "It's a dollar."

Drew retrieved the newspaper from the rack and returned to the register for his order. He paid with a twenty, pocketed his change and returned to his truck.

Instead of going back to the ranch, he settled in the cab, opened the small-town paper and searched for the Dear Debbie column.

There it was. Right next to the obituaries.

He took a sip of coffee, which hit the spot, then read the first of two letters. It was written by a woman who'd been taken in by a lying boyfriend. But it was Lainie's response that drew his interest.

> *I know exactly how you feel. It's painful to learn that a man you thought was Mr. Right lied to you—or even worse, that he doesn't trust you. And if that's the case, he's not the hero you thought he was.*

Lainie must be referring to Craig's deceit, but Drew had hurt her, too. He was the one who hadn't believed her. So he wasn't feeling very heroic right now.

He continued to read the next letter. The writer was a woman who'd gotten angry with her family and, on principle alone, refused several of her sister's attempts to make amends. Just as he'd done moments before, Drew focused on Lainie's response, which was especially personal—and telling.

My own family was far from perfect. After my mom died, my sister and I were raised by an alcoholic father who couldn't keep a job. Needless to say, life was far from easy.

Not long after my seventh birthday, my dad died in a bar fight, and my sister and I were placed in foster care. I'd been suffering from several medical problems that had never been addressed, one of which was life-threatening and required surgery, so the state stepped in and split us up. We ended up in different homes, and she was adopted. I haven't seen her since.

Forgive me for not feeling very sympathetic to your anger or your plight. I lost the only family I had, and you're willing to throw away yours. Please reconsider. Love and forgiveness are powerful gifts. But even more so to the person who offers them freely.

A pang of sympathy balled up in Drew's chest. He grieved for the child Lainie had been, yet he admired the woman she'd become. How could he have forgotten the kindness she showed the retired cowboys or the compassion she had for Andre and his brothers?

He didn't deserve a woman like her, but he wanted her in his life—if it wasn't too late. Yet he didn't move. He continued to sit in his pickup, staring at the newspaper in his hand without reading another word.

With each beat of his heart, he realized it wasn't just admiration he felt for Lainie. He loved her. Somehow, he had to make things right with her. And between her and Kara, too.

So he started the engine and headed back to the ranch. When he arrived, he spotted an unfamiliar car parked in the yard and Lainie walking out onto the front porch, her curls softly tumbling along her shoulders. She wore a somber expression and carried both a suitcase and a purse.

Panic rose up from his gut, and he crossed the yard to meet her. "Where are you going?"

"Back to town."

"What about the Rocking Chair Ranch? The men need you." Drew needed her. "What about your job?"

She didn't even blink. "I found a woman to cover for me until Joy gets home. I'll be back for the party."

Drew had no idea how to bridge the rift he'd created between them, but he had to give it his best shot. "Before you go, I want to apologize."

She studied him for a moment, then gave a slight shrug. "Okay. You're forgiven."

So she said. But Drew couldn't read an ounce of

sincerity in her expression or in her tone. And he really didn't blame her.

"Can we talk privately?" he asked. "It's important."

She continued to stand there, gripping the handle of her bag and clutching her purse. For a moment, he thought she was going to refuse. Not that he wouldn't deserve it if she did.

He reached for her suitcase without actually taking it from her. "Please?"

She sucked in a deep breath, then slowly blew it out and handed him her bag. "All right. But just for a minute."

He scanned the yard, spotting several ranch hands coming out of the barn and a couple of the old cowboys rocking on the porch. "Let's go to my cabin. I'd rather not have an audience."

She fell into step beside him as they crossed the yard to the cabin. Minutes later, he opened the front door ahead of her and waited for her to enter. Then he joined her in the small living area and set down her bag near the sofa.

"I've been a jerk. I assumed the worst about you, and in that sense, I didn't treat you any better than Craig did." When she didn't object, he continued. "I've seen you with the elderly men, watched as you served them meals and laughed at their jokes. And I've seen you with Andre. You've got a good heart, and only a blind fool would've missed that."

Her expression softened a tad, and she ran her hand through her glossy curls. "I told you that I forgave you."

"Yes, but you really didn't mean it then. Do you now?"

The corner of her lips quirked, revealing the hint of a smile. "Yes, I suppose I do. But it was more than just your distrust and lack of faith in me that hurt. You questioned my competency as a journalist, and…" She clamped her mouth shut as if having second thoughts about going into any more detail than that.

"Again," he said, "I'm sorry. There's so much about you that I admire. I'd really like to start over."

Her brows knit together. "In what way?"

"It would be great if we could roll back the time to when you offered me that sugar cookie. Or when the wagon's tailgate broke."

She didn't seem to see any humor in that suggestion.

"Let's just start at an hour before that call with my sister the other night."

"When we were in the kitchen?" she asked.

"Yes. If we were to start again there, I'd take you outside on the porch with me. Then I'd ask about your early years. And I would've really listened. I would have admitted that it broke my heart to think of you losing touch with your twin."

A tear spilled down Lainie's cheek, and she swiped it away with the back of her hand and sniffled. "Rickie was my only sister, my only family."

The reason he'd wanted to backpedal was to introduce her to Kara in another way, a better one.

"I have a sister, too," he said, "and she's my only family. She's pregnant and going through a divorce."

Lainie blinked back her tears. "I didn't realize Craig was…"

Drew placed his index finger on her lips to halt her explanation. "I believe you, Lainie. And I should have from day one."

"It's weird," she said, her voice as soft as a whisper. "People think I went after him, but it's the other way around. I'd been reluctant to date him at all. Looking back on it now, I realize that I'd always craved having someone to love, and he picked up on that need and used it to his advantage."

"Craig's a womanizer," Drew said. "And apparently, he's pretty damn good at it."

Lainie shrugged. "I'd only met him two weeks before—at a coffee shop next to the office where I'd worked at a temp job after graduation. He picked up the tab, and we chatted awhile. I don't normally talk to strangers, but when he told me he was nursing a broken heart and grieving a failed marriage, I felt sorry for him.

"When he asked me out the next day, I agreed to meet him for lunch at a nearby deli. He asked about my sun sign, which should have been my first clue that he was a player. But I went along with it and mentioned that my birthday was coming up. He surprised me by having a gift delivered to the office—a red dress and an invitation to meet him at Sterling Towers for a birthday dinner. I'm sure you know the rest."

"Pretty much."

"It rankles me now, but I went. But I wouldn't have if I'd known what was going to unfold."

"Kara found you together," Drew supplied.

Lainie nodded. "She'd been crying, and she stormed to our booth and asked Craig what in the hell was going on. He told her, 'Nothing,' and called her 'sweetie' and insisted I was 'nobody.'"

"I'd like to punch his lights out," Drew said.

Lainie smiled. "For a moment, I thought your sister was going to do just that. Instead, she snatched the margarita I'd been drinking and splashed the rest of it in my face. I don't know what stung worse, the icy cold on my skin, the humiliation or hearing Craig call me a 'nobody.'"

Drew's heart ached for Lainie. And for a lot of reasons—Craig's deceit, Kara's blame, the rumors that claimed Lainie was a villainess.

"Several diners held up their cell phones," Lainie said, "recording the ugly scene. And before I knew it, I became the night's social media entertainment."

"I'll explain all of this to my sister," Drew said. "She'll get over it. Eventually."

"That's okay," Lainie said. "I doubt that she and I will ever see each other again."

As a tear spilled over and trailed down her cheek, Drew brushed his thumb under her eye, wiping it away. Then he cupped her face with both hands and gazed at her. "Sure, you'll see her. That is, if you'll give me a chance to prove myself and go out with me."

Drew was asking her out on a date?

Lainie hadn't seen that coming. "Seriously?"

"You bet I am. My sister will get over blaming you, especially if I vouch for you."

This conversation wasn't at all what she'd expected. As she pondered his words and let them settle over her, she kept quiet.

Drew's thumb made a slow circle on her cheek, singeing her skin. "I've never met anyone like you, Lainie. I never expected to. And now that I have, I've rethought the future I'd laid out for myself."

To include her? She wasn't about to make a leap like that. "I don't know what to say."

"Tell me you'll let me show you that I'm a much better man than Craig."

"You've already proven that a hundred times over."

Drew brushed his lips against hers in a whisper-soft kiss that stole her breath away.

She was tempted to lean into him, to wrap her arms around him and let him take the lead, but she rallied. "First, before you say anything else, there's something I need to tell you."

His hands slipped from her jaw to her shoulders, but he didn't remove his touch, didn't remove his heated gaze. He didn't even blink. "Fire away."

He trusted her to lay everything on the line?

She sucked in a fortifying breath, then slowly let it out. "When I was a kid, I used to get tired doing the simplest things. But no one ever cared enough to worry about me or take me to the doctor. If they had, my congenital heart defect would have been diagnosed and corrected sooner. As it was, I didn't have surgery until I was eight."

"And that's when you lost touch with your sister."

She nodded. "It was a lonely, scary time. But don't get me wrong. I'm thankful that the state stepped in because then a skilled pediatric surgeon made me healthy. Things were better after that, but I was still very much alone and would have given anything for someone to love. At least, someone special."

"Has there ever been anyone special?"

"My college roommates, but we all went our separate ways. And there was one guy—for a little while. But he wasn't the man I thought he was."

"You mean Craig?"

"No, Craig was my second mistake. Right after I started college, I met a guy named Ryan and thought he might be 'the one,' but he wasn't. I can see that now. He kept pressuring me to have sex, but I wasn't ready. Then one night, I decided to give in, just to please him. But things never even got that far. It turned out badly, and we broke up."

"You don't have to talk about it—if you don't want to."

"I need to." It was the lead-in to what she had to tell him. "After I removed my blouse, Ryan froze up. You see, I have a long, ugly scar that runs along my sternum from my open heart surgery, and he was turned off by it."

"Oh, Lainie." Drew pulled her into his arms, holding her in a way she'd never been held.

She leaned into him, savoring his clean, woodland scent, his warm, comforting arms. "You're an amazing woman—beautiful, sweet, warmhearted. I don't want *you* to freeze up on me, but I'm falling in love with you. And there's nothing more I'd like than to take you to bed and show you just how much. But I'm a patient man. I'm willing to wait until you're ready."

Drew loved her? Could that be true?

She gently pushed against his chest, freeing herself from his embrace. "You haven't seen that scar yet."

"I don't need to." He pulled her back into his arms and kissed her long and deep. His tongue swept through her mouth, seeking and mating with hers until her knees nearly gave out.

She wanted to cling to him for the rest of her life, but she stopped the kiss before it was too late and took a step back. For once, she needed to let her head rule over her heart.

"Just so there aren't any surprises..." She unbuttoned her blouse, slipped it off her shoulders and dropped it onto the sofa. Then she unhooked her yellow satin bra and pushed the straps off her shoulders.

As she tossed it aside and stood before him, baring her flaw, his breath hitched. But not in revulsion. His expression was heated, fully aroused with desire.

"Aw, Lainie. You're beautiful."

Her hand lifted to her collarbone, a habit she couldn't seem to break, but he stopped her.

"Don't." He gently fingered the faded ridge, then bent his head and kissed the length of it. The warmth of his breath soothed her like a balm, healing the very heart of her.

He caressed the curve of her waist and along the slope of her hips, cherishing her with his touch, telling her without words that she mattered to him. Yet he was providing her with more than comfort, he was stirring her hormones and arousing her senses.

Her nipples hardened, and an ache settled deep in her core. When she thought she might die from pure sexual need, he pulled his lips from hers and rested his head against hers.

"I want to make love with you," he said. "But I won't press you until you're sure about me. About us."

She could hardly believe this was happening. "I'd like that, too. And to be honest, I'm ready now."

"You have no idea how glad I am to hear that. But are you sure?"

"It scares me to say this, but I love you, Drew. More than I ever dreamed possible."

He took her hand and led her across the small living area to the bedroom. "Is this your first time?"

She nodded. "I'm sure you're probably used to women with more experience—"

He squeezed her hand. "That's nothing to be sorry for. You're giving me a gift. And it's the best one I've ever had."

He removed his shirt and pants, while she kicked off her shoes and peeled off her slacks. Then he drew her into his arms again and kissed her, caressing her and taunting her with his skilled touch.

Lainie took the time to explore his body, too. Her fingers skimmed his muscular chest, the broad width of his back.

Drew trailed kisses along her throat and down to her chest. Then he took a nipple in his mouth, suckling it,

lavishing one breast then the other. She moaned, unable
to stand much more of the amazing foreplay.

Before she melted to a puddle on the floor, Drew
lifted her in his arms and placed her on top of the bed.
He joined her, and they continued to kiss, to taste and
stroke each other until Drew pulled back and braced
himself up on his elbow. "This might hurt the first
time."

"I know. And it's all right." She'd been waiting for
Drew—and for this—all of her life.

He entered her slowly at first, letting her get used to
the feel of him, the feel of them, until he broke through.
It stung, and her breath caught as she gave up her vir-
ginity, but her body soon responded to his, taking and
giving. Loving and being loved.

As they reached a peak, she cried out, arched her
back and let go. An amazing, earth-shattering climax
set off an overwhelming burst of love and a sense of
absolute completion.

When it was over, they lay still, basking in a sweet
afterglow.

Moments later, Drew rolled to the side without letting her go. "It'll be better next time."

"I thought it was pretty amazing now."

He brushed a loose strand of hair from her brow,
then traced her scar with his finger, gently and almost
reverently. "Don't ever hide this again. Not from me
or from anyone. It's a part of the miracle of *you*. Without that surgery, you might not have been here to meet
me, to love me."

"You're right. I'm still trying to wrap my mind around it."

"Me, too," he said. "I never expected this to happen, but I can't imagine my life without you in it. I want to marry you—but only when you're ready."

Her heart soared. Christmas had come early this year. For the first time ever, Lainie had a real future stretched out before her and the promise of the family she'd never thought she'd have.

Only it wasn't that simple.

"I might have a deal breaker," she said.

"What's that?"

"I want to apply to be a foster parent so I can take Andre and his brothers. I don't like the idea of them being separated. I realize the state might find me lacking. But I'm determined to do whatever it takes to get those kids into the same home—either mine or in another where someone will love and care for them."

Drew slowly shook his head. She waited for his objection, but instead, one side of his mouth quirked in a crooked grin. "I have to admit that getting a wife and family in one fell swoop was never on my radar, but a lot's changed since I met you."

"You mean you're up to being a foster dad?"

"I am if we're in this thing together. Hell, maybe we can help find more foster families or adoptive parents in the area."

Her breath caught and excitement built as the wheels began to churn in her mind. "We can create a blog, highlighting kids who need forever homes."

Drew laughed. "Maybe we've found a higher calling than rodeos and advice columns."

"That's true. But my biggest and highest calling is you. I love you, Drew." Then she kissed him, sealing those words the only way she knew how.

The Christmas party had been a huge success, and everyone seemed to have had a great time.

Joe and Chloe Martinez, the ranch owners, arrived earlier that morning and had been pleased at how Lainie had pulled things together in such a short period of time.

"I had a lot of help," she'd told them.

Drew had purchased the tree, as well as the ornaments. And the retired cowboys had all pitched in to help him with the decorating.

Molly, Brad's mother, had slipped away from Kidville several different evenings to help Lainie with the baking. They'd also wrapped all the presents and placed them under the tree.

Sully had returned a few days ago with his brother Homer, a happy-go-lucky fellow who seemed to fit right in with the other retired cowboys. As soon as Homer unpacked his things, he'd jumped right in to party mode, offering his help whenever needed. So Lainie had gladly put him to work.

While Homer made himself useful by decorating the tree, wrapping gifts and frosting sugar cookies, Sully practiced his ho-ho-ho to perfection. The wise old man was a natural Santa as he chatted with the children and passed out candy canes.

Lainie couldn't believe how well the party turned out. Or how many great photo ops she'd had that day.

There'd been a few disappointments, though. Andre's brothers had yet to arrive. And Kara, who'd been invited, hadn't been able to come because she was still taking it easy. But she'd invited Drew and Lainie to her house to spend Christmas Day. Somehow, Drew had convinced Kara to give Lainie a chance. Lainie hoped they'd be able to get past the whole Craig fiasco, and Drew insisted they would.

Dark clouds had gathered all morning, and the rain began just before noon, so they'd canceled the hayride and rescheduled it for a warmer, drier day.

Now, as the party was coming to an end, the children sat amidst torn wrapping paper and open boxes, admiring their gifts and munching on cookies. Lainie was glad she'd been able to offer them a few hours of fun.

"Congratulations," Drew said. "Things didn't go exactly as planned, but from the looks on those little faces, the party's been a huge success."

"Thanks, but I couldn't have done it without your help."

When he slipped his arms around her, she leaned into him and rested her head on his shoulder.

"I have a present for you," Drew said.

"You didn't have to do that." Just having him in her life, sharing his bed and loving him was gift enough for her.

"I've been working on it for a week, and..." He

glanced out the window and grinned. "Looks like it just arrived."

Lainie wasn't sure what he was talking about, but moments later a knock sounded at the door. Jim Hoffman, who'd been standing nearby, opened it for a petite woman and two small boys.

It had to be the social worker, along with Andre's brothers. But why would Drew say he'd been working on getting them here all week? She'd been the one to invite them. "Come on in," Jim said. "I'm glad you finally made it, Mrs. Tran." Then he called out, "Andre. Look who's here."

The boy, who'd been reading his new cowboy book, broke into a happy smile and shrieked, "Mario! Abel!" He scrambled to his feet and hurried to the door, his limp hardly noticeable.

The boys greeted each other with hugs and kisses.

"That's *my* present?" she asked Drew. "Looks like it's Andre's."

"It's the paperwork in Mrs. Tran's folder that's your gift," he said.

Bewildered, Lainie cocked her head and looked at the man she loved. "I don't understand."

"Congratulations, foster mommy. It's a boy. Actually, it's three of them."

Lainie's jaw dropped. "Are you kidding? They're going to let me take them? I... Well, my little studio apartment is going to be cramped, but I'll make it work. Somehow."

"No need." Drew reached into his back pocket and pulled out a folded sheet of paper. "I just signed a lease for a three-bedroom house in Wexler. It'll have to do for now."

"You did that for me?"

"I did it for *us*. Kids need a daddy, too. Don't you think?"

"Drew Madison, you're amazing. Have I told you lately that I love you to the moon and stars?"

"Just this morning, but I'd like to hear it again." He tossed her a dazzling smile.

"I plan to tell you every single morning and night for the rest of our lives."

"I have one last gift for you," Drew said.

"What more can you give me? My gosh, look at them. Their reunion is heartwarming. And so is their excitement." She pointed to the tree, where the three adorable brothers gazed up at the twinkling lights in wide-eyed wonder. "This has been the best Christmas ever."

"It's just the first of many—and it's not over yet." Drew reached into his shirt pocket, withdrew a business card and handed it to her.

DISCREET SERVICES
Damon Wolfe, Owner

She studied it carefully. "What's this?"

"The guy I hired to find Rickie."

"But it was a closed adoption."

"Damon is the best of the best. He told me to leave it to him. If Erica "Rickie" Montoya can be found, he'll find her."

She looked at him, her eyes glistening with tears. "I can't believe this. Drew, this is the very best gift anyone could ever give me."

He held her in his arms and kissed her again. "That's nothing compared to the gift you are to me. Come on, honey. Let's ask the Hoffmans to take a picture of us and the boys so we can have more than a memory of our first Christmas together."

"Good idea."

Lainie had always found the holidays to be depressing. But not any longer. She couldn't wait to create more of her very own family memories from this day forward.

And next Christmas couldn't come too soon.

* * * * *

Will Elena be reunited with her long-lost sister?
Find out in the next installment of
ROCKING CHAIR RODEO
The new series by
USA TODAY *Bestselling Author Judy Duarte*
Coming in July 2018

And catch up with everyone on the
Rocking Chair Ranch:

ROPING IN THE COWGIRL
THE BRONC RIDER'S BABY

And if you loved this book
Look for NO ORDINARY FORTUNE
Judy Duarte's contribution to
THE FORTUNES OF TEXAS:
THE RULEBREAKERS
On sale February 2018
Wherever Mills & Boon books and ebooks are sold.

MILLS & BOON®

Cherish™

EXPERIENCE THE ULTIMATE RUSH OF FALLING IN LOVE

MILLS & BOON®

EXCLUSIVE EXTRACT

With just days until Christmas, gorgeous but bewildered billionaire Max Grayland needs hotel maid Sunny Raye's help caring for his baby sister Phoebe. She agrees – only if they spend Christmas with her family!

Read on for a sneak preview of
THE BILLIONAIRE'S CHRISTMAS BABY

'Miss Raye, would you be prepared to stay on over Christmas?'

Oh, for heaven's sake…

To miss Christmas… Who were they kidding?

'No,' she said blankly. 'My family's waiting.'

'But Mr Grayland's stranded in an unknown country, staying in a hotel for Christmas with a baby he didn't know existed until yesterday.' The manager's voice was urbane, persuasive, doing what he did best. 'You must see how hard that will be for him.'

'I imagine it will be,' she muttered and clung to her chocolates. And to her Christmas. 'But it's…'

Max broke in. 'But if there's anything that could persuade you… I'll double what the hotel will pay you. Multiply it by ten if you like.'

Multiply by ten… If it wasn't Christmas…

But it was Christmas. Gran and Pa were waiting. She had no choice.

But other factors were starting to niggle now. Behind Max, she could see tiny Phoebe lying in her too-big cot. She'd pushed herself out of her swaddle and was waving her tiny hands in desperation. Her face was red with screaming.

She was so tiny. She needed to be hugged, cradled, told all was right with her world. Despite herself, Sunny's heart twisted.

But to forgo Christmas? *No way.*

'I can't,' she told him, still hugging her chocolates. But then she met Max's gaze. This man was in charge of his world but he looked...desperate. The pressure in her head was suddenly overwhelming.

And she made a decision. What she was about to say was ridiculous, crazy, but the sight of those tiny waving arms, that red, desperate face was doing something to her she didn't understand and the words were out practically before she knew she'd utter them.

'Here's my only suggestion,' she told them. 'If you really do want my help... My Gran and Pa live in a big old house in the outer suburbs. It's nothing fancy; in fact it's pretty much falling down. It might be dilapidated but it's huge. So no, Mr Grayland, I won't spend Christmas here with you, but if you're desperate, if you truly think you can't manage Phoebe alone, then you're welcome to join us until you can make other arrangements. You can stay here and take care of Phoebe yourself, you can make other arrangements or you can come home with me. Take it or leave it.'

Don't miss
THE BILLIONAIRE'S CHRISTMAS BABY
by Marion Lennox

Available December 2017
www.millsandboon.co.uk